Painless

The Story of Samantha Smith #3

Devon Hartford

COPYRIGHT NOTICE

Want to get an email when Devon's next book is released?

Sign up here:

http://eepurl.com/B7crf

DEDICATION

This book is dedicated to Jenn Hedge, for kicking ass and reminding me how important stories can be.

And, like the last time, I also have to dedicate this book to ALL of my enthusiastic readers. Every single comment you gals made about Reckless factored into my thoughts while I wrote Painless in one way or another. You gals helped make this a better book!

Thank you! :-D

Chapter 1

SAMANTHA

Dread.

The gloom of the deserted Manos Mansion pressed in around me, suffocating me. I sat on Christos' bed in his empty bedroom, clutching his sketchbook to my chest in my quivering hands. His haunted words echoed in my mind.

"Alone
I must brave this day
Alone
I have sealed my fate
Alone
I will touch the sky
Alone
I must die"

No! I must have read them wrong! Christos would never...

I couldn't even think it.

My heart rabbited in my chest and threatened to seize as I re-read his lonely poem under the dim light of his bedside lamp. Christos was in dire torment. His heart was breaking. I could feel his pain as if it were my own. He was in trouble, and he needed help.

Panic and a sense of helplessness spun through me. How could I help Christos if I didn't know where he was? He hadn't answered any of my calls or texts for over an hour. I desperately wanted to do something otherwise I was going to splinter into a million pieces.

But what?

The heavy silence pressing in around me was broken by the clatter of the front door opening downstairs.

"Christos!" I yelped as I shot up from the bed. I sprinted out of his bedroom and down the darkened hallway. Relief washed over me as I pounded downstairs. I was going to throw my arms around my man and hold onto him and tell him everything was going to be okay. I knew my love would heal the pain and self hatred that had been eating him up from the inside out for way too long.

At the bottom of the stairs, I turned and skidded into the entry hall. "Christos!"

"*Samoula?*" Spiridon smiled, his keys jingling in his hands. "What are you doing here?"

"Where's Christos?" I blurted anxiously.

"Isn't he with you?"

"No," I muttered, disappointment darkening my voice.

"He's not in the studio working?" Spiridon asked.

"No, I checked. He's not in the house anywhere." For a moment I felt nervous, worried I would have to explain to Spiridon why I was wandering through his house uninvited. Which was weird, because Spiridon had already invited me to move in with him and Christos. He'd even given me a house key. So why did I feel like a snooping criminal? Oh yeah. My parents. The Source of All that is Evil.

Them.

Telling my parents over the phone that I was moving in with Christos had freaked them out. Which led to me hanging up on them and Christos freaking out because my parents were freaked out.

And the worst news of all: Christos' pending Valentine's Day trial, only two days away.

Why hadn't Christos told me until now? Was the trust we'd built together a lie? What else was he hiding? A shudder shook me to my bones. My heart accelerated into overdrive as the stressful events of the last few hours reignited in my mind. My life was unraveling by the second. I felt light headed as my chest tightened, making it nearly impossible to breathe. Was I having a heart attack? Was that possible for a nineteen year old? At that moment, it definitely felt like it. Every cell in my body screamed that Christos was in immediate danger, wherever he was. My eyes flashed panic. I needed to protect him any way I could. "I need to go find Christos!"

"Calm down, *koritsáki mou,*" Spiridon reassured. "Come into the kitchen, *Samoula.* Maybe you should sit down. You don't look well."

My hands shook uncontrollably as he led me into the kitchen, pulled a chair out from the table for me, and opened the refrigerator. He grabbed a pitcher of water and poured a glass for me as I dropped into the chair.

"Tell me everything," he said as he set the glass on the table and sat down. He took my hands in his and rubbed the backs of them affectionately. "Whatever it is," he smiled, "everything is going to be fine."

My throat closed to a pinhole as I realized the bitter truth. Even if I could somehow find Christos and rescue him from whatever fate awaited him tonight, he faced the likely possibility of going to jail for who knew how long after his upcoming trial.

I rambled, "Christos, he's...I don't know...I think he's..." I was torn between my worry for Christos and the warm, loving way Spiridon was comforting me. His compassionate gaze made me oddly nervous. I wasn't used to any kind of tenderness from other people, or the way it lowered the walls around my emotions.

Other than the intimacy I'd shared with Christos over the last five months, I'd never opened up like this in front of anyone. Especially not an adult. And never in front of my parents.

I had *never* let my guard down around *them*.

The night Damian Wolfram had run over Taylor Lamberth, I'd freaked out big time. There was no way I would have shared my feelings about it with my *parents*. I'd made sure to avoid them until I'd had a chance to collect myself and stuff my feelings back inside the box I'd built around my heart when I was little.

I don't know when I'd started building that box. It was never a conscious thing. It was a defense mechanism. Probably one that everyone had. The idea of sharing my naked feelings with my parents had always felt like an invasion of my privacy. They didn't understand feelings. When I was little and showed my feelings to my mom, she frowned and scowled at me and told me to get a hold of myself like a big girl, or else. When my dad saw my feelings, he pulled out a calculator and tried to solve them like a math problem. If that didn't work, he tried to sterilize them with logic. That was why I never shared anything with my parents. Not anything that mattered.

But looking into Spiridon's deeply compassionate eyes, I felt safe. He wasn't freaked out. He was calm, confident, and loving. I wish he could give my parents lessons. In that moment, I felt like I could tell him everything, and he would understand. He wouldn't lecture or reprimand, and he wouldn't measure, calculate or solve. He would simply listen. And in that listening, healing occurred. Christos had taught me that. Had he learned it from Spiridon? It seemed likely, looking at him now.

Sitting in the Manos' kitchen, I felt comforted, swaddled in the warm embrace of the tangible love emanating from Spiridon, a love that circulated throughout his house, as if it had gently flowed out of his being for decades and soaked into the wood. This home, this kitchen, was a sacred space.

My tears welled. I was about to spill everything, tell Spiridon about the nasty things my parents had said, and the threats they had made on the phone. I knew in my heart that Spiridon wouldn't judge. He would listen with understanding and love. I longed for that sort of comfort, the kind of comfort Christos had shown me many times already.

But more than anything, I wanted it from Christos.

Christos…

Coiled resolve unwound inside me. My feelings about my parents could wait. Christos was in mortal danger right now. I needed to do something to save him. Could I tell Spiridon that deep in my bones I felt certain his grandson's life dangled on the precipice of disaster? I would sound like a lunatic. To my parents, anyway.

"What is it, *Samoula?*" Spiridon asked softly. "You can tell me anything."

I believed him and trusted him completely. I lifted my heavy head and met his eyes with mine. "Christos is in terrible trouble." It frightened me to say it, as if voicing my fears might magically make things worse.

"I know, *koritsáki mou.* I know," he said heavily as his head bowed solemnly and his eyes darkened.

His words carried such sadness, such poignancy, I felt my heart beginning to shrivel and sink into blackness…

Christos…

Oh no…

===

CHRISTOS

In darkness, I stood balanced on one bare foot, my toes curled around the frigid steel of the balcony railing of Nyyhmy Hall, ten stories above cement.

Cold winter wind billowed around me. Far below, a lone car slid silently down North Torrey Pines Road. I was in another world, separate from the invisible people in that tiny car. I wondered if they were happy or sad. No way to know.

But I knew I was on the verge of losing my shit. My trial was in two days. My pre-trial was in less than twelve hours, after which my future would be in the hands of the court and the twelve strangers who would be my jury. Would they convict me and send me to prison, or would I be found innocent and go free?

I hated not knowing. I hated not having any control over the outcome.

Did it even matter?

That was a million years from now.

Right now, in this eternal moment of insane danger, I had total control. Live or die. Fight or fly. It was all up to me. If I wanted, I could relax the tension in my knee. Just relax. Let it go. Everything would be over within a few seconds, all my stress gone. All my worries would become irrelevant.

Fall into the darkness and soar into eternity.

Samantha.

Fists knotted my guts with agony. My face squeezed and twisted with frustration and rage and guilt.

What had I done to her?

I'd made a mess of things big time.

Samantha now knew what a fuck up I was beneath my flashy exterior. While I'd slapped her with the truth, punched her with all the criminal shit I'd done in my past, the conviction I'd seen in her eyes was worse than what any jury could hand me at my trial. So what if twelve strangers decided I was a fuck up and sent me to jail to sweat out my guilt? My heart was already imprisoned in self hatred. For what I'd done to Samantha. For lying to her by not telling her about who I really was, for hiding my terrible past while she innocently fell in love with me.

How could I have done that to her? How could I have jeopardized the trust she willingly gave me by not telling her up front that I was no good?

The cold wind chilled my skin, but my heart was colder, shivering in my chest.

I glanced down at the tempting cement a hundred feet below.

It would be so easy to fly and let all my troubles fall away...

===

SAMANTHA

I clamped my hand around Spiridon's wrist and pleaded, "We have to do something!"

Spiridon raised his brows thoughtfully. "What do you mean?"

"Christos ran out of my apartment earlier and sped off on his motorcycle. I'm afraid he's going to..." I couldn't say it.

Worry and recognition weighed on Spiridon's face. "Have you tried to call him?"

"Fifty times!" My voice crackled with fear. "He won't answer. That's why I'm so worried. I hoped maybe he'd come here."

Spiridon folded his arms across his chest and huffed a nervous sigh. I think my fear was seeping into him.

"Did he tell you where he was going?" Spiridon asked.

"No! I have no idea! He could be anywhere."

"Perhaps the best thing we can do is wait here. He's bound to come back sooner or later."

"But what if..." I was ready to rocket out of my seat through the ceiling with anxiety. I couldn't sit here and wait. I needed to take action. "Wait, maybe Christos is out with Jake!"

"So call Jake," Spiridon said calmly.

I didn't have Jake's number, so I dialed Madison.

She answered after two rings. She sounded sleepy. "What up, girlfriend?"

"Mads!" My voice was way more panicked than I wanted, considering I was waking her up in the middle of the night. "Is Jake with you?"

"Last time I checked," she sighed. "Unless the hot guy sleeping next to me is someone else. Hey buddy," she giggled to whoever was in the room with her, "is your name Jake?"

I heard Jake's faint, grumbling voice over the phone, "Don't tell me you're bored with me already, babe."

"Men have such fragile egos," Madison whispered to me. I heard her turn away from her phone again and say to Jake, "Go to sleep, King Dong. Your man cannon is the only one that bombards my baby box every night. Quick! Everyone to the dong shelters!"

Crap. There went my theory about Christos and Jake being out at a bar. "Mads, ask Jake if he knows where Christos is."

"Why would he know where Christos is? He's been with me all evening."

"Can you please just ask him?" I pleaded.

"Jake," Madison said, "Sam wants to know if you know where Christos is."

"I haven't talked to him since yesterday," Jake mumbled.

Great.

Madison relayed the news, "Jake said he hasn't seen—"

"I heard," I interrupted.

"Is something wrong?" Madison asked, obvious concern in her voice.

I didn't have time to explain everything to her. I needed to go look for Christos. "It's, ah, it's nothing." I tried to sound like it was no big deal so she wouldn't start worrying. "I just need to talk to Christos. If for some reason he calls Jake, call me right away, okay?"

"Are you sure nothing's wrong, Sam?"

"Yeah. Everything is fine. Go back to sleep."

I heard the rustling of covers.

"Mmmm," Madison murmured, "I don't think Jake is going to let me. Call me tomorrow, Sam. But if you really, really need me, call me right away." Madison made a purring noise. "Scratch that. Don't call for at least twenty minutes."

I heard Jake scoff, "Twenty minutes?"

"Okay," Madison said to Jake, "make it forty. But that's all you get, cowboy. I have class in the morning."

"Don't worry about it, Mads," I said. "We'll talk tomorrow."

"Okay. Bye, Sam." She giggled before the phone line went dead a second later.

I envied her in that moment. She was snuggled up with her man, the two of them safe from all the harm in the world. I set the phone down on the kitchen table and looked at Spiridon.

He laid a comforting hand on mine once again. "I know you're worried, *koritsáki mou*. Why don't you try calling Christos again?"

"Okay."

He winked at me, "Isn't there an old saying, the fifty-first time is the charm?"

===

CHRISTOS

A shadow blurred past the corner of my vision. Something huge and dark whipped past my head from the side and was gone before I could register what it was. I followed the motion as the thing curved out over the ten story drop below.

A lone barn owl had beat wings past my face, only a few feet in front of me. I'd never heard him coming. He was dead silent. Totally in his element.

I watched in awe as he soared out past the distant moon, floating above the canyons between me and the ocean. He sailed through the air languorously, searching for prey. I was transfixed by the hunter in his natural environment. What a simple life he led.

Without warning, the owl's wings folded and it dove into the darkness. I followed it's plummeting path, watching intently as its wings exploded mere feet above the ground, the owl landing in a pool of amber beneath a streetlight. A second later, the owl flapped furiously and rose into the air, a mouse dangling from its talons. Then the owl disappeared into the black night with its prey.

I was in awe of the swiftness with which all of that had transpired. One life ended so another could flourish.

I realized I had a choice to make.

My life…or Samantha's.

I wanted her to flourish.

My face knotted in agony. My chest tightened as jagged knives of regret stabbed me from the inside out. How the fuck had I fucked things up so badly? I inhaled deeply, ready to shout my lungs out in an attempt to release some of the tension ripping my heart apart.

Then I realized shouting would call attention to myself.

Nyyhmy Hall was shaped like a blocky letter H when you looked at it from the top. The balcony was on the top side of the fat horizontal bar of the H. The thick vertical columns of the H held all the dorm rooms, the windows of which faced the balcony where I stood. Because it was San Diego, and it was no cooler than sixty degrees outside, many of those windows were open. Since this was a college dorm building, several of those windows had lights on, and some had their curtains open. If I started shouting, I had no doubt heads would start popping out of those windows like gophers checking for eagles overhead. The last thing I wanted was an audience or someone calling campus security and telling them there was another jumper on the tenth floor. I was enjoying my peace and quiet.

I took a deep breath. My stabbing regret eased a fraction. I took another breath.

That was when I realized I'd been looking at my situation all wrong. Eagles, owls, gophers and mice.

First, the owl and the mouse. For all I knew, that was a mama owl with baby owls back in her nest that hadn't eaten in weeks. No one wanted baby owls to go hungry. I know I didn't.

Second, the eagle and the gophers.

We all know which animal I was in that scenario.

No matter how much confusion and pain writhed in my guts, I would never be a gopher. I was the predator in my life, not the prey. I was not going to live my life cringing away from danger, always wondering when the death strike might come raining down from above.

I was going to step boldly into life and dance with danger.

I wasn't going to give up.

Like the eagle and the owl, I was going to bare my claws and teeth and do what I did best.

Fight.

For myself. For Samantha.

For my life.

No one was going to bring me down and tear me apart. Not even the judicial system. I never took the easy way out. That's how I'd ended up in this predicament in the first place. Because I liked living dangerously.

I was up here because the day I'd met Samantha, it had taken me less than half a second to decide that Horst Grossman, the fat fuck who was up in her face, was way out of line, and needed to lay off her shit. The easy thing would've been to ride away and forget all about her.

But that wasn't how I rolled. Not that day, not tonight, and not at my trial. If I was going down, I was going down fighting.

I still hadn't told my attorney, Russell Merriweather, whether or not to accept the plea bargain from the District Attorney. The offer was one year in jail in exchange for a guilty plea. Probably only nine months with time off for good behavior. That was the sure thing. If I went to trial, I risked up to four years in state prison if the jury found me guilty. Fuck it. I liked risks and I liked fighting.

I was going to roll the dice and go to trial.

I grinned and shook my head. I don't know why I'd been so stressed about all this. Like most women, Lady Luck had the hots for my shit. No reason why she wouldn't back me up at my trial.

Still balanced on one foot with my knee in the air, I lowered my foot down to the railing and stabilized myself.

As I was about to hop back onto the balcony, my phone rang, startling me.

The sound cut through the nighttime silence.

I hissed and pitched forward, I was so surprised. My arms whirled automatically and my hips thrust back violently, counter-balancing my weight. If I over compensated, I was over the edge of this railing and three seconds later, over with permanently. I strained to regain my balance. Agonizing seconds later, I recovered my center of gravity and hopped onto the cold cement balcony.

Was Lady Luck calling to tell me something?

Before Your Love by Kelly Clarkson continued playing through the tiny speakers on my phone.

Not Lady Luck.

Samantha.

I rolled my head back and chuckled. "Fuck," I mumbled to myself. She'd almost killed me. Tragic irony was a funny thing, as long as it didn't happen to you.

I answered her call. "Hey," I mumbled.

"Where are you?" Samantha begged.

"Out getting some fresh air." I sat down on the cold cement balcony and slid my socks and boots on.

"Are you all right?" she asked, worried.

"I'm fine, *agáp*—" I stopped myself short. Calling her that right now felt like an empty promise I couldn't keep for long. Shit was going to get real when I went to trial. I didn't want Samantha getting her hopes up if things went bad. If I was acquitted, great. But if the jury found me guilty? Nobody was going to throw a party.

"Please tell me where you are, *agápi mou*," Samantha said, her voice resonating with a penetrating fear tempered by her bold, fearless love.

Her confidence peeled back some of my reckless resistance. If I said nothing and kept her completely in the dark, I'd feel like a stubborn dick. "I'm at SDU," I sighed. "Everything is okay."

"I need to see you, Christos."

"Now isn't a good time." I shook my head at how lame I sounded.

"What do you mean?" she pleaded. "We were talking about some really important stuff and you ran out. Why?"

Did I tell her I'd run because I felt like an idiot? That I was embarrassed by my past? Shit, I could barely admit it to myself. Or did I talk about how my life still balanced on a knife edge thinner than the balcony railing I'd just been standing on?

If I ended up in jail, I'd end up going back to my old ways. I'd have no choice but to harden up and fight my way through each and every day I was stuck in lock up. I knew from experience that prison would get under my skin and dirty my fingernails no matter how hard I tried to hold onto the life I'd been building for the last two years. What kind of institutionalized prick would I be after four years in prison? Would Samantha want to know me then? Would I want to subject her to whatever damage I was sure to suffer from living like a barbarian?

Who was I kidding?

She needed better options than that.

I stifled an insane laugh as I considered how her parents might feel about the whole thing. I was pretty sure I would agree with them.

I shook my head. "Look," I said gruffly, "I really don't want to talk about this right now. I need time to think."

"Come home, Christos. No matter how bad you think things are right now, I love you. Your grandfather loves you. We're here for you."

Why did her words tear my guts apart?

Fuck, I couldn't deal with this.

"Samantha, I need to go."

"Christos! Please don't hang up! Tell me exactly where you are and I'll come right now."

Her voice sounded jumpy, like she was running with the phone in her hand. I heard the beep beep beep of her VW's warning bell and a door chunking shut.

"Are you in your car?" I asked.

"Yes. I'm driving out of your driveway right now. Don't move a muscle. I'm coming for you."

She wasn't going to let me get away. It's not like I was going to run down to my bike and bolt before she got here. I'd already done that earlier.

I shook my head and grinned. I hated to be predictable. Besides, I needed to talk to her sooner or later. And what the hell else was I going to do tonight anyway? Get some quality sleep before my pre-trial hearing?

Yeah, right.

"Fine," I said. "I'll meet you at the Adams College parking lot, where the motorcycles are."

"Okay, I'll be there in ten minutes."

"Don't speed," I said ironically, "I wouldn't want you getting in an accident." I meant it. Although my safety was low on my list of priorities, hers was still at the top of my list. "Why don't we hang up so you can focus on your driving?"

"No!" she shrieked. "Don't you hang up your phone until I'm standing right in front of you!"

I had to admit, her insistence was endearing. "Okay, I'll stay on the phone. But at least put yours on speaker and put it in your lap, or in a cup holder or whatever."

"Okay. My phone is in my lap. Keep talking."

"Ahh, do I recite poetry now?"

"If you've got anything memorized."

"Twas brillig, and the slithy toves did gyre and gimble in the wabe…"

"What language is that?" She giggled.

"English?"

"Are you sure?" She sounded like she was smiling.

"Yeah. It's the Jabberwocky by Lewis Carroll. I had to memorize that shit in the seventh grade. Wanna hear the rest?"

"Do you know the translated version?"

"No," I chuckled. "But it's about some kid who slays a crazy dragon. It's pretty ridiculous."

"What, slaying a dragon?" she asked.

"Yeah."

"That's not ridiculous. Isn't that what you do all the time? Slay dragons?"

I shook my head. "Not the last time I checked."

"What do you mean? Remember Big Foot? That hairy biker guy at that coffee shop in Pacific Beach? Xanadu? The guy who tried to kidnap me so he could mate with me and make missing link babies?"

"Oh yeah. That guy was like the cyclops from legend or some shit. If I remember correctly, he only had one eye. Didn't that guy have a pirate eye patch?" I chuckled.

"No! He only had one eye, in the center of his forehead!" Samantha squealed with laughter. "Can you imagine a cyclops with a pirate eye patch? He'd be blind and running around in circles!"

"I hear pirate cyclops only ever wear ear patches," I quipped.

"Ear patches?" Samantha laughed.

"Christos?" a voice asked from behind me.

I turned to face whoever it was. What a surprise. "Hey, Kamiko. What up?"

"What?" Sam asked on the phone.

Kamiko wore an SDU sweatshirt, sweatpants, and her hair in a sexy knot at the back of her head. A book bag was slung over her shoulder. She looked at me curiously, "What are you doing up here?"

"Enjoying the view," I said casually, flashing a dimpled grin at her.

"Are you talking to Kamiko?" Samantha asked.

"Yeah," I said to the phone.

Kamiko asked, "I'm sorry, are you on the phone? I didn't mean to interrupt."

"No worries," I said to Kamiko. To Samantha, I said, "Hey, can you hold on a second?"

I suddenly remembered Samantha telling me about what happened with her and Kamiko when they went to visit Brandon at Charboneau Gallery to show him Kamiko's work. Poor Kamiko. From the sound of the story, Brandon had been a many-quilled prickupine. I sensed an opportunity to work some of my magic. Helping other people always put me in a good mood.

"How come you're up so late?" I asked Kamiko.

"I was studying O Chem with my friend. We just finished."

"Are you going back to your room?"

"Yeah," she said.

"You want me to walk you?"

"Sure," she smiled.

"Cool. Let me tell my buddy I'll call him back." To Samantha I said, "Hey, I'm gonna walk my friend to her dorm room. Can I call you back later, bro?"

"Christos," Samantha said in my ear, "tell Kamiko I'm sorry about what happened with Brandon."

"Yeah, totally," I said to Samantha, "as soon as I get a new wet suit, we'll totally carve some waves. Later, bro."

"Christos!" Samantha chirped in my ear. "Wait! Don't hang up!"

I hung up my phone and smiled at Kamiko. We walked toward the elevators across the hall from the balcony.

When the elevator door opened, I motioned with my arm, "After you."

"Thank you," Kamiko grinned and stepped inside.

After the elevator ride, I walked Kamiko along the dark pathway between Nyyhmy and Paiute Hall.

"How's the painting coming along?" I asked. "You still working on submissions for Brandon's Contemporary Artists Show?"

She stuck her tongue out and groaned. "Ugh. I don't even want to hear that name. Brandumb is so meh."

I arched an eyebrow. "Brandumb?"

"Yeah," she shivered. "Just saying it makes me want to gag."

We stopped in front of the double doors to Paiute while Kamiko dug her keys out of her bag.

I raised an eyebrow. "What happened to you being the gung ho painting ninja?"

She brightened. "Oh, I'm still totally the painting ninja." She suddenly spun around and snapped a back kick at me, stopping her foot two inches from my chest.

"Look out! Ninja alert," I chuckled. "Did you study martial arts at some point?"

"Yeah, I studied shotokan when I was in grade school. It was the only way I could stop my brothers from beating me up," She grinned. "They called me the Kamiko Kid."

"What, like the Karate Kid? Your brothers called you that?"

"Yup. But I didn't study with Mr. Miyagi. The guy who trained me was Mexican." She lowered her leg and pivoted forward, punching me in the stomach.

I tightened my abs automatically. Her tiny hand met solid muscle.

"Ow!" She yelped.

"Don't be messing with the man of steel," I joked. I could tell she wasn't trying to hit me very hard, but she had put some power behind it. "Nice right hand. Much better than your Karate Kid reference," I quipped.

She wrinkled her nose. "Do I have to crane kick you in the chin, mister? Because I will."

I towered over her. "You're going to need an airlift."

"Fine! I'll go for your shins." She snapped a kick at my shins but I hopped back, out of range. "Let that be a lesson," she warned.

"Easy, Bruce Lee. I apologize." I smiled at her.

"Don't try to be cute," she grinned.

"Hey, I'm using the only defense I have left before you beat my ass." I winked at her. "But seriously, are you still working on any paintings?"

"Hells yeah! Even if Brandumb is a total jerk, I'm going to get one of my paintings into his stupid Contemporary Artists Show, just to show him I can."

I nodded approvingly at her. "I take it you're over him?"

"Screw him," Kamiko snarled. "I'm too good for that stupid snake charmer! I refuse to live my life as a mopey dick-whipped chick any longer. I am woman! Hear me paint!" She stomped her foot for effect.

I grinned and chuckled, "I'll tell Brandon to run the other way when he sees you coming or you'll go Hunger Games on his ass."

"That's a great idea! I totally need to carry a bow and arrow!"

"Next time I see him, I'll pin a bull's eye to his ass so you'll have something to aim at."

"Who are you going to pin a bull's eye on?" Samantha asked, walking around the corner toward me and Kamiko.

I flashed a conspiratorial grin at Samantha.

Kamiko frowned, looking between the two of us. "Hey! You guys tricked me!" She leered at me, both her eyes turned up to full stink. "That was Sam on the phone earlier, wasn't it, Christos?" she asked in an accusatory tone.

"Maybe," I smiled coyly.

Chapter 2

SAMANTHA

"We trapped you, Kamiko," I said, a big smile on my face. "Now you have to listen to my apology. For the millionth time."

Kamiko folded her arms across her chest. "No, I refuse." She scowled at Christos. "Traitor. Now I can't trust either of you guys."

Christos chuckled.

Oddly, all of my fears about Christos evaporated the moment I'd seen him chatting with Kamiko. Whatever I'd been worried about seemed crazy now. Christos looked like he was in a good mood. Regular old Christos. Why had I been so worried?

"Do you guys need a moment alone?" Christos asked. "For some naughty girl time?"

"Do you want to watch?" I blurted. "We charge admission. A hundred bucks a head for front row seats."

Christos pulled his wallet out and held up a bunch of twenties. "I've got cash to spare, ladies. Where's the nearest mud-filled kiddie pool?"

I giggled, "I'm game if you are, Kamiko."

"Mud wrestling?" Kamiko shook her head at me, "You're as bad as he is." She glanced between me and Christos. "Okay, no fair you guys, ambushing me like this."

"I'm sorry, Kamiko," I said. "That day at Charboneau was all a big misunderstanding. Brandsome—"

"Dumb," Christos interjected.

"What?" I asked, confused.

"Brandumb," Kamiko said, examining her fingernails.

I smiled, "That sounds about right. He's too dumb to see a good thing when it's staring right at him."

"He's a total fuck bucket," Kamiko grumbled.

Christos and I both chuckled.

"I can corroborate that," Christos grinned. "I have personally caught Brandon fucking buckets on more than one occasion, when he thought no one was around."

"Did you take photos?" I asked. "Because if you did, maybe we can blackmail Brandumb into accepting Kamiko's work into the Contemporary Artists Show."

"I don't need to blackmail that art fart!" Kamiko said confidently. "I'm going to paint something so awesome, he's going to offer *me* oral favors just to get my painting into his stupid show."

Confused, I asked dumbly, "Do you mean he'll give you a Lifesaver or a Mentos or whatever?"

Kamiko frowned, "Huh?"

"Didn't you just say you wanted Brandumb to give you oral flavors?" I asked.

Kamiko arched an eyebrow, "Flavors?"

Christos erupted with laughter.

Kamiko chuckled and shook her head, "You have finally lived up to your blondness, Sam. All that time you spent at the beach with Mads has broiled your brain. You might want to think twice before you quit your job at Grab-n-Dash."

I think that was the first time Kamiko had smiled at me in weeks. "Does that mean you accept my apology?" I asked hopefully.

"If you insist..." she sighed.

"I insist." I reached out to give her a big hug.

"...and give me five dollars," she finished, her palm held out expectantly. Her brows knit into a menacing frown and one of her eyes narrowed suspiciously.

"What?" I scoffed. "I'm so not paying for your forgiveness!"

"Why not? It goes for ten times that on the open market. I declare a guilt glare!" She lunged her face toward me threateningly.

I took a step away from her. "Get your guilt glare away from me! It's heinous! Where'd you learn how to make that face anyway?" I circled behind Christos.

Kamiko followed. "From my mom. She's a master at it. It always worked for her. I think she did it so I had to give back all of my allowance."

Confused, I paused my circumnavigation around Christos. "Wait, are you saying whenever you did something bad at home, your mom made you pay her?"

"Yeah," Kamiko said uncertainly, looking between me and Christos, "isn't that what your parents did?"

"Uhh..." I stammered.

Christos shrugged.

"Fine," Kamiko said dismissively, "my mom is weird and my allowance was nothing more than a cruel ruse designed to humiliate. But you still have to pay up." She jammed her expectant palm at me again and tightened the screws on her super powered guilt glare. It was disturbingly effective. She followed me around Christos.

I circled cautiously backward.

Kamiko was in hot pursuit. "Now it's ten dollars. You feel bad because my mother robbed me of my rightful childhood income. Think of all the dishes and vacuuming I did. For free."

"Guilt, guilt, guilt," Christos chanted.

"Not helping," I singsonged.

"Is Kamiko guilting you?" Romeo asked, suddenly standing behind me.

We all turned to look at him. He looked like he'd just come back from being out all night. He wore his fanciest black steampunk greatcoat. It had at least two hundred studs and buttons. Buckled black boots poked out from the bottom of the coat. His trademarked monocle was squinched into place.

"She won't quit until she gets paid," Romeo said, nodding toward Kamiko. "You'll have nightmares about that face of hers until you pay up. She's taken me for at least two grand since the start of high school."

Kamiko smiled smugly. "He's right." She was still creeping toward me.

I couldn't look at her guilt glare any longer. I dug a ten spot out of my purse and slapped it on her palm. "Make it go away!"

Kamiko's horrid expression relaxed into a pleasant grin. "Thank you, Sam. You're so kind."

"You can't be mad at me anymore," I insisted.

Romeo snickered.

"What?" I said.

"Kamiko's been playing you for over a week," Romeo said. "I talked her down from her Sam hating ledge over fish tacos last

Tuesday. I convinced her that boy Brandumb was bing bong in the ding dong if he couldn't see how hot she is."

I leveled an accusatory look at smiling, innocent Kamiko. She was no saint. She was the devil. It was time to flip the guilt trip. I turned up my own guilt glare to full power.

"What?" she said defensively. "I've been busy working on new paintings for Brandumb's show. I didn't have time to tell you."

It was my turn to frown. "Not good enough."

"My mom robbed me of my childhood earnings?" she said uncertainly. "Making me nothing more than an indentured servant?"

I shook my head and intensified my frown.

Kamiko screwed her face back into a glare and wiggled her wrinkled nose at me. "You can't guilt glare me! I studied with the master!"

I grabbed for the ten dollar bill in her hand and growled, "Gimme my money back, con artist!" She danced away and jammed the money into her book bag.

"Fine. Keep it." I rolled my eyes. "So, Romeo, what are you doing out so late?"

"Me?!" Romeo blurted. "What the hell are you guys doing out so late? Wait! I know! You missed me! You couldn't get enough Romeo into your day, so you waited until you could bask in more of my awesome sauce!"

I grimaced at Romeo. "Why does you saying that make me want to take a bleach bath?"

Romeo wrapped his arms around me and jumped up and down aggressively. "Come on, Sam, you know you want my awesome sauce all over you!" He tried to lick my face.

Still caught in his grasp, I dodged my head from side to side. "Stop! Help!"

"If I keep jumping," Romeo said suggestively, "maybe some awesome sauce will pop out the top of your head!"

Kamiko grimaced. "Seriously Romeo? I think I can taste vomit sauce in my mouth."

"Okay," Romeo said, ceasing his jumping. "Nobody likes to swallow vomit sauce." He paused thoughtfully, hands on his hips. "On second thought, I just met this guy tonight who said he—"

"Hush!" I snapped, "We don't want to know!"

"Yeah, Romeo," Kamiko pleaded. "We've heard enough."

"Actually," Christos said, "I'm kinda curious where you met the vomit sauce guy."

"Hillcrest," Romeo said.

"That explains it," Christos nodded thoughtfully.

"What's in Hillcrest?" I asked.

Romeo rolled his eyes. "The gays, dearest."

Christos chuckled. "True that."

"What were you doing in Hillcrest?" I asked.

Romeo and Christos exchanged a look of utter disbelief.

"Duh," Romeo scoffed.

"What?" I said defensively. "Am I supposed to believe you can drive to wherever Hillcrest is and random gay men are walking around the streets trolling for vomit sex?"

"Yes!" Romeo and Christos blurted in unison.

Okay, I admit it. I still had a few things left to learn in life.

===

The four of us stood outside Paiute Hall for awhile, continuing to chat and joke with each other. Christos had his arm draped casually around my waist most of the time. I don't think I'd ever hung out with friends in the middle of the night like this before, and definitely not with a super hot boyfriend for me to lean against. I felt like the star of my very own college romcom.

It must have been after one in the morning, yet it seemed so normal, which was awesome. If I had been out this late in high school, my parents probably would've tried to send me to juvie for criminal loitering and felony curfew breaking. Screw them. I was nineteen. I could stay out as late as I wanted. I was having so much fun with my friends, I'd almost forgotten that my parents were doing everything in their powers to interfere with this awesome life I was building for myself.

"What's up with the coat, Romeo?" Kamiko joked. "Were you on set for the filming of The Matrix Rebloated?"

Romeo smiled at her. "Hilarious, darling. I love you too. But I promise you it's the bulky coat. Underneath, I'm as svelte and sexy as ever."

"You should totally get a mirrored monocle to complete the look," I said.

Romeo ran his splayed fingers sensually down his chest and

flicked his tongue at Kamiko.

"Ew! Frog tongue!" she squeaked.

Five brawny guys turned the corner of Paiute Hall and emerged from the shadows while Romeo continued to flick his tongue scandalously. Three of the guys wore T-shirts that said 'SDU Rugby'.

One guy said, "Dude, did you see the way that guy turned bitch when I threw my beer in his face and told him to shut the fuck up?"

"Totally!" his buddy replied. "He was ready to piss his pants!"

"Fucking pussy!" another chimed in.

The five of them laughed uproariously.

Great. Here came Team Testosterone.

As the group passed us, one of the guys, who had a crew cut, took one look at Romeo and coughed out the word, "Faggot!" while covering his mouth.

Romeo batted his eyelashes at Crew Cut and said, "Mmm, aren't you mantastic."

Another guy in the group said to Crew Cut, "I think that guy has the hots for you."

Crew Cut scowled at his friend then flipped Romeo off.

Romeo responded by flicking his tongue suggestively at Crew Cut.

"Don't, Romeo," Kamiko hissed.

Crew Cut came to a stop in front of Romeo and said, "You want a piece of me, fag?"

"Depends on which piece," Romeo smiled, hands on hips. "Do I get to choose?"

The four other guys came to a stop beside Crew Cut. The five of them surrounded Romeo.

"Mmm. Gang bang. I like," Romeo smiled confidently. "Who goes first? Or do you guys want to take me all at once? I've got enough orifices and hands to go around."

"Stop, Romeo!" Kamiko pleaded while pulling on Romeo's coat.

"Who are you?" Crew Cut asked, "His fag hag?"

"Are you blind?" Romeo asked, offended. "She's no hag."

The guy with a lumberjack beard standing on the right said, "Fag's right. This asian chick is pretty hot. You guys can have the fag while I chat up his friend."

"Easy boys," Christos said, stepping forward.

Crew Cut glared at Christos. "Who the fuck are you? This guy's fag boyfriend?"

"Yeah," Christos said. "You gotta problem with my boyfriend, you gotta problem with me."

Romeo clearly liked the sound of that. He smiled up at Christos.

The rugby guys started sizing up Christos.

Oh no. What was Christos doing? I mean, I didn't want Romeo to get hurt, and Christos was awesome for standing up for Romeo and Kamiko like this, but if Christos was already going to court for fighting, surely more fighting was not a good idea? I had to put a stop to this.

I stepped toward the mass of men, putting myself between Christos and the rugby guys. The unmistakable aroma of alcohol and asshole immediately assaulted my nostrils. I held up my phone and snapped a photo. "Now that I've got a picture of you guys, I'm calling campus security. I've got them on speed dial. You guys should leave before they get here." My phone was already dialing.

Crew Cut snatched my phone out of my hand and hurled it into the darkness like a champion discus thrower. I was truly astonished at how far it flew. I mean, it sailed over the dining hall next to the dorms like it had wings and literally disappeared into the night sky. I didn't even hear it land, it went so far.

"Fuck your phone," Crew Cut said.

I backed up a step and glanced at Christos from the corner of my eye.

"Bad idea, buddy," Christos said to Crew Cut. "Now you owe her a phone."

"It's okay," I said nervously. "I don't mind. I needed a new one anyway. We should go." I tugged on Christos' arm.

Romeo and Kamiko were cringing together, slowly stepping backward.

"Where you going, babe?" Lumberjack asked Kamiko. "I was just getting to know you."

"No, this is bullshit," Christos said, his eyes locked on Crew Cut. "This guy owes you a new phone."

"It's okay," I insisted. "My contract is up and I'm sure I can get a new one for free." I didn't mention I needed the old phone if I wanted to exchange it for a new one. Oh well, it didn't matter. Getting us out of here unharmed was more important. I'd buy a prepaid phone if I had to. "Let's go, Christos."

Another rugby guy took a step toward Christos and said, "Better do what this silly little bitch tells you, if you know what's good for you."

===

CHRISTOS

Five on one was never good odds, even for me. Especially not when Samantha, Kamiko, and Romeo were likely to get sucked into things. Most men never hit women, but that didn't help Romeo any. I was pretty sure he'd need protecting. And if Samantha or Kamiko tried to help out and protect me, they'd probably get punched up in the process.

If I was by myself, I would've bolted. I didn't need more court trouble than I already had. And I doubted any of these pricks could catch me in a foot race, rugby or no rugby. I didn't give a shit if they called me a pussy for running away. But if I ran, there was no way Samantha, Kamiko, and Romeo would be able to keep up.

What to do?

Samantha was right. Her phone didn't matter. Best to just walk away.

I took a step back and put my arm around Samantha. "All right, let's go, you guys."

I felt Samantha breathe a sigh of relief.

The four of us turned around and started walking toward the front doors of Paiute Hall.

I quietly said, "Kamiko, get your card key ready so we can walk right into the building."

"Okay," she said. The card key was already in her hand, attached to her key ring.

Something slammed into my back and I went careening forward. Samantha stumbled, almost tripping, but caught herself.

"Get the fuck back here, bitch!" Crew Cut shouted. "We're not finished!"

The four of us turned to face him. Crew Cut stood proudly, cracking the knuckles of his fists, his four buddies right behind him.

"Open those doors, Kamiko," I hissed. "Get inside right now."

"Stop it!" Samantha shouted at Crew Cut.

"Too late for that, bitch."

Kamiko had one of the doors open. "Come on, Romeo!"

Romeo was overwhelmed by what was happening. Kamiko reached out and pulled Romeo into the building.

"Get inside," I said to Samantha.

"Not without you!" she pleaded.

"Now!" I backed toward the door.

Samantha stepped inside. "Come on, Christos!"

Crew Cut was advancing toward me.

Samantha reached out for my arm.

I pushed the door to Paiute Hall shut, forcing her inside. "Don't open that door," I growled.

Crew Cut rushed at me. I ducked and pivoted under his right arm and launched a looping left into his liver. He folded like a sack of potatoes and banged his shoulder against the doors of Paiute Hall with a rattle.

Four guys came at me like charging rhinos. I danced to the side and slammed my fist into one guy's left temple. Lights out. He was on the ground.

But Crew Cut was getting up, and the three other guys pounded me with a hailstorm of fists. One caught me in the chest, another in the jaw, another in my left eye. My own fists were flying and I whipped an elbow into the bearded guy's nose. Blood gushed from his face. The other two guys tried to wrestle me down but I snaked out of their hands and ran like hell for my bike in the parking lot.

I heard heavy footsteps pounding behind me, but there was no way they were keeping up. I had my bike key out when I made it to my Ducati and hopped on. I started the bike and heeled the kickstand up while revving the throttle. I had the bike turned around as the guys rounded into the parking lot and I was off like a rocket.

In my rearview, I saw them sprinting after me, but they gave up after ten yards. I flew out of the far end of the parking lot, turned onto Adams College Drive, which led out to North Torrey Pines, and cranked the throttle.

What the fuck was that?

My mind raced over the situation. I wasn't too worried about those guys following me now that I was on my bike. One, they couldn't catch me unless they had sport bikes, and two, with three of them banged up pretty good, I doubted they'd be in hot pursuit.

I wanted to call Samantha and tell her I was okay, but her phone was gone. I didn't have Kamiko or Romeo's numbers, so I couldn't call them. And I didn't want to head back to campus too soon, because I wanted to wait until those guys were long gone, and because someone would probably have called campus security by now.

The one thing that couldn't wait was putting my helmet on. A quarter mile from campus, I rolled to a stop on the side of the road and grabbed my helmet from where it was strapped to the side of my bike. No need getting pulled over for riding without a helmet on top of everything else.

After my helmet was on, I cruised toward La Jolla Village. I ended up at the La Jolla Village Square mall and parked outside the Ralph's grocery store. I swung my leg over the seat and took my helmet off. I was sweating good from the exertion of the fighting and the running. My helmet liner was damp with perspiration. I strolled inside Ralph's. Pausing at the liquor aisle, I considered grabbing a bottle of bourbon, but I had to ride my bike home. So I snagged a huge bottle of water off the shelf in the beverage aisle and went up front to pay for it.

I set the water on the conveyor at the cash register. The clerk, a young woman with a sleepy expression and too much eye makeup, looked up at me and grimaced.

That wasn't the reaction I was used to with the ladies.

"What happened to your face?" she asked.

I reached a hand up and touched my cheek. Now that the adrenaline from the fight was wearing off, I felt the throb on my cheek bone where one of the rugby guys had clocked me. He'd hit me harder than I'd realized. A dozen lame excuses raced through my brain. Ran into a door. Tripped on the sidewalk. Fell down the stairs. Stepped in front of a forklift. Wrestled a bear. Went twelve rounds with an elephant. Etc., etc., etc.

I winked at her, "Got in a fight with a drunken rugby team." Sometimes the truth sounded too ridiculous to believe. That was my plan.

She arched an eyebrow, "All by yourself?"

"Yeah."

She frowned skeptically, "Really?"

I chuckled. What was it about my physical appearance (muscles, tats, banged up face) that said, "this guy *doesn't* get in fights"? It always amused me when people didn't believe the truth.

"Really," I said.

She flashed a big smile, and her sleepy expression gave way to a pretty set of teeth. She had a rocking little body and was actually cute when she wasn't halfway to slumberland. "Do you need someone to put ice on it? My shift is over in half an hour."

I hid my grin. Much better. This was the sort of treatment I'd come to expect from the ladies.

I saw her eyeing the tattoos on my arms, and the script of my Fearless tattoo which peaked out of the notch in my V-neck T-shirt. I grinned back. "I'm good. Just the water." I flashed her a dimpled grin.

"You sure?" Her eyes narrowed into bedroom territory, but not the sleepy kind.

Yeah, too much eye makeup. Not that I cared. I had a girlfriend who was going to move in with me unless her parents put her under house arrest. "Totally sure."

The cashier harrumphed in a cute way, kind of like a sleepy kitten, then rang up my water bottle.

I paid cash and walked out to my bike, guzzling down the entire bottle before climbing on my Ducati and riding back to SDU.

===

SAMANTHA

Romeo called campus security on his phone while we watched in horror through the glass doors as Christos fought with the jerks of Team Testosterone outside of Paiute Hall.

"There's five guys with SDU rugby shirts beating up my friend!" Romeo shouted into his phone. "What? One guy! Yes, he's fighting them all by himself! Please send someone right now! They're in front of Paiute Hall!"

"Ohmygod!" Kamiko screamed. "They're hitting him!"

I was freaking out because Christos was in danger from the guys outside, but possibly worse danger if campus security showed up. SDU had actual police on campus. They were the same ones who'd arrested Christos the day we'd met.

I had to do something to stop this.

I was about to push the doors open when Crew Cut fell into

them, blocking them shut.

The next thing I knew, two more guys were out of commission and Christos was sprinting out of sight with the last two guys chasing after. Everything had happened so fast, there was no time to do anything.

Crew Cut and his buddy with blood running down his face were trying to lift up their friend who had been knocked out.

"Pick him up," Crew Cut grunted.

Bloody Face draped one of the unconscious guys arms around his neck.

The two of them hoisted their friend and started walking across the lawn in front of Paiute.

"They're going to get away before security gets here!" Kamiko growled. "They'll get away with it! That's not right!" Kamiko pushed the panic bar on the door with a loud thunk and strutted outside.

"Kamiko!" I called after her. "Don't! Stay inside!"

She ignored me. "Get back here, you guys! I'm pressing charges as soon as security shows up! You guys are going to get expelled!"

Crew Cut turned awkwardly while trying to support his buddy. "Back off, bitch."

"Stop!" Kamiko shouted, striding toward them.

I couldn't leave her alone with those guys, so I jogged out to join her.

"Don't make me tell you twice," Crew Cut said to Kamiko.

"Come on!" Bloody Face said to Crew Cut, "we need to go, man!"

Crew Cut snarled at Kamiko. "Fucking cunt."

"Fuck you, you stinky assbag!" Kamiko shouted.

I grabbed her by the shoulders. "Stop! Don't make this worse."

"But they started this, Sam!" she pleaded.

"I know." But all I could think about was the cops showing up and asking questions and Kamiko or Romeo blurting out Christos' name. Before I had time to explain myself, two uniformed cops walked across the big lawn in front of Nyyhmy and Paiute.

"That's them!" Kamiko shouted.

Two flashlights flicked on and danced across the three remaining rugby guys. "Stop where your are, sirs," a voice commanded.

Fuck.

"Oh, thank god! They're here!" Romeo said to his phone, now standing beside me and Kamiko. "Yes. Two cops just walked up. Thank you." He lowered his phone to his side.

I wasn't sure if Romeo had hung up his phone or not. I grabbed it from his hand.

"Hey! What are you doing?" he asked.

I ended the call on his phone. Had I not, I worried the operator might have heard what I was going to say.

"All three of you, put your hands up!" one of the cops shouted.

"We can't!" Crew Cut said. "Our friend is unconscious."

Shit. I was pretty sure whoever got knocked out in a fight looked like the innocent one.

"Some guys jumped us," Bloody Face said to the cops. "Beat the shit out of us."

WTF? Were they blaming us for starting this? At least they wouldn't be able to pin it on Christos if they didn't know who he was.

The cops were getting closer to all of us. I had only a few seconds to strategize with Romeo and Kamiko before the cops could overhear everything I said.

"Don't mention Christos' name," I hissed.

"What?" Kamiko asked, confused.

"Sam," Romeo said, "why'd you take my phone?"

I thrust Romeo's phone back into his hand. "Listen! Tell the cops that Christos was a stranger walking by and he tried to help out. Don't say his name. You don't even know his name. And don't mention his tattoos. Just say he was some random guy."

Kamiko and Romeo still looked confused, their eyes getting big. I couldn't blame them. They had no idea what was going on with Christos' trial.

"Trust me," I said. "And please do what I asked. Please. I'll explain everything later. Okay?"

"Yeah," Kamiko nodded.

"Okay," Romeo said. "But what if those jerks say something different? We talked to them for awhile."

Romeo was right.

"Uh," I said, "I don't know. We'll play it off. Just don't mention any names!"

I noticed then that the two cops were cuffing Crew Cut and

Bloody Face while their friend sat on the grass cross legged, hunched over. When the cops finished cuffing the two guys, they made them sit on the grass about ten feet apart from each other, near one of the lamps that illuminated the walkway between Nyyhmy and Paiute.

"Are you the people who called in this fight?" the taller cop asked.

"I did," Romeo said. He glanced at me nervously.

The other cop was calling in something on the radio attached to his shoulder. He was stocky and had a stumpy neck and broad shoulders. "Backup and EMTs are on the way," he said to the tall cop.

The taller cop walked up to us while stocky cop stood sentry over the rugby players. I hoped their asses were getting soaked and cold from sitting on the damp lawn. Jerks.

"I need to see everyone's Student IDs," the tall cop said.

We all pulled them out and handed them to him. He shone his flashlight on each one and looked us each in the face in turn. He handed the IDs back to us. "Can you tell me what happened?" he asked Romeo.

Romeo looked at me for approval. I didn't want to look like I was some kind of criminal mastermind, so I shrugged my shoulders.

"Um," Romeo said, "me and my friends were chatting over there," he pointed, "and these guys came walking up and started harassing us."

"Were any of you involved in the fight?" the cop asked.

"No," we all said.

"So, who was fighting them?" he asked Romeo point blank.

"This...guy?" Romeo said sheepishly.

"Which guy?" the cop asked.

"The...stranger?" Romeo said uncertainly.

I repressed an eye roll.

"Me and my two friends," I said, motioning to Kamiko and Romeo, "were talking for awhile, then this cute guy walked up to us and started chatting with us."

"Which cute guy?" Tall cop asked. Then he pointed at Romeo and said, "Him?"

"No," I said.

"Hey!" Romeo frowned, "I'm cute!"

"Shut up, Romeo," Kamiko said.

The cop hooked a thumb behind him toward the rugby goons. "Do you mean one of those guys back there?"

"No," I said. "He's gone. The cute guy, I mean."

"Why did he leave?" the cop asked.

"I guess because it was five on one?"

"What do you mean?"

"Me and my two friends here ran inside Paiute Hall when the guys all started fighting. The cute guy punched a bunch of them before he ran off. That's why that guy over there has a bloody nose or whatever. Then the two other guys who are gone chased after cute guy."

"Let me get this straight. Cute guy was fighting those three guys plus two more?"

"Yes," I said.

"And you don't know who this cute guy is?"

"No."

The cop nodded. "So how did the fight start?"

Did I have to answer? I was afraid anything I said was going to sound so ridiculous I was going to get caught in a lie and get Christos in trouble.

"One of those guys called me a faggot," Romeo said, "and I happen to be gay, which makes this a hate crime."

"Did you do anything to provoke them?" the cop asked, eying Romeo's steampunk attire.

I was starting to dislike this cop.

"No!" Romeo said. "Me and my friends were talking to each other and one of those guys went—" Romeo mimicked the coughing and hand covering thing Crew Cut had done, "—Faggot!"

The cop nodded, "Sounds like a potential hate crime to me."

Maybe this cop wasn't so bad.

"But none of them hit you?" he asked Romeo.

"No," Romeo said.

The cop glanced over at the rugby guys in the grass, then asked Romeo, "Do you know any of them personally? Are they aware of your sexual orientation?"

Romeo shook his head. "No, not that I know. I mean, I thought I looked pretty fabulous when I got dressed up to go out tonight.

Does that count? Some people do tell me I'm too fashionable for my own good. Is a crime of fashion considered a hate crime? I think it should be," Romeo said earnestly.

Kamiko glared at him.

"What?" Romeo frowned at her. "You said I looked like The Matrix."

"Rebloated," Kamiko jabbed.

The cop was obviously doing his best not to smile at their tomfoolery. He cleared his throat and said, "In any case, their use of such a derogatory term is unacceptable. Were either of you two ladies involved in the verbal altercation?" the cop asked me and Kamiko.

"The same guy who called Romeo a faggot called me a fag hag," Kamiko blurted. "Then his friend, the guy with the beard, called Romeo a fag too."

"Romeo?" the cop said, confused. "Who's Romeo?"

"I am." Romeo squinched his monocle into place and did a courtly bow while twirling his hand. "Romeo Fabiano, at your service."

"That's not what your Student ID said," the cop cinched his brows.

"Romeo is my middle name," he said nervously.

My jaw dropped. I turned to stare at Romeo.

A pained look weighed on Romeo's features as he said, "My first name is Elmo. Elmo R. Fabiano."

I was shocked. "Elmo?" I glanced at Kamiko and she nodded. I turned back to Romeo. "Are you serious? Is Elmo even Italian?"

"It is," Romeo said proudly. "Look it up."

I felt betrayed. It showed on my face.

"Hey," Romeo said defensively, "Can you blame me? Elmo has so many negative connotations nowadays. And that voice of his?" Romeo shuddered. "Anyway, Elmo was my great-grandfather's name. He was a member of the Resistenza Italiana during World War II and he fought against Mussolini and the Nazis. He was a total badass, and he was an Elmo long before that stupid puppet ruined it for the rest of us. Besides, Romeo is more romantic, don't you think?"

I didn't know what to say.

"Elmo's not stupid," Kamiko crooned. "He's cute."

Romeo rolled his eyes. "You're only defending him because Elmo was your boyfriend until the sixth grade."

"No he wasn't!" she protested.

"Was too!"

"No, if you remember," Kamiko frowned, "once I discovered Ash from Pokémon in the second grade, I forgot all about Elmo."

"That's right!" Romeo smiled. "Ash was your very first cartoon crushationship! You were always telling me how jealous you were of Pikachu for spending so much time with Ash!"

"I hated that bitch!" Kamiko grinned.

"Is Pikachu even a girl?" I mumbled, mostly to myself. "I thought he was supposed to be a boy."

"Ahem," the cop interrupted. "Anyway, miss, You mentioned a guy with a beard? Who ran off?"

"Yes," Kamiko said, trying to calm herself.

"And none of you hit anyone, or were hit by those three men?" he asked.

"No," I said, "we all ran inside Paiute and made sure the door was locked."

"And who was this cute guy again?"

"We don't know," I said a bit too forcefully. "I've seen him around campus and in class, but I don't really know him. I just say hi to him."

"Yeah, Sam's too shy to ask him his name," Kamiko insisted. "I don't know his name either," she giggled.

"Which one of you is Sam?" the cop asked.

Waving my hand meekly, I said, "I am. Sam...I am. Green eggs and ham...I mean Samantha. My name is Samantha. Green eggs and hamantha." I trailed off into a feeble giggle, then grimaced, rolled my eyes, arched both brows and kicked myself mentally for sounding like a schizophrenic Dr. Seussette. At this rate, I was pretty sure the cops were going to order up straight jackets for the three of us. As long as it took the heat off Christos, I was okay with that.

"And none of you know the cute guy's name?" Tall cop asked skeptically.

Romeo and Kamiko shook their heads.

"No," I answered meekly.

The cop drilled his eyes into mine for what seemed like an hour.

Finally, he adjusted his gun belt and sighed audibly. "Okay. You guys stay put. I'm going to confer with my partner." He walked over to Stocky Cop and the two of them started chatting.

Two more cops came walking around the corner of Paiute from the opposite direction, followed by two EMTs who were carrying plastic medical boxes. Tall cop nodded at them and waved them over.

"Did I do okay?" Romeo asked nervously.

"Make sure you never break any laws, Romeo," Kamiko said. "You're a terrible liar. You'd end up going straight to jail if you committed a crime. And you know what happens to men who go to jail."

"I know!" Romeo said enthusiastically. "The possibilities are endless! All those desperate men with nothing to do but lift weights and brood all day long. They get all pent up and even the straight guys are forced to seek 'alternative' sexual gratification. It sounds like a dream come true!"

Kamiko gawked. "Are you cray-cray, Romeo?"

"Nope. Just gay-gay," he winked.

"No jail for anybody!" I hissed insistently.

Romeo's playful expression mellowed into seriousness. "What about those jerks over there? I think they deserve jail. And a rusty shiv up the butt."

"Maybe them," I said. "But let's not talk about it, okay?" I noticed that Tall Cop was questioning Crew Cut. "Now be quiet so I can hear what those cops are saying!"

Their voices were faint, but I heard most of their conversation.

"How many guys did you say jumped you?" Tall Cop asked Crew Cut.

Jumped? Great. Those douche nuggets started this, and now they're trying to blame us?

"Four," Crew Cut said.

"And you say they started it?"

"Yeah. They were mouthing off about how SDU Rugby sucks and how we're a bunch of pussies. We tried to blow them off, but they wouldn't let up."

Maybe I was being too hasty. Perhaps Douche Cut Crew Cut was going to do my work for me and lead the cops on a wild douche chase, taking the heat off Christos.

"Can you describe any of them?"

"Not really. Everything happened so fast—"

Even better.

"—But I do remember one guy. Big dude. Had lots of tattoos on his arms. Dark hair."

Fuck.

Tall cop was jotting this down in a small note pad. "Had you ever seen the guy before?"

"Yeah. I've seen him around campus."

Oh, no.

"Do you recall anything about the other three?"

"Not really."

I shook my head. Douche Crew Cut was putting all the blame on Christos.

"Sit tight," Tall Cop said, "while I talk to your friend."

I saw Crew Cut shoot a glance at his bloody buddy, who was being tended to by the EMTs. Stocky cop was talking to the two new cops. Tall cop chatted with the three officers before he went over to Bloody Face and the EMTs.

Bloody Face was holding one of those quick freeze ice packs to his nose. I had a hard time hearing what he was saying. But I distinctly heard, "He started it," and, "tattoos on his arms," and, "I think he goes to school here."

My stomach knotted.

Then Bloody Face stabbed me in the heart. He said, "She called him Chris. Chris something. I can't remember exactly."

Tall cop turned and fired bullets from his eyes directly into mine.

My stomach twisted my remaining internal organs into a wad that dropped down to my toes like lead. I was ready to vomit up my insides, including the bones in my toes. But I resisted the urge to unravel. I kept my innocent face in place and tried to appear as casual as possible.

Tall Cop must've run out of eye bullets because he turned back to Bloody Face.

"Those guys are lying," Kamiko whispered.

"I know," I said morosely.

With painful clarity I realized that Christos' confession to me only hours before, the one about him being a criminal and having gotten into tons of fights and trouble with the law was ominously accurate. Bad luck found him, no matter what he did to avoid it. Was he cursed? Was I a fool for loving him? Would it always be like this? Would he constantly be on the verge of getting arrested, or worse, locked away for long stretches? What kind of life was that? I shivered and hugged my elbows to my chest. I needed to think of something fast.

"Officer!" I hollered while waving at Tall Cop.

He was still questioning Bloody Face. I noticed the two EMTs were now kneeling next to the guy who Christos had knocked out and shining a pen light in the guy's eyes. Stocky cop saw me waving and he nodded to the two other cops before walking over to me.

He had a broad, sullen face and seemed rather gruff. I needed to win him over. Just because these guys were supposed to uphold the law didn't mean they were going to believe our story over the rugby goon's version of events.

"Yeah?" he asked. "Can I help you with something, miss?"

"I forgot to tell that other officer something," I said. I'd been so focused on not saying anything to betray Christos, I'd missed the obvious.

"What?" he grunted expectantly, as if expecting something astonishing, like film footage of the second, third and perhaps fourth President Kennedy shooters.

My plan to win him over was not going well. "When those guys started harassing us," I said tentatively, "I took a picture of them on my phone and told them I was going to call campus security. Before I could, that guy with the crew cut grabbed my phone and threw it."

"Where?"

"Where what?"

"Where'd he throw your phone," stocky cop said impatiently.

"Oh. Over the dining hall."

Stocky cop turned to look. He frowned. "From here?"

"No. We were standing over there when he threw it." I pointed.

"You sure he threw your phone?" the cop asked, as if I was suggesting Crew Cut had thrown my car or perhaps an elephant over the dining hall.

"Yes, I'm sure! Do you want to search me? My phone is gone."

"How do I know you had a phone to begin with?"

A better question was, how did this get turned around on me?

"She did," Romeo said. "And I saw that guy throw it."

"Me too," Kamiko said.

Stocky cop looked between the three of us, doubt curling his lips. Yes, he had the teeth of an ogre, or perhaps a rotten goblin. Take your pick. "Okay," he sighed heavily, like I was asking him to clean his room for the tenth time. "I'll go tell my partner." He walked over to the other three cops and started chatting with them. Tall Cop looked at me again and nodded while Stocky Cop explained things. A minute later, Tall Cop walked back over to us.

"You say that guy over there grabbed your phone and threw it over the dining hall?" Tall Cop asked me.

"Yes," I said.

"Was that when the fight started?"

"Yes."

"Between those guys over there, and your friend, the cute guy?"

"Yes."

"And what was cute guy's name again?"

Brakes! I clamped my mouth shut before it could open. I'd almost fallen for the cop's trick line of questioning. "I told you before, I don't know his name. Like I said, he's more of an acquaintance."

He narrowed his eyes at me. "Do you remember if he had any tattoos?" he asked suspiciously. "Your *acquaintance*?"

"I don't think so," I said, making my best Little Miss Honesty face.

"No," Romeo added, "he didn't have any tattoos. I would've remembered. Guys with tattoos are hot!"

Tall Cop raised an amused eyebrow. "And you said there were five guys fighting your one friend?"

"Yes! And I have a picture of all five on my phone!"

"But your phone is gone?"

"Yes! I can totally go look for it, if you want."

"No. Hold tight here until we sort this out."

Tall Cop rejoined the other three officers. The EMTs had helped the guy who'd been knocked out to stand up. Crew Cut and Bloody Face still sat in the grass. Stocky Cop uncuffed them and they stood up. Stocky Cop gave them what appeared to be a stern talking to. Crew Cut and his buddies nodded solemnly and repeatedly like they were law-abiding citizens who'd been wrongly assaulted for no good reason. When the cops were finished lecturing Crew Cut and Crew, they let the three rugby goons walk across the quad and out of sight.

The four cops walked up to us.

"We're going to let you three go for the evening," Tall Cop said. "I suggest you all head to bed."

"What about my phone?" I asked.

He handed me a business card. "If you find it, give me a call."

Wow, big help he was. "Okay. So, um, are those rugby guys in trouble or anything?" I asked.

He sighed heavily. "Obviously, the three guys we talked to were in a fight. But we're missing several of the participants involved. Like your *acquaintance*. Unless we can round up everyone, there's not much we can do."

Great. Those rugby jerks got away with behaving like Upper Division Pricks while the man who had protected me time and time again was going to court in two days and possibly to jail.

How was that fair again?

===

CHRISTOS

Flashing reds and blues from a pair of police cars strobed across the pavement when I rounded the south end of the SDU campus and came up North Torrey Pines Road. The squad cars were parked behind Paiute Hall. I noticed them before I got to Adams College Drive, so I decided to drive right on by.

I wondered if Samantha had found her phone. If she had, did I want to ring her up while she was talking to a bunch of campus cops? Better to call her later.

I rode home. The house was silent when I walked inside. Not wanting to wake my grandfather, I slid my motorcycle boots off in the entry foyer and crept up to bed.

I needed to get my beauty rest before my pre-trial in the morning.

Fun stuff.

Chapter 3

CHRISTOS

Gravity had me by the balls and was hurtling me down toward oblivion like a boulder with a rocket pack strapped to its back. Faceless winged demons swirled around me, taunting me, clawing at my flesh, cackling with savage glee. Every time I swung at one of them or tried to grab an arm or a leg, they disappeared in a puff of black smoke only to reappear on my back, scaly limbs wound around my torso in a wicked embrace. Fangs sunk into my neck. I kept twisting and swinging and throwing knees, but there were too many of them. I couldn't stop the onslaught.

"Christos?"

I flailed awake in my bed. "What the fuck!"

"It's me, *agápi mou*," Samantha whispered. I felt her lay a soothing hand on my shoulder. "I think you were having a nightmare. Was it about those rugby guys?"

"Worse."

"Do you want to talk about it?"

"Not really. It won't make any difference. It was just a stupid dream." My bedroom was still dark. I glanced at the clock on the bed stand. 4:17am. "Did you just get here?"

"No. I've been here for awhile."

"In bed with me?"

"Yeah," she said softly.

"Are you naked?"

"Yes." Her voice was sultry and promised pleasant things.

I twisted and slid my arm around her waist, pulling her body into mine. Our taut stomachs kissed, delicious heat radiating from her skin into mine. Her soft breasts melted against my muscled chest and I was instantly hard. Samantha had no idea how completely womanly she was. Even in total darkness, she was incredible.

"Why didn't you wake me when you came in?" I asked.

"You were sleeping so soundly, I didn't want to disturb you."

"Yeah, my body must've crashed after all the adrenaline from the fight was gone." I kissed her softly on the lips and felt the tip of her tongue tease mine. "Mmm, but you definitely should've woken me."

"You're awake now," she said. "I didn't miss my window of opportunity, did I?" she giggled.

"Gee whiz, I don't know. Let me check." I rolled on top of her, skin to skin, and wedged my fingers under her ass, lifting her hips. Her knees parted freely and I slid between her legs. My cock was already throbbing, straining to be inside of her. I grabbed it in my fist and teased the tip against her. "Damn, woman, you're already wet."

"What did you expect," she joked. "I've been lying naked next to you for like two hours waiting for you to wake up."

"Did you touch yourself?" I asked suggestively.

"No!" she cried.

"Why not? It would be pretty damn sexy for me to wake up while you were getting yourself off next to me."

"You're such a perv, Christos!"

"Really? Why? Because I like the idea that you're so hot for me that you can't even wait for the real thing when I'm sleeping inches away? Sounds pretty damn hot to me..."

"Come here, you caveman," she giggled.

I planted my arms around her shoulders and lowered my mouth to hers. Our tongues snaked together as desperation fired down my spine.

"Yeah, definitely should've woken me sooner." I slid myself slowly inside her waiting warmth. "Fuck, *agápi mou...*"

We made so much noise, I couldn't hear those demons until long after we finished.

===

SAMANTHA

The scent of sex tickled my senses as I sighed pleasantly after making love to Christos.

I snuggled into Christos' arms. I couldn't get close enough to squeeze the unfinished business of his trial out of the way. I wanted to talk about it. I also wanted to forget about it and never mention it again. But it wasn't going anywhere. The heat of our infinite love could not burn it away, no matter how much I wished it would.

I considered Christos' feelings. Would bringing up his trial make him feel better so he could get it off his chest? Or would enjoying the comforting afterglow of our intimacy best soothe him into restful sleep? I didn't know.

Inadvertently I heaved a huge sigh. I couldn't help it. My indecision was driving me nuts. I was a terrible girlfriend.

"What is it, *agápi mou*?" he asked.

"Nothing."

He chuckled. "Come on. Tell me. I admit I ran out of your apartment somewhat hastily earlier tonight."

"Is that an apology?"

"It is. I apologize for bolting. But I've got all this heavy shit weighing down on me. I've got to get up and go to my pre-trial in a few hours."

"What's a pre-trial, anyway?"

"More legal bullshit before the actual trial. The D.A. and my attorney tell the judge what's going to happen at the trial, what they're going to say in court. But mainly it's my chance to officially accept a plea bargain, or turn it down."

"What's that mean?"

"The D.A. is giving me a chance to plead guilty in exchange for a shortened sentence."

He was talking about it like it was a news story that was happening to a total stranger. But this was real. Christos was going to court. Worse, I really didn't know anything about it. So far, all he had told me in the last twenty four hours was that he had punched a guy out and the trial was on Valentine's Day. Beyond that, I was totally in the dark. Not knowing anything made it somehow more frightening.

I asked, "Are you going to plead guilty?"

A heavy silence filled the room.

I'd watched TV shows about court in the past, I'd seen news footage of people in court, but none of it was real to me. It was always happening to someone else. In fact, the most memorable courtroom scene I could think of was the one at the end of the movie Legally Blonde. Somehow, I didn't think Christos' court experience was going to be candy-coated with a bunch of laugh track moments starring Reese Witherspoon.

"We don't have to talk about it if you don't want to," I said.

"It's okay. I'm going to plead not guilty."

"Wait, I thought you told me you hit some guy?"

"I did."

"Doesn't that mean you're guilty?"

"No, because it was self defense."

"Oh." I hadn't expected that. The way Christos had described it initially, I'd thought maybe he'd had a bar fight or something equally stupid. "Now I'm confused."

"The District Attorney is going to try to make me look like a bad guy. Like I started it for no reason. My attorney has to convince the jury that it was actually self defense, that the other guy started it."

"Did he?" I blurted. I slapped my hand to my mouth. I shouldn't be doubting Christos like this. "I'm sorry, I shouldn't have said that. Of course the other guy started it." I meant it. Every time Christos had ever fought someone in my presence, the other guy *had* started it.

"It's okay, *agápi mou*. Yes, the other guy started it. Despite all the shit I've done in the past, I haven't started a fight in years."

"So tell the jury that. Tell them you don't start fights."

"It's not that simple," Christos sighed. "There's all these rules about what constitutes self defense and what doesn't. It's different in every state, and I don't understand half of it myself. That's what my attorney is for. But I do know that we have to prove that the only option I had in that split second moment was to defend myself."

"Was it?" I asked.

He looked at me thoughtfully. "Without a doubt," he said confidently. "I had no choice."

"Then you're going to win!"

"That's my plan." Christos stood up from the bed. "I need a glass of water. Do you want any?"

"Sure."

I heard the faucet running in his bathroom and he returned a moment later with a glass.

"Thanks." I took the glass and sipped at it.

"Hey," he asked, "what happened after I left you guys back at SDU?"

I gulped down several swallows of water. Did I want to tell Christos that, aside from his trial, those rugby jerks were now blaming him for starting the fight? Not really. "Oh, uh, Romeo called campus security and a bunch of cops showed up. What happened to the two guys who chased you?"

"I have no idea. I hopped on my bike and ditched them. That was the last I saw of them. Did you get your phone back? I tried calling you."

"Eventually. After the cops left, Romeo and Kamiko kept calling my phone while we looked around behind the Dining Hall. It took forever, but we found it in some bushes."

"Sorry it was such a hassle. Those rugby buttplugs were a bunch of Upper Assmen."

I giggled. "Is the upper ass like a high quadrant of the anus near the colon? Or is it someone who's taking advanced courses in assery?"

"Both," he chuckled. "Hey, if your phone is all banged up now, and you need money for a new one, let me know. I feel like I owe you."

"Thanks, Christos. You don't owe me. Those guys were to blame, not you. Anyway, if I need a new phone, which I don't, I'll pay for it," I lied. I didn't have any cash to spare, but I didn't want him worrying about yet another thing.

"You sure? Are you getting a quarterly bonus from Grab-n-Dash?"

"Yeah. My boss promised me a free ICEE," I grinned. "I'll see if I can use it as a down payment on a phone."

Christos and I crawled into bed after I finished my glass of water.

I had no idea what the next 48 hours would bring, but for the moment, Christos was in my arms, and I was in his.

===

CHRISTOS

Thoughts of my pre-trial had me wired and jolted me awake before Samantha. I showered and dressed as quietly as possible. I don't think I'd put as much effort into going out on hot dates as I was for going to court. There was something fucked up about that.

After I shaved, I examined my shiner in the mirror. Nice. Black ringed in red. You couldn't miss it. Loved it. I grinned at myself. My upper lip was redder and fuller than usual, but I didn't think anyone would notice. With my rugged good looks, maybe the judge would attribute it to a recent collagen injection. Yeah, right. While the bruise didn't say, "This guy went twelve rounds with Mike Tyson and lost," it did say, "This guy fights more than most people."

I considered bugging Samantha for some concealer, but then I remembered she'd worn progressively less and less makeup since we'd met. If she had any, it was at her apartment, and I didn't have time for a detour.

Whatever.

After buttoning my shirt, I knotted my tie in the mirror.

"Sexy," Samantha said, standing in the bathroom doorway. "I don't think I've ever seen you dressed up before. Or clean shaved."

I flashed a cocky grin at her while cinching the tie up to my collar. "You like?"

"I love," she smiled as she walked up behind me and slid her hands over my chest. "Do I get to see you with the jacket on?"

"Sure." After giving her a quick kiss, I walked into the bedroom, pulled the jacket off the hanger, and slipped it on. I buttoned it and smoothed it down. "There."

"Wow, Christos, I knew you could pull off ruggedly sexy like no one else, but damn, I think you put that guy from 50 Shades of Grey to shame!"

"I think my shiner adds that hint of street danger that the 50 Shades guy was missing."

"Definitely," Samantha purred. "Do I have time to shower?"

"What do you mean?"

"Before we go?"

I arched an eyebrow. "We?"

Her face sunk. "Don't you want me to come with you?" she asked meekly.

I sighed and walked over to her. I grasped her arms and looked her in the eyes. "*Agápi mou*, it means a lot that you want to come with me. But this is just the pre-trial. Nothing is going to happen today. It's going to be a lot of boring talk from the lawyers about technical details, and which arguments they're going to use. Shit like that. Besides, you have classes, right?"

"Yeah, I guess. But I want to be there for you."

"You're here for me right now, *agápi mou*. I promise, you won't miss anything."

"Promise?"

I kissed her gently on the lips. "Promise. Now, I gotta run out the door. Don't wanna be late for court. You still have your key, right?"

"Yeah," she sighed.

"There's food in the kitchen if you're hungry. Take anything you want." I kissed her again and went down to the garage and hopped in my Camaro.

===

SAMANTHA

After Christos left, I showered, dressed, and went downstairs. I opened the refrigerator in the kitchen and stared at the contents. Who was I kidding? I couldn't think about eating when Christos was going to court. I gently closed the door and nearly jumped out of my skin.

Spiridon was standing right there.

"Oh!" I gasped. "I didn't hear you come in."

"Good morning, *koritsáki mou*," he said. "My apologies. I didn't realize you were still in the house."

I was always amazed by how much Spiridon looked like an older, silver-haired version of his blue-eyed grandson. Spiridon's eyes still shone as brightly as Christos'. I had no doubt that Spiridon had been quite the ladies' man in his day and I suspected he still was, but I had yet to meet any of the women who most certainly were pursuing him. I knew he went out in the evenings all the time, but I wasn't quite sure where he went or who he saw. Christos had hinted frequently about the women in his grandfather's life, but so far it was nothing more than juicy insinuations.

"Would you like me to make you some breakfast?" he asked.

"Oh, no thank you. I don't have much of an appetite."

"You have to eat something, *Samoula*. You can't go through an entire day without food." Spiridon pulled out a loaf of olive bread and spread soft cheese onto a slice. He handed me the plate. "Try this."

I took a bite. The cheese was salty and very peppery. It had some kick to it. It went great with the olive bread. "What kind of cheese is this?"

"You like?" he grinned.

"It's delicious!"

"It's called Kopansti. A friend of mine imports it from Mykonos."

"Wow, it's so good!" I chomped another bite and savored it. Somehow, the Manos men always managed to set me at ease, as if everything in the world was just right, and every moment was a decadent celebration of life. I hadn't had an appetite five minutes ago, but now I was ravenous. "Can I have another slice?"

"Certainly, *koritsáki mou*," he said, spreading more cheese on a fresh slice of olive bread. "I take it Christos made it home safely?"

"Yeah. Safe and sound." For now, I thought. I knew his pre-trial wasn't supposed to be a big deal, but I felt a doomsday clock ticking down to Valentine's Day on Friday, the day of his actual trial. Lameness. Could I petition to have Valentine's Day pushed forward a day? Probably not. "Spiridon?"

"Yes, *Samoula*?" Spiridon smiled.

"Do you, um, ah, I feel like maybe I shouldn't be asking this, but do you, uh...do you know about Christos' trial?" I was afraid maybe he didn't know and I was going to break his heart, but I also felt like I was stuck in the dark on this whole trial topic, and I needed some emergency support.

His smile faded. It didn't turn sour, like I could imagine my mom or dad doing, after which yelling and condescension would commence. Instead, Spiridon looked sad. "Yes, *koritsáki mou*, I know."

Phew. One obstacle out of the way. "Are you worried?"

"Yes," he said softly. "As many times as Christos has been in court, it never gets easier. There's little I can do but pray for him and hope that the jury sees the good boy I know my grandson to be."

"Yeah," I sighed thoughtfully. "Are you going to go to the trial?"

"Of course."

"Why didn't you go to the pre-trial today?"

"Because, based on my experience, it's largely a matter for the lawyers. But I will be at the trial on Friday."

"Oh."

I sort of felt left out because Spiridon knew all the details. But it made sense. Christos lived with him, so I'm sure he'd told his grandfather about it awhile ago. But I felt hurt that Christos hadn't told me. I wanted to be supportive in any way that I could, but that was impossible if he didn't include me in the process. I sighed to myself and shook my head.

Spiridon patted my shoulder. "It's okay, *Samoula*. Christos will be fine."

I hoped so. But the tortured look in Spiridon's eyes ignited the smoldering worry that had been twisting my guts in knots for the last twelve hours.

===

I drove to campus along the Pacific Coast Highway, slumped over the wheel of my VW. Class was the last thing I wanted to think about today. Worse, today was Sociology 2, starring my sleep-inducing Professor Tutan-yawn-yawn, and American History 2, where I always managed to draw cartoons in my sketchbook while conveniently avoiding putting notes in my laptop.

I contemplated bailing on class entirely. One of the perks of being a college student. But what was I going to do if I didn't go to class? Fret? Wring my hands together?

The beach was visible as I drove out of Del Mar. Too bad it was foggy and gray and I could barely see the ocean. Not much of a beach day, otherwise I might very well have parked my car and strolled down with my towel so I could lay out and catch some rays. Tanning under the buttery San Diego sun always soothed me.

Stupid fog.

The light at Carmel Valley turned red and I came to a stop. This was the intersection where I'd first met Christos last fall. I'd driven through here a hundred times since that day. The view of the beach never got old. I was so lucky to live in San Diego. I swear, it was a crime that people had to live anyplace else in the country. I felt bad for my parents, who were still stuck in the arctic urban wasteland of Washington D.C. It was probably snowing there right now. All I had to contend with was a little fog. The thermometer on my dash said sixty degrees.

A little fog wasn't so bad.

I reached for the Venti Americano I'd bought at the Starbucks in Del Mar. They didn't have a drive thru, so I'd had to park and it had taken forever. But today, I didn't care if I was late for class.

Not like that first day when I'd spilled my coffee everywhere. I shook my head and smiled. I'd been such a spaz that day. I remembered that fat guy behind me who'd been yelling at me.

Bitch...

He'd called me all kinds of crazy names.

Slut...

And he'd practically bitten my face off, he was so mad at me for holding up traffic.

Whore...

What a tool that guy was. Thinking about all of it now brought back Taylor Lamberth and Damian Wolfram, and the roller coaster my life had been for three long years. Was it ever going to stop? I felt like I'd left some crazy loop-de-loop behind me in D.C., but now I was headed into six more.

Agápi mou...

At least I had Christos to ride with me through life's twists and turns. Christos...

I started to tear up. I wiped my eyes, no longer worried about smearing the mascara I never wore anymore. My life had changed so much in the last six months. But was any of it for the better?

The light at Carmel Valley Road turned green and I drove the rest of the way to SDU.

===

I pulled into the parking lot on the north end of campus and searched for a space. The lot was packed with cars. I turned down yet another aisle and spotted an open space. As I drove toward it, a black Mercedes whipped around the corner at the far end of the aisle and raced for the space. I was closer and reached it well ahead of the Mercedes. The slick black car screeched to a stop as I was turning into the space, jamming its nose in the way of my VW.

"Hey!" I shouted. "What are you doing! This is totally my space! Move your car! I was here first!"

The Mercedes revved its engine. I couldn't see the driver because the overcast sky painted the front windshield over with a light gray glare.

I held my ground in my VW. This space was mine by right. First come, first served and all that.

The Mercedes' horn blared at me and the car inched forward like a menacing cobra.

"You're insane! I was totally here first!" I shifted my VW into park and got out of my car. For a second I thought it might be Hunter Blakeley, the figurative sculpting model who'd been stalking me all quarter. Then I remembered he drove a Porsche Boxster. I knocked on the window of the Mercedes sharply.

The power window whirred down.

"You," sneered Tiffany Kingston-Whitehouse, eyes narrowed.

"Yes, me," I smirked confidently. "Move your car."

"Move *my* car? You've got it wrong, Merry Maid. Shouldn't you be cleaning up fecal matter somewhere?"

As always, Tiffany looked like a team of stylists had done her hair, makeup, and nails this morning. She was dressed in the latest San Diego winter fashion: a sexy studded leather motorcycle jacket over a white scoop neck T that emphasized her ersatz rack, skinny black jeans, and a rugged belt. A super cute studded black leather clutch with white piping sat on the empty seat next to her. I had to admit, the girl knew how to dress. But it didn't make her any less of a bitch.

Which was why I was seriously considering grabbing a fistful of her fuck me blond hair and giving it a good yank. Could you scalp someone by yanking? Or did you need a knife to do it right?

"I hate to disappoint you, Tiff, but I was here first. Kindly remove your Mercedes from my way."

"I'm not moving anything, you shit stain. Get your car out of my way before I push it." She revved the engine of her Mercedes.

Her blond locks were within easy reach. I flexed my fingers in anticipation. Where was that knife? Screw it. I wasn't going to need it. I had nails. I was tired of taking shit from Tiffany Buttplug-Nuthouse.

"Go ahead," I laughed lightly. "Scratch your paint job and mine. I'm sure your daddy pays for the best insurance money can buy."

She glared at me and revved the Mercedes. "Move," she growled around gritted teeth.

"No." I stared her down.

She screamed in my face, "*MOOOOVE!!!*"

I winced and leaned back.

Wow, that girl sure had a set of lungs on her. And a voice that could cut glass. I think I was going to need to get my ears checked after that. But I stood my ground.

She thrust her head out her car window. "I've had it with you, you little bitch. You've been meddling in my life since you came to SDU. I'm sick of your ugly face. I'm going to make you regret the day you crawled out from whatever rock you lived under before you came to San Diego."

"Are you threatening me, Tiff?" I asked cooly, an amused smile on my face.

"No. I'm warning you. Because it's going to happen."

"Okay," I scoffed and waved a dismissive hand at her. No matter how many times Tiffany had tried to make my life miserable, she never succeeded. She was nothing more than a pesky housefly as far as I was concerned. I wasn't going to take any more of her dramatic threats. She was a spoiled brat who didn't know how good she had things.

Tiffany's eyes narrowed and her brows dove into a tight, threatening scowl. She looked hawklike. "Don't underestimate me, Samantha Anna Smith."

Surprise lit up my face.

"That's right," she hissed, "I know who you are. Don't think I'm some dumb blond you can laugh at. You have fucked with the wrong woman, you infected cunt."

How the hell did she know my middle name was Anna? Had Christos told her? That seemed unlikely.

"Watch your back, bitch," she said, then threw her car into reverse, backed up dramatically, and floored it. Her Mercedes growled a low threat as it disappeared at the end of the parking aisle.

Great. As if I didn't have enough troubles already.

Chapter 4

CHRISTOS

Half an hour after leaving my house, I walked through the cool marble interior of the San Diego Hall of Justice, looking slick in my dark suit. People in similarly formal and conservative attire milled about the wide main hallway, conducting impromptu meetings before going into the various courtrooms. Uniformed deputies in tan shirts, olive pants and bulky gun belts were scattered throughout the space, as were a few members of the S.D.P.D. in dark blue uniforms. It was all so formal and civilized.

A woman in one of those sexy fitted business suits carrying a briefcase peered at me over a pair of reading glasses. Her hair was in a neat mess on top of her head. Sexy librarian or sexy attorney? Same difference. I tossed her a dimpled smile and her composed, professional expression crumbled into a school girl grin.

May as well amuse myself before going into battle.

Russell Merriweather, my attorney, stood head and shoulders above the crowd in a dark charcoal suit, chatting on his cell phone. His ebony dark skin contrasted brilliantly against his impeccable amethyst button down shirt and striped tie. When he noticed me, he narrowed his eyes and flicked a nod in my direction. As always, he was all business while inside the courthouse.

I walked up to him as he ended his call. He slipped his phone inside his suit jacket and turned to me. "What the hell did you do to your eye, son?"

I opened my mouth to answer.

He held up a halting palm. "Stop. I don't want to know. Buy some concealer before the trial. We don't need the jury jumping to conclusions about you at the trial Friday."

I smiled. "Actually, I was thinking about getting the other one banged up so they match."

Russell repressed a smile and shook his head. "You do that," he said sarcastically. "But get some concealer either way." He put a fatherly hand on my shoulder. "On a more serious note, have you made a decision regarding the plea bargain offered by the District Attorney?"

I grit my teeth. "Fuck the D.A. I'm not guilty."

Russell nodded. A glint of approval passed across his eyes. "I expected nothing less from you, son. But may I remind you," he said ominously, "once you enter a plea, it's set in stone. No going back. If we go to trial and the jury finds you guilty, you run the risk of up to four years in prison. Are you okay with that?"

"Yup."

Russell nodded toward the doors to the courtroom. "You ready?"

"One other thing."

Russell raised his brows. "Do I want to hear it? The look on your face tells me I don't."

I grinned. "I'm going to testify."

Russell nodded, his eyes narrowing while his lips pursed thoughtfully. "As your attorney, I would be remiss if I didn't remind you that it's never wise for a defendant to testify. If you do, the Deputy District Attorney will have free rein to ask you anything he wants. Including questions about your criminal record. They will dredge up all of the demons from your past and parade them in front of the jury like a marching band. In the eyes of the jury, you will go from looking like a man who punched another man in a single case of self defense to Crime Spree Christos."

I knew he was right. But I hadn't started that fight with Horst Grossman. No matter how hard the D.A. tried to convince the jury I was a piece of shit, I knew the truth. I was going to stand up for myself. I was going to look every member of the jury straight in the eye and tell my story. If they didn't believe me? Fuck 'em.

They could all rot in hell.

"What other evidence do we have that I didn't start the fight," I asked, "other than my version of events?"

"Not as much as I would like," Russell said curtly.

"Then I have to testify," I said. "We don't have any other options."

Russell looked me in the eye. Hard. He didn't shout. He didn't lose his temper. He didn't try to argue me out of it. I'm pretty sure he could see the resolve in my eyes. All he said was, "You're sure?"

"Yeah."

"All right then. I'll make it work. Let's do this thing," Russell said, opening the door to the courtroom for me. He motioned inside. "After you, sir."

===

SAMANTHA

Professor Tutan-yawn-yawn was working the ancient Egyptian sleep magic in Sociology class better than the sandman today. I'd drained my Venti Americano within the first five minutes of class. If I was going to make it through the rest of the day, I was going to need more coffee.

I texted Madison.

I have a coffee emergency. Meet me at Toasted Roast after class?

Her reply, *Can't. I have Managerial Accounting with Dorquemann and Spanish after that. Lunch?*

I replied, *K. C u then.*

I heaved a sigh. Maybe I could find Kamiko or Romeo. I was seriously in need of some moral support. I didn't want to stew in my own thoughts about what might happen to Christos for a second longer.

I did my best to concentrate on the Sociology lecture and take notes until class was finished. Still in need of coffee, I got a fresh cup at Toasted Roast by myself before heading over to my History lecture.

I squeezed into a seat and pulled out my laptop. There wasn't enough room for my coffee and computer on the little fold out armrest desktop.

Did the University have a suggestion box somewhere? Because they totally needed to install cup holders in all the lecture halls.

"Well if it isn't Cathy Guisewite," some guy in the row behind me said over my shoulder in a smooth, smoldering voice.

I turned and looked into the eyes of a cute guy sitting behind me. He was chewing on the corner of a pen and grinning at me. He had this clean shaven boy band look going. No tattoos, and not especially muscular, but great hair and totally swoon worthy. I could imagine him sitting behind a piano and crooning while women threw underwear at him onstage.

I frowned but sort of smiled at him. "You must have me confused with someone else."

"Nope."

"I'm not Cathy Whoever."

"Sure you are," he grinned.

This poor boy had a screw loose. I arched an eyebrow. "Uh... no?"

"Don't tell me you've never read Cathy?"

"What?" I was totally confused. Maybe I had the loose screw. I'm sure if I shook my head something would rattle around inside.

"The comic strip? By Cathy Guisewite?"

Still not getting it, I shook my head.

"Do you even know what a comic strip is?" he smiled.

"Duh." I wasn't an idiot.

"Didn't you ever read the comics in the newspaper? I know it's totally unhip for people our age to admit to such a thing, but you can tell me," he winked, "I won't out you on Facebook or Twitter or whatever."

Now that he mentioned it, my parents still got the newspaper. My dad couldn't go to the office without first reading the comic strips at breakfast. He called them 'the funnies.' I used to look at them when I was a kid and try to copy the drawings, but I hadn't done that in a long time. Then a hazy memory locked into place. "Oh! You mean Cathy, the comic strip!"

He nodded, smiling. "Yeah. I mean, I know the series ended three and a half years ago, but I figured you may have seen it once or twice before all the newspapers started going out of business."

Who was this guy? He was bizarre. He was way too cute to be into something as last century as comic strips. "So, um, why are you calling me Cathy?"

"I've seen you drawing cartoons during class. Do you ever take notes, or just doodle?"

Guilty as charged. I blushed. "Is it that obvious?"

"Probably not to the professor and the T.A.'s, so your secret is safe with me," he winked. "You know, your work is pretty good. Have you ever considered submitting some of it to the school paper?"

I'm pretty sure he was pulling my leg. "No, those guys are all

Snooty McSnoots-a-lots." The SDU school newspaper, The Sentinel, had a reputation for being a high-brow elitist newspaper for preppie journalism majors. And considering I'd been ejected from high school society back in D.C., I didn't have any desire to go before a tribunal of hip socialites and have them tell me I wasn't good enough to join their club.

"The Analites at the Sentinel are totally snooty," he smiled. "I was talking about The Wombat."

The Wombat was SDU's comedy newspaper run by the Associated Students of SDU. It was full of funny spins on current events, humor about college life, party reviews of actual parties (on and off campus), and the ever famous Wombat comic strips. I'd read the comic strips before. They satirized the seedier social aspects of college: drinking, drugs and doing it with members of the opposite sex, same sex, or even different species. Some of them were hilarious and some of the art was amazing.

I raised my eyebrows. "You think I should submit my cartoons to The Wombat?" I didn't think my stuff was good enough.

"Yeah. I'll put in a good word for you with the editor."

"Who's the editor?" I asked.

"Me," he smiled. "Justin Tomlinson." He leaned down and offered his hand.

I had to awkwardly turn in my seat to shake it. "Samantha Smith. Isn't Tomlinson the name of one of the guys in One Direction?"

He rolled his eyes. "Don't remind me. If I'd had a choice at birth, I would've had the stork deliver me to another house," he smiled.

He sure had a great smile. Now all he needed was four more cuties and a boy band anthem and the girls would come out of the woodwork like termites. If they weren't already. For all I knew, Justin had a limo filled with fan girls waiting outside.

"Anyway," he said, "nice to meet you, Samantha. Email me some of your samples and I'll show them to my peeps at the paper."

"I've never written a comic strip. I mean, I just doodle in my sketchbook."

"Do you have your sketchbook on you now? I've seen you drawing in it before."

Ah, creepy stalker much? Or, had I been drawing in my sketchbook in History so often that it had become obvious to anyone who sat near me? That seemed unlikely. I religiously took notes in History class as if it was the most interesting topic ever invented. Not. "Yeah, I have it in my book bag."

"Can I see it?"

I had never shown my sketchbook to a stranger. I was somewhat reluctant. Oh well, if he mocked me, then he was a jerk, boy band cute or not. I pulled my sketchbook out and handed it to him.

He flipped through it casually, smiling the entire time. He stopped to linger at various pages, I didn't know which ones. He even chuckled a few times. "Yeah," he said, "these are great. Do you have any strips? Like multiple panels telling a cohesive story?"

"Not really,"

"No worries. What do you think about working with a writer?"

"What do you mean?"

"Some of the strips in The Wombat are written by one person and drawn by another. I could team you up with a writer if you needed help. Until you get the hang of it. But I get the sense you'll figure it out pretty quick, based on what I see here. Then you can write your own if you want. It would be up to you."

Wow, this guy was really nice. And cute. Not that I was interested in him. But he was being totally helpful, and he didn't even know me. "Okay. When do I start?" I wasn't sure how this was supposed to work.

"I have to show your stuff around first. But, like I said, I think the other guys will dig your work. Gimme your number and I'll give you a call after our next meeting—"

Oh. How smooth of him. I'd almost fallen for it. He was a master pickup artist.

"—or better yet," he continued, "why don't you come to our next staff meeting? It's this Friday."

Maybe I was getting ahead of myself. Maybe he was being genuine. "This Friday?"

"Yeah. We meet at 4:20 at Toasted Roast."

I did a double take. "You guys meet at Toke Time? Do you smoke joints during the meeting?" I smiled.

"It's up to you," he grinned. "so bring your own joints. But usually we stick to coffee."

"Sounds like my kind of crowd." But it was on Valentine's Day. The day of Christos' trial. Shit. My guess would be that I wasn't going to make their meeting. "But I don't think I can make it. I have…something really important to do that day."

"That's cool. If you want, I can snap some pics of your sketchbook and show them on Friday."

"Okay."

"Shoot me an email and I'll let you know what everybody says."

Wow, he backed off quick. Maybe I had judged him too hastily. Maybe he was totally just trying to help. "What's your email?"

"Look up The Wombat website online. You can find it there."

The professor walked into the lecture hall and set his briefcase down, getting ready to start.

"Okay," I said to Justin, "I'll do that."

Why did I suddenly feel like my life was being pulled in one too many directions at once? The one direction it was already heading was stressful enough.

And why was I thinking in boy band puns all of a sudden?

Groan!

===

I secretly wondered if Justin Tomlinson would try to chat me up after History class, but he was gone when I finished packing up my laptop.

On my way to the Student Center to meet Madison for lunch, I texted Romeo and Kamiko to see if they wanted to join us.

Madison was already waiting in line for fish tacos, decked out in an SDU hoodie, Hollister sweats and flip flops. For a certain contingent of students, sleepwear was acceptable school dress. I couldn't blame her. I knew she was jonesing to be back in short sleeves and board shorts. "What up, girl!" she cheered and gave me a big hug.

"Hey, Mads," I smiled.

"Did you find Christos last night?"

"Yeah."

"So what was the emergency?"

Hmm. How to explain that I was secretly worried he was going to commit suicide last night and still had no idea whether or not he had tried? And he was going to trial in two days? Yeah, not exactly an easy breezy topic. I wanted Madison to distract me from my pressing troubles, not dredge up my drama.

She nudged against me. "Come on, girl. Dish. I've got a scoop right here."

I sighed. Was there something else we could talk about, like boy bands? No, not that either. There had to be at least one topic I could come up with that wouldn't leave me dramatized.

"Can you believe that fight last night?" Romeo asked as he walked up to me and Madison, Kamiko at his side.

Eye roll.

"Fight?" Madison asked, looking between me and Romeo. "What fight? Between you and Christos?" she gasped. "And you didn't tell me?!"

I bugged my eyes at both of them. "Geez, you guys are worse than the National Enquirer! Christos and I didn't have a fight. And, Romeo, stop being such a dramaholic!"

"Can you blame me?" he asked. "I almost had my face bashed in by the jock squad last night."

"Wait," interrupted Madison. She looked at me pointedly. "What does the jock squad have to do with you calling me in the middle of the night asking where Christos was?"

Romeo, Kamiko, and Madison raised their eyebrows in tandem. They stared at me, dumbfounded.

"Don't hold out on us, Sam!" Romeo demanded. "If you have secrets, you have to share."

"That's what I said," Madison said, folding her arms across her chest. "Spill it bitch!"

"Fish tacos!" I cried.

Madison frowned, "That's not an answer,"

"Look!" I pointed and everyone turned to look at nothing. I considered running away while they were distracted, but luckily, we'd made it to the front of the line and it was time to order. I was spared further accusatory looks from my friends. For a few precious minutes, anyway. After everyone had their food, we carried our trays outside to an empty table.

"Well?" Romeo asked me after everyone sat down. "We're waiting to hear all about your fight with Christos."

My fish taco was halfway to my face when I said. "Reel it in, Rumor Romeo. There was no fight."

"Then what's the story, Sam?" Romeo asked. "We all want to know what we missed."

I scoffed. "You were the one who spent the night in Hillcrest with the vomit squad. Care to tell us about that?"

"Gladly," Romeo smiled. "It all started when I met this guy outside The Brass Rail, down in Hillcrest."

"What's The Brass Rail?" Kamiko asked.

"A gay bar in Hillcrest," Romeo answered. "Anyway, the vomit guy was—"

Madison cringed. "Can we table *that* discussion until after I've finished eating and digesting? Maybe after Winter Quarter is over or sometime next year?"

"I second that," Kamiko grimaced. "I don't need to know any more about Romeo's alternative lifestyle than I already do."

I would've gladly endured Romeo's graphic tale if it meant taking the heat off of my back.

The three of them stared at me.

If I couldn't tell my closest friends about my problems, who could I? Wasn't that part of what friends were for? To help you deal with your problems when you needed it? But how would Christos feel if I told the gang all about his trial? It's not like he'd willingly told me about it. I'd had to drag it out of him word by word. I contemplated waiting until Romeo and Kamiko were gone and just telling Madison. She seemed more leak proof than Rumor Romeo. I wasn't worried about Kamiko, but she and Romeo were practically attached at the hip. I secretly believed that if neither of them ever met their one true love, they'd eventually move in together and live like spinsters.

"We're waiting," Romeo said, chewing on his fish taco.

Screw it. They were my friends. They had a right to know. "Okay, but you guys have to promise to keep this a secret," I said.

"Oooh! Secrets! I love secrets!" Romeo cooed.

"I'm serious," I growled. "You can't tell anybody. This is a big deal. No fooling around. Especially you, Romeo. You. Can't. Tell. Anybody."

Madison and Kamiko turned to glare at Romeo.

"What, you guys?" he whined. "I've never spread gossip about any of you three and you know it, or my name isn't Romeo Fabiano!"

"You mean Elmo?" I chided.

"Who's Elmo?" Madison asked, confused.

Romeo looked distinctly embarrassed.

I arched an eyebrow at Romeo. "You keep my secret, I'll keep yours. Deal?"

"Deal," he nodded.

"Christos has to go to court on Friday," I said.

"Court?" Romeo blurted.

"Friday?" Madison said. "That's on Valentine's Day!"

"I know," I groaned.

"Why does he have to go to court?" Kamiko asked.

"Because he got in a fight."

"So?" Madison shrugged. "Guys get in fights all the time."

"Yeah," Romeo said, "I bet nothing is going to happen to those rugby buttplugs from last night."

"Rugby buttplugs?" Madison asked.

"I'll tell you later," Romeo said. "Right now we need to hear all about Christos' court date." Romeo sucked on his soda straw like he was in the middle of a movie theater watching a juicy drama.

I sighed and said, "He hasn't really told me much—"

Bitch...

"I just know he punched a guy out—"

Slut...

"—and I think it happened the day I met him."

Whore...

Oh my god. That was it! Christos punching that fat guy who'd yelled at me! That had to be why he was going to court. Why hadn't I seen it sooner? And why hadn't Christos told me? I was a witness and I could help!

"What, Sam?" Madison asked. "You look like you just swallowed some bad sushi."

"I think I just figured it out!" I shouted.

"What?" Romeo asked, on the edge of his seat, clutching his soda.

"I saw it!"

"Saw what?" Kamiko begged.

"I was there when Christos punched that guy! I'm the only other person who knows he started it! I have to call him right now!"

"You're losing us," Madison said, looking confused.

I whipped my phone out and dialed Christos. It started ringing. To the gang, I said, "I can help Christos win his trial! I saw everything!" Christos' phone went to voicemail. Damn. He was probably still in court. "Christos, you have to call me right now. It's about the trial. I was there! I can help." I hung up and texted him the same information. With any luck, he'd at least look at his phone and call me.

I just hoped it wasn't too late for me to be a witness for his trial.

===

CHRISTOS

"Are you saying that whatever we tell the judge today is what we have to say in the trial on Friday?" I asked Russell while we walked into the courtroom.

"Yes," Russell said as we sat down behind the defense table. "The judge gave us several months to get all our shit in order so there won't be any surprises on Friday. She's assuming that by now we've turned over every stone there is to turn."

There was still one stone nobody had turned. But I'd resolved to keep Samantha safely out of this mess from the beginning. It was my problem to deal with, not hers. "Got it," I said.

Russell pulled a laptop and several folders out of his briefcase while I looked around.

Everything in the room was wood paneled in dark tones or upholstered in muted grays. The color palette of serious business. It almost made court seem like the hip place to be. Chuckle.

At least the pre-trial would be short. Things would get serious in two days when the actual trial commenced. For now, I could entertain myself by studying inconsequential details like the color of the chairs.

The Deputy District Attorney was already at the prosecutor's table with two young assistants, the three of them going through files and murmuring softly about how they were going to hang my ass up on a spike.

The jury box was empty, as were the benches in the spectator gallery. No TV crews or reporters were present either. Nobody came out to watch pre-trials unless it was newsworthy. A one punch fight between two random citizens didn't qualify.

Russell turned to me and said quietly, "Once the judge walks in, the D.A. is going to lay out the basic framework he intends to present on Friday, then I'll lay out our proposed defense. We tell the judge up front about all the evidence and witnesses that we plan to bring into the trial. If we're lucky, and Judge Moody feels like the D.A. has a weak case, she may dismiss it right here on the spot. If that happens, you're a free man. If not, we step into the ring on Friday."

Man, I hoped everything went as smoothly as Russell made it sound.

He squeezed my shoulder and looked me straight in the eyes. "Don't worry about it, son. I've got you taken care of. No matter what the D.A. throws at us, I'll have a work around."

"Tell me you've got a getaway car ready just in case."

He winked at me, "Gassed up with the engine running." Russell turned to the Deputy District Attorney and said casually, "Good morning, George."

"Russell," the man nodded in reply.

I recognized George Schlosser from my arraignment. He was a tall man with short cropped hair dusted gray at the temples and a serious yet boyish face. A wolf in altar boy's clothing. The civilized kind of guy who offered you a cup of tea after whacking the bamboo stakes under your fingernails.

"How are Judy and the boys?" Russell asked him.

"Good," Schlosser said dismissively. "Has your client made a decision regarding our plea offer?" he asked, all business.

"After careful consideration, my client has decided to respectfully decline," Russell replied.

George Schlosser's lips curled minutely into a feral grin. He looked pleased. "So be it," he said.

With a blank expression on his face, Russell leaned over and whispered in my ear, "Rumor has it, old George over there cooked and ate his wife and children, hence his reluctance to answer my inquiry as to their health and well being. I almost asked him if human flesh went better with white wine or red, but I didn't think it would be in the best interest of your case."

I was ready to crack up laughing from what Russell had just said, so I dropped my chin to my chest and held it in.

I'd been in court with Russell many times in the past, and I always appreciated his effort to keep things light behind the defense table, no matter what was going on in the rest of the courtroom.

The door behind the immense judge's bench opened and

Geraldine Moody floated out like a black robed phantom.

"The Court will now come to order," the uniformed bailiff said. "All rise for the Honorable Geraldine Moody, presiding."

Judge Moody was as harshly beautiful as she was the last time I'd seen her at my arraignment. Her hair was perhaps a bit longer and blonder than before. Her makeup was subtle but effective. A queen taking her throne. Her leather executive chair was flanked by two flags, the U.S. on the left and the State of California on the right. The California State Seal, a large brass bas relief disc, hung behind her on the wood paneled wall.

"Please be seated," she said formally from her executive chair. Then she glanced at me briefly. "We meet again, Mr. Manos," Geraldine Moody said from behind the ramparts of her immense bench. I couldn't decide whether it was good news or bad that she remembered me. Considering she had been kind enough to set my bail at $150,000, even though the D.A. had only asked for $25,000, I was guessing bad. I couldn't escape the nagging feeling she was holding something personal against me.

At my arraignment, I'd been wearing an orange prison jumpsuit with my tats on display. Maybe she thought I looked like any other criminal that passed through her court room on a daily basis. At least now I was in a conservative suit, my ink hidden. But my shiner was incriminatingly obvious, even at a distance. I was starting to wish I'd put on that concealer. The smallest detail could sway her opinion for me or against me. If worse came to worse, and the jury found me guilty, her opinion would influence the sentencing, which could mean the difference between two years in prison or four. No small thing.

The only thing I could do was look as innocent as possible. I'd buy some concealer the second I stepped out of this courtroom. No more bullshitting around. From here on out, I was Mr. Clean, I was a Boy Scout. I helped old ladies across the street. Maybe I could squeeze some charity work in between now and Friday. Maybe Mrs. Elders at the library could arrange for a last minute Crayons with Christos session in front of Judge Moody during my trial. Fuck, who was I fooling? The time to be a Goody Two Shoed Samaritan had passed.

Russell whispered, "I think Geraldine might be sweet on you, young man. Perhaps you can slip her your phone number and make dinner plans. Sweeten her up before your trial."

I rolled my eyes and suppressed a chuckle. "Yeah, right."

"We are now on record for the State vs. Manos," the judge intoned gravely, "case number SD-2013-K-071183A. Counsel, please announce your appearances for the record."

"George Schlosser, on behalf of the state of California."

"Stanley Whitehead, on behalf of the state," Schlosser's assistant said. Stanley flung me a scoffing glance like I'd stolen his milk money one too many times in grade school. I'd like to pop his whitehead with a pin and shove a gallon of benzoyl peroxide down his throat.

"Natalia Valenzuela, on behalf of the state," Schlosser's other assistant said with a fluid hispanic accent. I hoped Natalia was as kind hearted as she looked. For all I knew, it was just an act to make people forget to take her seriously. She worked for the D.A.'s office after all, not as a nun or a nurse.

"Russell Merriweather, on behalf of Mr. Manos."

The judge shuffled papers and files on the desk in front of her, setting everything in order. When she was finished, she folded her hands on the desk in front of her. "Thank you, counselors. We have a number of motions to work through. I suggest we begin with the State. Mr. Schlosser?"

George Schlosser stepped up to the podium between the prosecution table and the defense table and said, "Mr. Manos is identified through witness statements and descriptions as the perpetrator in the assault and battery in question."

Schlosser then proceeded to dive into a litany of evidentiary motions. In other words, Schlosser told the judge all the things he was going to do at my trial to prove I was the bad guy, that I had swung first at poor old Horst Grossman for no good reason.

It was all uncomfortably familiar.

How many times had I sat behind the defense table for similar reasons? I'd lost count. In the past, I'd never cared. But I hadn't had much to care about. Now things were different.

Now I had Samantha to worry about. Seeing her flourish and find success in life was my number one priority.

I grit my teeth. I couldn't wait for this shit to be over.

When Schlosser finished sketching out what the State would argue on Friday at my trial, he returned to his seat and Russell took over the podium.

The entire time Russell spoke, Schlosser watched him closely, taking notes and periodically whispering to his assistants. I knew Schlosser was strategizing, looking for any weakness in Russell's case that he could exploit during my trial. For the most part, nothing was whetting Schlosser's carnivorous appetite. He almost looked bored. Russell Merriweather ran a tight ship, and I knew he'd worked up a solid case for my claim of self defense. The real action wouldn't really start until Friday.

"Will you be calling any other witnesses at trial, Mr. Merriweather?" Judge Moody asked, her eyes on her desk while she jotted down a note on some paperwork.

Before Your Love by Kelly Clarkson began playing from my suit jacket. It wasn't very loud, but in the crypt quiet courtroom, it sounded like a primo sound system at full blast. Shit. I thought I'd turned the ringer off before coming into court. I must've done it wrong. I fumbled with my jacket, trying to shut the phone off through the material. No good. I had to pull it out.

The judge cannoned a hard glare at me. "Do we have a problem, Mr. Manos?"

"No, I, uh," I mumbled as I fished my phone out of my suit.

"Perhaps we can reconvene when it's more convenient for you, Mr. Manos?" the judge asked sarcastically. I wasn't scoring any points with her today.

Schlosser and his team shared a chuckle at my expense.

Finally, I dug the phone out and shut it off, but not before noticing who had called. Samantha. Why the fuck would she be calling me now? Whatever it was, it could wait. I made sure the ringer was off and stuffed the phone back in my suit.

"Are you finished?" Judge Moody asked.

"Yeah, sorry. It won't happen again."

"I should hope not, Mr. Manos. For your sake."

Fucking great. Nothing like a bad first impression. In this case, it was more like a bad first, second, and third impression.

"As I was saying," the judge fired a final glare at me, "before we were so rudely interrupted," then she turned to Russell, "Mr. Merriweather, do you intend to call any other witnesses at trial?"

Russell flicked me a pointed glance. Just loud enough for me to hear, he said, "We gonna do this?"

My phone jumped in my pocket and vibrated once. I almost flinched, but managed to hold my shit together. I could tell from the vibration pattern that it was a text coming in. I ignored it.

I nodded at Russell.

He turned to the judge, and in a confident voice said, "Yes, your honor. I will also be calling Mr. Manos to testify on his own behalf."

A hush fell over the courtroom.

The three D.A.s looked like a pack of hyenas whose ears had pricked up and noses had twitched the moment they'd caught scent of a wounded wildebeest limping by. Schlosser dug his fingers into the armrests of his chair. He was practically climbing out of it. The greedy smile on Stanley Whitehead's face had curled into a twist. I was just waiting for his tongue to snake out and hungrily lick his lips. Kind hearted Natalia Valenzuela's cheeks had reddened as if she was suddenly turned on. Yeah, her earlier demeanor had been nothing but a front. She got off on desperation. I could feel it. These three had smelled my blood and were thirsty for a drink.

So what? Fuck 'em. I wasn't a wounded wildebeest. I was always ready for a fight. Because you knew the second the badass male lion came bounding out of the bush with his big mane on display, those hyenas scattered like ants in a sandstorm.

Too bad I wasn't allowed to throw punches and elbows in court. Not by law, anyway. But Russell could. In the courtroom, he was a bigger lion than I was.

He was going to eat those D.A. fuckers for lunch.

Somebody hand me a knife and fork.

Chapter 5

SAMANTHA

After lunch, I went to the Main Library to study. No matter how many times I called or texted Christos, he never answered. I tried to concentrate on my Sociology and History reading, but it was tough going. I was too worried about Christos.

Eventually I gave up on homework and packed up my books and laptop. On my way to the north parking lot where I'd parked, I texted Christos one final time.

Meet me at ur place 4 dinner?

When I reached my VW, I was pleasantly surprised to see that it was right where I'd left it, seemingly intact. I'd sort of expected to find it either gone, somehow towed away by Tiffany Shitstain-Hateface, or perhaps a mangled heap. I wouldn't put it past Tiffany to hire some guy to drive a bulldozer over it.

I strolled around my car, looking for any fresh key gouges or slashed tires. Nothing. Somehow, I imagined Tiffany was simply biding her time. Waiting for the most opportune moment to strike.

I climbed in my car and turned the ignition, wincing in anticipation of a car bomb going off. Nope, the engine started smoothly.

A moment later, I heard my phone jingle. A text from Christos.

Dinner is waiting for you at your new home, agapi mou.

Yay! I heaved a sigh of relief. I really needed to talk to him about his trial. I just hoped it wasn't too late to make a difference.

I backed out of my space and drove down the aisle. Maybe Tiffany had cut my brake lines? How did one check brake lines anyway? I had no idea. Oh wait, I know!

I glanced in my rearview mirror. When I saw no one was behind me, I braked hard. My car stopped abruptly. The brakes seemed to be working. For now. Maybe it took awhile?

Screw it. I didn't have time to worry about whatever that vengeful bitch Tiffany might be planning. I had more important things to worry about than her petty jealousy. I had to get home to my man.

Traffic was light and I made it to Christos' house in record time. I parked in the driveway next to his Camaro. I pulled out my key to let myself in. I really needed to pack up all my stuff and move in ASAP. I'd already given my apartment manager my 30 day notice to vacate.

Sadly, I doubted there was time for me to move everything before Friday. I hadn't even started packing. Then what? Would I be sharing this huge house with Spiridon while we waited who knew how long for Christos to be released from jail?

I didn't want to think about it.

I jammed my key in the lock and walked inside.

For now, I was going to enjoy our time together as best I could.

"*Samoula!*" Spiridon smiled as I walked into the kitchen. "Dinner is almost ready." He wrapped me up in a huge hug.

Christos walked in with a huge platter of lamb kebab skewers. "I just pulled these off the grill outside. I hope you're hungry, *agápi mou*," he smiled.

"You bet," I grinned and tip-toed up to circle an arm around his neck and kiss his cheek.

Christos was so tall, he had to lean over for me to reach him. He twisted at the last second, holding the kebabs in one hand while he wrapped an arm around my waist and smooched me on the lips. "That's more like it," he said. "I've been waiting for that all day."

"Your Spanakopita is almost ready," Spiridon said to Christos. "It smells delicious."

"Awesome," Christos said as he set the platter of skewers on the counter top. I noticed chunks of grilled onions wedged on the skewers between the lamb. He grabbed an oven mitt and used it to pull a baking pan out of the oven.

"Wow, that looks uber yum!" I said. "What is it?"

"Spanakopita. Spinach pie."

The crust was a perfect golden brown and looked flaky. I couldn't wait to dig in.

"Sit down, you two," Christos said while he cut up slices of Spanakopita and dished them up with the lamb skewers and cucumber salad.

"Mmm, Tzatziki! I can't wait," I smiled as Christos set plates in front of me and Spiridon.

Christos joined us at the table and we dug in.

As usual, conversation with Christos and his grandfather was fun and full of laughs. I relished these simple moments. Dinner with my parents was never like this. I was starting to believe my parents had no idea how to enjoy themselves, as if they consciously avoided laughter and joy. Groan. Maybe Spiridon and Christos could give them lessons. Not.

I continued to enjoy the good dinner vibes, but Christos' trial kept nagging at the back of my mind. I couldn't decide if Christos was avoiding the topic. He'd probably talked with Spiridon about it at length when I wasn't around. It had been five months since Christos' arrest, so they were probably sick of it. I wasn't going to spoil dinner by bringing it up for the billionth time. I'd wait until afterward.

When we finished eating, I got up to clear the plates and do the dishes.

"Let me get those, *koritsáki mou*," Spiridon said. "You go spend some time with my grandson.

"Are you sure?" I asked.

"Yes," he smiled, a faint sadness swirling in his eyes.

"All right," I said uncertainly.

"Go," he said, "enjoy yourselves."

"What the man said," Christos grinned. "Wanna help me clean up the grill?"

"Sure," I said.

We walked onto the back deck and Christos grabbed a steel brush to scrub down the grill. His muscles flexed and popped as he worked the brush, hypnotizing me instantly. I couldn't concentrate. What did I need to talk to Christos about that was so important? Was it the fact his tattooed arms made me dizzy and my thighs were now quivering? No. Something else. Was it the way my stomach was somersaulting and my cheeks glowed red when his sexy lips curled into a smile as he glanced over at me like my mere presence had made his day? No, couldn't be that either.

"Admit it," he said, "once again, seeing me cleaning something is turning you on."

Guilty. I rolled my eyes. "Totally not turned on."

He flashed me a dimple grin. "Uh huh. I see the way your eyes are spinning in circles. You can barely stand up."

So what if he was right? I wouldn't admit it, not even in front of a jury after swearing on a stack of Bibles. Crap. That broke the spell. We needed to discuss his trial. I sighed sadly. "Did you get my call today?"

Christos chuckled as he scrubbed. "Yeah. Right in the middle of court. The judge gave me a ton of shit because my phone rang."

"Oh no! I'm so sorry, I'm such an idiot. I should've waited to call."

"It's not your fault, *agápi mou*," Christos reassured. "Don't worry about it."

No matter how anxious I was, Christos' even demeanor could always calm me down. I took a deep, cleansing breath. "Did you get my text or have a chance to listen to my message?"

He set down the wire brush. "I did."

"And?"

"And what?"

"And," I said, "I can testify for you. It's not too late, is it?"

Christos ran a heavy hand across his stubbled cheeks. His always sexy cheeks. Why did he have to be so damn handsome? I could never get enough of my magazine cover model boyfriend. He was eye crack. I'm surprised my eyes didn't go into withdrawal when he was out of my sight. At least I could get a fix right now. Wait, he was doing it again! Trying to distract me with his sexiness!

"Please, Christos, can you stop being sexy for one second so we can discuss this?"

"I'd rather be sexy," he smirked. "It amuses me to watch your eyes cross like that."

"My eyes aren't crossing!"

"They were a second ago," he winked.

"You're such a man," I groused.

"Yup."

Wow. Cocky as ever. If it was me who was two days away from going to court, I'd be freaking out. Maybe Christos could give confidence lessons to packed stadiums and make a mint in the self help industry. Or maybe we could just bottle his ego and put heroin out of business. Either way, we'd retire young and rich.

I remembered thinking of him as Good Time Christos at the Halloween party at Jake's house last year. It turned out that had been an accurate title for him.

Christos lowered the lid on the grill and hung the brush on the side. "Shall we go inside? All this exercise has got me all worked up. I need to relax."

"Okay," I fawned dreamily. Then I shook my head. "Wait! Stop! Quit charming me with your hotness powers. We need to talk about your trial."

He raised an eyebrow. "Must we? I wanted to enjoy this evening with you. And I've got a present for you." He smoothed a loose lock of hair behind my ear and kissed my forehead.

Swoon.

"You do?" I sighed. Who didn't like presents? Wait a second, he was doing it again! I squinted at him and jammed my hands on my hips. "Is this another distraction tactic, Christos?"

"No, I really have a present."

"Fine. Do we discuss the trial before or after the present?"

He considered. "Before. That way, my present will get you back in the mood."

"Mood?" I said skeptically. "Are you trying to get me into bed, Christos Manos?"

He nodded confidently and slid an arm around my waist.

I rolled my eyes and smiled. "Fine. But not until after we talk."

"Works for me." He leaned forward and kissed me passionately.

After a minute, I could barely stand up. My legs had officially melted because of the forest fire deep in my…forest.

I shook my head and pushed away. "Stop! We need to talk," I pleaded. Who needed talking when the hottest man on the planet had his arms around my waist? I'm pretty sure that was the devil voice on my shoulder talking. Devil voice liked to have a good time. But Angel voice reminded her that there would be no more parties in my panties if Christos was in jail. Sigh. "Christos, you know I want you, but I don't want you just for tonight. I'd also like to have you tomorrow night, and the night after that, and the night after that, and—"

He smiled. "I get the idea. Look, my attorney has got everything wrapped up. I totally appreciate your desire to help. But everything is going to be fine."

"Christos, I don't know much about how court works, but I do know that I was there that day. You're going to trial because of that guy who yelled at me the day we met, aren't you?"

He nodded. "You figured it out. I'm not surprised. Your smarts are half of what attracted me to you in the first place."

"Really? I'm not just a pretty face?" I struck a fashion model lip pout pose and piled my hair on my head with both hands.

He chuckled. "You're a pretty face too. The prettiest."

"Then you'll totally want me in your trial so I can win over all the male jurors. I'll have them wrapped around my finger after I'm through."

"I'm sure you would. But you don't need to do anything. It's going to be fine."

"Come on, Christos. We both know I was an eyewitness. And my eyes were closer to that jerk than anyone else's. My version of events would totally help you. Am I wrong?"

"No."

"Then how do I get into the trial? What do I have to do to tell my side of things?"

"You don't."

I frowned at him. "Why not?"

"It's too late."

"What? Can you please explain in detail?"

He sighed. "We had to tell the judge at the pre-trial today which witnesses we're going to call to the stand on Friday. It's too late to add more."

"That's stupid! Why?"

"Because the D.A. has to have a chance to hear whatever testimony you might give *before* the trial starts. So they have time to prepare."

"No problem. I'll call them right now!" I stomped my foot.

"It doesn't work like that. You have to go through the system. It takes time."

"That's ridiculous!" I felt my anger rising like a volcano. I wanted to protect Christos more than I wanted to draw another breath. "We still have two days!"

"No, we had two days two days ago." he said calmly.

"What if I—"

He shook his head.

"I could—"

"No, *agápi mou*," he said. "It's too late."

"Why didn't you tell me sooner?" I wanted to pound him on the chest in frustration. "I could've helped!"

"You've already helped me more than you will ever realize."

"Who cares?" I was raging at him now. "If you're in jail because I didn't tell everyone what happened in court, it doesn't matter! I don't want you behind bars for even a second! Don't you get it? This is so stupid!" I pushed out of his arms and stalked across the deck until I was standing at the edge of the swimming pool. I suddenly had the desire to dive in and swim a hundred laps in my clothes. I was furious. But swimming wouldn't get me where I wanted to go.

I felt warm arms wrap around me from behind. He kissed the top of my head and I leaned into him.

I was crying now. "Why didn't you tell me, Christos?"

"Because I didn't want you to waste your time on this. I got myself into this mess, I'll get myself out."

"But I want to help!" I cried.

"*Agápi mou*, you need to focus on your classes and your jobs. Speaking of which, didn't you have a shift at Grab-n-Dash tonight?"

I stiffened in Christos' arms. Oh shit. Oh fuckity shit! I'd forgot all about it. I was so stressed about Christos not answering my calls, I had gone space cadet.

"You forgot, didn't you?" he asked.

I winced, "Uh…maybe?"

"Samantha, this is what I'm talking about. You're so wound up worrying about me when you should be worrying about you."

I spun around in his arms. "Don't you get it? You're always helping me, Christos. This is finally the one time I can do something to really help you, and you won't let me. My stupid job at Grab-n-Dash doesn't matter. I'm not going to be a convenience store clerk for the rest of my life. I can find another job. But if I'm not mistaken, you only get one trial, right?"

"Unless there's a mistrial. But yeah, usually there's only one."

"So quit being so bull headed and let me help you, damn it!"

He smiled his dimpled grin at me. "I would if I could, but it's out of my hands. Anyway, the trial is not until Friday. I have tonight and all of tomorrow to enjoy my freedom. And you, *agápi mou*. Can't we enjoy tonight and forget about what's around the corner?"

The pleading look in his eyes melted my heart. I snuggled my cheek against his rock hard chest. Stupid muscles. Stupid dimples. Stupid Christos! I wound my arms around him and squeezed him as tightly as I could. I would do my best to block out the trial and focus on the now.

I sighed. "I believe you'd mentioned a present of some sort?"

"I did," he said seductively. "But before we get to that, maybe you should call your boss and tell him you can't make it?"

Groan!

My boss could take his neon urine colored Grab-n-Dash uniform shirt and shove it up his ass. Since I was moving in with Christos, and would be saving on rent, did I really need the job? Oh wait, ever since my parents had gone bonkers and decided to stop sending me any money for college, yes. Not only did I need Grab-n-Dash, I could use three more jobs on top of it. There was no way I could pay my tuition with what I made working at the SDU art museum and Grab-n-Dash combined.

My life was truly screwing me in every orifice. Worse, not only were my main orifi getting the shaft from every direction, including my ears, nostrils, and eye sockets, but I imagined millions of tiny microscopic dicks busily raping every pore on my body.

Screw it. I may as well enjoy my evening with Christos.

Because things couldn't get any worse, could they?

===

Christos and I went inside and I immediately called my boss at Grab-n-Dash on my phone. I apologized profusely for not coming in and asked what I could do to make it up to him.

He promptly told me I was fired.

"Oh yeah?" I shouted into the phone, "Well, your uniforms look like pee and they smell like hot dogs! I don't need your stupid job!" I heard him hang up on me. "And your eyebrows look like caterpillars!" I screamed.

"That went well," Christos said dryly.

"I always hated that place anyway. I didn't even get free ICEEs when I was on the clock! My boss was a total miser."

"You'll find something better," Christos encouraged. "Who knows, maybe you'll sell some more art."

I wondered if The Wombat paid for comic strips? I'd have to ask the editor, Justin Tomlinson. Gulp. I could worry about that later. Christos now.

"So, you said something about a present?" I asked sheepishly. I admit it. I was greedy for a good gift. It had been a long day.

"Yes," he grinned. "You're going to love it. Come on, I'll show you." He led me through the house until we ended up in the garage. He flipped on the lights.

The first thing I noticed was an old station wagon with wood paneling on the sides and white wall tires. I'd never seen one like it before. I wrinkled my nose. "Did you get me a car?"

"What," Christos looked confused, "the Woody?"

I snorted a laugh.

He narrowed his eyes, "You don't know what a Woody is, do you?"

"Christos!" I giggled. "Of course I do."

He smirked at me. "Okay, what is it?"

"Duh. A woody is a hard on."

"A what?" he asked, amused.

"You know," I insisted.

"No. Tell me. I'm all ears."

"An erection."

"A what?"

"Christos, how could you of all people not know what I'm talking about?"

He shook his head, totally confused.

"An erect penis?" I said uncertainly.

He still looked confused.

"Am I not speaking English?" I asked.

He shrugged his shoulders.

"Okay," I blurted, "now I know you're messing with me."

He cracked up laughing.

I swatted his arm. "Jerk!"

He dodged away from another swat and cackled, "You're super sexy when you're mad! I totally need a picture of your face right now!"

"Boys!" I folded my arms. "So, what is woody, Mr. Smarty Pants?"

"This particular Woody is my grandad's 1949 Plymouth station wagon. He bought it when my dad was a kid and they restored it together back in the 1970s."

"Oh. It's really nice. How come I never see your grandfather driving it?"

"It's a classic. He only takes it out now and then. Before they finished restoring it all the way, my granddad would load up the surfboards and take my dad surfing up and down the coast when he was a kid."

"That sounds like fun." I'd never done anything nearly that cool with my parents. Once again, I felt that pinch of jealousy every time Christos told me yet another casual story about his family life. I don't think he thought anything of it. To him, it was normal. To me it was exotic, romantic, and almost unbelievable. Did people really enjoy their lives this much? My parents hadn't. For them, everything had been about work, taking precautions, planning for the future. What about living in the moment? I don't think they knew what that was.

"So," Christos said, "the first part of your present. Boxes."

"Boxes?"

He walked over to a stack of new boxes leaning against the wall of the garage. "Moving boxes. And packing supplies. For you."

"For me?" I looked at the boxes. There was a bunch of different sizes, including one of those wardrobe boxes for hanging clothes.

"If we're going to get you moved in with me, we're going to need to pack everything up, right?" He smiled at me.

My heart melted instantly. I'd been running around like cray-cray for the last two days, yet somehow Christos had managed to keep his eye on the prize, so to speak. I said tentatively, "Are you sure?"

He scoffed. "Of course I'm sure."

"But, the other night you flipped out and bolted from my apartment after telling me about your trial. I thought maybe you'd changed your mind." I wanted to hide my face. I was about to cry. I willed my tears to stay put, lest they ruin my dreams, which were coming true right before my eyes.

"I owe you an apology for that, *agápi mou*. I totally flipped out." He wrapped his arms around me and pulled me close.

I stared up into his lustrous blue eyes. They pierced my heart so easily. I felt warmth drizzling into me as my eyes drank the love shining from his. "It's okay, Christos. I understand."

"You didn't deserve for me to run out like that, especially after your parents blew gaskets about your plan to move in with me. I should've been there for you. I think I was so freaked out by what your parents said, combined with the stress of my trial, it was like I couldn't do anything to stop the landslide. After I cooled off, I had to remind myself that I can't control what your parents say or do, and I can't control the outcome of my trial. But that doesn't mean the rest of my life has to grind to a halt. We talked about moving in together, and I meant it. Shit, you already have a sweet art studio here. May as well seal the deal. This house is your house. I want you to live with me, no matter what happens."

I think I was floating outside my body. Any second I expected to see a light at the end of a dark tunnel and hear a choir of angels welcoming me to heaven. Oh wait, the light was just the love glowing in Christos' eyes. "Yes," I said hoarsely. I had to clear my throat, I was so choked up. "Yes!" I laughed. "I totally want to move in with you!"

"Awesome," he smiled, his eyes darkening with tangible desire. "I've already got Jake and a bunch of my buddies lined up tomorrow. One of them has a big pickup. If you're willing, I thought me and the boys could go to your apartment while you're at school and pack everything up for you. We can put your furniture in the garage. We'll have all your stuff moved in before you're back from campus. What do you think?"

"Wow! That sounds awesome! Are you sure? I mean, moving isn't usually people's number one social activity."

"It's totally cool. As long as you're cool with us doing it. I'd need to get your apartment key. And you should probably tell your manager and your neighbors so they don't think we're robbing you."

I laughed. "I'll do that. Oh, one thing."

"What?"

"Don't let any of your buddies sniff my underwear," I giggled.

He chuckled. "They won't have a chance. I'll be too busy hogging all of it for myself." He inhaled loudly, "Ah yeah, that's the shit!"

I swatted his arm again. "I can't decide whether that's disgusting or a total turn on."

"I like how your pussy smells, so I'm going with turn on."

I winced. "Gross!"

He shook his head and smiled. "One day we're going to have to break you of your prudish ways, *agápi mou*. I like how your pussy smells. I like how it tastes. I generally think about jamming my face between your legs every five minutes."

"You are so crude!"

He smiled his dimpled grin. "What can I say? You turn me on more than any woman has ever turned a man on in the history of men. I'm the luckiest guy on the planet and I like to indulge in it. Your pussy, that is. Nectar of the Gods and shit."

I had to admit, the hot throb between my legs was totally unintentional. I took no responsibility for being turned on by Christos' crass behavior. I was a proper girl without a single slutty bone in my body. Christos, on the other hand, had the soul of a male slut, and for some reason, I wanted his slutty bone in my body. Err, I meant, I wanted his slut bone in parts of me for which I was not responsible, the wet drenched center in particular.

He arched a cocky eyebrow, emphasis on the cocky part. "Ready to go upstairs?"

"Why do we have to go upstairs?" The hood of the Woody seemed like as good a place as any to me.

"To see your other presents," he murmured.

"Presents are good," I said softly, gazing up into his eyes.

Christos squatted down and scooped me into his arms.

Okay, I admit it, he'd carried me places a thousand times by now, and I liked it better every time. We went upstairs and he carried me into his bedroom. This time, I really felt like we had just crossed an important threshold. We had stepped into something permanent. Wow, I was hot from head to toe.

He flipped on the lights.

The bed was now covered in a new comforter and piles of pillows were stacked against the headboard.

"I thought the bed could be plushed up a bit, since you'll be spending so much time in it," he said.

"I love it!"

Still cradled in his arms, he walked me around the room.

"I also bought you a chest of drawers for your clothes." A new dark wood chest stood angled in one corner. "And I made room in the closet for you to hang stuff." He opened one of the mirrored doors. Plenty of room. "And you can put shoes and shit on the shelves and the floor. If you turn into a shoe whore, we can rent a storage locker," he grinned.

"Lucky for you, I'm broke," I smiled.

"That won't stop you from going to Goodwill or the thrift shops. Shoes are shoes. I know how you ladies get when it comes to footwear."

"Are you encouraging me?" I grinned. "I'm not above bargain hunting."

He rolled his eyes. "Give me at least a month before you go nuts. I'd at least like to enjoy the illusion of a shoe free household for that long."

Christos was still holding me in his arms. I snuggled my cheek against the large muscles of his chest. I inhaled his manly scent. Wow, I was living in a fantasy world. Somebody wake me up! On second thought, don't!

"When did you do all this?" I asked.

"Today. My pre-trial went pretty quick. There's still one or two more things."

"Oh? How many presents do I get?"

"As many as you want," he winked as he opened the bathroom door and walked me inside.

"Oh my god," I murmured. I couldn't believe my eyes.

Lit candles lined the room. Rose petals carpeted the floor and the edge of the jacuzzi tub, which was full of bubbles. Two big bouquets of fresh red roses were positioned on the counter top between the sinks. In the middle of everything was a big heart shaped box of chocolates.

"Happy pre-Valentine's Day, *agápi mou*," he said softly.

Okay, now I was officially crying. Tears streamed down my face. "Oh, Christos. My *agápi mou*. I can't believe you did all this."

"I can," he grinned.

"But it's so much," I said looking up into his eyes.

"It's not enough," he smiled.

"But I haven't gotten you anything, *agápi mou*," I said.

"Yes you have, *agápi mou*. You've given me you." He gazed deeply into my eyes. "Samantha, with you in my house and in my heart, I have everything I will ever need on this earth. You are my all. All that I need, all that I want, all that life has to offer."

I lifted my head up to kiss him. He worked his arms around beneath me and lifted me closer, until our lips met. The warm embrace of our kissing lips sent shimmers of desire cascading down my throat. Warmth spread across my chest and lit my breasts with pleasurey tension. His tongue entered my mouth and melted into mine. I grabbed a fistful of his shirt as his warm breath caressed me.

We kissed for a time, then he gently pulled away. "Your bath awaits. Don't want it to get cold." He set me down on the edge of the tub and pulled my flats off and massaged my feet.

"Mmm, that feels wonderful," I said.

He smiled and massaged for awhile. When he was finished, he slid his hands up my jeans and worked his thumbs between my thighs until they teased between my legs. I giggled as he tickled his hands up my sides and pulled my sweater and T shirt over my head. He tossed them onto the floor, took my hands, and pulled me to standing.

"What?" I asked.

"Pants," he grinned as he unbuttoned my jeans, slid the zipper down, and slowly worked my jeans and panties down to my ankles. He was kneeling beside me, his face inches from my center. He tilted his head up at me and cocked his dimples while he inhaled slowly.

"Fucking incredible," he said, closing his eyes to savor my scent. He leaned toward me and exhaled on my wet folds. His hot breath made me tingle. I wanted to dance nervously, but my jeans trapped my feet. He put one knee between my legs, pressing my jeans down and binding my feet. I wasn't going anywhere.

"Christos," I murmured. "I can't move."

"Nope," he chuckled. He cupped my butt with his hands and jerked my hips toward him, burying his face between my legs. His tongue laved between my lips, hot and hungry. He lapped up my wetness like a parched man stumbling into an oasis.

The pleasure was intense and electric, spasming out from my core into my chest, glowing up my throat. I felt faint, and propped an arm against his muscled shoulder, steadying myself as he licked away my equilibrium. Contractions seized my core as an orgasm rose up inside me, spinning through my body in liquid waves of heat. I moaned throatily and collapsed onto Christos' shoulders as pleasure stole gravity and lifted me into the air. "Oh, oh, oh..."

He drove his tongue into me as I came all over his face. He wouldn't stop, and my pleasure mounted, intensifying as another orgasm took flight on the wings of the first.

He didn't stop. He wouldn't relent. He growled and moaned as his fingers clenched my ass in his mesmerizing grip. He was ravenous and tore me open with his tongue. I wept pleasure between my legs, raining all over his face.

I was gone.

===

My legs were quivering when he finally finished. My torso was draped over his shoulders so I levered up with my arms. My hair hung in my face as I gazed down at him.

He tilted his head up at me, a wicked gleam in his eyes. He looked carnivorous as his slick lips spread across his teeth. "I told you I've been dying for a bite."

I giggled. "You sound like a vampire."

He chuckled and pulled off his shirt, revealing the intricate tattoos on his arms and shoulders as well as the 'Fearless' script across his chest, then slid himself up my body, pressing pectorals against my swollen breasts and the knots of my nipples, shooting electric tingles that stopped my breath. He unhooked my bra and peeled it away, his face still glistening as he kissed me deeply and caressed my neck.

"Mmm, so good," he said. "Ready for your bath?"

"What about you?" I asked.

"What about me?"

"Aren't you, you know, like totally worked up?"

"I can wait," he said cockily.

Ab alert! I looked down at his always amazing abs. I would do laundry 24/7 if his abs were my washboard. I ran my fingers down them, caressing all eight as they arrowed down to the waistband of his pants. "I don't know if I can." I grabbed his belt and pulled his hips into me.

"I would never refuse a lady," he grinned.

I unbuckled his belt and unbuttoned his jeans. I wanted to recreate the same move he'd used on me. I grabbed his underwear and jeans and started pulling. "Damn, your jeans are tight." I needed some leverage, so I stepped out of my jeans and panties and kicked them aside before setting my legs and yanking unsuccessfully on his jeans. "A little help?"

"Blame fashion," he said casually. "Skinny jeans are in." He shimmied his hips as I slid his pants down.

His cock sprung out of his boxers and waved in my face.

"Look out for my heat seeking missile," he joked. "It's got target lock."

I snickered. "You are a complete dork, you know that?"

"Only for you, *agápi mou*."

I managed to push his jeans and boxers down to his ankles. When I rose up on my knees, his throbbing cock was pointing right at my mouth.

"Uhhh…" I said, "What do I do?"

"You got yourself into this mess," he said.

I arched an eyebrow and glared up at him. "I think it's time for my bath?"

"Whatever you prefer. My dick's not going anywhere. I can fuck you later. It's up to you."

Still staring at him, I shook my head. "You have a dirty mind, young man."

"The dirtiest."

I lowered my eyes back to his manhood. Wow, it was really big. Thick veins wound around the shaft. The head was dark and purpled with blood. It literally pulsed, thump, thump, thump, probably in time with his heartbeat, getting slightly bigger with each thud. Pre cum dribbled from the tip. I licked my lips. I couldn't help myself. It looked so lickable.

I leaned toward it and felt heat pouring off of it before my lips even touched it.

"Do you know what you're getting yourself into?" he asked thoughtfully.

"Not really?" My mouth had never been this close to a cock in my entire life. I'd always maintained a safe distance at all times. Maybe it was finally time to throw caution to the wind.

"We can jump in the tub if you want, and enjoy the suds," he said softly. "It's up to you."

I smiled up at him and batted my eye lashes.

He grinned.

I leaned forward and gingerly kissed the top of the tip once.

"How was that?"

"Wow. Amazing. I've never felt anything like it," he quipped. "Best. Blow job. Ever," he winked.

I frowned at him. "Excuse me. I haven't had a lot of experience swallowing elephant trunks, hot shot."

He cocked a dimple at me. "I've got a hot shot waiting for you, whenever you're ready."

I rolled my eyes. "That was epically lame, Christos."

"And?" he grinned. "Make your move or I'm jumping in the tub."

"Fine. You asked for it," I growled. I leaned forward and licked the pre-cum right off the tip and swallowed. A salty hint of ocean. Not what I'd expected. But I wasn't done. I slid my lips around the head of his cock and licked the underside.

"Fu-uh-uh-uck," he moaned.

I glanced up and saw him throw his head back. There was no way I was getting all of him in my mouth so I grabbed his shaft with both hands and continued to lick and slide with my mouth.

He hissed in ecstasy. "Oh, damn, that's amazing…"

I wasn't entirely sure what I was doing. I had seen porn, and had some basic ideas about how this worked. What I hadn't expected was how much it was turning me on. I felt the muscles in my core shaking with need, like there was a direct connection between these lips and those. I slid my head forward as far as I could go, until he touched the back of my throat. Red alert! I pulled back abruptly.

I'd heard about gag reflexes, and those fabled women who had none. I did.

I could work around it.

I continued to lick and stroke with mouth and hands. I moved my left hand down and cupped his balls and massaged them with my fingers. I suddenly remembered seeing people working those silver meditation balls in their hands, the ones that rang when you circled them around in your fingers.

Meditation, my ass.

Those silver balls were for blow job practice.

===

CHRISTOS

The funny thing about blow jobs was that a good number of

chicks sucked at them. In a bad way. I mean, they were terrible. Like sticking my dick in a meat grinder.

I had no doubt an equal number of men were terrible at going down on women, but that was another topic.

The worst thing in the world was when a chick was going down on you, grinding the skin off your dick like a belt sander, having the time of her life, thinking she's all that. The last thing you wanted to do was burst her bubble and tell her she sucked at sucking. I'd never done that. I'd always manned up and endured the pain. Most of the time, I could force out a wad as quickly as possible and be done with it. But on one or two rare occasions, the chick was so bad, there was no way I was going to come before my dick was ground down to a nub. I don't even remember how I got out of that one. I think I had just shouted, "Oh shit, who's that outside your window!" and ran out her front door when she was looking the other way. Not one of my finer moments.

Lucky for me, Samantha was easily the best I'd ever had. World class. Gold medal performance. She'd barely started and already I couldn't tell up from down or left from right.

"Holy fuck" I said, "I have to sit down."

"Did I do something wrong?" Samantha asked, pulling her mouth off my dick.

"Fuck no. But I'm going to pass out at the rate you're going."

"Is that bad?" she asked innocently.

I shook my head and chuckled. "No." My knees were jelly as I lowered myself until I was sitting on the edge of the tub.

Samantha kept one hand around my dick the whole time, like she didn't want to let go. She had no idea how fucking sexy that was. And the fact she didn't know, made her ten times sexier. Not because she was innocent, but because she wasn't doing an act. Some women thought the cameras were rolling while they were in the bedroom and they were busy mugging and moaning for the lens. But Samantha was right here with me, focused entirely on me. It was a rare and unique experience for me as much as I knew it was for her.

She knelt down on the rug in front of the tub between my knees. "Shall I continue?" she asked.

"Hells yeah," I grinned.

Her hot lips slid back down my cock like a silk glove. Damn, she was such a natural. She worked her way up and down my dick, pulling me inside her deeper and deeper. I closed my eyes and my head fell back, lolling against my shoulders. Whatever she was doing with her hands and mouth was magic. I swear, my entire package was glowing with pleasure, like my entire awareness was collapsing into my cock in a tight ball of hot ecstasy straining to be released.

I don't know how long she went on. I lost all track of time. At one point, I looked down and saw she was putting her whole body into it. The head of my dick was on fire. Every lick made my body jerk. It felt so fucking good. I think my balls were wound up so tight there was nothing left to grab, so she released them and put both hands to work on my shaft.

"Fuck, Samantha," I whispered hoarsely, "I'm going to come. Oh, fuck, oh fuck..."

She intensified everything and I think my penis turned into a black hole because it was sucking the entire universe into the center of my body. Right when I thought I was going to blow, waves of heat flooded through my body and everything released. All my tension faded from existence. All the stress that had knotted my body for the last three weeks thinking about my trial finally let go. It was the most relaxing sensation I'd ever felt.

I was at peace.

And I still hadn't come.

I'd read about guys having multiple orgasms. I thought it was some kind of myth. But I hadn't yet shot my load and I was riding on a wave of intense, relaxing pleasure. It was amazing.

And Samantha kept going and going.

Orgasms had always been an explosion for me. A shooting, pounding, pulling thing. This was just total, peaceful release.

It felt so damn good.

The glow spread through my whole body. I slumped against the wall by the corner of the tub and slid down to an elbow, but Samantha kept going.

I could stay like this forever, enjoying the flying freedom the love of my life was giving to me.

I don't know how long it went on. I never wanted it to stop.

Then something started to build. A winding tighter than I'd ever felt before. I was going to blow. Someone had shoved a nuclear bomb up my ass and it was going to rip me in half. I welcomed it.

My awareness shrank down like the beginning of the universe between my legs: infinite mass crushed into a microscopic space. And then it was all over.

BOOM.

Every atom in my body disintegrated into protons and neutrons and shot across the universe at the speed of light, engulfing all of existence.

Release.

Peace.

I was at peace.

For the first time in my life, I was at peace.

Agápi mou…it was always you.

===

SAMANTHA

Christos' cock grew thick as it strained in my mouth. He'd been slumped over for awhile, but I was determined to finish him. I was starving for his cock, thirsting for his sweet release. I wanted to take him into me through my mouth, swallow his energy into my belly.

He was moaning continuously, almost absently, his eyelids fluttering, nearly catatonic with pleasure. It was kind of weird, but at the same time it was the biggest turn on. He was truly putty in my hands, his body a puddle of muscle and moans.

Then his cock suddenly strained harder and harder, veins bulging, jutting and swelling beyond all proportion. This was it.

He suddenly lurched forward, his knees pressing against my sides as his whole body contracted.

"Fuuuuuuuuuuuuck!!!" he shouted.

Hot cum fired into my mouth, hitting the back of my throat. I was surprised by two things simultaneously. It was very salty, and there was a lot of it. Way more than I expected.

I stopped moving my head but continued to pump his shaft. I was determined to milk every last drop out of him with my tongue. He kept coming and coming and I tried to hold it all in my mouth. I had no choice but to swallow.

I expected to gag, but I didn't. I was so turned on by all of this, I just went with the flow. No pun intended. He flowed right into me. I continued to slowly stroke his cock with my tongue.

With my lips still wrapped around him, I glanced at Christos. His eyes were closed, his face sagging unconsciously. He was totally gone. Was he asleep? After awhile, I stopped, pulled back, and smiled at him.

I don't think I'd felt nearly this slutty in my entire life, not even when I kissed my own wetness off of his mouth on several occasions. What really surprised me was that I liked feeling like this.

I gave head!

There, I said it! My first blow job! Yay, me! I couldn't get over how much I had enjoyed it. I'm pretty sure it had worked for Christos too, judging by the look on his face.

One of his eyelids opened into a slit. His pupil flickered in my general direction.

"Anybody home?" I joked.

A slow smile spread across his mouth. He lifted an eyebrow. "Am I dead?"

"No, silly." I placed my hands on his legs and leaned toward him for a kiss. I slid my tongue into his mouth and he welcomed it. I half expected him to wince for some reason, like maybe he wouldn't want to taste his own cum. But he sucked away at me ravenously.

"Mmmmm," he moaned.

"Was it good?" I asked.

"Mmmmm-hmmm. I don't think I can move."

"Ready for that bath?"

"You might want to run some hot water. I feel like we're into next week and the tub's probably cold," he joked. "What year is it? I don't even know."

I checked the tub and it was cool, so I ran hot water and added more suds. When it was ready, I climbed in. "You joining me?"

Christos' only response was to melt into the jacuzzi tub like a limp eel from where he sat on the edge, his legs following as an afterthought.

"Oh my gosh! Christos!" He was totally submerged. I didn't want him drowning. I cleared some suds away and I saw him smiling up at me from under water.

Eventually, his head raised above the surface, his hair glued to his forehead. "I really don't know what planet I'm on right now," he said as he slid around the tub until we were shoulder to shoulder and he leaned his body against mine. "That was really amazing, *agápi mou*. I've never felt anything like it."

"Really?" Despite Christos' sated behavior, I was still somewhat insecure about my performance, having never done it before. There was no shame in fishing for a few compliments, was there? Besides, it was almost as fun to talk about sex as it was to do it, especially when you were basking in the after glow of having just done it.

"Really," Christos smiled smugly. "I think you melted my dick off," he murmured sleepily. "I can't even feel it right now. I think my balls are completely empty. Like I shot my testicles out of my dick. Did you feel them going down your throat at any point? Can you check if they're still there, or has my scrotum deflated completely?"

I reached under the water, between his legs and cupped his balls. "Still there," I grinned. I gave them a gentle squeeze. "They seem like they're still kind of full. Maybe you need to drain them some more?"

"In awhile."

"What?" I gasped. "I thought you were the minute man when it came to recovery time."

"Not after what you just did. I might need an hour."

"No way!"

"Yes, way. Come to think of it, I think my blood sugar took a hit from all that action. I may need some chocolate after that."

"Are you crazy?" I barked. "After what I swallowed, I think I need to go on a diet!"

He snickered. "I'm sure you swallowed no more than two thousand calories."

"That many?" I gasped seriously.

"That's what they say. But that has to be a myth. A load is no more than a few teaspoons. I mean, a twenty ounce porterhouse is a thousand calories. How the hell would you squeeze two thousand into two or three teaspoons? Doesn't make any sense. In other words, you don't need to go on a diet."

"Are you sure?"

"Man, you're such a girl. I guess you won't have room for the chocolate I bought you, what with swallowing my load and all," he said dismissively.

"That's where you're wrong! Women always have room for chocolate!" I hopped out of the tub and grabbed the heart shaped box off the counter, then slid back into the water. I looked at the box. "What's See's Candies? I've never heard of it."

"That's right," Christos said, his mouth just above the surface of the water, a sleepy expression still hooding his eyes, "they don't have See's on the east coast. See's is Mary See, the little old lady who invented them. Prepare for the best chocolate truffles you've ever had."

"I've had Godiva. Some old lady named Mary can't possibly be as good as exotically sexy Godiva," I scoffed.

"Try one," he said, uninterested in my argument.

I opened the box and looked at all the different milk, dark, and white chocolate morsels. "Which one should I pick?"

"It doesn't matter, they're all awesome," he said.

I grabbed one and took a bite. Rich chocolate and butter cream filling melted my taste buds in a chocolatey rush of yummy scrumptiousness. "Oh my god. That is unreal." I swallowed. "I think I just had my first foodgasm."

"Told you," Christos chuckled. "Happy Valentine's Day, *agápi mou*." He leaned over and kissed me passionately.

We took turns kissing and eating See's chocolates. I couldn't decide which was yummier.

It didn't matter because I was sharing both with my man.

I was in heaven.

Chapter 6

SAMANTHA

The next morning I was in hell.

I'd had nightmares all night about Christos being in jail. I slept like crap and woke up exhausted.

At least Christos was next to me in bed. For now.

His trial was tomorrow.

I stared at the ceiling, my head spinning like a hurricane.

His trial felt like an eternity from now and I just wanted it to be over. It also felt like it was a second from now, and my time left with Christos was so fleeting that I needed to hold onto him for dear life.

"You awake?" he asked softly.

Tears dribbled down my cheeks. "Yeah," I said softly.

He rolled over onto his stomach and his face was inches from mine. He kissed my cheek gently.

I smeared tears from my cheeks and held back the hitching sobs that tried to force their way out. I wanted to be strong for my man.

"Let it out, *agápi mou*," he said softly. He wrapped an arm around me and pulled my naked body into his.

"Oh, Christos," I sobbed, finally letting go. My body shook with pain and fear. I shut out all the terrible future scenarios dancing through my head and did my best to concentrate on Christos' loving embrace.

I cried for a long time as he kissed me softly, showering love all around me, my lips, my eyes, my cheeks, the tip of my nose, my ears, my hair. I sank into his comforting love.

"I love you Christos. I can't let you go," I said desperately. "I need you. Right here. I don't want you going to court tomorrow." I knew it was ridiculous, but I said it anyway.

"I need you too, *agápi mou*, forever and always. I need you in my life to guide my heart, to keep it open, to keep me grounded, to remind me why life is worth living, why I have to keep fighting, why I will never give up on you or us. You are my life, *agápi mou*. I have nothing without you."

My heart opened to his in that moment wider than it ever had before. Christos was my one true love. I knew it as certainly as I felt his heart opening wide to mine in that moment. I literally felt energy flowing between us, the ruby jewel of my own heart absorbing and projecting back his love in a completed circle.

Together at last.

I treasured this man like no other thing in my short life. He was my gift.

I would do anything to keep him safe.

Anything.

Without thinking, I reached between us and felt his hot heat in my hand. I slid him inside my waiting wetness and we made tender love.

It was slow, soft, connected, and precious. The wings of my heart fluttered in the bath of his love. Our bodies spiraled up and out of the room as one, the hot breath of our love lifting us effortlessly into the sky on billowing sheets of ecstasy.

Eventually, we reached orgasm together.

"I love you, *agápi mou*," we murmured simultaneously.

After, as we laid in bed, we returned to Earth and came to rest in our own bodies once again.

To my surprise, I was on top of him. I hadn't even realized I had ended up here. It had happened unconsciously, without insecurity or anxiety.

I really had been out of my body, connected with Christos on some strange spiritual plane that existed outside of this bedroom.

But that moment had passed.

I was now intimately aware of my physical body once again. Christos' manhood, the most sensitive part of him, was still deep inside of me, quivering within, pulsing faintly and intermittently. I savored knowing that his fluids were mingling with mine as he emptied the very last of himself into me. I wanted to keep his tender manhood inside of me like this forever so I could protect him from all the terrible things in the world. I wanted to sustain the open flow between our hearts in that moment, this connection that was proof his heart was bound to mine.

Forever.

===

At some point, stark reality prodded its way into my awareness. I could feel Christos' semen puddled between us on his stomach. The gooeyness didn't bother me. It just reminded me that I would need to clean up, need to separate from Christos, breaking our physical connection so we could go about our day.

Why was it that sex always led to an ending? I felt sadness stirring in my belly. I knew the French called orgasms 'little deaths'. It had always seemed morbid to me, but in this moment, I realized they were right. I felt something dying. I hoped it wasn't prophetic.

Groan! This was not how I wanted to start what might be my last day with Christos for a long time.

I hugged Christos as tightly as I could, my face burrowing into his muscled chest. I never wanted to let him go.

Never.

"We should get cleaned up," Christos said.

"No," I whispered.

He wrapped his arms around me and held onto me for a long time. I appreciated that. His manhood was still inside me and I still wasn't ready to let him withdraw from the protection of my body.

Just a few more minutes.

For consolation, I reminded myself that after every ending comes a new beginning. It felt like false hope, but I did my best to rally. Life was filled with the rhythm of change. I'd seen it first hand.

Now I just had to walk into a new chapter.

Just get up off the bed and start.

Any time now.

I sighed.

Did I have to?

Finally, I sat up on top of Christos.

He smiled up at me, his jeweled blue eyes piercing my heart.

He gave me courage.

He gave me hope.

He gave me strength.

No matter what happened.

"We're a mess, aren't we?" I asked.

He chuckled. "I wouldn't have it any other way. Want me to lick you clean?"

I hung my head and lifted my hips off of his. There was a swimming pool down there. "I hope you're thirsty," I joked, totally unselfconscious. I felt like a new me. I don't think I'd ever been this relaxed around Christos, or even when I was alone.

I climbed off of him, cupping my hand between my legs to catch any errant drips. Why was reality always full of annoying details like this? "I'll be right back," I said as I walked toward the bathroom, "Stay right where you are."

Rose petals still covered the bathroom from top to bottom. All of the candles had gone out, save one.

One candle.

I looked around the room. Wasn't there one other candle still burning? Two strong flames burning bright, side by side?

No. There was only the one.

The one.

I shuddered and blinked away fresh tears. I almost doubled over in agony.

Christos…

"You okay in there?" he called from the bedroom.

"Yeah," I choked out hoarsely, "just a second."

After I composed myself, I looked around and grabbed a hand towel off the rack and returned to the bedroom. I crawled onto the bed and kneeled next to Christos. I gently wiped him clean, swirling the towel around his stomach and his thighs.

"Ready to shower?" I asked.

"After you," he said as he propped himself up on his muscled, tattooed arms.

I held out my hand to him and he took it. I led him off the bed and into the bathroom, where we showered together.

After we dressed, we went downstairs.

"What do you want to eat?" he asked.

"I'll make it," I said confidently. "Sit down and relax."

"Giving orders now?"

"Yep," I grinned.

"We have leftovers from last night," he suggested, "tons of lamb. I always love protein for breakfast."

"Zip it. I've got it." I opened the fridge and scanned the

contents. There sure were a lot of leftovers. I hated to let food go to waste and I wasn't above taking suggestions. I grabbed some veggies, the lamb and onions from last night, and cooked omelets for both of us. I also made toast and poured some orange juice.

"What are you going to do today?" I asked.

Christos finished chewing on a slice of buttered toast and wiped his face with a napkin. "Move you in, remember?"

"Oh yeah."

"I need your key. Don't forget to call your apartment manager."

"I'll do it right now. I don't want you getting hassled." I jogged upstairs and dug my phone out of my purse. I called my manager and explained everything before going back downstairs. "Christos, are you sure you don't want me to help move stuff?"

"No, I'll handle everything," he smiled. "You won't have to lift a finger. It's my gift to you."

"That's so sweet, *agápi mou*," I said, "but I kind of feel like ditching classes today."

"Which classes?"

"Today? Oil Painting and Figurative Sculpting."

"Oh, you can't skip those," Christos said firmly. "I mean, Marjorie would totally miss you in sculpting."

"The Bitchinger?"

Christos chuckled. "Yeah. Can't let her down. How's she been treating you lately?"

"Like her favorite student," I grinned.

"You must've done something to please her."

"I think please is too pleasant a word," I grinned.

Christos arched an eyebrow. "Do I want to know?"

"No, otherwise I'd have to kill you," I winked.

We finished breakfast and headed out the door together. I stood in the entryway as Christos locked up behind us. I felt like we were a married couple heading off to work. It was so domestically romantic I wanted to hug myself.

"Isn't Spiridon home?" I asked.

"No, he had to take care of some stuff. I think he'll be back late."

"Okay. If I get back to the house before you, is it okay for me to come in?"

"Of course, *agápi mou*. You live here now. Come and go as you please."

Wow, I really liked the sound of that.

Christos started loading up his Camaro with the packing materials while I hopped into my VW and drove to campus.

Getting through my day was harder than I'd expected. Nagging in the shadows of my mind, like someone continuously tapping the back of my head with two stiff fingers, was the awareness that Christos was going to court in less than twenty-four hours.

I tried to joke around with Romeo and Kamiko in Oil Painting to distract myself, but it didn't help. Somehow, everything made me think of jail. The paint that was trapped in the tube until I uncapped it and squeezed some out onto my palette. The fruit stuck in the bowl on the pillar in the middle of the studio until someone else decided to move it. Sure, Christos wasn't an inanimate object, but if he ended up in jail, he'd have as much control over life as paint or fruit did. None.

Lameness.

After class, I had no appetite, so I left Romeo and Kamiko to get lunch by themselves.

I went to the library to study some Sociology and History. My grades in both classes had continued to sink.

Despite the quiet environment of the library, no matter how hard I tried to concentrate, I couldn't remember a single word of what I read. I packed up my bags and went to Figurative Sculpting. Hunter Blakeley was still the model, but he had become invisible to me. He was just a big brainless slab of tanned muscle and blond hair. Whatever. He didn't even look at me anymore. Thank goodness for small favors.

When class was over, Romeo and I walked out together.

"Did you give your photo of the rugby buttplugs to the campus police yet?" Romeo asked as he squinched his monocle into place.

"Oh, I totally forgot about those jerks. Do you think there's any point in giving it to them now? I mean, what if they go track the other guys down and the next thing we know, the cops are looking for Christos so they can ask him questions? Or worse?"

"Good point."

"I'll hang onto it for now. Who knows, maybe I'll need it later to prove Christos' innocence." Something clunked into place in my head the moment those words were out of my mouth. I felt my eyes saucer in surprise. "Oh my god! That's it!"

"What's it?" Romeo was totally confused.

"Thank you so much, Romeo!" I hugged him and shook him vigorously. "I have to go to the library and look something up right now!"

"You look like you just won the lottery or something," Romeo smiled. "Care to share?"

"No time! I'll tell you later!" I kissed Romeo on the cheek and sprinted to the Main Library, which had a super fast internet connection.

"If you win more than ten million bucks," Romeo hollered at my back, "you have to give me at least a hundred grand!"

"Will do," I laughed over my shoulder.

===

My search online proved fruitless. After two hours of trying, I gave up and trudged to my car. Maybe my idea hadn't been so smart. Grrr.

I drove to my apartment out of habit, mulling over other options in my head. Nothing came to mind by the time I parked in my assigned space in the parking lot. I walked upstairs and opened my door. Everything was gone. My furniture, my clothes, my art supplies, my dishes. Everything.

"That was quick," I said out loud. For a second, I nervously thought perhaps I had been robbed, but I knew it was just Christos. There was a Post-It stuck to the front door that read simply, 'All Finished!'

The carpet was immaculate and didn't have a single foot print in it, just overlapping diagonal lines from the carpet machine. I was loathe to mar the perfect surface, but I wanted to check the kitchen and bathroom. I stepped inside to investigate. Yup, everything had been scrubbed to a sparkling shine.

I locked up and drove to Christos' house. I meant, my house. Grin!

A big pickup truck was coming out of the driveway as I was turning in. Jake was driving. Two blond and tan surfing buddies of his sat in the cab next to him.

Jake stopped and rolled down his window.

I stopped my VW beside his cab. "Oh my god, Jake! You guys cleaned me out! And cleaned up too! My place is spotless. I didn't think guys were capable of such things," I grinned.

Christos came walking up between our cars at that moment. "You kidding? Haven't you heard of the Twelve Labors of Hercules? One of them was to clean all the shit out of the Augean Stables in a single day. They had thirty years of built up filth. Your place was worse."

I swatted at Christos from my seat in my VW. "Jerk!"

He dodged away easily and chuckled. "Hercules wouldn't have stood a chance at your apartment!"

"My apartment wasn't that dirty!" I shouted. "Tell him, Jake!"

Jake smiled, his teeth a bright white stripe shining from his tanned face. How did he manage to stay so tan, even in winter? I guess surfing seven days a week was better than a tanning club membership.

"Between you and me," Jake chuckled, "Christos took a lot of breaks." He shot a glance at Christos. "I mean, a *lot* of breaks."

"Totally," the two cute guys sitting next to Jake chorused.

"Dude," Christos sneered, "you guys were asleep the whole time. If it wasn't for me, you'd still be napping on Samantha's couch."

Jake rolled his eyes. "You're smoking crack, bro."

I smiled at Jake. "I'm sure Christos didn't lift a finger, so thank you Jake, and you guys too," I said to Jake's cute surfer buddies sitting next to him in the truck.

I noticed the large steam cleaning vacuum in the back of the pickup. "You guys even shampooed my carpet."

"Yeah," Jake said, "a buddy of mine has a steam cleaning business. He let me borrow one of his rigs for the day."

"Do I owe you guys any money?"

"It's on the house," Jake smiled.

"Thanks, Jake. So, how did you guys work so fast? I mean, everything is finished and it's still early."

"Elbow grease," Christos said.

"He's right," Jake said. He flexed his left arm and the muscles popped. I forgot how muscular Jake was. I guess he was always so relaxed, I never noticed how cut he was. Madison probably licked Jake's arms at every opportunity. I was so happy for her.

"You should've been there watching us work," Christos said. "You would've been creaming your jeans watching the four of us scrub and scour."

"Me and Madison could've sold tickets," I joked. "Who are your buddies, Jake?"

"This is Lucas and Logan Summer," he said, nodding to the two hotties on the bench seat beside him. "They're brothers."

"Twice the summer, twice the brother," the one with blue eyes said.

These guys were the epitome of summer, all right. Beaches and bathing suits were made for them.

"Dude, you know that doesn't make any fucking sense," the one with green eyes scoff-smiled and shook his head.

Blue eyes rolled his glittering orbs. "So what? I like how it sounds."

Yeah, they were brothers. Cute as hell, but definitely brothers.

I smiled at them and they beamed their winning smiles back at me. I gave them a wave. "Hey, guys. I'm Samantha. Which one of you is which?"

"What up, Samantha. I'm Lucas," he waved. He had blue eyes. "This is my kid brother, Logan."

"Hi," Logan nodded, his green eyes sparkling at me like emeralds. He seemed shy compared to his brother.

These guys were total heartbreakers. Both were as tan as Jake and had shaggy blond hair with a natural curl. The only visible difference between them was that Lucas had blue eyes and Logan had green. Girls everywhere swooned at the sight of them and envied their awesome hair, I had no doubt. They also projected a very homey, genuine energy. No wonder they were friends with Jake and Christos.

"So, do hot guys always travel in packs or what?" I asked.

"Normally, me and Logan do," Lucas said, "but today we're slumming it with these two trolls." He motioned toward Jake and Christos with his thumb.

"Dude, you're totally walking home," Jake joked.

"Whatever, dude," Lucas scoffed.

Jake rolled his eyes. It was obvious he was close friends with Lucas and Logan from the way the three of them behaved.

"Hey," Lucas said to me, "If you guys aren't doing anything this Saturday night, you should totally come watch our band play."

"You guys are in a band?" I goggled.

"Totally," Logan said softly.

Yeah, they were perfect.

Lucas nodded, "We've got a show at the Belly Up."

"The Belly Up?" I said. "That's right near where I live."

"You guys should come check us out," Lucas smiled.

Saturday night. I felt that lead ball that had been weighing me down for the last few days roll around in my stomach. If luck was against me, I'd be crying my eyes out while Christos started a long stay in jail. I glanced at Christos and I could tell Lucas' offer hadn't sat well with him either. "Oh," I said, "I don't know. Can we decide later? Christos and I have some...family stuff."

Christos nodded, a hint of sadness tightening his smile. "Family stuff," he echoed.

"Yo, we gotta jet," Jake said. "Get this rig back to my buddy at his shop before he goes home for the night. Anyway, me and Mads are going to see Lucas and Logan play on Saturday, so call us if you want us to pick you up."

"All right," I smiled. "Thanks again, you guys!"

"Any time," Lucas said.

Logan nodded and smiled.

I waved as the truck drove off.

When they were gone, I parked my VW in front of the garage and got out. Christos still stood at the end of the driveway near the street. He seemed a million miles away. I started walking toward him, but he didn't move. I broke into a run until I was in his arms.

"Christos...oh, *agápi mou*..." I wept as he enveloped me into his warm embrace. I felt the world crumbling around me by the second, and his arms were the last safe place in the universe.

Words could not do justice to my sadness and fear in that moment.

His trial was tomorrow morning...

===

Christos and I walked into the house together after I'd calmed.

"Welcome home, *agápi mou*," he said.

"That's right!" I smiled. "I live here!"

"Yup. You're all moved in. I even put your ice cream in the freezer in the kitchen."

"All of it?" I grinned.

"All nine pints," he smiled.

Christos led me upstairs and showed me all my clothes, neatly folded in the chest of drawers or hanging in the closet. My old shoes from D.C., which I rarely wore in warm San Diego, were neatly arranged on the floor of the closet.

"Your furniture is in the garage," Christos said. "If you want any of it, let me know. I'll put it wherever you want in the house. Otherwise, make yourself at home. This is your house now."

I smiled at him. "I love you, Christos."

"I love you too," he smiled.

The pleasant knowledge that I was now moved in was blown out of my chest when I remembered that my parents didn't know. Now that I was actually situated in the Manos' house, I sensed they would not be happy. But there was no going back. Since they'd stopped paying for anything, did it really matter? Was there any way they could make my life worse than they already had? I sighed harshly, not wanting to think about it.

Christos and I went downstairs and had a somber dinner together. Spiridon wasn't back from wherever he'd gone, and the usual relaxed, social atmosphere was crushed by the weight of what tomorrow might bring. Not even Christos was his usual easy going self.

After dinner, I tried to do some sketching at my drawing table in the studio while Christos worked on the background for one of his unfinished paintings. It was useless. I couldn't concentrate.

I walked over to Christos, who sat at his easel, and put a hand on his shoulder. "I can't get anything done. Do you want to go to bed?"

He sighed loudly and dipped his brush into a jar of turpentine and swirled it around. The turpentine spligged and splogged around the jar until he wiped the brush dry on some paper towels. "Sure."

When we reached the threshold of the studio that led back into the house, Christos turned and took a long, meaningful look at the studio.

I wanted to cry, but I held back my tears, for his sake. This wasn't the last time he was going to see it. It couldn't be. The jury *had* to find him not guilty. Christos wasn't a bad man. I knew it in my heart.

Christos sighed again and turned out the lights.

We walked quietly upstairs and got ready for bed in silence. We slid under the covers together and laid side by side, holding hands, staring at the ceiling.

I was miserable.

Christos was distant, almost like he was in shock. I couldn't blame him.

I squeezed his hand, and he squeezed mine back.

I don't know how long we laid like that.

At some point, I needed to talk. The stress inside me needed to be vented before I vomited up my dinner. If that happened, I knew I wouldn't hesitate to run downstairs and fill my stomach with ice cream until I had to vomit that out too.

"Christos," I whispered in the darkness, "are you sure there's no way I can testify at your trial tomorrow?"

He didn't answer.

"I mean," I said, "I was there. I saw the guy. My version of events should make a difference, shouldn't it?"

After a long time, a thin, tired voice said, "It's too late, Samantha. Whatever happens, happens. I'll deal with it."

"But, what if—"

"I really need to try and sleep, *agápi mou*."

I couldn't argue with that.

He slid his hand out of mine and rolled onto his side, his back to me.

I felt like he was a million miles away. I almost snuggled up against him, but decided to let him sleep. I laid in bed quietly for awhile.

My stomach was churning like a sailboat in a super storm. I couldn't take it anymore. I had to do something about my stress. I slipped silently out of bed and went downstairs.

I passed right by the evil ice cream in the freezer.

I had work to do.

I skulked around the house until I found an office. It was lined with bookcases filled with art books. A beautiful, ornate wooden desk sat in the center of a Chinese area rug. Probably Spiridon's office. There was a computer on the desk. I switched on a small desk lamp and a yellow disc of light fell onto the blotter. I clicked the mouse and woke the computer. I checked that I could access the internet. Yup, working.

For a second, I drummed my fingers quietly on the desktop

while I considered what to do next.

I finally broke down and tiptoed back to the kitchen. I spooned two modest scoops of Peanut Butter Fudge Bomb into a small bowl then returned to the office. I was going to need at least a little sustenance while I worked.

I didn't care what the stupid courts said. It was never too late to make a difference.

Chapter 7

SAMANTHA

I jolted awake.

Where the hell was I?

Ow! My cheek was killing me. Had I slept on a bed of nails?? I opened my eyes carefully, on the lookout for sharp objects. No nails.

But I had fallen asleep at the keyboard, my face resting on the keys. I sat up and rubbed my cheek. I felt keyboard grooves waffling my skin.

Nice.

I leaned back in the antique chair in Spiridon's office. Something creaked and popped. I couldn't decide if it was the antique chair or my antique back. When I stood up, more popping. Definitely my back. I would need to get it refurbished later.

Light slipped into the office around the window blinds. I yanked the cord and sunlight blared inside.

Morning already?

How late had I worked? There was no way to know what time I'd fallen asleep. But it didn't matter. I'd found what I'd been looking for online last night. I now had a way to help Christos.

I couldn't wait to tell him the good news!

The house was so quiet, I imagined Christos was still in bed. I tiptoed out of the office and back to Christos' bedroom. *Our* bedroom.

The door was open.

He was not in bed.

I walked into the bathroom. It was empty, and all the roses from Valentine's Day were gone, as if they'd never been there.

"Christos?" I called.

The house was silent.

I went from room to room.

This search felt eerily familiar. I'd done the same thing only days before, but it had been at night. Now the sun shone through windows all over the house.

Fuck! What time was it? I ran downstairs, hoping to find Christos and Spiridon eating breakfast together, hot coffee in the pot waiting for me.

The kitchen was empty. The clock on the stove said 8:30am.

"Christos?" I called loudly. "Spiridon?" My panic started to rise. Tears began dripping down my cheeks.

I ran to the studio and shouted, "Christos! Spiridon!"

Silence.

I even checked the back deck, but no one was outside.

I ran into the house and toward the front doors. A note was taped to one of them. It read, 'Went to court'.

I opened the front door and sprinted down the driveway.

I screamed when I reached the street. "Christos!" I started sobbing uncontrollably. "Noooo!!!!"

How could I help my man when I didn't know where to find him?

I fell to my knees on the cement of the driveway and wailed.

===

CHRISTOS

The sky was clear blue as I drove my '68 Camaro south on the 5 freeway toward downtown. Great day for a trial, right? What I wouldn't do to strip out of the shirt and tie that were strangling me so I could head down to the beach with my board and catch some waves with Jake instead.

Not today.

Maybe not for the next four years.

I grit my teeth, doing my best not to think about it.

Morning traffic was light and my car cruised along at sixty-five. I thumbed on the MP3 player mounted in the dash and skipped through songs until I hit Mouth For War by Pantera. I cranked the volume and the music rumbled the interior of the car. My left foot pounded on the floor board in time to the bass drum and my hands slapped out the rhythm of the snare drum on the steering wheel. Guitars screamed into my eardrums.

Yeah, I was going to fucking fight.

Time to testify, mother fuckers.

I desperately wanted to floor the gas pedal. Take my Camaro up to one-forty and start weaving through the cars on the road. But these people weren't my enemies.

That's what was driving me crazy.

There was no one to fight. No one to punch. No one to kick, claw or bite. Damn, I needed to punch someone in the face.

I glanced over at the Buick next to me. An old woman was at the wheel. She had the seat pushed way forward and could barely see over the dash. Her hands were at ten and two and her chin jutted forward, pinning her eyes on the road in front of her.

Yeah, not exactly what I had in mind.

Where was that Hunter Blakeley when I needed a punching bag? I'd barely scratched his nose the night me and Jake had run into him coming out of the downtown Hooters. He deserved a proper ass kicking for being such a shit magnet.

I took a deep breath and tried to release my frustration. I started shouting along with the lyrics of Mouth For War.

A couple miles later, I pulled off the freeway at the Front Street exit and headed toward the courthouse. I drove into a parking garage. The lower levels were already filled with cars so I hammered the gas and squealed tires up the next four floors, leaving trails of rubber around every corner, until my car was on the roof. Plenty of spaces. I parked in the far corner. After throwing on my suit jacket, I headed for the stairs.

When I was on the sidewalk, I turned the corner at Broadway. The sun shot hot bullets off the glass front of the courthouse, punching my eyes. I squinted at the glare and felt like some western cowboy at high noon. Time for the final shootout. Too bad a trial took way longer and was way more boring than a six gun duel on a dusty street cut between rows of whorehouses and saloons.

I shot my cuffs and adjusted my tie. Man, I hated suits.

I strode up the courthouse steps.

Time to kick fucking ass.

===

SAMANTHA

After screaming my lungs out on the driveway for the better

part of two minutes, I stood and dusted off the knees of the sweats I'd slept in and ran into the Manos house. I sprinted upstairs and jumped behind the desk in Spiridon's office and frantically searched online for San Diego court houses while wiping tears from my eyes.

There was more than one. I ruled out the obvious ones, like Juvenile Court and Family Law Court. There were two Superior Courts. One downtown, and the other in Kearny Mesa. They were fairly far apart. I hoped I didn't pick the wrong one.

I had no idea how long a trial actually took. I mean, most court TV shows took an hour or less. But what about in real life? I had zero clue. Best to get cracking.

What I did know was that I couldn't run into court wearing sweats and slippers.

I ran into my new bedroom and rifled through my closet. I didn't have a second to savor the fact that this was my first morning in my new home with Christos. Welcome to Sucktown, population: Me.

The remnants of my Washington D.C. wardrobe were perfect for putting together court-appropriate attire. I selected a black blazer and a gray pencil skirt, plus a cute white blouse, black hose and conservative pumps to go with.

I dashed into the bathroom and slathered on antiperspirant. Too bad I was out of industrial strength. I would have to go with Extra Dry. I pulled my hair back in a harsh pony tail, then applied minimal makeup.

I was out of the house seven minutes later.

Who said women had to take forever to get dressed?

I was on a mission.

I was going to save Christos.

I tried calling him as I hopped into my VW, but he didn't answer his phone.

It didn't matter. I had proof of his innocence in the palm of my hand.

===

CHRISTOS

Footsteps echoed throughout the crowded marble hallway inside the courthouse as I snailed through security in slow motion. I had to remove my belt and shoes when I went through the metal detector. It was almost like going on a plane trip vacation, except there was a fifty-fifty chance my flight would crash into the side of Mt. Guilty.

I paused to glance back at the sunlight shining through the tall windows of the courthouse's main entrance. I took a good look, in case it was the last time I saw freedom for four years.

No, fuck that.

I was going to fight this shit until I won.

I found Russell waiting outside our courtroom.

"Eye of the Tiger?" Russell said as I strutted up to him.

"What?" I asked.

"You got that Rocky Balboa look on your face when he fought Clubber Lang the second time at the end of Rocky three."

I chuckled. "Fucking eye of the tiger, man."

As always, Russell was sharply dressed from top to bottom. His suit was freshly pressed, his cufflinks glittered, and the white of his collar and cuffs contrasted brilliantly against his ebony skin. "Speaking of eyes, I see your concealer did the trick. You look like Joe Citizen now."

"Yeah." I'd borrowed some from Samantha's makeup bag this morning.

"We win this," Russell said, "I'll have to take you out for a fancy dinner, considering we're both dressed up."

"Yeah," I smiled. "I'm shooting for lunch. I plan on being in and out of here by noon."

Russell chuckled and slapped my shoulder firmly. "Eye of the tiger."

A tall, beautiful dark-skinned woman in a tight navy blue suit stood next to Russell, holding the handle of her briefcase in front of her hips with both hands. She smiled at me.

"Christos," Russell said, "you remember Ms. Johnson? She will be assisting today at trial."

"Of course." I smiled down at her, "Brianna." At 5'11" in her heels, she still seemed short to me. We shook hands. She had the same firm grip I remembered. I'd met her at Russell's offices numerous times.

"Christos," she smiled and nodded.

I knew Brianna was still on the lookout for quality husband

material. Before Samantha had taken me off the market, I'd offered to fill the bill for Brianna several times. She was a good woman, smart and hellaciously funny the second she was off the clock and hung up her lawyer's costume. But she'd said I was too young. I think I was eighteen at the time and she was thirty. I couldn't blame her. I was still a mess back then. "Any good men been able to catch you yet, Brianna?"

"Not yet," she grinned. "None of them are fast enough." Brianna had trophies and photos of her running college track in her office.

"When are we going to head down to the SDU track to see who runs the fastest hundred?" I chided.

"Your muscle bound ass wouldn't stand a chance," she chuckled. "Too damn top heavy."

"Keep dreaming," I smiled. I was damn quick, but I knew Brianna would give me a run for my money once she put her track spikes on.

Russell said to me. "We get you off today, I'll drive you both out to the track myself. But my money's on Brianna."

"I hope you like losing," I grinned.

"I never lose," Russell said shrewdly. "We ready?" He nodded toward the courtroom.

"Let's do it," I said.

Russell opened one of the heavy wooden doors and his game face slid into place like Sir Lancelot's visor.

I followed Brianna and Russell into the belly of the beast.

The big door latched shut firmly behind me.

===

SAMANTHA

I was excited and anxious as I drove out of my new home, the one I shared with Christos!

I was sure fate was with me and good things were going to happen once I got to the court house downtown. Everything was going to work out for me and Christos in the end

The only problem?

At that moment, everything started going wrong.

Halfway to the freeway, the needle on my gas gauge decided to lay down on the job. It pointed right at the E like a lazy bastard. No problem. I was all about solving problems today. I would not be deterred. Luckily, there was a gas station right before the on ramp. Yay! There was also a long line. Lame! But there were no other convenient gas stations.

Waiting in line wouldn't take that long, would it? There were four lines of cars, so I picked the shortest one, hoping it was the quickest one.

I waited.

Why was it so crowded? Were they out of gas? I hadn't heard about any looming gas shortages or oil embargoes.

I pretended to be patient while I waited. The sedan two cars ahead finished and pulled away from the pump. The guy in front of me drove forward and climbed out of his huge truck to gas up. I was next.

Too bad truck guy had a gas tank the size of an oil field. It took forever for him to fill it up. Then he had to go inside to pay. Didn't he have a credit card or a debit card? Who used cash anymore? Maybe he was going to pay with gold doubloons?

I tapped my foot impatiently. "Any time, cowboy!" I shouted. He had been wearing boots. All men who wore boots and drove trucks were cowboys. I'm sure he had a gun rack in his truck somewhere. I grew up in Washington D.C. Sue me.

Were had he gone? Was he using the bathroom? Did he fall into the toilet, or was it just diarrhea? Geez, how long did it take to wipe your butt?

I drummed my fingers on my steering wheel. If I tried to drive around the island to another pump, I might lose my spot. Truck guy's truck was too big for me to push out of the way with my tiny VW, otherwise I would have. And the gas hose was too short to reach my car because the bed of his truck was about a mile long, and it had forced me to stop way far from the pump.

When I noticed moss starting to grow on the tip of my nose, Cowboy finally walked outside. Molasses slow. Slow motion scene in a movie slow. The shifting of continents slow. "Move it!" I shouted inside my car. He hadn't heard me so I rolled down my window to shout again.

Before I could make a peep, he turned on his cowboy boot heel and walked back into the store. No! Where was my lasso! I need to wrangle his ass and throw him behind his steering wheel.

I scanned around me. Unfortunately, the lines for the other

pumps were wall to wall cars. It was really smartest for me to wait.

Two minutes later, Cowboy came back outside with a big pepperoni flavored Slim Jim and a bottle of Mountain Dew. He climbed into his truck. Did he immediately drive off? No. Did he even start his engine? No. Did he do anything other than play with the meat stick in his hand while in the comfort of his cab?

I had no idea what he did with his meat stick, nor did I want to.

Days, weeks, even months later, he started his truck. A gust of exhaust billowed through my window as he drove off. I should've rolled it up. I coughed out a portion of my left lung before the air cleared.

I gassed up my car then sped to the onramp for the 5 freeway. I swear, every light I hit on the way there was red. At one intersection, I got stuck behind a line of cars waiting to turn right because a woman with a stroller out for a Sunday stroll had decided to use the cross walk. Didn't anyone tell her it was Friday? No Sunday strolling on Fridays! I swear, I saw three snails racing past her. Why was she walking? Who walked anywhere anymore? Didn't she know it was rush hour and people had places to go?

Eventually, the right turners turned and I made it through the light. I was on the 5 heading south a few minutes later.

Nothing could stop me now.

Except a traffic jam.

As I crested the hill at Del Mar Heights Road, I nearly crashed into a blanket of brake lights. The cars had all slowed from 65 to 35 in less than a quarter mile. A few minutes later, my VW crept along at 10 mph.

Had I jinxed myself by hoping things would turn out for the best?

===

CHRISTOS

Russell led Brianna and me to the defense table inside the courtroom.

The judge's bench was still empty. Only a few random heads populated the seating in the spectator gallery.

I noticed that George Schlosser and his assistant hangmen, Stanley Whitehead and Natalia Valenzuela, were already set up at the prosecutor's table with three laptops open and humming, and file folders neatly arranged between them.

George Schlosser looked calm and sure of himself. Whitehead looked like a smug fuck who I'd very much like to bump into in some dark alley when no one was looking. Natalia was a bright eyed and bushy tailed vampire jackrabbit.

Whatever.

I knew that me, Russell, and Brianna looked like three gladiators stepping into the Coliseum in Ancient Rome as we walked up to the defense table. We were going to slice some heads off. I could feel it.

I sat down while Russell and Brianna arranged their laptops and files on the defense table. It was a quiet moment for me to settle into my seat. I was going to be doing a lot of sitting for the next few hours. At least it was peaceful in the courtroom prior to trial. Almost like enforced meditation. I could roll with that. Then my stomach dropped through a hole in the floor and plummeted to the center of the earth.

"Paidi mou," my father said from somewhere behind me.

I recognized his voice instantly.

Holy fuck. How the hell did he get here?

My stomach bounced back from the earth's core and flew through the ceiling to shoot into the stratosphere. This was not going to be my day, was it?

I hadn't told my dad about the trial. I'd considered it after discussing the topic with my grandfather, but at the last minute decided not to. Maybe if my dad actually came by my grandfather's place now and then or showed some interest in something other than drinking, I would've told him.

I glanced back as he squeezed my shoulder.

He was leaning over the thigh high partition between the court floor and the gallery, wearing a sharp dark suit. He looked like a slightly older version of me, but with a hint of gray at the temples. To my surprise, he looked healthier than when I'd last seen him almost a year ago.

Ever since my mom had run out on us, my dad had stayed locked up in his house where he drank away his days. His split with my mom had turned him into an absentee human being. I couldn't stand watching him throw away his life and tremendous talent, so I rarely visited him, and we never talked on the phone. He was always too damn drunk to hold a conversation.

Russell and Brianna both turned to look at my dad. Russell knew him on sight. He'd met my dad many times in my youth, but I don't think Brianna knew him.

"Mr. Manos," Russell nodded, standing to shake my father's hand.

Brianna stood as well and introduced herself. "Brianna Johnson."

"Nikolos Manos," my father said.

Reluctantly, I stood and turned to face him. My grandfather, wearing a light gray suit, walked up behind my dad, looking nervous and apologetic. Yeah, he knew why I might possibly be irritated that he'd brought my dad. Fuck.

"*Pappoús*," I said as I leaned over to hug my grandfather.

He whispered in my ear, "I thought your father should be here. For you. For his son."

That explained where my grandfather had been last night. Probably sobering up my dad so he wouldn't be sloppy drunk in court. I ground my teeth together.

Still whispering, my grandfather continued, "Your father was worried you wouldn't want him to be here but I told him it would be all right with you."

Yeah, right.

I pulled away from my grandfather but dropped my eyes to my hands. My hands were already clenched into fists. My fucking dad was the last person I wanted sitting behind me during my trial.

"I can see where Christos gets his good looks," Brianna said warmly. "You three could be brothers."

My grandad smiled proudly and nodded. "That's my boys."

"Say hello to your father," Russell said softly, nudging my elbow.

I glared at Russell but saw compassion in his eyes. He'd been encouraging me to forgive my dad for years.

Without looking at my dad, I leaned toward him. He threw his arms around me and squeezed, stifling me. I expected to smell booze, but I did not. That was a surprise.

I pulled away and glanced at him briefly. "Hey," I mumbled.

"*Paidi mou*, it's so good to see you," he said earnestly.

As I was about to take a step back, my dad threw his arms around me again and crushed me to his chest. He'd let his body go to shit years ago. But now, he was much stronger than I remembered. Had he been working out again? That seemed impossible. I sighed as he patted my back repeatedly. "Okay, dad. That's enough."

He softened when I'd said 'dad'.

He released me and I glanced at him again. His eyes were moist.

"You look handsome as always, son," he smiled, his mouth shaking. "Bet the ladies have been chasing you, no?"

I arched a noncommittal eyebrow.

"I heard all about your sellout show at Charboneau," he continued, "I went down to see everything the day after opening night. Amazing work, *paidi mou*. Your female figures put mine to shame."

I gave him a solid, long look.

"I'm not bullshitting you, *paidi mou*. At my best, I did not paint like you do now."

My chest tightened and my eyes went hot. For my father to say that and say it sober blew me away. My father never exaggerated when it came to painting. He wasn't harsh, but he never piled on false praise. He was honest, direct, and encouraging. But he never said what he didn't mean. I'd been waiting to hear words like that from him my entire life. He was so fucking talented, I never thought I would. I was shell shocked.

My voice cracked as I spoke, "Thanks, *Bampás*."

My dad's smile widened across his even white teeth. Silent tears dripped from his eyes, staining his suit jacket. He grabbed me and hugged me more fiercely than before.

I let him.

My grandfather rubbed my dad's back affectionately. His eyes were wet as well. Then he turned to Russell and said, "My grandson is such a good boy."

"Yes he is," Russell stated firmly.

I was ready to cry myself. When my dad released his hug, I happened to glance at Russell who was marveling like he was witnessing a miracle. Maybe he was.

"The Court will now come to order," the uniformed bailiff announced from the front of the room.

So much for happy reunions.

Time to fight.

===

SAMANTHA

Traffic ground to a halt before I reached the 805 split. I was literally parked in my VW in an ocean of other frustrated drivers.

Just north of the SDU campus, the 5 freeway split into two roads, the 5 and the 805. Usually traffic lightened up at that point because there were suddenly twice as many lanes.

I'd hoped that the slow down through Del Mar would be temporary.

No such luck.

I was stuck. I couldn't get to an off ramp to take surface streets because traffic had not moved in the last ten minutes. I know, because I was watching the clock on my dashboard.

I considered driving along the shoulder. Several drivers had done just that in the last couple of minutes. Desperate times called for desperate measures. The only problem was, I was in the number three lane and there was an eighteen wheeler between me and the shoulder on the right. There was no way he could move out of the way, and I was boxed in by cars on the front, back and left.

If my VW had been shorter, I would've driven beneath the eighteen wheeler's trailer, between the sets of wheels. I'd seen it done in a movie once, but I didn't have a low slung sports car.

Maybe I needed to hop out of my car and hitch a ride with one of those people driving down the shoulder?

A second later, a California Highway Patrol car sped by, lights flashing, siren blaring. He was probably going to pull over those shoulder drivers and ticket them.

Groan!

Could I charter a helicopter and call in an airlift? Probably not. What if I called 911 and told them I needed to get to the hospital? Too bad that wouldn't help me get to court.

What was I going to do? It was fifteen miles to downtown. Wait. I could run fifteen miles. It wouldn't take me more than, oh, I don't know, two hours?

Too bad I was in heels.

Where were Taylor Lamberth's running shoes when I needed them? I should've learned my lesson. Never wear heels. Heels were evil.

I laugh cried at my own morbid joke.

I'd now been stopped for twenty minutes.

That was when I noticed black smoke billowing up into the sky in the distance.

There must have been an accident.

I knew the fire trucks were going to drive by and clear the road at any minute, right? Open up the road and get at least one or two lanes moving?

Right?

Ten more minutes passed without a single firetruck or ambulance. Where were they? People could be dying in their mangled cars. Somebody needed to help them so I could get to the courthouse!

How long would it take to walk? How fast could I walk? Three miles an hour? I could make it to downtown in five hours! Would Christos still be in court?

But could I walk fifteen miles in heels?

Fuck.

As soon as this day was over, I was throwing away any shoe I had with a heel on it. I was going to be one of those women who wore business suits and running shoes during their power walk lunch breaks, but I was going to do it around the clock. I would spearhead the movement to rid the world of shoes with heels! Ladies! Throw away your chains! Burn your heels! Right, like that was going to work. When it came to addictive substances, women's shoes were worse than crack cocaine. I knew from experience.

Another ten minutes passed without moving an inch. People had gotten out of their cars to look around and see what was happening.

An ambulance finally drove by, followed by a fire truck.

My good humor was gone. I was really stuck. Maybe I could walk to the nearest off ramp and call a cab? But with traffic stopped, how would a cab get to me? Crap.

What was I going to do?

I tried calling Christos. No answer. I'm sure he was in the courtroom in the middle of the trial. He wouldn't answer.

This was killing me.

I had cold hard evidence that Christos was innocent, incontrovertible proof that he had acted in self defense. All I needed to do was to give it to him and his lawyer. They would know what to do.

But what did it matter if I couldn't reach them?

I didn't even know the name of Christos' lawyer, otherwise I would've called his office to tell them what I knew. I'm sure the guy had a secretary who could send an assistant over to the courthouse or whatever.

I slammed my palms repeatedly against my steering wheel.

"Fuck!!!!!!!!!" I screamed.

In that moment, I was completely useless.

Chapter 8

CHRISTOS

"All rise for the Honorable Geraldine Moody, presiding," the bailiff said.

Third time was always the charm. The last two times I'd heard that phrase, during my arraignment and pre-trial, it was no big deal. Now it was the real thing.

After my trial, I was walking out of this courtroom into one of two places. Freedom or prison.

Judge Moody walked to her throne. She wore more makeup than I'd seen previously, and her hair was up in a careful bun. She was all dressed up, an attractive woman who could fuck me over with a single bang of her gavel. Not the kind of banging I liked to think about.

I huffed out a sigh as she settled in.

I was tired of waiting. Let's get this shit on.

George Schlosser and his assistant D.A. fucks Stanley and Natalia looked ready to drool over my corpse.

Fuck them. I was still kicking and breathing. Watch out, motherfuckers.

"Please be seated," the judge said gravely from her bench. "We are now on record for the State of California vs. Christos Manos, case number SD-2013-K-071183A. All parties are present. And so we begin," she finished ominously, "Bailiff, please call in the jury."

The bailiff opened a side door and twelve jurors, a mix of men and women of various ages and ethnicities, filed into the jury box and sat down. Some of them looked bored. Some looked excited to do their civic duty. Some looked like they'd rather be anyplace else but here.

That was when the truth of my situation slapped me full in the face. Who was I kidding? This wasn't a fist fight. For the next however many hours, I had to sit still and keep my mouth shut. No fists, no knees, no elbow strikes, nothing. All I could do was wait and hope the jury paid attention, kept an open mind, and didn't bum rush to judge me.

This was going to be torture.

Fucking Christ. Did they serve bourbon to defendants? I could use a shot or twelve.

Deputy District Attorney George Schlosser walked up to the podium to give his opening statement to the jury. He took his time, looking each of the twelve members of the jury in the eye before he opened his mouth. Was he going to say anything, or just smile pleasantly all morning?

The court room was completely silent.

"Yeah, I hit the guy," Schlosser said, nodding dramatically, looking at various jurors. "Yeah, I hit the guy," he repeated before pausing for further dramatic effect. "Ladies and gentlemen of the jury, these are the defendant's own words, given during an interview with the San Diego Police Department, a few days after he assaulted Horst Grossman."

Schlosser put his hands on his hips, pushing his suit jacket behind him with his arms, and in a voice dripping with accusation and harsh judgment said, "The defendant himself *admitted* that he did in fact *violently* punch Horst Grossman in the stomach on September 26, 2013." Schlosser nodded authoritatively.

Violently? What did you expect when good old Grossman called me a fucking prick and tried to jump me? Was I supposed to give him a friendly punch or maybe a gentle one? Fuck me.

Based on Schlosser's delivery, you'd think he'd already won the trial. What a fucking douche. He wasn't there. He didn't know what happened. I grit my teeth and did my best to look calm, cool, and bland. Russell had warned me not to show my emotions, or the jury might latch onto whatever I did as if it was proof of my guilt.

Schlosser smiled at the jury like they were old pals. "You may be asking yourself why we're even having a trial today, if the defendant already admitted to hitting Horst Grossman. He's guilty, right?"

Fuck. I knew exactly what Schlosser was doing. He was planting seeds in the minds of the jury. He was good. I knew a few tricks of my own. Too bad I couldn't use a single one in the courtroom.

"The reason we're here today, ladies and gentlemen of the jury, is because the defendant wants you to believe he struck the victim in self defense," Schlosser sneered, as if it couldn't possibly be true.

I noticed that Schlosser's assistants, Stanley Whitehead and Natalia Valenzuela, were watching his performance with obvious admiration. I could tell the two of them bowed and scraped at Schlosser's feet. I couldn't blame them. If I wanted to be the best bottom feeder ever, I'd probably pucker up for Schlosser too. Fucking low lifes.

"Members of the jury, I ask you to take a look at Exhibit 86 B on the projection screen," Schlosser said, clicking buttons on his laptop at the podium.

A huge photo popped on the screen mounted on the wall across from the jury box, filling it like a drive in movie theater. The image was split down the middle with me on the left and Horst Grossman on the right. I looked like the Incredible Hulk standing next to a little old man.

The reason for this discrepancy was obvious.

The picture of me was from the day I had been arrested. I wore a white V neck short sleeve tee. My muscled arms, covered in tattoos, were popping out of my shirt. In clear black letters on the gray wall behind me was a horizontal measurement line with the numerals 6'5" skimming the top of my hair.

Horst's photo had been taken at a different time in front of a random white wall. There were no measuring lines behind him. Horst could be 3'2" or 8'11", but without any numbers, there was no way to know. Whatever his actual height, his head was positioned much lower than mine, creating the illusion that he was much shorter. Finally, the photo of Horst had been zoomed out. Not so much as to be comically misleading, but enough that Horst seemed like a small, inconsequential man standing next to a mammoth titan.

This was fucking absurd. I knew from standing two inches from Horst Grossman that he wasn't nearly as tiny as this image made him seem.

The split photo had been on screen for all of two seconds before Schlosser said, "The defendant wants you to believe that Horst Grossman put him in fear for his life that day—"

"Objection, your honor," Russell cut in authoritatively, "this evidence is blatantly prejudicial."

"Sustained," Judge Moody said. She leveled a stern look at Schlosser and said, "Counselor, take that slide down immediately."

"Absolutely, your honor," Schlosser said agreeably. He clicked on his laptop and the screen went black.

"Members of the jury," the judge said, "you will disregard that photo. Let the court transcript reflect that exhibit 86 B has been stricken from evidence."

It didn't matter. The jury wasn't going to forget the photo now that they'd seen it. Worse, none of them had yet seen Horst Grossman in person because he wasn't even in the courtroom. If he had been, the fair thing would be to have me and Horst stand shoulder to shoulder in front of the jury so they could see for themselves our actual size differences. But that wasn't how it worked.

George Schlosser knew exactly what he was doing. He was pushing the rules of law to the breaking point, and he was getting away with it.

It wasn't the first time shit like this had happened to me when I was in court. All I could do was sit still and suck it up in silence.

The rest of Schlosser's opening statement was almost as heinous and misleading as that split photo, but there was nothing overt that Russell could object to. It was all in the way Schlosser delivered his argument: his sneering judgmental tone of voice, body language, and choice of words. Schlosser was a despicably brilliant man.

When Schlosser finished and sat down at the prosecution table, Russell leaned over and very quietly whispered in my ear, "After nine years working under the head District Attorney, Schlosser is still nothing more than a young buck trying to prove himself. His only goal today is to sharpen the points of his glorious career on your hide while climbing the political ladder. The only problem is, there's a mountain lion in this here courtroom ready to take his shit down a rung. And that mountain lion's name is me. Don't worry, son. I'm going to have Schlosser's head mounted on my wall before the day is over."

I cracked a smile.

"No smiling," Russell ordered sharply as he stood and stepped up to the podium.

Russell was a consummate badass during his opening statement.

He was gracious, level headed, straight to the point, focused on the facts, and he dismantled the bulk of Schlosser's inflammatory arguments with ease.

The men and women in the jury box, who had looked ready to string me up from the nearest tree in a tight noose, nodded thoughtfully at Russell's words, enthralled by his confident, no bullshit presence.

When Russell finished and sat down at the defense table next to me, I breathed an obvious sigh of relief.

I couldn't imagine a better attorney in my corner of the ring than Russell Merriweather.

The only problem was that it was going to be back and forth like this all day. Russell Merriweather and George Schlosser were evenly matched. When it came down to it, this trial hinged on my word against Horst Grossman's, and whether or not the jury believed a word I said after Schlosser titillated them with tales from my true crime lifestyle.

People weren't inclined to believe a convicted criminal.

Schlosser had the advantage.

If only we had something better to work with.

===

SAMANTHA

It had been over an hour since traffic had stopped. There was a black haze in the air that stank of burning rubber and cooked meat. It was nauseating to say the least.

I finally got word from some guy standing outside his Toyota Camry that it wasn't a pile of burning corpses. Thank god for that. Apparently, a refrigerated Ralph's grocery store semi truck had over turned and gone up in flames. Several other cars were involved, all of them burning. The CHP weren't letting anyone drive through the inferno.

But I did see a Life Flight helicopter land up ahead. Had my wish been granted? Was it possible?

Of course not.

I'm pretty sure they needed it for someone who was seriously hurt. Yes, I considered asking if they could give me a lift after they dropped off the injured people at the hospital. No, I didn't walk up to the scene of the accident and actually ask.

The grapevine rumors about when traffic would be moving again ranged anywhere from one hour to four. I could only cross my fingers and hope.

I called Christos several more times. No answer.

I called Madison who called Jake to ask if he knew who Christos' lawyer was. Jake never answered. Madison said he was surfing and it could be hours until he checked his phone. What was it with professional surfers spending all their time in the waves?

Damn it. There was nothing I could do but wait.

===

CHRISTOS

George Schlosser called a series of witnesses to the stand, all of whom had been at the scene the day I'd punched Grossman. They all sounded reasonable and credible.

The problem was that none of them had a clear, uninterrupted view of the whole thing from start to finish and no one had heard anything Grossman or I had said that day because the traffic noises were too loud, or they'd been too far away, or their windows were rolled up and they hadn't heard anything at all.

You would think this would work to my advantage. Unfortunately, the law said that if I couldn't prove I had acted in self defense, the jury would have to find me guilty of assault because I had punched Horst Grossman. It was that simple.

And right now, what the jury had to work with was like handing them a mystery novel with half the pages torn out, including the ending, and asking them who the killer was. They could only guess.

In other words the score was, the State: 1, Me: 0.

In Ice Hockey and Soccer, after a whole bunch of running around, many games finished with one to nothing on the scoreboard. I hoped things went differently for me. I needed someone to run a six point touchdown into the end zone. Too bad no one with legs had the ball.

"The state will call your next witness," Judge Moody said.

From his seat at the prosecution's table, George Schlosser said, "The state calls Edna Holloway."

A uniformed deputy walked outside the courtroom to fetch her. A minute later, the deputy led an old woman up to the podium. She wore a shin length navy blue dress and a pill box hat that floated in the foam of her white hair. She firmly clutched a gold clasped old lady handbag in her gloved hands. Despite her age, she walked erect and with purpose.

My first impression was that she'd probably chopped open kegs of beer and liquor with a wood axe during prohibition, or had led an army of suffragettes during the early charges to secure voting rights for women in the U.S. during the 19th century.

The bailiff motioned for Edna to raise her right hand while he said, "Do you solemnly swear that your testimony will be the truth, the whole truth, and nothing but the truth, so help you God"

"Yes," Edna Holloway said.

The bailiff led her to sit down at the witness stand.

George Schlosser asked Mrs. Holloway a series of questions establishing that she was an 83 year old retired high school math teacher who lived in Del Mar and never missed a Sunday at church. I'd been slightly off about her age. Edna also told the jury how she had been out walking her German Shepherd Greta on the trail running alongside Pacific Coast Highway when I'd punched Horst Grossman. She'd had a clear view of the incident, and had hung around to do her civic duty and tell the cops her version of events.

George Schlosser smiled at her from the podium. "Mrs. Holloway, please tell the court what happened in the moments leading up to the assault."

"I saw that man," she pointed at me forcefully, "get off of his motorcycle, walk up to Horst Grossman, and hit him without provocation." She nodded once for emphasis, her wrinkled lips pursed as tightly as the handbag she clutched in her gloved hands. You'd think she was worried about purse snatchers.

Russell stood up and said, "Objection to the use of the phrase 'without provocation', your honor. Mrs. Holloway was not privy to the conversation between Mr. Manos and Mr. Grossman. She had no way of knowing what was said between the two men. Therefore, she can't speak to matters of provocation."

"Sustained," Judge Moody said. "Please strike the phrase 'without provocation' from Mrs. Holloway's testimony. Members of the jury, you will disregard her remark."

Schlosser cast a snake's smile in the direction of Russell before he turned back to the witness stand. "Mrs. Holloway, at any time, did you see the victim punch or kick the defendant?"

"No."

"Did he attack the defendant in any way before the defendant punched him?"

"No. I saw the entire thing, from the time the defendant got off his motorcycle until the time he rode away. I never saw Mr. Grossman attack him."

Schlosser nodded victoriously. "What happened after the defendant punched Mr. Grossman?"

"I'll tell you what happened next. Mr. Grossman fell over. Then I watched in horror as the defendant dragged Mr. Grossman to the side of the road and threw him down on the curb like garbage," she spat. "Just like garbage. I've never seen a young person show such blatant disrespect for an elder in all my life. Then he walked away with no concern for the health and well being of Mr. Grossman. After that, he got on his motorcycle and drove off to who knows where."

That was wrong. I'd asked Grossman if he wanted an ambulance. He'd said no. Of course, Edna Holloway didn't know that.

"Thank you, Mrs. Holloway," Schlosser said to her. "Nothing further."

Schlosser sat down and Russell stepped up to the podium.

"Mrs. Holloway," Russell said in a friendly tone, "did you happen to overhear any of the conversation between Mr. Manos and Mr. Grossman?"

"I did not." Edna Holloway's eyes flashed at Russell like he was the mugger who would undoubtedly steal the purse in her gloved hands. She tightened her grip around it and sat up straight and stiff, her head held high.

"Did you see them speaking to each other?" Russell continued.

"I did." Mrs. Holloway glanced around defensively, as if Russell was trying to trap her in a lie.

"But you didn't hear any of the content of their conversation?"

"I did not," she said warily.

"How would you characterize the body language of Mr. Manos during the conversation?"

I remembered clearly that I'd been calm and relaxed that day. I hadn't gotten worked up until he'd told me to take a fucking hike.

"Aggressive," Edna Holloway said, "and confrontational."

Fuck me. Nothing like eye witness testimony to get to the bottom of things. Only in this case, Edna was shoveling dirt out of the grave she was digging for me with every word out of her mouth.

"You're sure?" Russell asked doubtfully.

"Yes," she said tightly.

"Did you at any time see Mr. Grossman move to attack Mr. Manos?"

"No."

That was wrong. Ten seconds after getting up in my face and shouting F-bombs at me, Grossman had lunged like a charging bull. That's when I'd punched him. Once. Sounded like self defense to me.

"You never saw Mr. Grossman lunge toward Mr. Manos?" Russell asked skeptically.

"No," she said firmly.

"Did you see Mr. Grossman step toward Mr. Manos?"

"No."

"He didn't move at all?"

"No. Mr. Grossman stood right where he was the whole time. I don't care how many ways you ask me, sir. That young man threw the first and only punch." After a pause, she glared at Russell and added, "Without provocation," as if she was spitting in his eye.

Russell ignored it.

She just had to slide that in, didn't she? Who the fuck was this woman?

Brianna gave my hand a brief reassuring squeeze under the table. She knew the story, I'd told her and Russell so many times. I glanced at her and she smiled briefly. Neither of us wanted to call attention to ourselves. She went back to taking notes on her laptop and preparing files while I went back to looking bland and calm.

Russell worked Edna Holloway over with questions for the next twenty minutes, coming at her from every angle, but Edna Holloway wouldn't budge. The last thing Russell wanted to do was look like he was badgering the witness, so he finally backed off and said, "Nothing further, your honor," before sitting down.

The score was now, the State: 2, and Me: 0.

===

After Mrs. Holloway left the witness stand, the deputy led Horst

Grossman into the courtroom to be sworn in.

Too bad I couldn't stand next to Grossman so the jury could see our actual size difference. Horst wasn't as big as me, but no way was he the tiny man that the District Attorney's side by side photo of me and Grossman had led the jury to believe.

Grossman's big gut hadn't changed. It tented out the flaps of his threadbare sport coat. The guy looked like he couldn't afford new clothes. I knew that was bullshit. He drove a custom Mercedes convertible, for fuck's sake. Gone was his gold jewelry and the expensive silk shirt and fitted slacks he'd been wearing the day I'd punched him.

Also missing was his fancy toupee. I remember thinking the guy had a great head of hair. Now he sported a stringy comb over. He looked the part of an ineffectual city bus driver hoping for an early retirement.

Horst Grossman limped his way to the witness stand. He breathed heavily, like he was climbing Mt. Everest. What a show boater. Give that guy an Oscar.

I repressed a desire to chuff out a comical laugh. Ridiculous.

George Schlosser leaned patiently against the podium and smiled while poor old Horst settled into the witness chair with a series of grunts and wheezes. I'm surprised they hadn't wheeled Horst in on a hospital bed with an IV tube sticking out of his arm.

Schlosser asked Grossman all the usual questions to identify who he was and where he lived. Grossman also rambled on about his family who he loved dearly, his selfless involvement in the community, and his considerable charitable contributions. In his spare time, I had no doubt that Horst sponsored thousands of starving children living in Third World countries, regularly rescued kitten's caught in trees and helped old ladies across the street. Somebody call the Vatican. They needed to officially recognize Saint Horst Grossman and make some statues of the guy.

Finally, Schlosser dove into relevant testimony. "The question on everyone's mind, Mr. Grossman, is why you got out of your car in the first place, putting yourself in harm's way?"

Grossman nodded respectfully, like a good little boy who always did what he was told. Uh huh. He made Sir Anthony Hopkins look like a ham actor in a Wayan's Brothers comedy. Grossman said, "I thought the woman driving the VW, the one who had stopped in front of me, was having some sort of car trouble. The stoplight had been green for a long time, and her car hadn't moved. So I got out of my car to check that she was okay."

It took everything I had not to blurt laughter. Grossman had wanted to kill her, not help her.

Grossman continued, "It turned out, she had spilled her coffee all over her car. I asked her if she needed any help. She said no, she was fine. I suggested that she should pull over to the side of the road to let traffic go by."

What? He was totally lying. He'd been shouting his ass off at Samantha and calling her names. The guy had been so worked up, I was surprised he hadn't given himself a stroke. That's why I'd walked up to Samantha's car in the first place. Grossman had been trying to pry her window down so he could get to her. When that hadn't worked, he'd started kicking her car door.

"Was this the point at which the defendant approached you?" Schlosser asked.

"Yes. He surprised me. I never saw him walk up. The next thing I know, he told me to 'back the F-word off' and leave. I had no idea what was going on. I had been trying to help the young woman in the VW. I turned to face him so I could explain myself. That's when he hit me. I was so surprised, I never saw it coming."

Was he serious? Or just fucking insane?

"Where did the defendant strike you?" Schlosser asked.

"In the stomach. I felt pain shoot out from my belly, and I think the wind was knocked out of me. I couldn't breathe or even stand up, so I fell to my knees. Before I could recover, he grabbed the back of my shirt and lifted me up. My shirt cut into my throat and I couldn't breathe. Then he dragged me to the side of the road. I was trying to stay on my feet, but he was pushing me so fast, I kept tripping. I think the only reason I didn't fall on my face was that he had me by the shirt collar. When we got to the curb, he threw me to the ground."

Schlosser continued asking Grossman a litany of questions: the severity of his injuries, how long he was off of work, how much pain he was in immediately after the attack and in the weeks following. It went on and on. Horst Grossman sounded like the most level headed, reasonable guy on the planet. George Schlosser was so smart with his questions, there was little Russell could object to.

I was on the edge of my seat when Schlosser finally turned things over to Russell.

Russell stepped confidently to the podium and went straight to work on Grossman. "Do you remember saying anything to Mr. Manos when he approached you?"

"Not that I recall," Grossman answered promptly.

"You didn't say anything to provoke him?"

"Not that I recall."

"You didn't make any threatening remarks?"

"Not that I recall."

Fuck, Grossman had the most selective memory of all time. If he was going to lie his way through cross examination, I was fucked.

"How long would you estimate it was between the time you turned to face Mr. Manos and when you claim he attacked you?"

"I don't know, maybe five seconds?" Grossman said thoughtfully.

Now he remembered. Too bad his recollection was a tad inaccurate.

"Did you make any moves that might have provoked Mr. Manos?"

"None that I recall."

"You didn't move toward him suddenly?"

"I don't think so."

Russell noticeably rolled his eyes. I couldn't blame him. I wanted to roll mine, but I stared straight at Grossman as blandly as possible. I hoped the jury didn't spot the daggers and bullets sneaking out of my eyes, because they were flying out at a thousand rounds a minute.

Russell asked Grossman, "You didn't move an inch?"

"I don't think so," Grossman answered.

"Did you stand immobile, like a statue?" Russell asked in a tone that bordered on comical.

Grossman chuckled agreeably. "Of course not. But I didn't make any sudden movements."

"You're sure?" Russell said doubtfully. "May I remind you, Mr. Grossman, that you are testifying under oath?"

Grossman's brows furrowed. "I know that, sir, and I didn't make any sudden moves."

"That seems odd to me, Mr. Grossman. You're saying that the defendant got off of his motorcycle, walked up to you, a complete stranger, and simply punched you in the stomach? Then he led you to the curb and asked you if you needed an ambulance?"

"It was the strangest thing..." Grossman mused thoughtfully.

"It was, wasn't it?" Russell marveled, a grin of disbelief tugging at the corners of his mouth.

I was marveling too. Grossman was totally lying. But there was no way to prove it.

Russell asked more questions about the attack and the aftermath, including Grossman's supposed injuries, but the man deflected all of Russell's questions like the greatest goal tender in the history of sports. I couldn't believe it. Grossman was a total pro on the stand.

Russell finally ran out of questions and sat down.

"Anything further, counselors?" the judge asked.

"No, your honor," Schlosser said from the prosecutor's table.

"Nothing further, your honor," Russell said.

"The State rests, your honor," Schlosser said.

Grossman stepped down from the witness stand.

"All right," Judge Moody said, "we'll take a short fifteen minute recess, then the defense will call its first witness." She banged the gavel with finality.

Fuck. The score was now: the State: 3, Me: 0

The only way I was going to score any points with the jury was when Russell called me to the stand, giving me the opportunity to finally tell my version of events. If I was lucky, this would win me a point with the jury, bringing the score up to 3 to 1. Too bad Schlosser would get to follow up with questions about my criminal past during cross examination. He could very well undermine any advantage I'd gained from telling my side of the story. If things went poorly, after I was finished testifying, the score could be back to 3 to 0, or worse, the jury might view me as a criminal. Because everyone knew: once a criminal, always a criminal. That would score a point for the prosecution. The way I saw it, that would put things at 4 to 0.

Sadly, it didn't matter. Whether it was 3-0, 3-1, or 4-0, I was the loser in every scenario.

I needed an NFL wide receiver to run right onto this soccer field and catch a Hail Mary touchdown pass, or I was fucked.

Too bad there were no wide receivers in soccer.

===

SAMANTHA

The traffic jam finally cleared enough for the emergency crews to let cars start going through. It took forever for everyone to merge into the one lane that was open and squeeze around the wreck.

The Ralph's semi and the other cars involved in the accident were all twisted, crunched, and blackened. The firemen were still milling about and hosing things down, but nothing appeared to be burning anymore. The people who'd been air lifted out by the helicopter were long gone. I took a moment to remind myself that their days were going way worse than mine.

I stuck to 65 mph on the way downtown, paranoid I might get pulled over by the CHP if I tried to speed. I didn't need any more delays. I kept a four second following distance from the cars in front of me. I didn't want to somehow get in a wreck of my own. That bitch Lady Luck had been working against me all morning, so I wasn't giving her any opportunities to further fuck me over.

I exited the freeway at Front Street and headed toward the courthouse. There were a bunch of one way streets and I got turned around several times before I found the courthouse on Broadway.

Did the courthouse have priority parking for panicky girlfriends? No. Did they have any parking whatsoever? None that I could see.

I was tempted to ditch my car on the steps of the courthouse and run inside. Crap. That wasn't an option. I drove around the block and stopped at the first parking garage I could find. They wanted twenty five bucks! I didn't care. I threw some bills at the parking attendant and parked on the third floor.

I took my heels off and carried them while I ran from my car to the courthouse. Lucky for me the San Diego sidewalks were relatively clean. The courthouse was a huge building with a bunch of Roman columns out front and the words 'Hall of Justice' in big letters above the entrance. Did Superman and Wonder Woman work here? Why hadn't Wonder Woman flown her invisible jet to pick me up from the traffic jam? Or Superman could've just hopped out his window and swooped me out of my car. Those guys were getting lazy.

I put my shoes on and walked through the doors. Then I got in line for the security check and promptly took my shoes back off. And my belt. Why? I wasn't flying anywhere. Couldn't they see I wasn't a terrorist? So what if my blouse was soaked with sweat? I know I was close to losing my cool because one more delay was going to broil my brain and send me into seizures, but it wasn't like I had a bomb in my purse.

After I finished with security, I stopped in my tracks. Where the hell was Christos' courtroom? There must've been a hundred rooms in this place! I grabbed several people walking by and asked if they knew where the Manos trial was, hoping that was what it was called. Every person I grabbed looked at me like I was insane. I wanted to tell them I didn't have a bomb in my purse, nor was I a terrorist, but I deduced that would not help matters any.

So I started opening courtroom doors at random. Every time I did, whatever was going on inside ground to a halt. Everyone turned to stare at me and the lawyers glared at me like I was ruining their lawyer mojo. What the heck was the problem? I was being quiet. It might have been because all of the courtrooms were so small. Where were the huge ones you saw in all the movies?

More importantly, were the heck was Christos?

I was never going to find him.

This building had at least ten stories. Did I have to go from floor to floor opening every single door? That could take hours. But nobody I'd asked had a clue where Christos' trial was.

What if I'd driven to the wrong court house?

Fuck!

Chapter 9

CHRISTOS

We all filed into the courtroom after the recess. The judge sat down at her bench and called in the jury.

"Mr. Merriweather," Judge Moody said to Russell, "you may call your first witness."

Russell leaned over and whispered in my ear, "You ready to do this?"

I took a huge breath. "Yeah."

Time to roll the dice.

Time for me to step up and testify.

I felt my balls crawl up inside my pelvis. I think the hair on my head was trying to crawl back into my scalp and my fingernails were retracting. Every part of my body was attempting to avoid disaster or injury. This was it. Up on the high wire without a net. Did I fall to my death in the middle of my performance or finish with a flourish to the sound of applause?

"Psst!"

I whipped around to see who was hissing in my ear.

It was Samantha.

I nearly jumped out of my seat.

"*Samoula?*" my grandfather whispered, looking confused.

Brianna looked up from her laptop and stared at Samantha like she had just stepped off the Crazy Train from Crazy Town.

Russell's head swiveled slowly around like a gun turret. He leveled a bludgeoning gaze at Samantha. He had no idea who she was. "Excuse me, young lady," he whispered sternly, "may I help you?"

"I have a video!" Samantha hissed.

"What?" Russell asked bluntly.

"You should sit down, *agápi mou*," I said softly.

"You really need to see this video!" Samantha whispered. "It's on my phone." She held it over the low railing between the observer's benches and the floor of the courtroom proper. She gave a little wave to my grandfather and smiled at him.

"Young lady, court is in session," Russell warned. "You keep talking, and the judge is liable to cite you for contempt of court. I suggest you return to your seat and behave yourself or I will have you escorted out of here myself."

"This is important!" Samantha pleaded. "Tell him, Christos!"

"Do you know this miscreant?" Russell asked me sharply, narrowing his eyes.

"Yeah," I sighed. "I sort of do."

Samantha slapped my shoulder and frowned at me. "Sort of?"

I repressed a chuckle. "Russell, meet Samantha Smith. She's my girlfriend."

Russell raised his eyebrows. "Pleased to meet you, Samantha," he said politely. "I don't know if you've noticed, but we're in the middle of a trial. I'm trying to keep your boyfriend out of the slammer. Unless you have a very good reason for interrupting, I suggest you sit down immediately and keep quiet."

"But I have video of what happened!" Samantha pleaded.

"What are you talking about?" Russell asked, perplexed.

"Mr. Merriweather," Judge Moody interrupted, "do we have a problem?"

Russell smiled at the judge. "No, your honor, not at all. May we have a moment?"

"Make it quick, Mr. Merriweather," Judge Moody ordered.

"I have video of him!" Samantha hissed.

"Of who?" I asked.

"I found a video online of you punching that guy sitting right over there!" She pointed at Horst Grossman who sat on the far side of the witness gallery, behind the prosecutor's table.

Both of Russell's eyebrows climbed up his forehead. "Come again?"

I couldn't believe what I was hearing. I said, "Samantha, are you serious?"

She nodded. "Yes!"

Judge Geraldine fired a stern look at the three of us. "Any time, Mr. Merriweather."

"One moment, your honor," Russell said. "I may have just received information that bears on this case."

"May have or have?" the judged asked impatiently.

"If you would kindly give me a moment, your honor, I will let you know."

"Do I need to call another recess five minutes after the last one?"

"No, your honor. This will only take a moment."

"You have two minutes, counselor."

Russell turned to Samantha. "Do you have the video on your phone?"

"Yes."

"Is it ready to play?"

"Yes."

"May I see it?"

Samantha handed the phone to Russell.

I leaned over his shoulder and he pressed play.

The video was amazingly clear. You could see Horst Grossman's face clearly as he shouted and screamed at Samantha in her VW. You could even see Samantha's face inside her car, and me when I walked up in my helmet, before and after Grossman lunged and I punched. Whoever shot it must have been planning on studying cinematography at USC film school. The audio was a bit choppy, but you could hear most of what Horst Grossman said.

Russell glanced between Samantha and the phone. "Is that you?" he asked, pointing at the tiny image of Samantha in her VW.

She nodded.

In a low voice, Russell said, "Christos, you're lucky we're in court. Otherwise I'd smack you upside the head. Then I'd turn you around and smack you up the other side. Why didn't you tell me your girlfriend was the girl in the car? Are you crazy? No, don't answer that. Because I know you're crazy." He turned to Samantha. "Where did you find this video?"

"On somebody's blog. It's not even a Youtube video. It was on Vimeo."

"We checked the road rage videos," Russell said, confused, "and we checked Vimeo. And Youtube. And everywhere else. Several times. We couldn't find anything."

"I think whoever uploaded just posted it. See, the upload date is two days ago and it only has a few hundred hits. It took me all night to find it because of how it was labelled."

"You're quite the private investigator," Russell said. "What was your name again?"

"Samantha Smith."

"Thank you, Ms. Smith. I think you just saved your boyfriend's ass." Russell smiled. "Would you have any objection to going up on the witness stand to testify in Christos' defense?"

"Me?" she gasped.

"Yes, you. If the judge will allow it, we can keep Christos off the stand."

"Of course! I'll totally do it!" she said.

"Do me a favor," Russell said, "email the URL of that website to my assistant." He nodded toward Brianna and said, "Ms. Smith, this is Brianna Johnson."

Brianna and Samantha shook hands then Samantha fired off the email to her.

"Got it," Brianna said a few seconds later. I watched her pull the video up on her laptop. It turned out the courthouse had great wi-fi service.

Russell stood up, faced the judge, and in his most charming, winning voice, said, "Your honor, may counsel approach the bench?"

"This better be good, Mr. Merriweather."

George Schlosser and his team were staring at us openly. They had no idea what was about to hit them.

"I think you're going to be amused, your honor," Russell said thoughtfully. "I certainly am."

"You may approach, counselors," the judge said.

Russell, Brianna, George Schlosser, and his two assistants walked up to Geraldine Moody's bench.

In a soft voice I could barely hear, Russell explained everything to the judge. He pointed at Samantha several times. When he did, Schlosser and his team gave Samantha dirty looks.

Brianna set her laptop on the corner of the judge's bench so that the judge could view the video. Schlosser and his team had to crane over to see the screen when Brianna played the video.

At first, Judge Moody was bored, but as the video unrolled, she became entranced and literally leaned forward on the edge of her seat. When the video finished, she said, "Can I see that again?"

"Certainly, your honor," Russell said. "Brianna, please play it again."

Brianna nodded and reset the video.

After the second viewing, Schlosser growled, "This is preposterous, your honor. There's no way you can allow this into evidence. I need time to verify that the woman in this video is the one standing over there."

"It looks like the same young woman to me," Judge Moody said, a hint of amusement in her voice.

"That may very well be," Schlosser huffed, "but if it turns out she is the woman in the video, I still need time to depose her properly. I have no idea what her testimony might be."

"Neither do I," Russell said.

Schlosser scoffed at him, then turned to Judge Moody and said, "Your honor, freshman tactics like these aren't fit for this courtroom," he said it like Russell was a known liar, "I suggest we leave them in trashy novels and circus tents where they belong."

"I'll decide what flies in my own courtroom, Mr. Schlosser," the judge said in a parental tone. "Mr. Merriweather, have you had an opportunity to interview this surprise witness of yours?" Judge Moody asked.

"No, I have not, your honor," Russell said. "I wasn't aware of her existence until she stepped into this courtroom today."

The judge raised a skeptical eyebrow at Russell.

He raised a skeptical eyebrow at her.

Schlosser rolled his eyes at both of them.

"I'll allow it," Judge Moody said.

"But—" Schlosser interjected.

The judge cut him off. "Mr. Schlosser, you've been doing this long enough. Improvise. In light of this video, you're lucky I don't dismiss this case on the spot. Would you like me to do that?"

Schlosser smiled endearingly, "Your honor, I—"

"Yes or no, counselor," the judge said.

Schlosser huffed a hard sigh. "As you wish, your honor."

"Excellent. Mr. Merriweather, please see that Mr. Schlosser gets the link to this video. We'll take a one hour recess, during which time both your teams can review the video in depth and formulate your arguments." She banged her gavel. "Court is in recess for one hour."

===

Samantha's testimony and the amazing video footage turned the trial on its head.

Russell played the video on the big projection screen while Samantha was on the witness stand. He paused the video intermittently to ask her questions to help clarify details of what was happening.

I watched with a minimal grin on my face while the moments before I'd gotten off my bike for the first time unwound on the screen. I did my best not to look smug in front of the jury. It was damn hard.

The video had close ups on Grossman's face as he shouted at Samantha and tried to pry her car window down. He looked like a raging lunatic. The jury watched in stark, wide-eyed amazement as Grossman frothed at the mouth in the video and turned beet red while he called Samantha a bitch, a slut, a whore, and a pinhead. One of the female jurors giggled in disbelief when Grossman kicked the door of Samantha's VW.

The knock out punch, both literally and figuratively, came when Grossman lunged at me in the video. I had been standing calmly in front of him. Everyone in the courtroom could clearly see that Grossman had tried to tackle me before I'd side stepped out of his way and punched him.

I glanced over and saw Deputy District Attorney George Schlosser running a hand through his hair. He looked defeated, like *he'd* just been punched.

When Russell finished asking Samantha questions and sat down, Schlosser was finishing a quiet discussion with his assistants. After a moment, they all nodded at each other.

Schlosser stood up and said, "Your honor, due to the unforeseen developments regarding the evidence in this case, the state has decided to drop all charges against the defendant."

"Are you sure, Mr. Schlosser? I don't want to come back and do this again," the judge said.

"Yes, your honor," Schlosser said.

"Let the record show that in the matter of the State of California vs. Christos Manos, case number SD-2013-K-071183A," the judge intoned, "the State has dropped all charges. She banged her gavel. "Case dismissed. Mr. Manos, you are free to go."

For a second, I couldn't believe my ears.

The huge smile that spread across Russell's face proved that I hadn't been hallucinating. "Congratulations, son," he said while shaking my hand and squeezing my shoulder vigorously, "let's agree never to do this again. Feel me?"

"Agreed," I said, grinning from ear to ear.

He pointed at me with a jabbing finger. "I mean it, son. No more bullshit. You've got better things to do than waste my time in a courtroom."

"You know me too well," I smiled. "I promise, no more courtroom bullshit."

With any luck, I'd be able to live up to my promise.

===

SAMANTHA

I practically jumped over the witness stand trying to get to Christos when the judge dismissed the case.

Christos came out from behind the defense table and I leapt into his arms.

"We did it!" I squealed.

He spun me around once and set me down. "No, you did it, *agápi mou*. You won this case single handed." He glanced at his lawyer and said, "I mean, Russell helped, but you, Samantha, stole the show. Samantha, meet my attorney, Russell Merriweather. He's an old friend of the family."

I shook Russell's hand, "Nice to meet you."

"Christos is right, Ms. Smith," Russell smiled. "You should send him a bill."

I grinned. "Nah, I'll figure out a way to make him pay for it with services rendered."

Christos chuckled. "Gladly."

Brianna Johnson walked around the defense table and frowned at Christos. "Christos, how could you forget to mention to Russell and I that your girlfriend was at the crime scene?"

Christos shrugged his shoulders noncommittally.

"You could've saved yourself a whole lot of time and trouble had you told us sooner," Brianna admonished.

Christos cracked out a dimpled grin. "I was trying to save Samantha a whole lot of time and trouble." He rubbed his hand against my shoulder. "She has better things to do."

I rolled my eyes at him. "Russell was right, Christos. You are crazy!" I looked at Brianna for agreement.

She gave me a sisterly smile and shook her head, "Men! I swear, if it wasn't for us women, they wouldn't be able to tie their own shoes!"

"I know, right?" I smiled.

"Hey," Christos quipped, "I'm standing right here."

"Good. Then maybe what we're saying might sink in." Brianna winked at me. "Despite his thick head, Christos is a good young man. But don't you let him weasel out of doing a few chores to make up for all the trouble he's put you through."

"I won't," I smiled.

Spiridon walked up a moment later with someone who could only be Christos' dad. They both exchanged big hugs with Christos.

"The Manos men," Russell said proudly, smiling at all three of them, "all up in this here thing."

"Samantha," Christos said, "I want you to meet my dad, Nikolos Manos."

I shook Nikolos' hand. He looked like a slightly older version of Christos. He was as dashing as his son and had the same priceless blue eyes. Seeing the three of them together, it was obvious that Christos was going to be painfully gorgeous at every stage of life. I know people said that George Clooney got better looking as he got older, but Nikolos and Spiridon put poor George to shame.

"I've heard all about you," Nikolos smiled. "My father tells me that you're a good young woman, and a talented artist too. Maybe you could teach my son a thing or two about painting. He needs all the help he can get," he winked.

Spiridon smiled at me. "Yes. *Samoula* has moved into the house to be Christos' private painting tutor. Isn't that right, *koritsáki mou*?" He patted me affectionately on the shoulder.

I was so overwhelmed by all of it, the relief that Christos' trial was over and the sense of having a family that I absolutely adored, that I couldn't speak. I smiled and nodded my reply as tears blurred my vision. I did my best to hold them in as the group of us walked out of the courtroom together.

Now that it was over, I secretly hoped that would be the last time I ever set foot in a courtroom. Between Taylor Lamberth,

Damian Wolfram, and Christos, I'd had enough trials to last a lifetime.

===

CHRISTOS

I inhaled a deep breath of mellow afternoon air as we stood in front of the Hall of Justice in the San Diego sun.

I was free.

It still hadn't quite sunk in. Part of me had been fully prepared to be led out of the courtroom in handcuffs and trucked off to prison after my trial. The foggy claws of that fear still nicked at the back of my neck. Not to worry. They'd fade. I was in the clear. I was with my family and friends, and I was free.

"Who wants to celebrate?" I smiled. "I was thinking drinks and dinner at the Yard House up the street? I'm buying."

"You've spent enough money on me already," Russell smiled. "We can all head over there and I'll pick up the tab."

"Christos Manos?" some random guy walked up and asked abruptly. He had come from the direction of the Hall of Justice and wore an expensive suit and held a briefcase. Was he a court clerk or something?

I narrowed my eyes. "Who wants to know?"

"Are you Christos Manos?" the guy asked again.

Now that I'd had a chance to look at him, he didn't seem threatening. But he held a thick white business envelope in his hand. "Yeah, I'm him. What do you want?"

The guy raised his arm and jabbed the envelope at me. "You've been served."

I shook my head and took the envelope from him. He immediately walked away.

"Christos, Christos, Christos," Russell sighed. "What is it this time, young man?"

I opened the envelope and read the paperwork.

"What?" Samantha asked, worried.

I sighed heavily. "Hunter Blakeley is suing me."

"What? Why?" Samantha frowned. "Because you tripped him that day at SDU?"

She was referring to the time I'd walked up on Hunter giving shit to her and Romeo in the Eucalyptus grove on campus. "No.

Because I punched him in the face."

"When?" Samantha asked.

"You don't want to know."

"I want to know," Russell interrupted. He took the summons from me. "And I want to know who all was involved. No more of these last minute surprises." He scanned over the paperwork. "This is a civil suit, Christos. He's suing you for damages. Did you hit him?"

"Yes," I sighed. "But it was self defense."

"I'm sure it was," Russell said.

I couldn't tell if he was being sarcastic or not. He was probably pissed that I'd walked out of one trial and right into another. I couldn't blame him.

"Look," I said, "A couple weeks ago, Hunter and three of his buddies followed me and Jake after we left Hooters. Hunter took a swing at me, so I back-handed him in the nose. Once."

Russell pursed his lips while his brow knotted over his dark eyes. "Sounds familiar. Unfortunately, a civil trial isn't like a criminal trial, son. If you hit him, you're probably going to have to pay. The only thing I can do is work to minimize what you'll owe him." He flipped through several pages of the document. "Which, in this case, is a whole hell of a lot. This guy's attorney is asking for a million in medical bills, lost wages, and pain and suffering. We can cut that down quite a bit. But I might not be able to make it all go away. May I ask, did you have a film crew on hand to save your ass in court this time around?"

"I doubt it," I said. "It was the middle of the night on an empty street. No one was there except Jake and the three guys with Hunter."

"All right," Russell said. "We'll figure it out. In the mean time, may I please beg that you not get in any more fights? Is that possible? Or am I asking for water from a stone?"

Everyone was staring at me expectantly. Samantha, my dad, my grandad, Brianna, and Russell. All had skeptical looks on their faces.

"Come on, guys," I pleaded, "the only reason any of this shit started is because I was defending Samantha. The first time at her VW, the second time in the Eucalyptus grove at SDU. Hunter never would've cornered me and Jake that night if I hadn't tripped him that day at SDU. He was still pissed I'd made him look foolish."

"While your actions have been honorable," Russell admonished, "the next time there's trouble, I encourage you to run the other way. Feel me?" He raised a doubtful eyebrow, but a slight smile betrayed his seriousness.

"What about Samantha?" I asked. "What if I need to protect her? I'm not going to leave her in trouble."

"You're a strong boy," Russell smirked. "Pick her up, throw her over your shoulder, and run."

I chuckled, "I can handle that."

Russell put a big hand on the back of my neck. "All right, you all. I've had enough courtroom drama for one day. Let's get some dinner."

We all walked east on Broadway and went inside the Yard House. Since it was early and the dinner rush hadn't set in, we got a table for six right away.

While we waited for our waiter to take our drink order, I checked my phone. Tons of texts and voicemails from Samantha. I felt like a jerk. She must've been freaking out trying to reach me. I'd make up for it later.

But the last text to come in was from Brandon Charboneau.

How are the paintings coming along? I want to book the gallery for your show, but I can't set a date until you give me one. Let me know.

Fucking great. I had never told Brandon about the trial. He'd been cracking the whip enough as it was without knowing. I hadn't wanted him going nuts thinking I had to get everything done before I ended up in prison. It would've created way too much tension between us.

Now that my trial was finally over, the last thing I wanted to do was jump back in the studio to continue painting a bunch of models I had no interest in painting.

Before, I had been painting them mostly to keep my mind off the Grossman trial. Work was always a good distraction. On the bright side, now that I had this ridiculous Hunter Blakeley civil suit hanging over my head, the work might be just what I needed to keep me motivated. I'd spent a huge amount of my money on Russell. His services weren't cheap. If I ended up paying out to Hunter, even if I only owed him a fraction of the amount he was asking, I'd be broke.

I needed to earn some cash quick. Cranking out the canvases for Brandon was a good a way as any to pull in more Benjamins.

And now that Samantha had moved in, she could watch me hanging out with hot naked chicks seven days a week. She wouldn't miss a moment of the excitement. I'm sure she'd have the time of her life.

Fuck. Like everything else, I'd worry about it later. When the waitress arrived, I ordered a double shot of Basil Hayden bourbon.

Let the drinking begin.

===

SAMANTHA

"How much did you drink?" I asked Christos as everyone walked out of the Yard House onto Broadway.

"Lost count," Christos slurred.

"You weigh a million pounds," I grunted. His arm was over my shoulder and he leaned against me. It felt like a building had fallen onto me.

"Let me help you, Samantha," Nikolos said, concerned. He grabbed Christos' other arm and stood him up easily, taking all of his weight.

"Where's my Camaro?" Christos asked.

"You're not driving, *paidí mou*," Nikolos said, "not like this."

Christos wasn't sloppy drunk, but he was in the neighborhood. This was the first time I'd seen him like this. I couldn't blame him. He'd had a stressful day.

"I can drive Christos' Camaro," Spiridon said to Nikolos. "You can take my car home."

Nikolos nodded. "Which way to your car, Samantha?"

"This way," I pointed.

"Brianna and I are parked this way," Russell said to everyone. "I should get her back to her car at the office so she can go home."

We all said our goodbyes. Spiridon and Nikolos walked Christos and me west on Broadway, toward the parking garage where my VW was. Russell and Brianna went the other way.

"Tell me about some of your paintings, Samantha," Nikolos said as the four of us walked along the sidewalk.

"She's awesome," Christos slurred, his eyes a little glassy.

"She's quite good," Spiridon agreed. "She's a fast learner. Christos has taught her a lot since they met in September. I've never seen such rapid improvement."

I blushed. "Gosh, Spiridon, thank you."

"I'd love to see some of your work," Nikolos said. "Has Christos been teaching you about the figure?"

"Yeah. He's taught me all about gesture drawing and studying anatomy, and how to draw from the model. I never knew you could do that. I always thought you had to make everything up out of your head."

Nikolos nodded and smiled, still holding Christos around the waist to help him walk. Christos was drunker than I'd thought.

"She's soooo good," Christos said.

Yeah, he was toasted.

Nikolos didn't seem to mind. I knew from Christos that Nikolos was a heavy drinker, but he hadn't drunk anything at dinner. He was completely sober.

"A lot of people think drawing is magic," Nikolos said. "They think you're either born knowing how or you're not. That's not true. You can learn, especially if you have a good teacher."

"That's what Christos said!" I smiled.

Nikolos nodded proudly.

We eventually made it to the parking garage where my VW was parked. Nikolos gently lowered Christos into the back seat, then the rest of us climbed in.

After dropping Spiridon off at Christos' Camaro, I took Nikolos to where Spiridon's car was parked in another garage. He pulled Christos out of the back seat of my VW and put him in the front seat for me. There was no way I could've done it myself. Nikolos moved Christos like he didn't weigh a thing. He was pretty damn strong.

"Thanks for everything," I said as I hugged Nikolos.

"I can tell, Samantha," Nikolos said as he patted my back, "you're a good girl. I'm glad my son met you. I'm just sorry it was that idiot Horst Grossman who brought you together."

"Oh, I don't care," I laughed. "That guy was a jerk and now we can forget about him. But if he hadn't been such an ass master in the first place, I never would've met your son."

"Ass master?" Nikolos chuckled. "In the old days, when I was young, I would've called him a fucking asshole and left it at that."

I shrugged. "But that sounds like any random asshole. Horst Grossman was like the master of all assholes. He's the one who gives all the orders," I grinned.

"I like how you think," Nikolos laughed. "Do you need me to follow you back to my father's house to help get Christos out of the car?"

"I think I can manage. If not, he can sleep in the car."

"Spiridon has a wheelbarrow in the garage if you need one. Well, good night, Samantha. I look forward to seeing your art sometime soon."

"Me too!" I smiled. I waved as he got into Spiridon's car and drove away.

I hoped that Nikolos would come by the house for a visit at some point. He seemed really nice. I don't know why Christos never spent any time with him. Based on the way Christos had talked about his dad in the past, I'd imagined Nikolos would be some rundown drunk. That's not what he seemed like tonight. He seemed healthy and was definitely sober. Christos had been the one doing all the drinking.

Maybe Christos and his dad would start spending more time together. I'm sure it would be good for both of them.

Despite all of the day's drama, I felt like things were starting to look up for me and Christos.

Finally.

===

My good mood took a nose dive when my phone rang on the drive home.

My parents were calling.

There was no way I was going to answer them right now. I couldn't deal with one more drop of drama tonight. After our last call, I could only imagine the nastiness they would slam me with if I answered.

I let it go to voicemail. I'd deal with them later. Maybe tomorrow.

Maybe never.

Maybe if I never called them back, my parents would slowly forget they ever had a daughter. I could hope.

So, so, so, SO GROAN!!!

I rolled my eyes and concentrated on the road as I drove toward home.

Home. To my new house where I lived with Christos. Swoon. The drunk guy slumped against the door of my VW. Sigh. Oh well, nothing was perfect. So what if he was drunk? It was better than him being in jail.

Besides, I'd been drunk plenty of times in high school as an outcast teenager. Sometimes things got so bad, it was the only thing I knew how to do to block out the pain and rejection when I was alone. Sometimes, not even ice cream was enough. But my drinking hadn't turned me into an alcoholic. I'm sure Christos would be fine. If his drinking somehow became a problem, I'd be around to help. I wouldn't let him throw his life away. We'd find a way through whatever obstacles life put in front of us. Together.

Spiridon was already back at the house when I pulled into the driveway. He helped Christos out of the car with ease and didn't need a wheelbarrow. All the Manos men were very strong physically. I didn't know how old Spiridon was, but he had to be at least sixty. He pulled Christos out of the car like he didn't weigh a thing. I couldn't have done it without a forklift.

Spiridon walked Christos upstairs and lowered him onto the bed.

"I can take it from here," I said.

"Okay. I feel like some tea. I'm going to go make some. You can join me if you'd like."

"All right."

Spiridon smiled, "It's so good to have you living with us, *Samoula*. It was far too quiet with only my grandson around. It's nice to have more family in the house."

My heart warmed at his words. "Thank you, Spiridon." The implication that I was family brought tears to my eyes. I'd known him for all of five months and I felt completely at ease around him. Maybe he could adopt me officially. Oh wait, wouldn't that make me Christos' sister? No, that would only be if Nikolos adopted me. If Spiridon adopted me, that would make me Christos' aunt. Not gonna work.

"What's so funny?" Spiridon asked.

"Nothing," I smiled. "Just random thoughts. Let me take care of Christos and I'll join you downstairs."

"Perfect. I'll be in the kitchen."

I hung my blazer in the closet and slipped off my heels. Then I slid Christos' dress shoes off. He was still in his suit, which was now quite rumpled. He'd been truly dashing in the courtroom. Now his rumpled face looked like it could use a press as badly as his suit. I loosened his tie and opened his collar. He moaned sleepily, but didn't seem interested in opening his eyes.

"You're completely at my mercy, Christos. Think of all the things I could do to you. Draw a mustache with a marker?" No, that reminded me of Tiffany's yacht and her painting. "Shave your head?" Why would I want to get rid of that perfect hair of his? I wouldn't be able to run my hands through it. "Oh, forget it. How about I give you a striptease then let you have your way with me?"

Yeah, that sounded like what the doctor ordered.

Christos moaned sleepily. He didn't seem to agree.

"How about I let you sleep?"

Silence.

I wasn't sure how drunk Christos was, but I didn't want to risk him choking on his own puke. I grabbed his wrist and pulled him onto his side, just in case. I had to really put my body into it, he was so heavy. I had a good sweat going by the time I finished. Who knew all that muscle could weigh so much?

I blew a wisp of hair out of my face when I was finished. "Sleep tight, *agápi mou*. I'll be downstairs."

As I walked toward the bedroom door, I remembered my parents' recent phone call. I pulled my phone out of my purse and looked at it. They had left me a voicemail.

The phone that had kept Christos out of jail was now the phone threatening to put me in a different kind of jail.

Screw my mom and dad.

They could wait.

I dropped my phone in my purse with a scowl and left the room. Screw them.

Chapter 10

SAMANTHA

I left Christos to sleep off his drunk.

Spiridon poured me a cup of tea in the kitchen and we made our way into the living room.

As tired as I was, all the stress of the past several days had my thoughts bouncing around inside my skull like a thousand ping pong balls. I needed to unwind.

I stretched out on the couch while Spiridon sat down across from me in his leather easy chair. He told me stories about his art career for hours.

The living room was the perfect location because Spiridon's glorious landscape paintings hung all around us. They set the perfect mood as he wowed me with tales from his life as a world famous painter. He recalled all the celebrities he had met, the countries he had visited, and the awards he had won in the course of his illustrious career.

Spiridon had lived an amazing life I couldn't help but envy. Art was in his blood. As was success. Art and success were also in the blood of his son Nikolos and his grandson Christos. The Manos family was truly blessed.

The Smith family hadn't been nearly so lucky. Oh well. Even if my upbringing had been bland and mediocre by comparison, at least now I got to be around the Manos family. Maybe I could absorb some of their good luck. I was still young. There was still time for my life to turn out awesome too.

Close to midnight, Christos clomped downstairs into the living room and collapsed on the couch next to me. He still wore his shirt and tie and his slacks. Even with his hair a mess, he looked ready for the cover of GQ.

"He's risen from the dead," Spiridon chuckled from where he sat in his leather chair.

Christos clutched his hair in both hands. "I feel like someone has driven a spike through my head. I think I'm still buzzed. How much did I drink?"

"You probably need some water," I suggested. Experience had taught me that water was a hangover's worst enemy.

Christos groaned, "I think I got dehydrated during court today. I was too stressed about everything else to think about water. Those bourbons at dinner went straight to my brain."

"I'll get you some water," Spiridon said as he stood up.

"I can do it," I said.

"No, you sit with my grandson." He smiled as he walked out of the living room.

"Christos, did you puke on the bed?" I asked.

He chuckled and snuggled up against me on the couch. "No. Like I said, I didn't drink that much. I think it was the dehydration. I was loopy after three drinks. That never happens. I'll be better after I get some water."

Spiridon returned with a huge glass.

"Thanks, *Pappoús*," Christos said. He gulped down the entire glass in several long swallows. "Let's see if it stays down," he winked then set the glass on the coffee table. "Can I use your blouse as a bib if I spit up?"

"Eww!" I giggled. "That's disgusting, Christos!"

He chuckled as he nuzzled his nose against my neck. "Gack!" he grunted, pretending to puke.

"Stop!" I laughed.

"I think I'll be heading to bed," Spiridon smiled, standing up. "It's been a long day and I think you two need some time alone."

"Good night, *Pappoús*," Christos said.

"Good night, *paidí mou*," Spiridon said as he rubbed Christos' shoulder. "And good night to you to, *koritsáki mou*," he said to me as he leaned down and kissed the top of my head.

My parents never did that. I would've flinched if they did. But it felt completely normal when Spiridon did it. "Good night," I smiled.

"See you at breakfast. I think I'll make French toast in the morning." He considered thoughtfully. "Yes, I'm in the mood for French toast. Sound good to you two?"

"I have class," I sighed, "I don't know if I'll have time."

"Tomorrow's Saturday," Spiridon said.

"Oh, duh!" I had been so caught up in the stress of the day, more like the stress of the last two weeks, I'd lost track of what day it was.

"See you two in the morning," Spiridon said as he walked upstairs.

Christos rubbed his nose across my cheek. "Mmmm. I missed you, *agápi mou*." His hand slid across my stomach and hooked around my waist. He pulled me into him as his hot tongue slid into my ear.

"Christos! Your grandfather's like ten feet away!"

"He doesn't care," he murmured.

"I do!"

"Then let's go outside."

"What?"

"There's plenty of comfortable lounge chairs out there. I'll get some blankets."

"I don't know, Christos. It's late. And you're tired. I'm tired, now that I think of it."

He lifted his head up and looked me in the eyes with his amazing blues. "You sure?"

Who was I kidding? Christos was the most amazingly handsome man I'd met in my entire life. He was breathtakingly beautiful. My heart accelerated and my body temperature spiked several degrees just looking into his eyes.

"We can go to sleep if you want," he said.

"Ahhh, maybe we can stay up for a little while?"

His dimpled grin widened over his beautiful white teeth. His lips looked so soft and I really needed to lick them. But his grandfather was upstairs and it was a straight shot from the living room to Spiridon's bedroom. I didn't want him to hear us. "Outside is good," I grinned.

Christos drank another huge glass of water in the kitchen before grabbing blankets from a closet.

We went out onto the deck together.

The sky was almost totally clear, a black velvet blanket overhead. A few scattered clouds drifted lazily past the glowing moon. Christos led me to a circle of chaise loungers on the far side of the swimming pool that had a great view of the dark ocean. Distant waves crashed in a silver drizzle against the shore.

Christos whipped a blanket out and it billowed down on a lounger built for two. We crawled on top and he spread the other blanket over us. It was almost warm enough without the top blanket, but it wouldn't be as cozy without it.

We snuggled together, our arms and legs entwined. There was no way I could imagine cuddling under the stars in Washington D.C. in February. Not without a winter sleeping bag, long johns, wool cap, and mittens.

"Exciting day," I said.

"Yeah," Christos chuckled. "Who knew my girlfriend could make Sherlock Holmes look incompetent."

"Thanks," I grinned. "You know, it's still Valentine's Day."

"That's right. Happy Valentine's Day, *agápi mou*."

Snuggled under the blankets together, I felt unbelievably peaceful in his arms. All the troubles of the world were far away. Whatever they might have been, they were no concern of mine.

I realized that Christos was gently stroking the side of my cheek with his hand. Swirling energy flowed out from his fingers across my face, relaxing away my remaining tension.

His thumb slid across my lower lip, tugging gently against it. I moaned softly.

"You never got your Valentine's Day kiss, *agápi mou*," he murmured.

I remembered all the flowers and candles and chocolates he'd given me the day before. And the love making that had followed, him inside me, inside my mouth. And how all my stuff was moved into the house the next day. I was living with my boyfriend! Woo hoo!

Over the last few months, I had experienced so many firsts with the most perfect man in the world. Christos never ceased to amaze me. He brought so much joy and excitement into my life. I was the luckiest girl in the world.

"I love you, Christos," I sighed. "You have no idea how much I love you."

"If it's even close to how much I love you, *agápi mou*, I have a pretty good idea."

My heart still melted every time he told me that, every time he called me *agápi mou*.

"My heart is yours, *agápi mou*," he murmured. "It always will be, and I believe it always was. I just had to endure the torture of waiting for you to finally show up in my life. It was a long wait," he grinned. "But now that you're here, I can't imagine life without you. Without us." There was a vulnerability in his eyes that warmed my heart.

"Oh, Christos," I sighed.

He leaned toward me, his lower lip brushing across my upper. That slight contact was enough to cause a heat wave to blossom in my chest and my mouth to tingle with anticipation. When our lips gently touched, his tongue slid inside and caressed mine. Hunger for more overtook me and I fell into our kiss like it was the first time all over again. My heart raced as heat poured down into my core. I breathed him in, inhaling the life force of love that flowed from him into me, and back out again. Our bodies united in a perfect exchange of our desire for each other and our need to be needed. Our hearts were beating in an intimate rhythm, completing an eternal, infinite connection.

Christos' intense desire to touch me accelerated into almost a desperate thing. His hands were all over my breasts, my ass, caressing across my stomach, my throat, touching all the tender sensitive places that only Christos had ever touched. It was like he couldn't touch me intimately enough, as if his fingers searched desperately for my very soul so that he could hold onto it and never let go. My heart was so open to him in that moment, I welcomed his need. I imagined my own soul flowing into his body to mingle with his. I was his to take, to embrace, to caress, to hold, to love.

I murmured, "I need you, *agápi mou*."

He responded by unbuttoning my blouse with intoxicated languor while he licked my neck, the curve of my jaw, the lobe of my ear. He tugged the tails of my blouse out of my skirt and unbuttoned it slowly. Then he planted his warm palms firmly on my taut stomach before sliding both hands over the satin cups of my bra and squeezing my cleavage.

"Your breasts are perfect, *agápi mou*. I swear, whenever I'm around you, just thinking about them gets me hard. I always want to touch them and grab them. They drive me fucking crazy. I've never been so obsessed with breasts in my entire fucking life."

For a second, I was startled by his crude language. But there was a humor to his words, a lightness, an unabashed desire. After a moment, I realized that Christos was expressing his joy. His simple, unadulterated joy. For me. For my breasts. His words had an innocence and honesty to them that warmed my heart, an innocence that I couldn't deny.

I encircled his neck with my arms and smiled up at him. "They're all yours, *agápi mou*," I murmured.

"Really?" he asked almost shyly. It was so unlike him to be shy. But he was. For me.

I nodded and smiled at him. "For you, *agápi mou*. Only for you."

He smiled wide while he unsnapped my bra in the front and it popped free, releasing my breasts. His eyes goggled and the grin on his face was now gigantic, like he'd never seen breasts before. "Fuck," he grinned, "look at them. Perfect. Absolutely perfect." He looked like he had discovered a treasure chest worth trillions of dollars. Maybe he had.

I glanced down at my breasts. They looked like my regular old breasts. I wasn't going to argue with Christos. If they looked like treasure to him, so be it. My own smile widened.

I was all his.

He brushed his fingertips across my nipples and moaned, "Fuck, just touching your nipples makes me want to come in my pants."

Him? The butterflies taking wing in my chest made me want to come in my panties. My nipples tightened into hard buds. Christos leaned down and flicked one with his tongue until it was wet and slick and straining. Then he showered the other with similar attention while massaging both with his hands.

My eyes were rolling into the back of my head as the familiar whirlwind in my chest coiled me into a tight knot of ecstasy. Every time he kissed and caressed my breasts like this, I was transported out of my body. I don't know if I had an orgasm or not, but it really didn't matter. The pleasure was immeasurable.

After a time, he paused and sat back on his heels. He gazed longingly down at my chest. "Fuck!" he smiled, staring at my swollen, heavy breasts and my engorged nipples. "You are a work of art, *agápi mou*," he sighed.

Christos was excruciatingly happy now, a happy bomb waiting to go off. His happiness flowed into me, and I welcomed it. I felt relief washing over me. Christos' joy was cleansing my soul, purging all the horrible stuff that had led up to today. The anxiety and worry and fear were all gone. Water under the bridge, a fading memory.

Joy was what lay ahead for me and my man.

He laid down beside me, propped on his elbow. He grinned, "Do you have any idea how fucking hot you looked in court today?"

"Mmm?" I moaned, still half dreamy with the pleasure circling between my sensitive breasts.

"After my case was dismissed, all I wanted to do was hike up your skirt and throw you on top of that defense table."

"With an audience?" I snickered. I couldn't decide if the idea was totally weird or a total turn on.

"I'm sure we could've asked the judge to clear the courtroom," he smirked, "For a sidebar."

"You mean the one in your pants right now?" I giggled. His cock was a hot rod of iron pressing against me through his slacks. "I think your sidebar needs some attention."

I rolled onto my side and reached down to unfasten his slacks. Then my fingers snaked past the waistband of his boxer briefs and found his heat. The tip was hot and the shaft throbbed with need. I wrapped one hand around him and slid softly up and down.

He moaned in response to my touch.

"You like?" I asked.

He moaned again.

That was a yes.

I crawled under the blanket and he helped me get his pants and boxer briefs down far enough for his cock to pop free of the high zippered slacks. Under the blanket, I hunched over him in total darkness. I was going to have to use sonar, braille, or both. Who was I kidding? There was barely enough room under the blanket for me and his cock. I couldn't miss it if I tried.

I took him into my mouth and went to work. The wetter I got him, the slicker I licked, the wetter my crotch became, the hotter I throbbed down between my legs.

I couldn't wait any longer to have him inside me.

I surfaced from under the blanket and gave him a sultry smile while slowly stroking his manhood hidden beneath the blanket with one hand.

Christos unzipped my skirt with practiced ease. I think he knew his way around women's clothing better than I did. Under the circumstances, that was just fine. He helped me slide out of my skirt, then I pulled my pantyhose down frantically. My core was clenching with need.

Christos dove under the blankets and went for my crotch. He slid around and down between my legs and lifted me up with both strong arms. His warm breath washed across my wet folds. Then his hot mouth was all over my core a second later. My eyes rolled back into my head once again as pleasure erupted from my center.

I was bucking into him seconds later. I needed this so badly I was on the verge of passing out with desire. It didn't take long for a powerful orgasm to overtake me. I squeezed my legs against the sides of his head as I came against his face. My thighs and stomach quivered as my head lifted off the lounger. I didn't cry out because we were outside, and I couldn't escape the feeling neighbors were near, but I couldn't stop myself from moaning low and long, over and over again as my orgasm coursed through me.

When the spasms of pleasure started to subside, Christos snaked his way up my body, his chest sliding across my stomach as he levered himself up on both powerful arms.

"Fuck," Christos murmured while I floated in post orgasmic bliss, "you are soaking wet down there."

I nodded at him through half hooded eyes.

His head hung down and he kissed me passionately, his face still covered in my wetness. His tongue slid into my waiting mouth as his cock slid home. He was inside me. Deep inside, his heat burning me from the inside out. He began a steady rhythm, pumping his manhood into my womanhood. He filled me up completely. His cock was a perfect match. He thrust steadily and I floated toward another hot climax minutes later. I moaned loud and long as my body released yet more tension.

I think maybe I was carrying more stress than I had realized. It felt so good to let it all go.

"Wow," he whispered, "you're on fire tonight." Still inside me, Christos propped himself up on his arms and the blanket slid down his back, pooling behind him.

I felt a cool breeze across my breasts. I looked up at the moon and the stars twinkling overhead. Such a beautiful view.

"You okay down there?" Christos asked, slowing his rhythm.

That was when I realized that not only were my breasts exposed to the world, which wasn't entirely new for me, but I had Christos' throbbing cock inside my sopping pussy.

We were having sex outside. Passionate, hot, wet sex. I'd never done that before.

I nervously noted my outdoor surroundings. How loud had I been moaning? Was it possible that the neighbors had mistook my moans for air raid sirens and ignored us? Or had they been listening and snickering while I came? Was someone watching with binoculars? What about the squirrels in the trees? They slept outside. Surely we'd woken them. And the raccoons. They were nocturnal. They'd probably been watching during their lunch break. And what about the Man in the Moon? He had an unobstructed view the entire time.

I remembered some old black and white silent movie where the Man in the Moon had an actual face. Where had I seen that? Probably the internet. Wherever it was, I remember he'd looked pretty pervy. I'm sure I'd given him a good show.

I asked, "Can you pull the blanket back up?"

Christos raised his eyebrows and his thrusts slowed to a stop, "Aren't you getting hot?"

So what if I was broiling? At least it offered cover from prying eyes. "A little," I lied. "Why?"

"I'm dying under this thing. Mind if I get rid of it?"

"Uhhh..." I stammered, "what about the Man in the Moon?"

"Huh? Did I miss something?"

"He can see everything," I whispered.

"What are you talking about?"

I pointed behind Christos. He turned to look at the moon.

Christos laughed, "Yeah, that guy is a total creeper. He's always looking through bedroom windows around the world, watching people do it. Imagine all the times he's watched people fucking in the history of man? Before man learned to hide in caves or build the first grass huts? Geez, the moon has seen it all. I think that means he doesn't care. We're just two more people amongst billions. He's probably bored."

"Okay, I get your point," I smiled. "You can dispose of the

blanket and we'll behave like primitive man. Sex under the stars."

He threw the blanket aside.

Now we were really exposed. I was naked from head to toe, under the night sky, my legs spread, Christos and his hugeness deep inside me.

Screw it. I didn't care if the Man in the Moon or the squirrels or the raccoons were watching with binoculars or not. I wasn't going to let my worries ruin the mood. I'd had a bunch of orgasms already. Christos deserved his.

"Please continue, good sir," I quipped.

I was in heaven as Christos' cock slid cozily in and out of me.

He leaned forward and kissed me affectionately. "I totally love you, *agápi mou*."

"Me too," I sighed pleasantly.

I gazed into his eyes as he accelerated his thrusting. All I saw was his love, his devotion, and his passion for me. His joyous look from earlier had now eased into total, relaxed pleasure.

"*Agápi mou*," he moaned. "I love you…"

Before I knew it, I was overtaken by his mounting ecstasy. He increased his tempo and I fell completely into his unbridled desire for me. We weren't just having sex outside, we were fucking.

And I loved it.

Let the whole world listen. I didn't care.

"Take me, Christos," I hissed.

He responded by pounding into me. The desire in his eyes ignited into burning passion.

Each time he thrust, he grunted, "You. Are. The. Perfect. Woman. In. Every. Way. Imaginable…"

He continued to fuck me, grinding his pelvis into mine, for a long time. It felt incredible. Hot, wet pleasure stormed through my body, bouncing from head to toe. My body broiled with ecstasy.

My own pleasure built back up to maximum and soon I was floating out of my body, up into the stars. I felt connected to every planet and every solar system and every star I could see above me. I never noticed whether or not the Man in the Moon was watching. It didn't matter. He too was a part of the universe that held the infinite pleasure that circulated between my heart and Christos', and the hot heat that exploded between our legs as we came together.

I was one with Christos as powerful orgasms tore through both our bodies.

===

Christos and I spent the weekend relaxing together. Most of it was spent in our new bed. Then it was back to the grind on Monday morning for both of us.

I had a little matter of visiting the Financial Aid offices at SDU to attend to. I had no intention of changing my major from Art back to Accounting like my parents had demanded. That meant I had to get a bigger student loan now to cover the portion of tuition they had been paying previously.

After driving to campus, I walked into the Financial Aid offices and put my name down on the list. While waiting for my name to be called, I doodled in my sketchbook.

A little while later, a woman with curly hair who wore a frilly blouse and knee length skirt came walking out of a hallway. "Samantha Smith?" she asked.

"Me!" I waved and stuffed my sketchbook into my book bag before walking over to join her.

She led me down the hallway to a room full of cubicles. We stopped at hers and she motioned for me to take a seat. There were cat posters pinned up all over the walls of her cubicle, and framed photos surrounding her computer. She also had a stuffed cat wearing a miniature SDU hoody that had a zipper and little drawstrings on the hood.

"Hi" she said as she sat behind her desk. The name placard on the front of the desk read: Sheri Denney. She smiled at me and said, "My name's Sheri. What can I help you with today, Samantha?"

"I'm going to need more loan money for Spring Quarter or I'm not going to be able to pay my tuition," I sighed. Did I sound like I was complaining? I didn't mean to.

"I'm sorry to hear that. Can I see your Student ID?"

I pulled it out and handed it to her. She typed my info into her computer. "It looks to me like you've reached the maximum federal loan amount already, based on your parents' income and your calculated financial need."

"But I need more money," I scoffed.

She folded her hands on her desk. "I'm sorry, Samantha. But you have to understand, the federal government and the university consider it your parents' responsibility to pay for college. The loans are intended to subsidize whatever amount your parents can't cover. And you're expected to work to help pay for anything left over. I see on my computer that you have a work study job?"

"I do, at the campus art museum, but it doesn't come close to making up the difference I'm going to owe for Spring tuition."

"Have you considered finding a second job off campus?"

"I had one, but it didn't, uh…work out. It was at a convenience store. I smelled like hot dogs every time I came home from work."

She grimaced, "Hot dogs?"

"Yeah. I'll never eat one again. I'm traumatized," I giggled. "It totally gets in your hair, worse than cigarette smoke."

"Sounds like you're better off without that job," she winked. Sheri was nice.

"Anyway," I said, "I'm looking for another job. But I haven't found one yet. It may take awhile. Jobs are scarce."

She nodded sympathetically, "The job market is tough right now."

"But even if I do find one, I know it probably won't cover the rest of my tuition."

"How did you cover the difference Fall and Winter Quarters?"

I frowned, "My parents paid."

"Aren't they going to help pay for Spring?"

I held my palms up in frustration. "It's complicated, but…no."

Compassion knitted Sheri's brows, "I'm sorry to hear that. It happens more often than you might think."

"So what can we do? Without my parents' help, there's no way I can pay my tuition on time."

"You could pay in monthly installments," she offered. "Would that help? It's three equal payments with the first one due in March."

I did the math in my head. "With the loan money I'm supposed to get for Spring, I'll have enough to cover the first payment. But I won't have enough to make the second and third."

"At least that gives you some time to find another job," Sheri said hopefully.

"Yeah," I sighed, "but I'm not going to make thousands of dollars by April, and thousands more by May."

Sheri winced, "That sounds like a problem."

"You're telling me," I groaned and clapped my hands on my knees. "I don't know what else to do."

"The first step is talking to your parents. Try to work through whatever it is that's coming between you and them."

"Believe me, I've tried. It's been an ongoing discussion since I started at SDU last fall."

"But you're still talking. That's something, right?" she smiled optimistically.

"Maybe 'discussion' is too strong a word," I sighed. "More like them giving me orders that they claim I refuse to obey."

Sheri rolled her eyes. "I know how that goes. I was there once myself. My mom and I had it out all the time when I was a teenager."

"So you know what I'm talking about?" It felt good to have someone who could relate.

"Do I ever. But that doesn't mean you can't get through to your own parents."

"Believe me, I tried."

She took a deep breath while nodding her head. I half expected her to keep pushing me to talk to my parents, but she didn't. Instead, she said, "If you absolutely can't get your parents to understand where you're coming from—"

I shook my head emphatically no.

"—and nothing is going to change their minds, there is the option of overriding your dependency status."

I sat up on the edge of my chair hopefully. "Really?"

"Yes. But you have to meet certain criteria," she cautioned.

"What criteria?" I was sure I could meet something or other. Criteria and me were besties. We went way back.

"Are your parents incarcerated or presumed dead?"

Maybe me and Criteria weren't as close as I'd hoped. But the idea of my mom or dad in jail was hilarious. I couldn't decide if my mom would rule her cell block or be shived in the shower because she was such a bitch. My dad would probably be like Andy Dufresne in The Shawshank Redemption and do everyone's taxes while outsmarting the warden. As for presumed dead, did it count that they were dead to me? At least it felt that way. I sighed. Probably not.

"No to both," I said.

Sheri's friendly expression suddenly went serious. "This is difficult to ask, but were you physically or sexually abused by either one of your parents?"

"No. But does mental abuse count?" I joked.

I could tell Sheri didn't find that funny.

"Sorry," I said.

"That's okay. Don't worry about it. I know you're probably very stressed dealing with all these money issues when all you'd rather be focusing on is your studies."

"You can say that again," I sighed.

"Next criteria. Are your parents unable to be located?"

I had no interest in ever seeing them again, but that wasn't what she meant. "No. I mean, yes. They're in Washington D.C."

"And you weren't adopted?"

"No." But sometimes it felt like I was adopted by robots.

Sheri sighed heavily. "Well, unfortunately that means we won't be able to override your dependency status."

My shoulders sank and I slumped down in the chair. "Oh."

"But you might qualify as independent already."

"Oh?" I smiled.

"Yes. If you are twenty-four, you would automatically be considered independent, but I see here on the computer that you haven't yet turned twenty."

"No," I sighed. "Not until next school year."

"And you're not an orphan, or ward of the court?"

"Do you mean a ward like Robin is a ward of Batman's?" I asked hopefully

She grinned. "Well yes. But you don't happen to know any superheroes, do you?"

"One," I grinned, thinking of Christos. "But he doesn't have a costume. He has tattoos. Does that count?"

She chuckled, "Sadly, no. Maybe if you got him to wear a costume?" she winked

"Probably not," I sighed.

"Any chance you're a veteran?"

"No."

"A graduate student?"

"Still an undergrad. Geez, I'm nothing, aren't I?"

She smiled. "I wouldn't say that. I'd say you're a bright young woman with a financial hiccup. We can work through it. You don't have any legal dependents, do you? Any children or aging grandparents you care for?"

"No. But I could get pregnant, if that would help," I said sarcastically.

"I wouldn't advise it," she said with amusement. "Besides, even if you got pregnant tomorrow, you wouldn't have the baby until Fall Quarter, so your dependent status wouldn't change until then. That wouldn't help you pay your Spring tuition, now would it?" She winked at me.

"I guess not."

She leveled a serious but compassionate look at me. "Don't get pregnant, Samantha. If you think working two jobs is tough, having a child is ten times harder. I know what I'm talking about." She picked up a photo from her desk and spun it around for me to see. It was her smiling with a little boy and girl. Both kids were grade school age. "Don't let their cuteness fool you. Like toads, lizards, and demon spawn, the second they realize they're larger than you, they will try to eat you," she grinned.

"Got it. No kids."

"Gosh," she sighed, "there's only one other option."

I winced. "What? Do I have to be a member of the clergy or something? I'd totally become a nun if it would pay for school."

"No," she smiled, "just the opposite. You're not married, are you?"

A bullet of surprise knocked me into the back of my chair. "Did you say married?"

"Yes."

"As in, wed? As in, hitched?"

She chuckled, "I did. Can I take it that you have a husband? I only ask because I didn't see a ring on your finger."

I didn't see a ring on my finger either, but the idea made me woozy in the best way possible. I leaned forward in my chair and rested my elbows on Sheri's desk. My brain and heart swirled with possibilities.

What if Christos and I were married?

What if?

I suddenly wanted to do the happy dance on Sheri Denney's desk. But it wasn't like I could ask Christos to marry me, could I?

No. Such things weren't done. I could hint. I could hint like crazy twenty times a day. But Christos had to do the asking, assuming I didn't scare him away with all the hinting.

Sheri raised her eyebrows expectantly. "You are married, aren't you?"

"No," I sighed. "Not yet, anyway. But I have a serious boyfriend."

She deflated a little. "Don't rush into anything, Samantha. I don't want you coming back in here tomorrow with some adventure story about how you drove to Las Vegas tonight and got Elvis to marry you and your boyfriend at a drive thru wedding chapel for a hundred dollars. Marriage is a serious commitment. Don't take it lightly."

"I know," I sighed.

Sheri rested a hand on my forearm and looked me in the eye. "I'm not saying don't get married, I'm just saying don't rush into it. Get married because you love each other, when you're ready. Not because you need some financial aid money."

I really liked Sheri. She wasn't so hard core like my parents, trying to control everything I did. Maybe Sheri could adopt me? No. She had two kids already.

"In the meantime," she said, "try talking to your parents again. It's your best bet."

"I don't know. Ever since I changed my major to art, they've been flipping out. And my mom thinks my boyfriend is a bad influence."

"I see," she nodded. "I argued with my mom about boys all the time when I was your age."

"Really? What happened?"

She grinned conspiratorially at me and leaned forward to whisper, "I married the boy we argued about the most."

"See! Maybe I *should* marry my boyfriend!"

She rolled her eyes. "I know it sounds like getting married will fix everything. It doesn't. There's more problems, just different ones. Now, you said something about changing your major. What was it before?"

"Accounting. But that's just what my parents wanted. I changed my major to art because that's what I've dreamed about doing since I was a girl."

Sheri smiled, "I wanted to be a dancer when I graduated from high school. Getting married and having kids put a stop to that. Don't get me wrong, I love my husband dearly on all the days he isn't driving me nuts, and I love my kids more than anything. But I never got to move to New York to be a dancer like I had always dreamed." She gave me a serious look. "Samantha, you have to choose. If you want to be an artist, you might have to wait on marriage."

"But my boyfriend is an artist! And he's successful too!" A sudden rush of optimism and hope swept through me. It felt like my life was suddenly coming together, despite everything my parents were doing to stand in my way. "Maybe I can have my boyfriend *and* an art career *and* get married!"

"Maybe you can," Sheri smiled. "But please, *please*, don't rush out and tie the knot. Try talking to your parents first. If they helped you before, it's because they love you."

I wasn't so sure about that. Loved me like fire loved to burn things, maybe. Groan. But I bet not like Sheri loved her kids. They were lucky to have her as a mom.

She continued, "Maybe if you explain to your parents how serious you are about art?"

"I have. They don't think I can make any money doing it."

"Can you?"

"Yes. My boyfriend makes tons of money selling his paintings."

"Then you need to show your parents that you can make money as an artist too." Sheri had stars in her eyes, as if she were suddenly living my dream with me. "This is your chance to be the dancer I never got to be. You go be an artist, Samantha. Live your dream. You're young, and there's no better time."

"You're right! I'm totally going to do it!"

She laughed, "And maybe you'll even marry your artist boyfriend someday."

"Someday," I swooned.

I think it was already spring time in my tummy because I could feel flowers blooming and an army of butterflies spreading their wings inside my heart. That, or every cell in my body was getting ready to explode with sudden happiness.

For the first time in weeks, I felt honest to goodness hope.

I was dizzy as I walked drunkenly out of the Financial Aid

offices.

Everything was finally falling into place for me!
All because I had Christos in my life.

Chapter 11

CHRISTOS

"Mmmm, Christos, my neck is so stiff. Can you massage for me?" Isabella asked in her broken and accented English.

Never in my life had a naked hottie sitting five feet away from me asking for a massage been so utterly fucking annoying.

Since I'd taken the last five days off from painting, I was way behind, and I had to juggle all the models' schedules. Hence, Isabella being in the studio today instead of her usual Wednesdays and Saturdays. I *could* have had Isabella here last Saturday, but I'd wanted to spend the weekend with Samantha. Not some random model, no matter how hot she may have been.

Isabella made a blatant show of rubbing her neck and working a hair toss into the mix. "You rub my neck, Christos," she insisted, "so I feel much better."

The pose she was holding was an easy one. Any other model I'd worked with wouldn't have been complaining.

Isabella was up to her usual games. She was looking for any excuse for me to touch her, especially when she was naked and vulnerable. Any normal man on the planet would've taken Isabella's cue and had their hands all over her luscious caramel skin and dark mane of hair a second later.

I wasn't any normal man.

I sighed and set my brushes down. "Why don't you take a break?" I suggested. "Put your robe on and walk around for a while. It'll help you loosen up. Maybe do some jumping jacks."

She frowned. "What is jumping jack? Is Jack a friend of you?"

I reminded myself that Portuguese was her first language. I cracked a smile. It was kind of funny when I thought about it. How had the word jack met up with jumping in the first place? I had no idea.

"What is funny?" Isabella smiled coquettishly.

"I'm sorry, it's nothing. Try doing some neck rotations. Like this," I demonstrated moving my head in circles. "And some shoulder shrugs," which I did.

Isabella stood up, revealing her naked body from head to toe in all its perfect glory. "Massage is better," she moaned, taking a tentative step toward me.

"I've gotta take a leak," I lied, hoping it would ruin her mood.

She cocked her head, not understanding.

Subtlety was not going to work with the language barrier.

"Bathroom," I said, "I've got to go to the bathroom."

"Oh."

"Walk around while I'm gone. Neck rotations will help." I raised my eyebrows while rolling and nodding my head. "Got it?"

"Yes," she pouted.

Instead of using the bathroom in the studio, I went into the furthest guest bathroom at the back of the house. I passed by my grandfather's office on the way. He was sitting at the computer. I stopped and leaned against the doorframe.

"That girl never quits," I sighed.

"Who? Isabella?" my grandad asked.

"Yeah. She keeps throwing herself at me."

My grandad leaned back in his chair and clasped his hands behind his head. A sly smile spread across his mouth. "Want me to handle her?"

"Go for it," I chuckled. "I'll be back in an hour?"

"An hour! I'll need at least three," he joked.

"Deal. But you have to finish my painting for me," I joked. My grandad was fully capable of doing the work and making Isabella's portrait look awesome. But he hadn't picked up a brush in a long time.

"Hah!" he chuckled. "If I have to work for it, forget it, *paidí mou*."

"All right, *Pappoús*. You're off the hook for now. But if she throws herself at me one more time, I'm carrying her in here and dropping her in your lap. Naked. Can you handle that?"

He blurted a laugh as I walked out of the room.

Instead of going to the guest bathroom, I went out on the balcony attached to my bedroom to enjoy the view for a few minutes. I hadn't needed to take a leak in the first place. While I was standing outside, my phone rang.

Brandon.

I rolled my eyes. He probably wanted to bitch about my unfinished paintings.

"What's up, man?" I answered.

"Christos!" Brandon said enthusiastically. "I was beginning to worry about you. You haven't answered my calls for the last five days."

"I was busy painting."

"Excellent. Can I assume you were busy completing some of your existing paintings?"

"Totally."

"Which ones are done?"

"Most of them," I said evasively.

There was a pause. "Okay…ahhh, it doesn't matter which ones. Hey, are you at the studio right now?"

"Yeah. I'm painting Isabella today. Why?"

"How's it coming along?"

"Great."

"Mind if I come take a look?" Brandon asked, "and bring a prospective buyer with me?"

Great. The last thing I wanted was an audience while I was working. "Who is it? Mrs. Moorhouse?" She was always trying to stick her nose into art studios all over San Diego. It made her feel special. Whatever.

"No. It's Stanford Wentworth. He flew in from New York to see your work."

I grunted out a sigh. Stanford Wentworth was one of the richest art patrons in the world. He owned a vast collection of world renowned artwork ranging from the Pre-Renaissance iconography of the 14th and 15th centuries, to the Impressionists like Monet and Degas in the late 19th century, to living masters like Chuck Close and Julian Schnabel. Wentworth was always on the hunt for new talent. If he bought your work, he could make your name and your career for life.

I'm not surprised Wentworth wanted to investigate my work, considering that he'd bought a number of my dad's paintings and my grandad's over the years.

"Couldn't you have warned me Wentworth was coming?" I asked.

"I didn't know," Brandon pleaded, "the man literally called me from the airport an hour ago. He flew in on his private jet and told me he wanted to see you at work. What was I supposed to tell him? Fly back tomorrow?"

I chuckled. I couldn't blame Brandon. If you were an artist, getting a call from Wentworth was like getting a call from the President, or maybe the Queen of England. "Fine. You can come by whenever. When do you think you'll be here?"

"Within the hour. Wentworth is already here at the gallery. He's getting antsy. And you know the drill. What Stanford Wentworth wants…"

"Stanford Wentworth gets," I finished. "Yeah, yeah. We'll be here. I'll leave the door unlocked. Oh, Brandon, one other thing?"

"What?"

"Did you kiss his right shoe or his left when he walked in today?"

"Both," Brandon chuckled. "I'll see you shortly."

I ended the call. The thing that amused me about Brandon was that he was never predictable. Never entirely an asshole, but never your best friend. It worked well for a business relationship. The long standing, vaguely personal relationship between his family and mine never got complicated. It was always business first.

I went to the office to warn my grandad that Wentworth was coming.

"No shit," my grandad said. "I haven't seen Stan in years."

"Yes, shit," I quipped. "I'm sure he'll be happy to say hello."

I went back to the studio.

Isabella stood in front of one of the French doors, bathed in soft light. She truly was ridiculously beautiful, even in her short butt length robe. Her hand rubbed her neck as she did neck rolls. Maybe she actually had a stiff neck. "Christos," she murmured, "you massage now?"

"No time, Isabella. We're going to have some special visitors."

"Who?"

"Brandon is bringing a famous art buyer to the studio in an hour. Guy's name is Stanford Wentworth. He's going to want to see me working."

"I work better after massage."

Poor thing. Weren't there any eligible men where Isabella lived in Los Angeles? Maybe I'd have to turn her loose on Lucas or Logan Summer. I owed them a solid after they'd help me move Samantha into the house. That gave me an idea. "Isabella, you know I have a girlfriend, right?"

Isabella pouted, but nodded acknowledgment.

I walked up to her and pulled my phone out. "Check this out." She watched expectantly as I thumbed through my photo gallery until I landed on a picture of Lucas and Logan smiling like idiots. "See these two guys?"

Isabella's face lit up in a smile. "Oooh, handsome. Are they friends of you?"

"These guys are brothers. Lucas and Logan Summer. Both of them are single. I'll make you a deal. You do what I tell you while that guy Wentworth is here, and I'll set you up with Lucas or Logan. Take your pick. Or pick both," I snorted a laugh, "it's up to you."

She frowned, but was still smiling at me. "For true?"

"Yeah. For true. Deal?" I held out my hand for her to shake.

She slid her tiny hand into mine and shook. "I meet your cute friends?"

"Totally."

"Ok."

"Awesome. I gotta get stuff ready before Wentworth gets here. Hang tight. And do more neck rotations and shoulder shrugs. It'll help."

===

When Stanford Wentworth arrived with Brandon, my grandad answered the door. I could hear them chatting in the foyer from the studio where I was painting Isabella. It sounded like Wentworth had brought someone with him. I didn't recognize the voice.

I wanted to look busy working when Stanford walked into the studio, so I left them to their small talk and concentrated on painting Isabella.

You couldn't miss Wentworth's voice. He sounded like he belonged behind a podium with a teleprompter and an audience of five thousand adoring constituents.

"Spiridon Manos," Wentworth said. "Always a pleasure. It's

been years, if I'm not mistaken?"

"It has," my grandad said.

"Mr. Wentworth just flew in this morning," Brandon said.

"Oh, then you must be tired from traveling," my grandad said. "Would you like something to drink, Stanford?"

"Since my assistant Fredrick will be doing all the driving today, I think I'll indulge. What have you got with some tooth?" There was a tinge of amusement in Wentworth's voice.

"Let's stroll over to the bar and see," my grandad said.

I heard some shuffling around and clinking of glasses in the living room. I knew that Stanford Wentworth was in his seventies. The story went that he'd made his fortune investing in computers before it was the obvious thing to do, and he'd gone into cable television big in the 1980s. For the last 25 years, he'd devoted all of his time and money to the world of art, where he'd enjoyed further financial success.

"I don't believe I've seen any of these paintings before," Wentworth said. He was referring to all of my grandad's landscapes hanging in the living room. None of them had ever been displayed in any gallery shows.

"No," my grandfather answered. "This is my private work."

"It all looks fabulous. Have you considered selling them?" Wentworth asked. "The Private Collection of Spiridon Manos?"

There was a long silence while I pretended to work in the studio. Isabella was posed naked in front of me, but I was too worried about what Wentworth might do or say to get any real painting done.

"I'm too old for the art business," my grandad sighed. "It's a young man's game."

"Balderdash," Wentworth said. "I'm older than you, Spiridon, and I'm still in it."

"But we're on opposite sides of the game board, Stanford."

"Touché. I'll make it easy for you. I'll give you seven million for everything in the room."

I think I could hear Brandon gulping all the way from where I sat at my easel.

"Thank you, Stanford," my grandad said, "but no. The memories in these paintings are worth ten times that. Many of them were painted when I was a young man, or when my son was but a child, or when I had my grandson sitting on my knee. I couldn't part with them."

"If you change your mind, give my office a call. But I promise, my offer will have changed, and not to your advantage, I assure you."

Nice. I hadn't yet met the guy, and already I didn't like him.

"Enough of that," Wentworth grumbled. "Now, shall we see the young artist at work?"

"If he's not too busy," my grandad said a bit defensively.

"I'll go check," Brandon said. He rushed into the studio a moment later, a pained expression on his face. "You ready for the dog and pony show?" he whispered.

"Do I have a choice?" I mumbled.

"No," Brandon said sharply.

Fan fucking tastic.

Stanford Wentworth ambled into the room, flanked by his assistant Frederick, Brandon, and my grandad.

Wentworth was a large, tall man with a thick head of tightly maintained aerodynamic silver hair. He wore an expensive suit and imposing tie.

Frederick was similarly slickly suited. Wire rimmed glasses were attached to his face and a cellphone earpiece was attached to his ear. He raised his hand to his earpiece and pressed a button. "Frederick Whitlock speaking?" After a pause, he said, "He's busy at the moment." Pause. "I'll check. Mr. Wentworth, it's Couteux Galerie in Beverly Hills. They want to know if you're coming by this afternoon?"

"Tell them I'll come by if I come by," Wentworth barked.

Nice. Wentworth sure had a winning personality.

Frederick relayed the message over his earpiece way more politely than Wentworth had said it. I had no doubt Frederick more than earned whatever Wentworth paid him.

I pretended to paint as they walked toward my easel, mixing paint on my palette. Isabella briefly glanced at them, but maintained her pose. I had explained to her earlier in detail that we should continue working while everyone walked in and watched.

I noticed Wentworth blatantly eyeballing Isabella's nakedness. He positioned himself to get the best possible view of her exposed breasts. His overt desire was as subtle as a volcano. He slid his hands into his pockets and arched his back, thrusting out his pelvis. I wouldn't have been surprised if he started jingling his change like he had a jackhammer running in his pants. Total douche. I liked him better and better. Not.

I would've thrown the guy out except for the fact he could ruin my art career with the snap of his fingers. The one downside to selling paintings for ten grand or fifty grand or more was that you were always dealing with rich shitheads.

Whatever. It's not like the guy had his hands on Isabella. If he crossed that line, I'd break his fingers. But Isabella was a big girl, and I'm sure this wasn't the first time she'd been ogled by an old dude. She worked as a model, after all. I could only hope she'd learned how to deal with it.

Wentworth let out a big sigh and pulled his hands out of his pockets. I'm sure by now he'd come in his pants. Fucking perv. He walked around behind my easel to see what I was doing.

I nodded at him.

"Don't mind me," he said. "Please continue."

The way he said it sounded dangerously close to a command. I'm sure he was used to telling people what to do 24/7. I rolled my eyes before glancing at Isabella. She seemed relieved that I was now positioned between her and Wentworth like a shield.

I had been in the process of painting Isabella's hips. The joint where the leg comes out of the pelvis was always tricky. Beautiful women had a softness, but you had to give it just the right amount of subtle structure or else it looked like carnival balloons stuck together. I'd always believed that softness was the secret of feminine beauty. Not hard muscle. All that modern shit about women having eight packs and guns for arms was ridiculous. If you wanted to fuck a guy, go fuck a guy.

I loaded up my brush with a mixture of burnt sienna and a hint of burnt umber. I swept the brush across the canvas at the hip joint in an elegant curve.

"Mmmm," Wentworth nodded.

I ignored him.

I needed to hit one of the planes on the front of the pelvis with a lighter mix, so I went back to my palette and added a hint of zinc white.

As I was about to apply the paint to the canvas, Wentworth

went, "Hmmm."

Was it going to be like this all day? I almost turned and tossed him a glare, but decided it was a bad idea. So I scumbled the paint onto the canvas instead. Then I took out a clean brush and used it to soften the edge between the light and dark areas.

"Uh huh," Wentworth mumbled.

Oh man, this was killing me. I set my brushes down and wiped my hands on a rag. I took a step back from my easel.

Wentworth immediately stepped in, getting his nose inches from the canvas. A simple "May I?" would've been nice. Nope. What Wentworth wanted, Wentworth got. He inspected the hip joint I'd just painted like a jeweler. Somebody give that guy a loupe so he could examine the molecules in the paint mix a little better.

He stepped back to view the whole painting and nodded thoughtfully. I couldn't tell if he approved or what. Then he lunged forward, getting in close on the portrait again.

This guy was a nut.

He continued lunging in and out for several minutes, examining different parts of the painting in detail. When he was finished, he stepped back and stood beside me.

"I like it," he said thoughtfully, "but it needs work."

Was he kidding? We hadn't even been introduced. Yeah, he knew who I was, and I knew who he was. But, fuck, there was this thing that had been around for thousands of years called common courtesy. I guess when you got rich enough, shit like that went out the window.

I glanced at Brandon, who gave me a sympathetic look that said, "Yes, he's crazy, but he's a hundred times richer than he is crazy, so suck it up."

I shook my head minimally and rolled my eyes for Brandon's sake.

He shot me a warning glare.

I sighed. Time for me to behave.

"Yes," Wentworth said, "a few revisions and I think this will be serviceable. The head is good, but have you considered altering the pose?"

I raised one of my eyebrows at least three inches.

My grandad chuckled and walked out of the room. I could tell he was offended for me by the way he laughed.

I guess I'd missed the part where Wentworth had been hitting the crack pipe like a high class hooker after a blow job bender. The guy was a lunatic. Oh, I forgot. Wentworth did what Wentworth did.

He said, "This is good work. It's not great. I wouldn't pay more than fifteen thousand for what I see here. But I believe if you were to change the pose to something more elegant, you could get it up to fifty thousand."

More elegant? Was he blind? Everything Isabella did was elegant, and my painting captured that.

Before I had a chance to tell Wentworth to go fuck himself, he asked, "What other paintings do you have on hand?" He turned away to investigate, and the second his back was to me, I rifled a glare at Brandon.

Brandon ignored it. "Christos," he said pleasantly, "can you show Mr. Wentworth the other paintings you've been working on? I know you have several in progress."

Thanks a bunch of fuck, Brandon. Wentworth started digging through some old canvases I had leaning against the wall like he owned the place. I had to restrain myself from planting my boot in his ass.

"The new paintings are over here," I said, pointing to the drying rack where I kept the canvases of Avery, Jacqueline, and Becca that I'd completed a few weeks ago. They stood in the tall vertical slots of the drying rack, which kept dust off the paintings while the oils cured. I carefully slid out the first one. "They're still wet," I warned subtly, half expecting Wentworth to run his fingers all over the art like he owned it.

Instead, he glanced at the first painting, then nodded commandingly, "Next."

Yes, master. I slid it carefully back into the rack.

I noticed Frederick answering his earpiece again. "Mr. Wentworth, it's Madelyn Cornett with Jah—"

"Can't you see I'm busy, Frederick?" Wentworth grumbled.

"Yes, Mr. Wentworth," Frederick said before turning away to handle the call.

Whatever Wentworth was paying Frederick, it wasn't enough. The guy needed a raise. My suggestion would've been for Frederick to find another boss, but that was just me.

"Next," Wentworth insisted, looking at me expectantly.

Man, Wentworth needed an attitude adjustment in a hurry. I'd be more than happy to take him to the garage where I kept my tools and no one would hear him shouting for help.

I slid out another painting. This was of Jacqueline, and I was pretty happy with it.

"No. Next."

I pulled out the last one.

He shook his head and turned away, looking for new distraction.

What a charmer. And I was doing whatever he said like a servant. Who the fuck did he think he was? I wanted to tell him he could take his money, light it on fire, and stick it up his ass. I didn't need him. There were other art buyers out there.

Wentworth's eyes fell on Samantha's easel in the corner. He walked over to it. Samantha's painting of three Calla Lilies in a vase sat on it. "What's this?" Wentworth asked. "It's not yours, is it?"

"That's my girlfriend's painting," I said.

"It's terrible," Wentworth chortled.

He turned away and started walking toward the door before I could respond. He stopped in front of the Isabella portrait on his way out and said, "If you change up your painting of this beautiful young model like I suggested, you might have something with it. Frederick? It's time to go. Call Couteux Galerie and tell them there wasn't anything worth my time in San Diego today."

I ground my teeth together. Wentworth had never once called me by name. He was prick royalty. King of All Dicks. I debated whether or not Frederick or Brandon would turn me in if I beat Wentworth to death and dropped his body in a ditch somewhere.

"Did you see those Calla Lilies?" Wentworth quietly asked Frederick as they neared the doorway leading back into the house.

"I did not, sir," Frederick replied quietly.

"They were god awful," Wentworth chuckled quietly.

"Hey!" I shouted at his back. "Fuck you, Wentworth."

Wentworth stopped in his tracks. He turned around slowly, like an old gun fighter at high noon. "Excuse me?"

"You heard me, Wentworth. Fuck. You."

Wentworth blinked. "You do know who I am, don't you, boy?"

"I do, but not because you introduced yourself like a normal person," I growled. "You came into my house like you owned the place and you've been acting like an entitled dick since you got here. I don't need to take shit from you. And I don't need your fucking money."

Wentworth narrowed his eyes. "Do you think a bunch of curse words and petulant puffery is going to rile me, boy? I've watched the likes of you come and go countless times in my life. At the rate you're going, in twenty years, no one will remember your name. They'll remember your father's and your grandfather's, but not yours. All you had to show me today was nothing but boorish scribbles. You're not a real artist, boy. At best, you're a copyist. Your work is lifeless. It has no art to it. Take a page from your father's or your grandfather's career, and maybe you'll make something of yourself."

"Fuck off," I scowled. "And get the fuck out of my house."

"Your house?" Wentworth laughed. "I imagine that your grandfather was the one who paid for this house with his own efforts. Not you. Maybe one day, you'll amount to something. But all I saw here today was garbage. I'll forget about you the moment I step into my car."

Wentworth walked out of my house with Frederick on his heels.

I'd never met a bigger prick in the art business in my entire life. Wentworth not only took the cake, he shoveled his cake down his throat like a glutinous troll. Why had I gotten into this business again?

"What the fuck was that?" I asked Brandon, who stood on the other end of the studio.

Isabella stood between us, now in her robe. She must've thrown it on the second I was busy with Wentworth. I couldn't blame her for wanting to cover up in front of his hungry lizard's stare. She hugged the robe tightly around herself and shivered, "That man a big jerk."

Brandon looked torn, like he wanted to rush after Wentworth and lick the man's asshole until Wentworth scratched him behind the ears. "My apologies, Christos. I've never met Wentworth in person. I had no idea what to expect. I should really go talk to him." Brandon jogged out of the room.

A minute later, I heard car doors chunking shut and an engine starting. Brandon must've left the front door open. I heard a car drive off. To my surprise, Brandon walked somberly back into the studio looking defeated.

"I'm going to need a ride back to La Jolla," he said.

"Huh?" I said.

"We drove here from my gallery in Wentworth's car."

I considered telling Brandon he could walk back after bringing that prick into my house. Lucky for him I was in no mood to paint after today's episode of The Stanford Wentworth Show. I told Isabella she could leave early and asked if she could drive Brandon to La Jolla before she went back to L.A.

She said yes.

When they were gone, I stomped into the living room and grabbed a bottle of bourbon from the bar. It was a forty dollar bottle of Basil Hayden's. It had a smooth caramel flavor I enjoyed. I wasn't in the mood for anything too fancy. I'd gotten more than enough high end bullshit from Wentworth already.

I walked out to the deck behind the pool and tipped the bottle back while enjoying the view of the ocean from one of the loungers.

Yeah, I was done working for the day, if not for the month.

There was only one thing on my mind as I worked my way through my bottle of bourbon.

Wentworth was right.

Those paintings inside were nothing more than illustrations. They didn't have any heart in them.

Wentworth had seen it instantly.

Fuck.

I sloshed more bourbon down my throat.

===

SAMANTHA

I walked across campus to the lecture hall for Sociology. I was in a good mood after talking to Sheri Denney about my financial aid options.

Marrying Christos?

Was that a real possibility?

I was afraid to think about it too much in case I jinxed myself.

Sociology with Professor Tutan-yawn-yawn was the perfect cure. The lecture turned into a sleepy blur. I may or may not have taken notes. After class, I stopped at the Toasted Roast to freshen up my Americano. I hadn't slept enough in the past four days, and I was going to need caffeine if I wanted to get through History without snoring.

When I walked into the lecture hall and sat down, a familiar face greeted me.

Justin Tomlinson, the editor of The Wombat humor newspaper. He was as boy band cute as ever. "Hey, Samantha," he grinned, "we missed you on Friday."

"Oh no! I totally forgot about your meeting," I smiled sheepishly. "I'm totally sorry, I was...ah, super busy with homework." Justin didn't need to know about my harrowing trip to the courthouse to save Christos.

"No worries," he smiled. "Everyone liked your stuff. You should join us at the meeting this coming Friday so you can meet everybody."

"You mean I'm not black balled for missing my first meeting?" I quipped.

"Naw, we're pretty laid back. You should totally come by. Same time, same place."

"4:20 pot time? Toasted Roast? Wait, aren't toasted and roasted both euphemisms for getting stoned?"

"Pretty much," he winked.

"Maybe I should draw a pot smoking wombat for you guys?"

He cracked a smile, "I'd like to see how you handle a pot smoking wombat."

"Cookies and potato chips," I said flatly.

He was confused. "What?"

"Don't wombats get the munchies like everyone else when they're high?" I smiled. "If I had to deal with a pot smoking wombat, I'd give him cookies and potato chips."

"Totally," he chuckled. "I have a feeling you're going to fit right in. Do you think you can have some sketches of Potty the Pot Smoking Wombat by Friday?"

"His name is Potty?" I arched an eyebrow.

"It is now," Justin smiled.

Wait, had I just inadvertently named their mascot? Maybe I had. "Can I do something combining toilets and pot smoking? Maybe have Potty on the john while he's smoking a big fat spliff?"

"You can do anything you want. Run with it. There. Are. No. Rules," he grinned.

Wow, I liked the sound of that. "Okay. I'll have some drawings on Friday!"

"Awesome."

I couldn't wait to tell Christos. I had my first real live art assignment!

Chapter 12

SAMANTHA

"You have to draw a what?" Christos asked. He was super drunk.

"A pot smoking wombat sitting on a toilet, for The Wombat newspaper," I said.

We were in Christos' studio, where my new drawing table was. I couldn't wait to start sketching cartoon wombats. I thought Christos would be working when I got home from SDU, but the model was gone and he had been sitting in front of his easel with a bottle of booze in one fist.

Christos slowly swiveled his glassy eyes in my direction. "Do you want me to sneak into the zoo and steal one for reference?"

"What, a wombat?"

"Yeah. I could go all ninja and climb over the fence at night. I know a way in," he nodded ultra seriously. Then he held his palm to the side of his mouth and whispered, "There's a grade school on the north side of the San Diego Zoo and their playground goes right up to the back of it."

I wrinkled my nose, "Does the zoo even have wombats?"

"Probably. We should totally take one and keep him as a pet. I'll name him Womby the Wombat. Wouldn't that be totally cute?"

"I guess?" As in, it sounded like a terrible idea.

"We can climb right over the fence," Christos slurred. "Let's you and me go right now. I'll drive."

"Ahh, you probably shouldn't be driving or climbing ninja style or anything else tonight. Maybe you should lie down for awhile?"

"But the wombat will get away!"

I chuckled, "I'm sure Womby will be fine for tonight."

Christos giggled fluidly and leaned his head against my arm, "You like the name Womby, don't you?"

He reeked of alcohol.

"It's perfect," I smiled indulgently.

In a high voice, Christos baby talked, "We'll make a wittle bed for Womby wight in da coner of da studio."

"Why don't we make a bed for Womby right now? You can test it out."

"'Kay," he slurred.

I led Christos into the living room and helped him onto the couch. I took his boots off and covered him in a blanket. After grabbing my sketchbook, I sat in the leather chair opposite him and turned on the reading light. I went to work on my sketches of Potty the Pot Smoking Wombat. It took about ten seconds to realize I didn't know what a wombat looked like. Maybe Christos had been onto something with his wombat kidnapping master plan.

Or I could just look for a picture on the internet.

I dug out my laptop and returned to the living room. With dozens of wombat photos on the screen and my sketchbook at the ready, I dove into cartoon dreamland as I drew page after page of toilet sitting pot smoking profligate wombats.

Who knew wombats were almost as cute as koala bears? I'd been expecting some kind of bat monster, but it turned out wombats had the same big black noses as koalas, and their ears were these tiny little button things.

So cute!

===

"Are you sure this is okay, Sam?" Romeo asked nervously as we walked across campus toward the Student Center on Friday afternoon.

It was just after four o'clock and we were on our way to The Wombat staff meeting at Toasted Roast. The sun was out and it was a warm end of February day.

"Why wouldn't it be?" I reasoned enthusiastically. "That guy Justin made it sound like anyone could submit stuff to The Wombat. He said some of the artists work with writers on the comic strips. I don't know anyone funnier than you, Romeo."

"What if it turns out Justin was just hitting on you and they don't need more writers? They're not going to need my gay super powers then," he said anxiously. "I become a liability."

"Relax, Romeo. I'm sure it'll be fine."

"Okay. But if something goes wrong, don't expect me to shoot rainbows out of my fingertips and save the day," he warned.

"No problem," I chuckled. "At no time will I require the use of your rainbow super powers. But I may call upon them later. Deal?"

"Deal. But you know how shooting too many rainbows drains me," he grinned.

"What happened to that infamous Romeo stamina?"

He smiled, "It's all a facade, Sam. Once I shoot my rainbow load, it takes at least a week to recharge. Don't tell anybody, or my rainbow reputation will be ruined."

"Your secret is safe with me." I crossed my heart with my fingers. "Hey, I bet if you found a bunch of unicorns it would speed up your rainbow recovery time."

Romeo rolled his eyes. "You've been hanging around with Kamiko and watching way too much Adventure Time. I wasn't talking about cartoon rainbows. The only place I can go in San Diego to recharge my rainbow is Hillcrest."

"Is that why you've been going there?"

"Of course."

We walked across the Student Center quad.

Outside the Toasted Roast there were a ton of free tables. This late in the day, most of the students were gone, especially on Friday. The only time it was ever crowded at the Student Center in the afternoon was when SDU had a band playing in the quad, but that usually happened in the fall or spring.

It was almost 4:20, so I looked around for Justin Tomlinson. He waved from a group of tables that had been pushed together. Five other students sat around him.

Me and Romeo walked over to join them.

"Hey, Justin," I said to him. "Everybody, my name is Samantha. This is my friend Romeo."

A girl with black plastic hipster glasses said to me sarcastically, "Shouldn't your name be Juliet?"

There was a long, drawn out moment of silence. I think she was being a bitch, but I wasn't one hundred percent sure. I thought Justin had said everyone on the paper was laid back?

Romeo glared at the bitchy girl with the hipster glasses. In a sarcastic voice, he said, "I have rainbow super powers. I promised Sam I wouldn't use them, but I will if I have to. They work especially well on hipster bitches."

I winced, expecting everyone to frown and turn their backs on us, or maybe just boo and hiss until we left.

Justin raised an eyebrow, and in a serious tone said, "Ever since Keith used his super powered farts at the last meeting, we voted to make this a super power free zone. We all agreed his super powered farts had lost their comedic effect," Justin grinned, now obviously joking around.

"But not their horrid stench," snickered the second girl, who had a nose ring, dark hair, and lots of black eye liner.

One of the two guys sitting at the table smiled guiltily and rolled his eyes. I imagined he was Keith, the super powered farter. He had a thick dark under-beard. It was just the beard part with no mustache. He had a lot of beard for a young guy.

The other guy, who was snickering at Keith, had long black emo hair that draped over one of his eyes and was died red at the tips.

"So," Justin smiled at Romeo, "even if you tried shooting rainbows, which I would pay to see, your super powers won't work here at the meeting because of all the magical fart repellant in effect."

"Oooh," Romeo said, super excited, "where do you guys get your fart repellant? I hear that stuff is expensive."

"Costco," Justin winked. "We buy in bulk."

Keith rolled his eyes once again. Everyone else laughed and smiled, except for the girl with the hipster glasses, who folded her arms across her chest and grimaced.

Everyone was laughing so much, me and Romeo joined in.

Keith of the Underbeard said, "What? I told you guys I had beans for lunch so I couldn't be held criminally responsible for bad gas."

"Dude," Emo Hair chuckled, "those were beer farts. Don't deny it."

"At 4:20?" Keith asked. "I was so not beer fart drunk that early."

"Bullshit!" said the girl with the nose ring. "You were wasted last Friday!"

"Maybe by 5:20, but I assure you I was not beer farting at 4:20," Keith sneered.

They all shared another laugh, even Hipster Glasses. Clearly, they knew each other well. I'd been expecting some kind of exclusive boy's club like in those college party movies like Animal House. I hadn't expected two girls.

"All I want to know is," the girl with the nose ring said, chuckling in advance of what she was about to say, "who would win in a fight? Keith with his toxic farts, or Romeo and his rainbows. I want to see them go head to head."

"Keith's farts would totally win," Emo Hair said, deadpan.

Nose ring laughed and Keith rolled his eyes.

"All right, guys," Justin said. "Samantha, Romeo, meet Keith, Micah, Alyssa, and everyone's favorite SDU hipster, Tammy Lemons."

They all waved as Justin called their names, except for Tammy, who made a sour face.

Micah was the guy with the red-tipped emo hair. Alyssa had the nose ring and wore a T shirt that had a picture of a Tyrannosaurus rex saying "Rawr!" The caption below read, "Rawr means 'I love you' in dinosaur." Tammy Lemons, of course, was the girl with the hipster glasses.

Aside from Tammy, I liked these guys.

"Pull up a chair," Justin said.

Me and Romeo sat down.

"So," Justin said, "you guys remember those drawings of Samantha's that I emailed everyone?"

"Yeah," Keith nodded, grinning.

"Totally," Micah chuckled.

"Funny stuff," Alyssa smiled.

"They were okay," Tammy shrugged. No surprise there. I think Tammy was going to take awhile to thaw out. Whatever.

"Well," Justin continued, "I asked Samantha to work up some drawings for a new Wombat mascot."

"We already have one," Tammy said snidely.

Yeah, she was a bitch. I was now one hundred percent sure.

"But it's just a plain old wombat," Alyssa said. "It's boring."

"Did you bring some new drawings for us?" Keith asked me.

"I did," I said and pulled out my sketchbook. I opened it up to the first wombat sketch and set it in the middle of the table.

The group started flipping through my drawings. There were at least a dozen. It didn't take long before the group was grinning and laughing, except for Tammy, of course. Tammy mostly frowned at my art.

"That one looks constipated," Micah smiled.

"Maybe he should drink more beer," Alyssa quipped, "then he'd always have beer diarrhea like Keith."

Everyone groaned.

"It wasn't beer farts," Keith said defensively while the group continued turning pages of my sketchbook, fascinated by my artwork.

I'd never experienced anything like it. I'd sort of expected them to nod politely and not say anything about my art at all, or maybe tell me I wasn't very good, not be obviously entertained and amused.

"Have you ever seen a blunt so fat?" Micah marveled, referring to the giant joint in the next drawing. "That's like an entire ounce of ganj."

"The only time I see that much weed in one place is when I buy a fresh ounce that you haven't gotten into yet, Micah," Keith groused.

"Dude, that's bullshit. You still owe me a bunch of blunts from over Christmas," Micah scoffed.

Keith shook his head and scowl smiled at him.

They continued turning pages, and found something amusing about each drawing.

I really couldn't believe it. I restrained the huge grin wanting to jump onto my face. They actually liked my art!

When they finished looking at the last drawing, Justin said, "Maybe we should take a vote on which one to use in the next edition of The Wombat as our official logo. What do you guys think?"

"I vote we don't use any of them," hipster glasses Tammy Lemons said. "I don't like her drawings."

Did Tammy not realize I was right here? Yeah, she was a Bitch with a capital Buttplug.

"Don't worry, Samantha," Alyssa smirked, "Tammy's on the rag this week. She's not usually this bitchy."

I smiled at Alyssa, but couldn't think of an appropriate response. For all I knew, they all loved Tammy like a BFF, despite her sour personality. I didn't want to offend by saying the wrong thing.

"I thought I smelled iron," Romeo said in response to Alyssa's rag gag about Tammy. He absently examined his fingernails.

Alyssa grimaced and leaned forward. Her head bonked against the table top. She started chuckling heartily, rolling her forehead from side to side on the table.

Keith whipped out his phone. "If this turns into a cat fight, I'm filming it." He pointed his phone at Tammy, who was scowling at Romeo.

"What?" Romeo said defensively to Tammy, "I have an acute sense of smell."

Tammy flipped Romeo off.

"Is that what you use to plug it up?" Romeo asked. "No wonder it doesn't work. Fingers aren't very absorbent, and it won't do any good if you don't keep it in your hole." He rolled his eyes dramatically. "Even I know that."

Alyssa sat up abruptly, her eyes wide. "Oooohh, damn! No he didn't!"

"Yes. I did," Romeo insisted.

Keith and Micah both suppressed snickers.

"Settle down, guys," Justin said. "No need for a grudge match with the new girl on her first day."

I couldn't tell if Justin was saying I was the new girl or Romeo was.

Alyssa leaned against Tammy and put a friendly arm around her. "Don't worry Tammy, we still love you."

Tammy shook her head and frowned. "You guys are dicks."

"You started it, Tammy," emo Micah chuckled.

"Whatever," Tammy snorted.

Justin said pleasantly, "Why don't we send these out to the rest of our artists, and have everyone vote in a few weeks? How does that sound?"

The group nodded agreement.

Justin continued, "And if any other artists want to do their own version of a wombat mascot, they can put their art in the mix. That includes you, Tammy."

So Tammy Lemons the hipster bitch was an artist too. I was curious to see what she came up with. For all I knew, she could be way better than me, or worse. I didn't really know.

"Agreed?" Justin asked.

Everyone said yes.

Justin took pics of my wombat sketches with his phone like before. "Samantha, I'll email these to everyone, and put you on the CC list, so you can See See all the other entrants."

"Did you just say 'See See'?" Alyssa asked.

"Yeah, why?" Justin grinned.

"Because that's Lame Lame," she sneered.

"Do you have something against the crippled?" Keith asked, quick as a whip.

"The crippled?" Alyssa asked, confused.

"The lame?" Keith said suggestively. "The lame have feelings, too."

Alyssa said sarcastically, "I twisted my ankle last week going down some stairs. Does that count?"

Keith shook his head, "Afraid not. The lame have feelings too, and your use of the term normalizes their struggles like they don't matter."

"Fine," Alyssa sneered. "Then I meant to say the Dumb Dumb."

Keith shook his head, "the intellectually challenged have feelings too."

Alyssa frowned, "Well, then who the hell can I make fun of? Snails?"

Keith arched an eyebrow thoughtfully, "That would work. As far as I know, snails haven't yet made any noises about fair and equitable treatment."

"That's because they don't have any mouths," Micah snickered.

"When did it get so politically correct around here?" Alyssa asked. She turned to Justin and said, "Justin, I want to apologize for saying that you were Lame Lame. I would like to retract that statement and change it to, 'you are Snail Snail'." She looked to Keith for approval, "Better, Keith?"

"Much," Keith snickered.

"Ass," Alyssa said offhandedly to him.

"I have a donkey, and he feels real bad right now," Micah said, "his ears are totally burning."

Alyssa wadded her napkin and threw it at Micah while he cackled.

"All right, you guys," Justin said. "Samantha, when I email your drawings to everyone, I'll put you on the Snail Snail list," he quipped.

"Okay," I smiled. I really liked these guys.

"Equal rights for snails!" Micah mocked, pumping his fist high overhead.

For the rest of the meeting, everyone discussed topics for the next issue of The Wombat. Well, except for Tammy Lemons who mostly sat sulking with her arms folded across her chest.

Romeo fit right in with the rest of the group and contributed lots of funny ideas. By the end, Justin was encouraging him to write a sample piece for the paper.

"Are you sure?" Romeo asked.

"Totally," Justin said. "If you come up with something good, we'll put it in the next ish."

"Sam and I talked about doing a comic strip together," Romeo said. "Can I do that?"

"Whatever you want," Justin smiled at him. "It's cool with me. Is it cool with you guys?" Justin asked the group.

Everyone except Tammy agreed.

"I promise," Romeo said to Tammy, "I won't write anything nasty about you or your period." He sounded sincere.

"Whatever," Tammy said.

"Come on," Romeo pleaded comically, "you're not still mad, are you? I promise, I never smelled your iron."

Alyssa winced and chuckled.

Tammy huffed out a sigh, "Fine. Whatever."

When the meeting was over, Romeo walked me back to my car. The sun had already set, but the sky was still pink on the horizon over the ocean, which was visible from the North Parking Lot.

"That went pretty well," I said.

"Except for Nasty Tammy," Romeo chuckled. "What a bitch."

"Maybe she's just defensive because you and I were invading her clique of friends," I suggested.

"Maybe she's just offensive because she smells."

"You didn't really smell her iron, did you?"

"No," Romeo laughed, "but it seemed like the right thing to say."

"I hope you didn't piss her off."

"Don't worry about it, Sam. What's she going to do? Rig the vote so they don't choose your drawing?"

I shrugged, "I don't know. Maybe?"

"Who cares if she does? It's just a stupid school newspaper."

He was right, but I sort of liked the idea that I might win a drawing contest. It would be one more piece of evidence I could show my parents that I wasn't an idiot for pursuing art. If I ever talked to them again.

I still hadn't listened to their voicemail, and I was starting to think maybe I never would.

===

I dropped my highlighter marker on my textbook in defeat. "Mads," I sighed, "I'm totally going to bomb my Sociology final."

Madison and I were studying in the Main Library, which was super crowded because it was right before finals week. Madison had arrived early and had secured a study room hours ago, so we had some privacy. But just outside our door, every study carrel in sight was occupied. There were even students sitting on the floor studying, leaning against the walls. It was this crowded on every floor of the library.

"I thought you were acing Sosh?" Madison said sympathetically.

"That's because the last time we talked was like the beginning of the quarter." Madison and I had barely hung out since I'd dropped my Accounting classes. "I've been tracking my grade all quarter and it's hovering on the edge of the toilet bowl, about to fall in. If I don't get a hundred on my Sosh final, you can flush my ass goodbye."

"I know what your problem is," Madison said confidently.

"What?"

"Christos has made you cum dumb," she said matter of factly, "making it impossible for you to concentrate on anything other than his cock."

"What?" I scoffed. "Are you totes cray cray?"

"Easy on the cray cray, Sam Sam. I told you we have to stop talking like thirteen year olds because it's totes inappropes," she grinned.

"So what if I like talking like a thirteen year old? I think it's totes adorb," I giggled. "You're just totes jelly that I know more totisms than you."

"That's totes fa' shotes," she grinned, then shook her head. "Now you're making me do it!" she laughed. "Stop!"

"Don't be totes ridics, I'll never stop. I'm the totestess with the motestess."

Madison groaned. "Oh my god, that is awful! You really are cum dumb!"

"Maybe dumb, but not because of too much cum."

"What, aren't you and Christos doing it every day?" Madison asked doubtfully.

I blushed like a beacon. "Mads! Must you be so blunt?"

"I'm trying to get to the bottom of things. Where all the cum is!"

I frowned, "What, like anal?"

Madison leaned back in her chair and laughed melodiously.

I threw my highlighter at her. "Shut up! You're a total horn dog tonight! Hasn't Jake been taking care of your business?"

Madison grinned, "Oh, he totes has been taking care of my business," she winked. "I swear, all I can think about is sex! More and more sex! Sex, sex, SEX!! I admit it! Jake has made ME cum dumb!"

We broke into a giggle fit. I noticed people were staring at us through the windowed walls of our study room, but I didn't care. It felt good to release some of my stress. I leaned back in my chair and sighed after our laugh attack passed.

"Was it good for you?" Madison asked.

"What, my laughgasm?"

"Yeah," she smiled.

"Totes magotes," I sighed.

Madison groaned and threw my highlighter back at me. It bounced onto the floor.

"Did I tell you my parents aren't helping pay for my tuition anymore?" I asked, staring at the ceiling, "And I can't get any more loan money to make up the difference?"

"You can work for me and Jake at the surf shop," Madison said.

"Really?"

"When it finally opens," she sighed.

"Oh. When's that gonna be?"

"I'm working on it. Not for awhile. But I totally promise, you'll be our first employee. When we take the company public, you'll be a millionaire overnight."

"Thanks, Mads. But I need money sooner."

"There's always stripping," she said casually.

"That's totes forbodst. There's no way I'm taking my clothes off for a bunch of drunken fraternity mouth breathers, or whoever goes to those places."

"I think it's usually serial killers and guys that smell."

"Do serial killers and guys that smell get along?" I mused. "Or do they hate each other and stick to opposite sides of the strip joint?"

"I think the strip joint separates them into two sections with a smell proof barrier between them."

"Would I get to pick which side I stripped on?"

"Probably not. I think it goes by seniority."

"With my luck, I'd be stuck in the stank tank," I grumbled.

"Wait, are you saying that you'd prefer being cooped up with a bunch of odor donors over stripping for smell-free serial killers?"

"Wouldn't you?" I protested. "I don't want to be killed by my clientele."

"After being locked up in the smell cell for an eight hour shift, you'd be begging for murder," Madison laughed. "I know I would."

"I'd wear a gas mask! Problem solved," I grinned.

"Nobody wants to watch strippers with gas masks," Madison chuckled dubiously.

"Come on," I insisted, "guys don't go to strip joints to admire the strippers' beautiful eyes."

"You might be right about that," Madison said.

"Totes mascrotes," I giggled.

"Stop!" she begged. "I think my brain is officially overdosed on totes quotes. Maybe we should take a study break?"

"I totes concotes."

Madison leaned over and threatened to smack me in the face.

"Okay!" I pleaded, "No more totes!"

We left our stuff in the study room and took the elevator to the ground floor and walked outside.

"Mads, do you want to go get coffee at Totested Rotes?" I quipped.

"Did you just say Totested Rotes?" Madison growled.

I started running before she could catch me and pummel my ass.

She chased me all the way to the Student Center. We laughed the entire time.

===

My blank blue book stared up at me, challenging me to write something that wasn't inane.

It was finals week.

Grrr.

I was sitting in the crowded lecture hall for my American History 2 final. I had to write several essay answers to various questions about 19th century America in the span of three hours. Timed essays? Whose idea was that? What happened to multiple choice? Groan!

The one nice thing about blue book exams was all the extra space for doodling. Did I get extra credit for drawing a picture of Abraham Lincoln? Probably not.

I scanned through the list of questions. Which one to attack first?

Discuss the War of 1812 and its economic consequences. I could barely remember what happened in 2012. How was I supposed to write about what happened in 1812?

Discuss the instigating factors and the political aftermath of the Mexico-American War. Didn't it start over drug trafficking? No? Well, I was pretty sure after the war was over, the U.S. got to keep New Mexico, but the Mexicans got to keep Old Mexico. That was enough of an answer, right? Maybe not.

There was one question I was happy to answer. It was about the James Gang, as in Jesse James. A real American outlaw. I remembered the photo of Jesse James in our readings about his gang. I was not surprised to discover that he was quite handsome. If they'd made a movie version about Jesse James back in the old days, he could've played himself. I'd wondered if he had tattoos beneath his cowboy outlaw garb. I knew one thing for sure, if he'd been alive today, he would've ridden a motorcycle.

I did my best to b.s. my way through the exam questions for over two hours before I finally gave up.

I trudged down to the bottom of the lecture hall and dropped my blue book on the pile of finished exams already on the table, then I trudged back up the stairs.

Justin Tomlinson was waiting for me outside the lecture hall. As always, he appeared fresh from a boy band music video, or like he had just finished hosting Saturday Night Live. Justin flashed his matinee idol smile at me. "How'd you do?" he asked.

I slumped my shoulders as I walked toward him and rolled my

eyes. "Kill me now," I groaned. "The T.A.'s will recognize my blue book because it'll be the one with all the flies buzzing around it due to all my stinky b.s. answers."

He chuckled, "That good?"

I sighed, "How'd you do?"

"It went pretty good, but I can't say for sure until grades come out."

I think he was trying to be supportive. He'd probably aced it. I said, "I don't know about you, but I'm desperately in need of caffeine before my next final. Do you want to get some coffee at Toasted Roast?"

"Sure," he smiled.

We walked toward the Student Center together and chatted the entire way. Ever since Justin had first approached me in History class, I couldn't decide if he was being flirty or not. Unlike Hunter Blakeley, whose flirtations were as subtle as Britney Spears climbing out of a limousine in a short skirt, Justin was hard to read. Whatever. I wasn't going to worry about it. If Justin was interested in me beyond my art contributions to The Wombat, he wasn't letting it show or get in the way, which I totally appreciated. If it became a problem, I'd deal with it then.

"Have you guys voted about which drawing to pick for Potty the Pot Smoking Wombat?" I asked.

"Not yet. I think people were too busy studying for finals. I want to give everyone a chance to submit their own drawings before the vote."

"That's cool," I said, hiding my disappointment.

I was really hoping one of my drawings would get picked because I was pretty sure my final grade for History was going to suck donkey balls. When the grades for Winter Quarter came out next week, I was going to need some good news to offset the inevitable bad. Because, sooner or later, I would have to talk to my parents, as much as I loathed the idea.

It would be nice if I could show them some proof that my desire to become an artist wasn't completely idiotic.

On second thought, I don't know what I was worrying about. It wasn't like my parents could do anything more than they already had to make my life miserable.

Chapter 13

SAMANTHA

"Spring Break!" Romeo, Kamiko, Madison and myself all squealed as we clinked wine glasses together. We stood on the backyard deck at the Manos Mansion. I had invited them all over for a house warming party. The weather was perfect for it. San Diego was having a heat wave. It was seventy-two, the skies were blue, and only a few cotton candy clouds puffed above.

Wine splashed out of our glasses onto our naked toes. Madison and I were in bikinis, already working on our tans.

"Where's your swimsuit, Kamiko?" Madison asked.

"In my bag," she said bashfully. She wore boy shorts and an Adventure Time baby tee.

"You gotta get that rockin little body of yours tanned up," Madison said. "You look like you spent all winter inside studying."

Kamiko groaned, "I did spend all winter inside studying."

"And painting," Romeo added. He wore a black short sleeve tee and black jeans. I think it was his version of swimwear.

"That's right!" I smiled at Kamiko. "Are you still working on paintings for Brandon's Contemporary Artists Show?"

"You bet I am," Kamiko scowled. "I'm not letting that stupid Brandumb bring me down. I'm getting my art into his show even if it kills him."

"Him?" I asked.

"Yeah," Kamiko smiled mischievously, "if I don't get a painting into his show, I'm going to assassinate him with my ninja skills while he's sleeping."

"Does that mean you're going to seduce him into bed, then kill him?" Romeo asked.

"Ew," Kamiko grimaced, "why would anyone want to sleep with a jerk like Brandumb?"

"I often wonder the same thing," Christos said as he and Jake walked up to join us. Both of them had beers in their hands and wore nothing but low riding board shorts. Their rippled abs Veed down to the waistbands of their low riding swimsuits. They were a sixteen pack attack of muscled manliness.

Romeo openly ogled Christos and Jake. "I just came in my pants," he said casually.

Christos rolled his eyes and smiled wide while giving Romeo a good natured fist bump.

"Ew!" Kamiko grimaced. "TMI, Romeo!"

"Admit it, Kamiko," Romeo goaded, "the second you have a moment alone and your fingers are free to roam, the first thing on your mind will be a slow motion replay of Christos and Jake walking up with their abs flexing. I know that's what I'll be thinking about."

"Dude," Jake joked, "if you keep talking like that, I'm going to put my shirt back on. I totally hate being treated like a sex object."

"Yeah, right!" Madison said. "I don't think I've ever seen you wearing a shirt except at my parents' Thanksgiving!"

"True," Jake smiled thoughtfully.

"And you had to borrow that one!" Madison continued. "Do you even own any shirts?"

"Nope," Jake grinned. "I never need 'em when all I do is surf."

"You give surf bums a bad name," Madison smiled at him.

Jake wrapped his arm around Madison, "And you love it."

Madison rolled her eyes at me and said, "Men. What would they do without their precious egos?"

"Hey, Madison," Romeo said, "if you get tired of Jake, let me know."

"Back off, buddy," Madison grinned. "He's all mine."

"Women," Jake quipped to Christos, "what would they do without our precious egos?"

"I'll drink to that," Christos said as he clinked beers with Jake.

"Romeos," Romeo said, "what would you all do without me?"

Everyone chuckled as we toasted again.

"Spring break!" Madison squealed.

"Spring break!!!!" everyone else shouted.

===

Shish kebabs sizzled on the grill as Spiridon turned everything over. "Meat's ready," he said, "come and grab a plate."

We all lined up and Spiridon served everyone.

Christos was busy putting out more pita bread to go with the fresh hummus he'd made. I noticed he had yet another fresh beer in his hand and was already buzzed. Oh well. It was Saturday. He could enjoy himself for the weekend. His paintings for Brandon could wait until Monday.

Once we all had plates full of food, we sat down at a table under a big sun umbrella and Spiridon joined us.

"Wow," Kamiko smiled, licking her fingers which were sticky from eating the juicy shish-kebab, "This is so yummy!"

"Thanks," Spiridon said. "There's more if you want it."

Romeo leaned into me and whispered, "Is Spiridon single? Because I've always had a thing for hot older men. If Christos looks that good in forty years, you'll never leave the bedroom. I know I wouldn't."

I chuckled and shook my head. "Geez, Romeo. You have a one track mind."

"What?" Romeo said defensively. "He's hot!"

"He's not gay. Even if he was, I wouldn't want you dating my boyfriend's grandfather."

"Oh, pish posh. We could totally double date."

I shook my head, "Eat your lunch, Romeo."

After lunch, we all jumped in the pool. Except for Romeo and Kamiko. There was a small diving board at the deep end, so I dove off and swam to the other end of the pool in one breath. Blue green glimmers danced across the bottom of the pool as I breast stroked my way to the far wall. I still kept up my running regularly, and the pool wasn't olympic sized, so it wasn't too hard to swim it in one breath. But I was totally ready for air when my head popped out of the water at the end.

"Look at you, Aqua Girl," Kamiko smiled.

"You should put your suit on, Kamiko," I encouraged.

"I don't want to leave Romeo alone," she smiled. In a low voice, she said, "he keeps staring at Christos' grandfather like he's going to eat him."

"I think Spiridon can protect himself. You should get in the pool."

"Maybe later," she smiled.

Christos and Jake took turns doing flips off the diving board. I think their goal was to splash as much water on me and Madison as possible. We moved to the far end of the pool and cheered them on.

Romeo and Kamiko were also egging them on.

Christos climbed out of the pool after his last jump, water dripping down his tattooed muscled body, and strolled to the diving board, where Jake stood ready to dive.

"Show us what you've got," Christos said to him.

Jake took a few quick steps on the short spring board and launched himself forward as far as he could and landed in a cannonball. He made huge splash and water rained everywhere. When he rose out of the water he did that wet hair flip thing that made him look like he was filming a TV commercial for men's cologne.

Madison and I were leaning against the wall in the shallow end.

I nudged her and whispered, "Do you think Jake could be any hotter?"

"No," she smiled proudly.

I laughed. "You know, he's totally spoiled all other men for you."

"I know!" she grinned. "He better marry me or I'll end up a lonely spinster. No other man can hold a candle."

I winked at Madison, "Well, I can think of one man."

"Dude!" Christos shouted at Jake, "that was nothing! Check this shit out!" Christos hollered as he backed up a few steps on the deck behind the spring board. He sounded a little slurry from drinking.

"What's he doing?" I asked Madison, suddenly concerned.

She narrowed her eyes and turned to look at Christos. "I don't know."

"Christos?" I said. "Maybe you shouldn't—"

Before I could do anything, Christos ran toward the board and leapt onto it, continuing to accelerate. He hopped and landed on the front edge of the board. For a second, I feared he would slip right off and hurt himself. But he didn't. The board bowed under his weight and he was flung high into the air at an angle. Instead of heading toward the middle of the pool, he was sailing diagonally toward the cement side. Everything that happened next happened in slow motion. His body turned languorously in a forward flip. But he was going too slow to get his feet back under him. His head was aiming right at the side of the pool. Oh my god, he looked like he was going to hit it head first.

Ohmygodohmygodohmygod—

My heart jumped into my throat and my eyes popped out of my head.

CRACK!!

At the last second, Christos' back flopped onto the surface of the water, making that sickening slapping sound you hear when someone does the most painful belly flop of all time, except on his back. He had missed the cement side by inches, yet he still sank slowly into the water.

Kamiko gasped, "Oh no..."

Was Christos okay? I didn't know. I swam toward him as fast as I could to check.

The backyard had gone suddenly silent.

Romeo stood up from his chair where he sat in the shade like he wanted to help somehow.

Jake had swum over to check on Christos too.

I was about to dive under the water to pull Christos out when he slowly rose to the surface head first, bubbling water out of his mouth. "Man," he laughed, "that fucking hurt."

"Are you okay?" I asked nervously.

"I'm fine," he smiled.

"What the fuck was that?" Jake asked.

"Did you miss it?" Christos quipped. "I can do it again if you did."

"No!" I shouted. "We don't need to see it again. Maybe we should be done with the diving board?"

"That sounds like a good idea," Madison said, now floating beside us.

We all climbed out of the pool and everyone stood around Christos. I think we were all still shaken.

"Are you okay, C-Man?" Romeo asked.

Christos nodded, "I'm good."

Spiridon had been inside and came walking out onto the deck. "Does anybody need anything?" He'd missed the whole thing.

"Maybe some towels?" I suggested.

Spiridon nodded and went inside. He returned with a stack of towels.

After toweling off, everyone laid out on the loungers in our damp swimsuits. Romeo and Kamiko sat under a sun umbrella around a circular glass table.

Ten minutes later, I think my heart was still doing a drum roll in my chest because of Christos' brush with disaster.

Christos stood up and stopped at the foot of my lounger. He asked, "You need another beer?"

I shook my head, "I'm good."

"Anybody else?" Christos asked the group.

"I'll take one," Jake said.

When Christos was gone, Madison leaned over to me and muttered, "Is it just me, or is Christos drinking too much today?"

"You noticed?" I winced.

"Yeah," she scoffed, "but I wasn't worried about it until his back flop. I don't remember him drinking this much before. Has something been bothering him?"

"I think he's just blowing off leftover steam from his trial."

"Oh," Madison said thoughtfully.

A few days after Christos' court case had been dismissed, I'd asked if he minded me telling Madison and the gang about it. He said he didn't care. So I'd given them a rundown of all the hair raising events over fish tacos a couple days later.

I said, "Do you think I should talk to him about his drinking?"

"Maybe you should," Madison said seriously.

I resolved to have a conversation with Christos about it tonight. In the meantime, I just needed to keep him out of the pool and off the diving board until he sobered up.

I eased back onto my lounger and closed my eyes, letting the warm sun wash over me. I should've been more relaxed, but something nagged at me, like I was missing some obvious looming threat that would inevitably injure Christos or take him away from me forever.

But I couldn't figure out what it was.

===

When people were ready for a shade break from tanning, Romeo and Kamiko asked Christos for a tour of his art studio, which neither of them had seen. Christos took everyone inside to check it out.

"Wow, Christos," Kamiko marveled, "these paintings are even

better than the ones you sold at your solo show at Charboneau."

"Thanks," Christos said casually, leaning against the nude portrait of Jacqueline, which he'd pulled out of the drying rack. I'd met Jacqueline several times while Christos was painting her. She was nice.

I felt better now that Christos was far from the pool. There wasn't anything he could really hurt himself on inside the studio. But I kept a close eye on him, just in case. I didn't want him knocking over an easel by accident and ruining a painting or something.

"Yeah, Christos," Romeo said, "these new paintings are awesome."

Christos frowned seriously, "Even better than my painting of Tiffany with the mustache you added?"

Romeo laughed nervously. "Your painting of her was awesome, but you have to admit, the mustache made her look way better."

The anger melted from Christos' face and he smiled at Romeo, "Yeah, totally."

Romeo heaved a sigh of relief. I think he still felt guilty about triggering Tiffany's tirade on New Year's Eve.

Madison rolled her eyes. "Tiffany was totally lameballs that night."

I had to agree. What a trip that had been on Tiffany's yacht. If I never saw that hot air ho-bag Tiffany again, it would be too soon.

Christos clinked his fresh beer against Romeo's glass of wine, then gulped down several swallows.

I sighed to myself. How much was Christos going to drink? I'd resolved that as long as he wasn't driving or diving, I wasn't going to stop him. He was over twenty one. He could drink all he wanted. If he ended up passed out on a couch, so much the better. I wouldn't have to worry about him breaking his neck. All I'd have to do was make sure he didn't drown in puke.

Christos pushed the painting of Jacqueline back into the drying rack. Then he tried to pull out another one, but it seemed stuck.

I think the real problem was that Christos was too fumbly drunk to manage it himself.

"Let me help," I said, stepping forward.

"I've got it," he said, wrestling with it. Suddenly, it popped out of the drying rack. Because of how he'd been standing, he stumbled backward and threw his hands out to keep his balance, causing him to release the painting, which started tipping forward. At the same time, Christos bumped heavily into the table behind him which was covered with painting supplies. The table rocked and a glass jar sitting on the corner containing a bunch of brushes fell to the floor and shattered on the concrete. Wooden brushes clattered and danced.

I was laser focused on stopping the falling painting. I clenched my teeth, and lunged for it, but Kamiko was in the way, and I would've had to put my foot right through the middle of the canvas to reach the falling edge because it was so tall. There was nothing I could do to stop it.

I was expecting the worst, but the painting acted like a big sail. It was so light, it caught enough air to cushion its fall. It landed softly on the floor of the studio. Phew. Disaster averted.

"Whoops," Christos slurred.

Romeo quickly bent to pick up the painting, a concerned look on his face.

"Don't worry, it's dry," Christos reassured from where he now sat on the floor. I could tell he felt a bit stupid for his drunken clumsiness.

I helped Christos to his feet and he dusted off his ass.

"I'll get a broom," he said.

I squatted and started picking up paint brushes.

"Be careful of the glass," Madison said.

Christos returned with a hand broom and dust pan, "I've got it." He squatted and swept up the mess.

Trying to defuse the awkwardness of the situation, Kamiko said, "Err, ah, who are all the women in the paintings, Christos? They're all so beautiful."

"Brandon hired them," Christos said as he shook the last of the glass out of the dustpan and into a wastebasket. "They're all kind of bland, don't you think?"

"Totally," Romeo joked, also trying to lighten the mood. "Maybe you could paint some hot muscled guys with big dicks?"

"Dicks and fine art don't go together," Christos chuckled.

"That is so sexist," Romeo growled. "I want more dicks in fine art! Dicks, dicks, dicks! I want to see them exploding all over the place like fire hoses!" Romeo was trying his hardest to make people laugh, but it wasn't working. Discomfort still filled the air.

Kamiko said, "So, Christos, how many paintings do you still have to do for your upcoming show?"

"I don't know," he dismissed, "a bunch."

"Who else are you going to paint?" Madison asked.

"More of Brandon's models," Christos said apathetically.

"Why don't you paint Samantha?" Madison suggested.

"Because Brandon wants nudes. That's what sells," Christos said.

"I'll pose nude for you," Romeo said enthusiastically.

"Who would buy a nude painting of you?" Kamiko asked.

"I would!" he said. "I'd pay a million bucks for a painting of me."

"Do you have a million dollars?" Kamiko asked.

"No," he sighed.

"Exactly," Kamiko frowned.

"Christos, I think you should paint Romeo," I winked at Romeo. "He is super sexy. But with clothes on. That's when he's at his sexiest."

"Thank you, Sam," Romeo smiled at me, then glared spears and arrows at Kamiko. "At least someone around here has good taste," he hissed.

Kamiko rolled her eyes.

Christos laughed, "I'll keep it in mind, Romeo."

At least no one was making a big deal out of how drunk Christos was.

===

A dog barked softly somewhere outside our bedroom the next morning. The winter sun was up, brightening the bedroom.

"Somebody shut that fucking dog up," Christos moaned. "It sounds like it's barking inside my head." He slid his head under his pillow and pulled it tightly around his ears.

"Do you need some water?" I asked.

He peaked out from under the pillow. "Can you add some vodka to it?"

"No. The bar is closed. I'll get you some cold water from the fridge." I threw on my robe and padded downstairs to the kitchen. When I returned with the glass, Christos was sprawled out in bed face up with the pillow over his face, the blanket pushed down to his waist, revealing his rippled abs.

I considered resting the cold glass on his stomach, but that would be cruel. I sat next to him and rested my hand on his abs instead. Yum. Even hungover, he was ten times sexier than mortal men.

He sat up and drank the water thirstily.

"Thanks," he sighed. "I could use five more of those."

"Do you want me to get the pitcher for you?"

"No, thanks, I can get it. I might have to crawl, but I can do it," he grinned.

"Christos, is everything okay?"

He blinked and looked at me seriously. "What do you mean?"

"Uh, um, you've kind of been drinking a lot lately."

Christos' brows drew together in a frown.

I winced, expecting an argument. Memories of short fused Damian Wolfram gnawed at the edges of my awareness. I reminded myself that Christos wasn't a hothead. He might be drinking more than he should, but never once had he raised his voice at me, or shown a single sign of anger. That was one thing I loved about Christos. He never seemed to get angry. He knew how to handle his emotions like an adult. I hoped this discussion wouldn't be the exception.

"Yeah," he sighed and laid his forearm across his eyes.

"Do you want to talk about it?"

"Maybe later?"

At least he didn't get angry at me for bringing it up. Maybe I should've waited until he wasn't hung over.

"Do you want some breakfast?" I asked.

"Sure."

"How about I make you breakfast in bed? You're always doing all the cooking anyway."

He lifted his forearm off his face and smiled at me with his dimples and brilliant blue eyes. "Sounds awesome."

"Eggs and toast?" I suggested.

"Perfect," he said sleepily.

"You wait here, and I'll be back in a jiffy."

I went down to the kitchen and made breakfast for both of us. When I brought it upstairs on a tray, Christos was fast asleep.

I didn't have the heart to wake him.

===

When Monday morning rolled around, I woke up to an empty bed. I threw on a robe and went downstairs to find Christos. I heard slashing and rattling noises as I approached the studio.

I leaned my head through the door to the studio, afraid of what I might find.

Christos stood behind the big canvas of Isabella, practically attacking it by throwing big gobs of paint at it with a loaded brush.

"What are you doing?" I asked tentatively.

Between slapping paint on the canvas, Christos said, "Getting the canvas..." WHACK! "...ready for Isabella..." SPLAT! "She's going to be here..." GLOP!" "...at ten."

I walked around behind Christos and the canvas. The painting of Isabella was almost entirely covered in wet brown paint. The only part that wasn't covered was the face. "Oh my god, Christos," I gasped, "what did you do to your painting?"

Now he was working the blobs of paint into the canvas with a big brush. "It needed some work..." SMEAR! "...a lot of work." SCRUB! "I'm going to change..." RUB! RUB! RUB! "...the pose." He took a step back from the canvas to assess it.

"But it was almost finished," I said, feeling an overwhelming sense of defeat. He had put a tremendous amount of work into this painting. It had looked amazing to me before. Now it seemed, I don't know, ruined. "You're starting over?"

"Yeah."

"Why? It was beautiful. Kamiko and Romeo and Madison and Jake all thought it was amazing. I thought it was amazing."

He grimaced, "It wasn't working."

I sighed. Oh well. I wasn't the one who'd sold hundreds of thousands of dollars worth of paintings. I trusted that Christos knew what he was doing. Besides, it was too late to do anything about it now. He really did have to start over, no matter how far it put him behind on his deadline.

Since I had the week off and Christos had to work, I decided to spend the day in the studio with him. When Isabella arrived and they went to work, I sat down at my drawing table to work on some cartoons for The Wombat based on ideas Romeo and I had discussed.

Isabella got undressed and Christos had her sit in a variety of different poses until he found one he liked. They all looked good to me, but based on Christos' brooding demeanor, I could tell he wasn't happy with any of them.

Once he started painting, he sighed audibly at least once every five minutes. He wasn't enjoying himself. Too bad the weather was so nice outside. It was the perfect day to get out of the house and take a road trip or do something relaxing in San Diego. There were a hundred options of fun things to do in town, but Christos needed to work. He didn't need to add more stress by losing another work day today.

So I sat quietly at my drawing table and worked. If Christos had to work today, I would too.

After painting Isabella for half an hour, they took a break. Christos walked into the living room and returned with a glass of bourbon and the bottle. When he went back to work, it seemed like every time I looked over, he was taking another swallow of liquor. I couldn't decide if the bourbon was helping his mood or making it worse.

I contemplated finding Spiridon and asking him if he could throw away all his booze or at least hide it until after Christos' gallery show. Too bad that wouldn't actually solve anything.

Around one o'clock, I was ready for a break. I set down my pencil and closed my sketchbook. "Does anybody want a sandwich or something?" I asked, standing behind Christos.

Christos laid down his brushes like they weighed a ton each. "Sure," he mumbled, sounding exhausted. I knew it was the stress.

"May I break, Christos?" Isabella asked demurely in her Portuguese accent.

"Sure," he huffed dismissively and walked through the French doors to the back deck.

"Isabella," I asked, "do you want a sandwich?"

"Please," she smiled.

It wasn't at all weird to me anymore that Isabella sat naked in front of my boyfriend on a regular basis. The jealousy I'd felt the first time I'd been in the room with Christos painting her nude had shrunk to almost nothing. It helped that she seemed to have lost interest in him, which was odd because before she'd been all over him. Maybe she had met a cute guy of her own. "I'll go make those sandwiches," I said. "Care to join me in the kitchen?"

She followed me and we chatted while I pulled ingredients out of the refrigerator.

"Have a seat," I said, motioning to the chairs at the kitchen table.

"Oh, no sitting. I sitting all day. Now I stand," she smiled. "Standing good."

"How's the modeling up in Los Angeles?"

"L.A. is good. I busy, all the time busy."

"That's good," I smiled as I pulled a loaf of sourdough out of its paper sack and sliced off several pieces with a bread knife. "I imagine you're making good money?"

"Very good. Also nice to work here with Christos. No cameras. He make me perfect without the Photoshop."

"Yeah," I grinned. "Christos is an amazing painter."

"I thought I heard you in here," Spiridon said as he walked into the kitchen.

"Do you want a sandwich?" I asked him.

"Please," he smiled. "Isabella, can I get you anything to drink?"

"Agua, por favor?" she said. "Oh, uh, I mean the water, please?"

"We have plenty of água," he winked at her as he pulled out the pitcher from the fridge.

A loud crash echoed in from the studio.

I jumped where I stood at the counter, "What was that?"

"I don't know," Spiridon said, setting the pitcher down. "I'll go look."

There was another crash.

"Fuck!" Christos shouted.

Was he hurt? I dropped the knife I'd been using to slice a tomato and ran past Spiridon into the studio.

Christos held the painting of Isabella over his head.

"Christos! What are you doing?" I gasped.

He smashed the painting into the cement floor, splintering one corner of the wood frame. Then he bent over, grabbed the broken pieces of the frame, and tore the canvas halfway down the middle.

"Stop, Christos!" I pleaded.

"I can't stand this piece of shit!" He snatched the broken painting off the floor, barged past me and stomped through the house to the front door, which he ripped open. I was surprised he didn't yank the door off the hinges, he pulled so hard.

With a growl, he threw the floppy remains of the ruined painting out into the entryway. He shouted a primal roar and chased after it, kicking at the heaped ruin of the broken canvas.

I jogged up behind him, "Christos, stop! This is insane."

"No, it's a PIECE OF FUCKING SHIT!!!" He clutched one corner of the remains of the painting in both hands and beat it against the driveway like a rug. With each swing, he shouted, "PIECE! OF! FUCKING! SHIT!!!"

I backed off. He was in a rage, There was no point in trying to stop him. I couldn't even if I'd wanted to. Christos was ten times bigger and stronger than me.

Christos continued beating his painting to death. I noticed Spiridon and Isabella standing behind me. Spiridon had a pained, sad look on his face. Isabella's eyes were popping out of their sockets.

A car I didn't recognize turned down the driveway and drove toward us while Christos pulverized the last shreds of the painting.

Christos was yelling, totally oblivious.

The glare from the sky overhead made it impossible to see who was in the car.

Christos bundled up the wad of torn canvas and the shattered wooden frame. He threw everything over the roof of the garage with a final primal roar. "PIECE OF FUCKING SHIIIIIIT!!!"

The car doors of the random sedan opened and two occupants stepped out.

"Sam?" my mom asked nervously, "is everything okay?"

Oh, fuck, no fucking way.

"Are you all right, Sam?" my dad asked.

Christos stormed back into the house, shouting "GOD DAMN USELESS MOTHER FUCKING PIECE OF SHIT PAINTING!!!"

I stared at my parents.

My fucking parents.

How the hell did they find me in San Diego?

Maybe I should've checked that voicemail they'd left weeks ago.

Chapter 14

SAMANTHA

Spiridon walked into the living room from the kitchen and handed a glass of fresh squeezed lemonade to my mom. She sat next to my dad on the couch in the Manos' living room. I sat on the leather chair opposite them.

"Thank you, uh...Spiridon?" my mom said, taking the glass from him. She hadn't gotten used to his name. I could imagine her thinking it sounded hippie dippie. Whatever.

"This is good lemonade," my dad said after taking another swallow.

"Thank you," Spiridon smiled. "There's plenty more. A warm day like today is perfect for it."

I never imagined my parents inside this house. Ever. It felt wrong, like my privacy was being invaded in the worst way possible, like my hope for a new life was being undermined by their presence. I wished they would go. Like, now. I beamed ESP suggestions to my mom:

you left the stove on

Dad left the back door unlocked

your pipes will freeze and burst because you didn't leave the faucets on a slow drip

GO THE FUCK HOME!!!

Nothing worked. Oh well. Maybe I should just tell them to leave? I could say, "Mom, Dad, you guys are such big jerks, I was thinking you could turn around and fly back to D.C., okay? It's only a six hour flight." Yeah, maybe not. I sighed to myself, fresh out of ideas.

"How are you two enjoying the warm weather?" Spiridon asked. "I bet it's not this warm in Washington D.C."

My mom smiled her office ass kissing smile, "I was just telling

Bill on the drive over that the weather is so nice, maybe we should move here."

My eyes bulged out of my head. No, please no. I buried my chin in my chest, hoping to hide my expression.

Dad said, "It was a smart move for you to choose San Diego, Sam."

I nodded in mundane horror as my lips peeled back over my clenched teeth.

My mom chuckled fakely, "You never told us San Diego was so nice, Sam."

Maybe because you never asked? Duh. All my parents cared about was whether or not I was taking all my Accounting classes in the right order and getting A's. The weather? Irrelevant. My desire to become an artist? Irrelevant. My wonderful boyfriend? Irrelevant. My parents were in total denial.

"If you had," my mom grinned, "we would've come to visit sooner," she chuckled.

Yeah, because me and my mom were totally besties. Was she insane? I was waiting for Rod Serling to walk out from behind a piece of furniture and welcome us all to the Twilight Zone.

I searched around the armrests of my chair for one of those James Bond control panels. I was hoping there were ejector seats beneath my parents so I could shoot them through the ceiling. Or maybe trapdoors that dropped down to a dungeon filled with ravenous grizzly bears or a shark tank. I hadn't yet found that control panel, but the leather chair had rivets on the front of the armrest, so I began meticulously pressing every single one. I was sure one of them was the trapdoor button.

"Sam, what are you doing?" my mom scoffed.

"Nothing," I said defensively as I folded my hands in my lap. Sadly, I don't think any of the rivets were switches.

Mom turned to Spiridon and chuckled, "Sam always was fidgety."

Dad joined in with the good times. "I remember when Sam was a baby, she always wanted to play with my old adding machine. Once I showed her how to make the paper tape spool out by adding numbers together, she couldn't get enough of it. She'd play with that adding machine until she'd used up the entire roll of tape. It was then that I realized my daughter's love for numbers. Just like her father."

I rolled my eyes. Was he serious? My dad was so oblivious. I don't think he realized that adding machine had been far more responsive to me than he ever had. I was now convinced the stork had dropped my baby basket off at the wrong house nineteen years ago. Maybe my real parents were wizards like Harry Potter's mum and dad. I rubbed my scalp, hoping to find a lightning bolt scar hidden there. Nope.

"Are you okay, Sam?" Mom frown-smiled. "Have you been using your dandruff shampoo?"

"I'm fine, Mom," I groaned. Where was my magic wand? Oh yeah, Christos had taken it with him when he went for a walk earlier. Yes, the wand in his pants. I repressed a secret smile.

"What's so funny?" Dad asked.

I needed to take some spy classes so I could learn to make my secret smiles more secret. "Nothing," I groaned.

"Where did Christos go?" my mom asked.

"I think he went for a walk," Spiridon said. "He'll be back sooner or later."

Christos had stormed past my parents after they'd arrived without saying hello, and gone out the driveway to who knew where. I couldn't blame him. I wasn't happy to see my parents either. It was for the best. My parents had been in shock for at least a half an hour after watching Christos murder his painting.

Wanting to change the subject away from Christos and his outrage, I said, "So, how'd you guys find the house?" I'd never told them the Manos' address.

"That was easy," my dad said. "We called the manager at your apartment and asked him for your forwarding address. Since we're your parents, and we co-signed your lease, he was happy to oblige."

Great. Thanks, Mr. Manager. What a great guy he was. Traitor.

"You're not staying at *Samoula's* apartment, are you?" Spiridon asked.

"Who?" my dad frowned.

"I'm sorry," Spiridon smiled. "*Samoula* is a nickname I use for your daughter. It's a common thing in Greek families to nickname everyone."

Mom grimaced. I don't think she liked the idea that I had a

nickname, like Spiridon was taking some sort of parental ownership of me. "We call her Sam," she insisted.

Spiridon nodded, "That's wonderful."

Did that mean he was going to stop calling me Samoula? I hoped not. I liked my nickname. Maybe he'd use it after my parents left.

"At any rate," Spiridon continued, "where are you two staying?"

"We're staying at the Motel 6 in Hotel Circle," my dad answered.

"What? That's half way across the city!" Spiridon laughed. "You can't stay there."

"The price was unbeatable," Dad said nervously, "and I found a coupon online—"

Spiridon cut him off with a dismissive grin. "You can't stay in a hotel. You're family and we have plenty of room here in my house. I won't have you and your wife staying in some rundown no tell hotel. I hear that place rents rooms by the hour." Spiridon chuckled.

No tell hotel? Since when did Spiridon start dishing out the jokes? I kind of liked it. He got awesomer every time I hung around him.

"Oh, no," my dad corrected Spiridon, missing the humor completely, "I assure you, Motel 6 doesn't rent rooms by the hour."

"Are you sure, Dad?" I said dryly. "This is San Diego. We do things differently on the west coast."

My dad frowned and shook his head. "Motel 6 doesn't rent rooms by the hour. I know better." He glanced at Spiridon, as if seeking agreement.

I arched a doubting eyebrow at Dad. "You're sure?"

"Yes, I'm sure," he insisted, "Motel 6 is not a flophouse." I could tell he was starting to get angry.

Whatever.

"I don't care if you have a suite at the Hotel Del," Spiridon said. "You are *Samoula's* parents and you can stay here with us." He winked at my dad, "And we have the cheapest rates in town."

My dad perked up at that and turned to Mom. "What do you think, Linda? We could save several hundred dollars if we stay here."

"I don't know, Bill," she said skeptically, "we've already checked in and I unpacked my bags."

"It'll only take a minute to cancel the rest of our stay and pack your bags," my dad said.

Rest of their stay? Geez, how long did my parents plan to be here? Despite the earlier failure of my ESP, I tried again. I stared at my mom.

Say no, say no, say NO, SAY NO!!!!!

Mom sighed and threw her hands up in defeat, "Fine."

Wow, my ESP had backfired. I needed some ESP lessons ASAP.

"It's settled then," Dad said. "I'll call the motel and let them know we won't be needing the room after tonight. Spiridon, may I use your phone?"

As always, in my parents' world, cell phones didn't exist.

"Of course," Spiridon smiled, "it's in the kitchen." Spiridon led the way for my dad.

I restrained a groan. Why did Spiridon have to go and invite my parents to stay? Yeah, I knew Spiridon was all about family. I was too, just not my family.

With Spiridon and my dad out of the living room, it was just me and my mom sitting alone together. I couldn't have been happier. I started pressing the rivets on the leather chair again, looking for the one that triggered an escape hatch under my ass so I could get the hell out of here.

My mom was pinching the bridge of her nose with her eyes closed. I knew this routine of hers well. I'd seen it a hundred thousand times since I was a kid. After the nose bridge pinch would come the rubbing of her temples with her fingers. Then she'd slide her palms down her cheeks into a prayer position beneath her chin while she stared heavenward for guidance.

While her eyes were closed, I punched both my fists in her direction and flipped her off. I opened my mouth wide and silently screamed, "Go the fuck HOOOME!!!" I'd already determined my ESP needed a little boost.

My mom suddenly stopped massaging her temples and her eyes popped open.

I instantly dropped my hands into my lap with a sheepish grin. Had she noticed? I couldn't tell for sure, but she didn't act like she had.

Mom closed her eyes and went back to rubbing her temples.

This was going to be a long Spring Break. Yeah, I'd always fantasized about spending my first ever college Spring Break with my parents.

Groanballs.

===

"Everything is taken care of," my dad said when he walked back into the living room almost an hour later. "I canceled our room at the Motel 6 after tonight. We can pick up our bags this evening."

Spiridon followed him into the room.

"I don't know, Bill," Mom said. "Are you sure you don't want to stay the night at the hotel since we already unpacked?"

Sounded like a great idea to me.

Dad smiled, "Spiridon was showing me the guest rooms upstairs. They're much nicer than the Motel 6. And the deck outside is better than the pool at the motel. We'll have plenty of privacy here."

Yay! But I wouldn't have any.

Were there any giant meteors in outer space hurtling toward San Diego? They couldn't get here soon enough.

"Plus," Dad continued with a big smile, "the price here can't be beat."

My mom huffed out a sigh. I knew she could only take so much of Dad's bargain hunting before she was sick of it. "Fine, Bill. Whatever you say."

The front door opened quietly and Christos walked into the living room. "Hey, everyone," he said softly.

I jumped out of my chair and ran to him to see if he was okay, but slowed halfway across the room because my parents were here. Their presence always, I don't know, restrained me. I stopped a foot away from Christos and didn't even touch him with my hand or anything. "Hey," I said.

"Sorry about the scene earlier," Christos smiled. "I was having a bit of a problem with one of my paintings."

Spiridon nodded sympathetically, "I've been there many times myself. Sometimes a painting goes south in the middle of the process and there's not much you can do with it short of starting over."

"You're an artist too?" My dad asked innocently.

"Yes," Spiridon said. "All of the paintings hanging in this room are mine."

It was weird, because there were literally dozens of them

surrounding us, and my parents hadn't said a word about them since they'd walked in. That just went to show how much my parents paid attention to art. It was nearly invisible to them. Just like my love of art. They had no idea it existed.

"There's a lot of paintings in here. Don't you ever sell them?" Dad asked.

"I do. As a matter of fact, I've sold over a thousand paintings in my career," Spiridon said.

"Is that how you paid for this house?" my dad asked.

Yeah, my dad was world renown for his social graces.

Spiridon smiled indulgently, "Yes. Everything you see in this house was paid for by the sale of my art."

Go, Spiridon! Tell it! This was exactly the kind of thing my parents needed to see and hear. An actual mansion, way bigger than my parents' house, bought and paid for by a real live art career.

"So why haven't you sold the paintings in this room?" Dad asked.

"I love them too much to part with them," Spiridon said thoughtfully. "Each one holds a special meaning for me. They're touchstones that remind me of moments in my life I never want to forget. I could never sell them, at any price."

"Oh," Dad said. He had no idea what Spiridon was talking about. Spiridon may as well have been speaking a foreign language when it came to talking about feelings with my dad.

"They're very nice," my mom said curtly. "You're a very gifted artist, Spiridon. I'm sure if our daughter could paint as well as you, she would sell paintings too."

Because I was turned away from her, my mom's words literally stabbed me right in my back. Fortunately my mom couldn't see my face burning with sudden rage and embarrassment. Had she seen my anger, she would've told me to get a hold of myself and stop acting like a child. I gave Christos a pleading look.

"You haven't seen any of Samantha's recent paintings," Christos said to my mom. "She's come a long way since I met her. Her artistic growth has been unreal. Your daughter is epically talented."

Take that, stupid Mom and Dad!

"She really is good," Spiridon said, walking over to me to rest his hand on my shoulder. "With my grandson tutoring her, she gets better every day." He flashed a smile at me, "Isn't that right, *Samoula*?"

Now I was blushing as tears of joy threatened to pour down my face. I nodded. The Manos men were defending me against my evil parents! I wanted to jump for joy. I wanted to happy dance all over my parents' faces while hungry sharks nipped at their toes. Yippee!

"You should see some of her paintings," Christos said.

The next thing I knew, we were all in the studio.

"This entire room is a painting studio?" my mom marveled. "It's as big as our house!"

My dad looked around, taking everything in. "I wouldn't say it's as big," he said defensively. "Perhaps two-thirds the square footage. Maybe less if you include our garage."

Yeah, whatever, Dad.

"And these are your paintings, Christos?" my mom asked.

"Yeah," he said casually.

I could tell Christos was still somewhat buzzed from all the bourbon he'd been drinking before my parents arrived. But now he was happy drunk, not angry drunk.

"You sure like to paint naked women," my mom scoffed judgmentally.

I couldn't take my parents anywhere.

"It's art, Mom," I said. "You know, like Rembrandt and Botticelli and Bouguereau."

"Who?" she frowned.

"William-Adolphe Bouguereau? The nineteenth century French realist?" I'd learned a thing or two about artists from hanging out at the Manos house all the time.

My mom shook her head. "I'm sorry, I don't know who you're talking about."

"He's really good. You should check out his work," I sneered. "One of Bouguereau's paintings is hanging in the San Diego Museum of Art in Balboa Park. It's awesome."

"Are any of your paintings hanging in the San Diego Museum of Art, Spiridon?" my dad asked snidely.

"Yes," he smiled, "in the permanent collection. As are two of my son Nikolos'. I imagine one day soon, one or more of my grandson's will join them," Spiridon said, patting Christos on the back. "And who knows, if she keeps at it, maybe one of *Samoula's* will end up there too."

I think I heard a shame plane fly over my parents' heads and start dropping suck it bombs all over them. Too bad the explosions weren't fatal. But the confused looks on my parents' faces made me rejoice.

Mom motioned at Christos' paintings as if they were garbage. "I assume all these nude women are actual people?"

"Yeah," Christos said.

Mom nodded, "Was that young woman who was here earlier one of the nude women you paint?" she asked acidly.

"Yeah," Christos said.

"And what," Mom continued, "she just takes her clothes off for you?"

Christos shrugged, "That's usually the way it works."

My mom huffed, as if Christos was forcing women like Isabella to strip for him while he watched with his pants around his ankles and did nasty things to himself. She said accusingly, "You know, you're setting the women's movement back thirty years."

"They're models, Mom," I said. "They get paid. It's a job."

"To take their clothes off?" she scoffed.

"Yes!" I growled.

My mom shook her head. "That's not art. That's pornography. I hope you would never consider debasing yourself by deigning to strip for Christos. I should hope I've taught you better than that."

I rolled my eyes. "Whatever, Mom."

There was a pregnant pause as the room went silent. I'm sure my mom would accuse Christos of getting the pause pregnant after having paid it to model for him naked. Dirty pause. Everyone knew the pause had no shame. Pause was a whore who had sex for money. I rolled my eyes. My mom was such a prude.

"You should show your mom and dad some of your drawings, Samantha," Spiridon encouraged.

Under any other circumstance, I would never have showed my art to my parents. Not after all those times in high school when they'd snarked about how bad my art was. But with Christos and Spiridon at my side showering me with supportive loving compliments, I felt like nothing too terribly bad could happen. I should've known better.

I walked over to my drawing table where my sketchbook sat.

"This is where I work," I said randomly as I picked up my sketchbook.

My mom put her hands on her hips. "It looks like you're all moved in, aren't you, Sam?"

Oh yeah, my parents and I hadn't yet had the discussion about my new living arrangements. I couldn't wait to discuss the topic further.

Maybe I would've talked to them about my move already if every conversation with them didn't turn into a minefield. I swear, I couldn't say a single wrong thing around my parents without triggering yet another one of their bullshit bombs. I needed more suck it bombs to defend myself. Too bad the shame plane was out of the area.

I clutched my sketchbook to my chest, suddenly reluctant to open it. I'm sure my parents were ready to lob insult bombs with abandon. Was there any point in showing them my art? Maybe I could change the subject.

"I haven't seen your newest work," Spiridon said. By newest, he meant the stuff I'd drawn in the last few days. Lately, he'd been asking to see my sketches on a daily basis. He always said nice things and offered me little pointers here and there.

Spiridon motioned with his hand, so I gave him my sketchbook, opened to the Wombat sketches I'd done recently. He blurted out laughter and Christos chuckled over his shoulder as they flipped through it.

"These are hilarious, *agápi mou*," Christos said.

"Your daughter has a definite talent for cartooning," Spiridon said before handing the sketchbook to my parents.

My mom took one look at my cartoons of Potty the Pot Smoking Wombat and grimaced as if someone had shown her crime scene photos of a beheading. She didn't say a word. She just nodded absently as my dad turned the pages.

My dad, on the other hand, surprised me. "Not bad," he said. "These drawings sort of remind me of Dennis the Menace, but not nearly as refined."

I had to pause. That was actually sort of a compliment. My dad loved Dennis the Menace. It was one of his favorite comic strips and he still read it daily.

"But I don't see how you can make any money with these," Dad finished. "Hank Ketcham has the Dennis the Menace market all locked up."

I think from now on, whenever I thought of the phrase, "thinking outside the box," I'd picture my dad literally building a wooden crate around himself with hammer and nails, and as he was about to lower the lid on his own head forever, he'd say "Bye bye, everybody. If you need me, I'll be inside my box. Where I live with all my thoughts. Which, by the way, are the only thoughts worth having." I'd gladly nail the lid shut for him. I glanced around Christos' studio for hammer and nails. Drat. I didn't see any.

Christos' phone rang, distracting everyone. He pulled it out of his pocket and examined it. "Excuse me," he said to everyone, "I need to take this call." He walked out of the studio.

"What could be so important he had to answer his phone while he's entertaining guests?" Mom muttered sourly, as if we couldn't hear what she was saying.

Because, yeah, this was totally entertaining. Maybe if your idea of fun was a weekend of water-boarding followed by hourly whippings.

Kill me now. Please.

===

CHRISTOS

I walked out the French doors of the studio to the back deck with my ringing phone in hand.

Russell Merriweather was calling.

Fantastic. I'd debated answering it in the studio and putting the phone on speaker so Samantha's parents could listen in. Yeah, right. I'm sure they'd want to hear all about the recent civil charges Hunter Fucking Blakeley had slapped on my ass. After her parents heard all the gory details, maybe I could get them up to speed about my recent criminal trial. Samantha's parents would totally love me after hearing about that shit.

When I was half way around the swimming pool and out of ear shot from the house, I answered. "What up, Russell?"

"Christos! How are you enjoying freedom, son?"

"Freedom rocks," I joked.

"Yes it does. I'm somewhat inclined to it myself." I could hear the smile in his voice. "The good news for you is, if you're smart, you can enjoy as much freedom as your heart desires. All you have to do is stay out of trouble. You think you can do that?"

"I can give it a shot," I chuckled.

"Don't shoot anything," he laughed, "just stay out of trouble. As in, no fighting. Feel me?"

"Yeah, yeah, yeah," I sighed.

"I'm serious, son. No fights. As in, none. Zero. Nada."

I shook my head and chuckled. "Man, you're as subtle as brass knuckles."

His voice turned humorous again. Russell was never long on lecturing. "I don't want you crying to me on the phone at three in the morning, waking my ass up to tell me that you're in the can again. I need my beauty rest," he laughed.

Russell always put me in a good mood. Not only was he a badass attorney, he was the nicest guy. "You know, you're pretty cool for an old dude," I said sarcastically.

"Watch your mouth," he said with good humor, "I can still whup your ass, young man."

"What, you trying to get me in more fights?"

"I won't press charges, so it's okay. And I will kick your ass into next year if I find out you've so much as given someone a dirty look."

"All right, all right," I smiled. "No fighting. So what's so pressing you had to call me so late in the day? Shouldn't you be relaxing behind a bloody steak at the Yard House by now?" I gazed at ruby clouds glowing in front of the golden sun hovering above the Pacific Ocean. My grandad's house had the best damn view.

"My dinner has been delayed because your pal Hunter Blakeley may have a valid claim against you, my boy. It turns out, he does in fact do a fair amount of modeling, and his broken nose has been costing him jobs."

I shook my head. I should've known Hunter was a total pussy. "What, does the prick want? A bunch of plastic surgery or some shit?"

"That's putting it lightly. He also wants lost wages and substantial pain and suffering. You should see the bills his attorney is sending me for the high class shrinks Hunter Blakeley has been visiting."

"Shrinks?" I rolled my eyes. "Why, because he has PTSD after the vicious beating I gave him?"

"You took the words right out of my mouth."

I sighed, "Do you have any good news?"

"I'm brimming over with good news," Russell joked, "I'm the Santa Claus of good news."

"Well?"

"I need the contact information of your friend Jake. I need to get his deposition and add it into the mix. Also, I've got people talking to the Hooters wait staff, see if they can corroborate your story that Hunter was in cahoots with three friends."

"Of course he was."

"Not according to his statement. He's making it sound like his friends watched the incident from a block away while you roughed up poor Hunter."

"Fuck. His buddies were ready to jump in until I put Hunter in his place. The guy is a total liar."

"A liar he may be, but if I can't prove he's whistling Dixie on the stand, the jury is going to have a hard time believing your side of things. Remember, this isn't a criminal trial, where the prosecution has to convince the jury beyond all reasonable doubt that you're guilty. This is a civil trial. If Hunter's attorney can convince the jury that it's 51% likely that you're at fault, instead of an even fifty-fifty, they will rule against you. That's not much elbow room for us. Even if I present the greatest defense of all time, Hunter's case need only be one percent more convincing than ours, and you're gonna end up having to pay damages. And right now, Hunter's attorney is asking for your left nut on top of all the other damages."

"Maybe we can send him my left nut and call it even," I grinned.

Russell chuckled, "Last time I checked, the nut market is in a recession, and you won't get a quarter of what you're hoping for."

"Fine. I keep my nut and you win my case. Deal?"

"I'll do my best. But I'd start looking into prosthetic testicles. I hear you can hardly tell the difference," Russell laughed.

"Thanks, man. You're all heart."

"Don't worry, son. I'll take care of this. I've got plenty of people looking into things. We'll track down Hunter's friends and drag the truth out of them with pliers and tongs."

"You do that."

"I'll have more good news the next time we talk," Russell said.

"Oh, and one other thing."

"Yeah?"

"No. More. Fights."

"I hear you loud and clear."

"Then my job is done. Now, I have a steak waiting for me with my name on it. I've got to run. Bye."

"Later, man." I ended the call. While I felt fortunate to have Russell watching my back, as always, his expert services weren't going to be cheap. At the rate things were going, I was going to run out of money before this case was over.

Too bad I'd destroyed that painting of Isabella. I could've gotten at least ten grand for it.

Whatever.

Stanford Wentworth had been right. That painting was a piece of shit. I wasn't going to lose sleep over it.

I walked inside to join everyone.

Maybe Samantha's parents could cheer me up.

Ha. Ha. Ha.

===

SAMANTHA

"Does anybody need a refill on their lemonade?" Spiridon asked.

Everyone, including Christos, was standing in the kitchen.

"I don't know about the rest of you," my dad said as he looked at his watch, "but with the three hour time difference, I'm starving. Are you ready to eat, Linda? Remember, we still need to stop by Motel 6 to get our luggage at some point."

My mom sighed heavily. "Sure."

She sounded so happy to be here. The feeling was mutual.

"Is there a Cheesecake Factory around here somewhere?" my dad asked.

Leave it to my parents to fly across the country and eat at the same chain restaurant they always went to back home. Their sense of adventure made Christopher Columbus look like a homebody. Not.

"Yeah," Christos said, "I think there's one near Hotel Circle."

"That's near our motel," my dad beamed. "We can kill two birds with one stone and get our luggage after dinner."

Dad could kill three birds with one stone if he smashed me over the head and put me out of my misery.

Then an idea hit me. "Why don't we invite my friends?" I suggested. "Then you can meet all the cool people I've met in San Diego!"

"I was thinking it would just be you, your mother, and I," Dad said soberly.

"I agree with your father," my mom said.

I knew what they were thinking. They wanted to corner me and berate me for being an idiot until I changed my major back to Accounting.

It wasn't going to happen.

"I'll text everybody right now," I said, undeterred. I invited Madison, Jake, Romeo, and Kamiko. I'd gotten Jake's contact info, as well as Spiridon's, after Christos' trial. I hated not being able to reach people in an emergency.

I briefly considered asking Christos to invite Tiffany Kingston-Whitehouse. I was pretty sure her and my mom would bond over their bitchery. In the end, I decided we could do without her. No surprise there.

I pressed send and crossed my fingers that everyone would be able to join us. If they all showed up, I'd be like the quarterback in a football game with all the offensive linemen protecting me from my parents. I wasn't going to let them blindside me. No way.

When we walked out to the driveway, my parents headed toward their rental car.

"Sam," my dad asked, "are you coming with your mother and I?"

"I think I'll ride with Christos and Spiridon," I said. Did I sound snarky? Only a little.

"Suit yourself," Mom said as she climbed into the car, which I noticed was a silver Honda sedan. Just like Dad's car back home. What a surprise. I'd have thought since he was on vacation, he'd go crazy and rent a red Honda. Nope.

"I think I feel like driving the Woody tonight," Spiridon said. The garage door was already open. "Do you mind, Christos?"

"Not at all," he said.

The three of us climbed into the classic car. Yeah, we were a million times cooler than my parents.

The engine of the 1949 Plymouth station wagon purred as it pulled out of the garage. Spiridon stopped the car beside my parents' Honda. My dad rolled the window down and Spiridon asked, "Do you know where we're going?"

"I'll follow you," Dad answered.

Didn't he know how to use the GPS? I'd seen it in their car earlier. Oh wait, we were talking about my dad. Of course not.

"Don't go too fast," my dad said nervously. "I adhere to the speed limit."

"Don't worry, Bill," Spiridon smiled, "I'll make sure you don't get lost."

I think Spiridon was being too optimistic. When it came to most things, my parents were already totally lost.

Chapter 15

SAMANTHA

"This sexy beast can only be your mother," Romeo said as he shook my mom's hand in the lobby of the Cheesecake factory.

Romeo actually lifted my mom's hand to his lips and kissed the back of it. She tugged her hand away with a hint of disgust before he was finished, surprising Romeo.

"I do have that affect on the ladies," Romeo winked at her.

My mom scowled at him. I'm sure she was confused. The only romance in her life came from my dad. He was as spontaneous with his romantic gestures as he was with his choice of rental cars.

Kamiko, Madison and Jake were also here. With Spiridon and Christos at my side, that made it seven on two against my parents.

I had high hopes for the evening.

The restaurant was packed, so we had to wait awhile for our table. Madison cornered my parents and asked them a million questions about Washington D.C. I think she was trying to keep them occupied. She understood. She was my own personal emotional bodyguard.

When we were finally seated and the waiter took our drink order, I wasn't surprised that Christos ordered a double bourbon. With my parents in town, I considered joining him. But I decided I needed to be alert, in case my parents tried to launch a sneak attack. For all I knew they'd blindfold me and throw me in a packing crate the first chance they got so they could ship me back to D.C.

But I could tell something was bothering Christos more than usual. The obvious answer was my parents, but I suspected it was something else. I leaned over and whispered to Christos, "Who called earlier? Is it something I should be worrying about?"

"No, *agápi mou*. It's fine," he smiled.

"You sure?"

"You let me worry about it. Enjoy yourself."

"Whatever it is, it can't be any worse news than my parents arriving out of nowhere," I groaned.

Christos chuckled. "True that." He rested his hand on my knee under the table and looked me in the eyes.

I couldn't get over how handsome Christos was, even in the middle of his bourbon buzz. His face was so relaxed and dreamy, I wanted nothing more than to fall into his enchanting eyes right at the dinner table. So what if my parents might see? I eyed Christos' luscious mouth and nibbled on my lower lip. His lips spread in a wide smile over his immaculate white teeth. His legendary dimples appeared. I teased my upper lip with my tongue and giggled softly. I was going to lick those dimples of his, no matter who was watching. I leaned forward, about to—

"Sam?" my mom blurted. "What are you going to eat?"

Dimples? I jolted out of fantasyland and frowned. No, I think my mom meant for dinner. Embarrassment and irritation crackled inside my chest.

My mom's voice was her special gift. Children everywhere clamored for my mom to read them bedtime stories and soothe their nighttime fears with that voice of hers. No, seriously. My mom was world famous for her bedside manner. She taught sold-out seminars in mothering to giant auditoriums packed full of people. Seriously.

Not.

The waiter was standing at the table with his notepad in hand, waiting to take my order. I hadn't even looked at the menu yet. I think Christos had hypnotized me with his beautiful blues. Time had slid right by. That was easy to do with Christos by my side.

The waiter arched an expectant eyebrow at me.

I glanced down at the menu, "Oh, um, I'll have the Asian Chicken Salad?"

"Excellent," the waiter said, "and for you sir?" he asked Christos.

"I'll have crab cakes for an appetizer and the grilled rib-eye with mashed potatoes and gravy."

How was it that Christos could eat like a horse and never have an ounce of body fat? It was ridiculous. Maybe all the drinking kept him slim? No, probably not. It had to be all the sex we had. But that was on hold until Mom and Dad were gone. Sigh.

Sometime later, after the waiter had dropped off everyone's entrees and people were eating and chatting, Romeo said to Kamiko, loud enough for the whole table to hear, "Our waiter sure is hot. Did you see the bulge in the front of his pants?"

Kamiko frowned, "Romeo! Do you *always* have dick on the brain?"

Romeo grinned, "Yes. I like them on the brain and anyplace else I can fit them."

"Them? As in, plural?" Madison asked.

"As in, a plethora," Romeo smiled, "A cornucopia."

Madison giggled. Jake and Spiridon chuckled. Christos smiled while he chewed.

My parents looked shocked. They weren't used to this sort of talk, especially not at the dinner table. It had become normal to me. Maybe my parents needed a good old dose of Samantha's San Diego. I wasn't their little girl anymore. I was tired of trying to be someone I wasn't, just to suit them. I needed to live my life my own way, not theirs. If they didn't like my friends, they could suck it.

"I think Romeo needs a dick intervention," Kamiko joked.

"I assure you, Kamiko," Romeo said, "I'll never kick the dick. I'm a regular Dickaholic, darling. You'll never catch me at an Alcoholdicks Anonymous meeting. Not that I'm suggesting you frequent such meetings. I know how much you hate the flesh pistols."

Christos raised his eyebrows, amused.

"Aren't the Flesh Pistols a band?" Madison asked. "Weren't they, like, a punk band from the U.K.?"

"That's The Sex Pistols, darling," Romeo corrected.

"The Who?" Kamiko asked.

Romeo shook his head. "No, that's Roger Daltry and Pete Townshend. I'm talking about Johnny Rotten? Sid Vicious? You have heard of them, haven't you Kamiko?" He raised his eyebrows expectantly.

Kamiko shook her heard vigorously. "What the hell are you talking about?" She was totally frazzled.

My parents were even more lost. They exchanged a perplexed glance like they'd woken up in an insane asylum.

"I know, I know, Kamiko," Romeo sighed. "If it's not on Cartoon

Network, you have no idea what I'm talking about. How about—"
Romeo lowered his voice to a conspiratorial whisper and leaned
over to Kamiko's ear, "Locally grown…Butter Lettuce…"

Kamiko's eyes lit up like fireworks and she beamed a smile.
"Butter Lettuce party!!!"

Romeo sighed and hung his head. "I swear, Kamiko, you can't
be more than nine years old."

"What the hell are you guys talking about," Spiridon laughed.
Even he was lost now, but he wasn't horrified like my parents.

"It's a line from Bravest Warriors," Romeo groaned. "A *cartoon*."
He said the word 'cartoon' like it was offensive.

Kamiko clapped her hands merrily. "I totally forgot! There's a
new episode of Bravest Warriors going up on YouTube tonight! I
can't wait to watch it when I get home!"

Romeo shook his head, defeated. He leaned toward my mom
and said, "I should've left Kamiko with the babysitter."

My mom leaned away from Romeo like he had leprosy or
carried a highly contagious strain of flesh eating bacteria.

Kamiko smacked Romeo on the arm.

My mom jumped in her chair and winced as if she'd been the
one Kamiko had hit.

"Ow!" Romeo shouted, turning to face Kamiko.

"Who's the baby now," Kamiko grinned.

"Why do you have to be so abusive, Kamiko?" Romeo rubbed
his arm. "I'm not a cartoon, you know."

"Maybe if you were, you wouldn't be such a baby!" Kamiko
squealed.

I secretly hoped my parents would be the ones who decided to
slip out unnoticed because of how weird everyone was acting. Let
them be the uncomfortable ones for a change.

This was my world, bitches!

Christos leaned over and kissed me on the cheek, "Having fun?"

"Totally," I smiled at him.

I had the best friends, and the best boyfriend, ever!

===

Acid spewed from my mom's mouth as she said, "I knew that
Christos was no good the first time I met him."

I stood beside her and my dad outside the elaborate chimpanzee
exhibit at the San Diego Zoo several days later.

She continued, "He acted like a Boy Scout when he was staying at our house in D.C., but I knew it was only a matter of time until a boy like him showed his true colors."

Christos and Spiridon had gone off to find some drinks for everybody because we were all thirsty. My mom had suggested the three of us stay and watch the chimps. I should've known she was scheming.

I had managed to make it through almost the entire week of my Spring Break without getting into any arguments with my parents. They hadn't made a peep about me or my living arrangements or my Art major while we'd gone to Sea World, the San Diego Wild Animal Park, Old Town San Diego, Pacific Beach, downtown to the Gaslamp, and to Coronado Island.

We'd even toured the USS Midway aircraft carrier, which had been Dad's idea. The Midway turned out to be amazing because our tour guide had actually worked on the Midway in the 1950s and told us lots of insider stories about his tour of duty.

I think my dad and Christos bonded a little while they looked at all the jet fighters on the deck and talked about how fast they went and all the missiles they carried. I was glad to listen to their man talk if it meant my dad wasn't giving me a hard time about my art.

The only time my dad had said anything remotely negative was when we'd gone to Balboa park to see the San Diego Museum of Art. When we ended up in front of one of Spiridon's paintings, my dad had said, "Well, I'll be damned," as he squinted at the title card next to the painting, as if maybe Spiridon had been lying about it.

Through all that, there had been no arguments. I think it had something to do with the fact that I made sure I was never alone in my parents' presence for even a second. Christos or Spiridon were always by my side. I had fantasized that maybe everything between me and my parents was fine. I should've known better. They were ticking time bombs. They hadn't flown all the way out to San Diego just for a vacation.

Leave it to my mom to finally go and ruin things. Her timer had ticked down to zero before my dad's. It usually did.

The second we were alone at the Zoo today, Mom had taken the opportunity to pounce. Had we been standing outside the tiger enclosure, I'm sure the hungry tigers would've cheered her on and licked their chops, waiting to take a bite out of my carcass when my mom was done with me.

"His true colors?" Dad asked.

"Yeah, Mom," I said, "what true colors?"

"Christos' drinking," she said with arch superiority. "I see the way he drinks at every meal. Every. Meal."

"What do you care?" I sneered. Christos had been drinking less since they'd arrived, and it was the last thing I was worried about. At the moment, my parents scared me ten times more than Christos' drinking.

"What do I care?" Mom frowned. "I don't want you shacking up with an alcoholic."

"I don't see where that's any of your business," I growled. I glanced around and noticed that for the moment, there were no people hovering around this part of the chimpanzee exhibit. The last thing I wanted was an audience while my parents treated me like I was a child. At least the chimpanzees on the other side of the glass didn't seem interested.

My dad said, "Sam, who you're living with is certainly of concern to your mother and I."

"Thanks for caring, Dad," I scoffed.

"Don't talk that way to your father," my mom barked.

"Why not? It's not like you guys are doing much in the way of parenting anymore."

"I beg your pardon?" my mom said stridently.

"I went to the financial aid offices, you know," I grumbled, "and they told me that I can't get more student loan money as long as I'm your dependent, because of how much money you guys make. The government says it's your responsibility to help pay the difference. Last time I checked, you refused."

"Now, Sam," my dad said with an edge, "we discussed this at length. If you are willing to change your major back to Accounting, like your mother and I asked, we'd be happy to pay the difference."

"But I don't want to change my major back," I said. I did my very best to keep any hint of whining out of my voice. Why was it that I seemed to have regressed around my parents since they'd arrived? I didn't like how their presence made me feel and act fourteen again. Like I was a little kid who didn't know anything and my parents had all the answers, which I knew they didn't.

"If you don't want to change your major back," Dad sighed,

"then there is very little your mother and I can do."

"Then why don't you leave me alone?" I whined. "Why don't you go back to Washington D.C.? I'm doing fine here by myself." I folded my arms across my chest. "I don't need your help."

My mom chuckled, "I doubt that."

"What do you know," I growled at her. "I have a place to live, a job, and I like studying art. And I have an awesome boyfriend who cares about me. If you're not going to help me, stop telling me what to do."

"Are you sure?" my mom scoffed. "With all those naked young women around him day in and day out, it's only a matter of time before Christos' eyes start to wander. Then where will you be? Without a place to live would be my first guess."

And like a bullet through window glass, my remaining confidence shattered into useless fragments. How did my mom manage to do that so easily? My heart skipped a beat or ten and my throat filled with porcupine quills as I tried to swallow a dry lump of dread that wouldn't go down.

If I'd learned one thing about Christos since his trial, it was that he didn't tell me everything that was going in his head. Was he thinking about the long term with me? Or was I passing fancy? Maybe he was interested in Isabella, or one of the other naked women he painted seven days a week. They were all gorgeous models. I wasn't. I was just a regular girl from D.C. trying to study art. Why would a stud like Christos be interested in plain old Sam Smith when he was surrounded by supermodels?

No, that couldn't be right. Christos had asked me to move in with him and had voluntarily hauled all my stuff into his house. That meant he was serious, right? He was in it with me for the long term. Right?

So why were my mom's questions making me so nervous?

I felt tears begin to well. I needed to hide them from my mom or she would use them against me and go in for the kill. Before she had a chance to attack, I turned away from her and my dad to watch the chimpanzees to distract myself.

One of the older female chimps had walked over at some point and sat beside the glass only a few feet away from me. She looked up at me with the deepest, darkest, most compassionate eyes I'd ever seen, like she was looking into me, communicating on some primal level and trying to comfort me. She puckered her lips at me in a strange gesture. Was she trying to tell me something? No, that was crazy.

A young chimp ambled over to her on all fours and fell into her lap like it was his favorite place to hang out. He wrapped his arms around his mother's neck and she wrapped her arms around him while making kissy faces at him. She began gently grooming him. He looked like he was in heaven.

I wish that mother chimp was my mom too.

"Christos isn't like that," I said timidly. I wiped tears from my eyes before turning to face my mom.

A maleficent smile curled her lips. She looked like the Evil Queen from every storybook ever written.

Oh, boy. I needed some ice cream.

"All men are like that," my mom said victoriously.

Quick as a blade, I asked, "Is Dad like that?"

A flash of anger danced across her eyes, but she didn't respond.

There was a long, tingling silence.

"Yes, Linda," my dad said with nervous humor, "am I like that?"

My mom's eyes widened noticeably in surprise. She flicked a quick glance at my dad, then chuckled and drilled me with her stare, "No, your father is not like that."

Wheels turned in my mind, "Mom, how do you know so much about men? This isn't the first time you've mentioned men cheating. It sounds to me like you've had some bad experiences? If not with Dad, then who?"

My mom was taken aback. Heck, I was taken aback. I couldn't believe I'd asked her that.

Mom chuckled, "That's none of your business, Sam."

"Is it any of my business, Linda?" Dad asked innocently.

"There you guys are," Spiridon said, walking up with an armful of water bottles.

"We got some ice cream bars, too," Christos smiled, "in case anyone wants a snack." He held one up to me. "Chocolate dipped vanilla with butterscotch filling. I thought you might like one."

"Thank you, *agápi mou*," I said warmly as I took the ice cream bar and peeled back the wrapper. I leaned against Christos while I ate my ice cream. He put his arm around me as he ate his and we watched the chimpanzees together. I was in heaven.

Christos was nothing like my mom wanted me to believe. The ice cream bar he'd brought me was proof because it was the yummiest ice cream bar in the history of ice cream bars.

My mom was such a bitch.

===

"When are you going to realize that you'll never make any money as an artist?" my mom asked as she sipped her tea on the couch in the Manos' living room.

Christos and Spiridon had gone out for dinner to give my parents and me time to talk alone. I'd begged them to stay, but Spiridon had insisted. I think he understood my parents wanted to talk to me in private.

"Your mother is right, Sam," my dad consoled, like he was being nice and supportive. "It's unlikely that you'll ever make any money as an artist. If you ever hope to have a career, pay a mortgage and a car payment, you need to pursue a sensible career path like Accounting."

I'd heard this argument a thousand times from my parents, and my dad had always provided facts and figures to back everything up. As a teenager, I had always believed them. Every time we'd argued, my resolve had crumbled and I'd reluctantly given in to their ideas.

I was done with that.

This was my world, not theirs.

"Look around you, Dad," I motioned at all of Spiridon's paintings hanging in the room. "You heard Spiridon yourself. He paid for this house with his paintings. What makes you think I can't do it too?"

Dad said thoughtfully, "Well, for one thing,—"

"Ha!" Mom interrupted, "you think a few cartoons can compare to the paintings Spiridon has done?"

"I can paint!" I whined.

"All I've seen is your horrid cartoons of that degenerate wombat," Mom cackled. "What do you know about painting?"

"I took an oil painting class last quarter, and I got an A."

"I'm sure you painted a bowl of fruit or two," she chuckled, "but any beginner can do that."

"I'm no beginner." I stood up and stormed out of the living room.

"Where are you going?" Mom snickered.

I stopped in my tracks. Minding my parents like always. Like their slave.

"It was always like you to give up easily," Mom said. "Your father is right. You don't have what it takes."

"I'm not giving up," I barked. I strode into the studio and picked up two of my best oil paintings. One was from my class and one was the calla lilies I'd done in the studio. I thought they were really good, considering I'd only been painting for three months. I shoved them into my parents' hands when I returned to the living room. "See?"

My dad held the calla lilies at arm's length. "This isn't half bad," he said thoughtfully. He hadn't said half good, but my dad was never an optimist.

Mom sneered at my painting of sunflowers she held in her hands. "So? What is this supposed to mean?" she asked. "It looks like any other painting of sunflowers."

"Exactly," I growled. "It looks like sunflowers. And it doesn't suck, like you seem to think everything I draw or paint does."

She shook her head and scoffed. "There's a long road between a painting of sunflowers and making any money."

Dad set the calla lilies painting on the coffee table gently. At least he didn't drop it in the trash. "Your mother is right, Sam. While these paintings of yours show promise, I don't know that painting will lead anywhere for you."

"Are you kidding?" I asked, my hands on my hips as I stood in front of them. "Look around this room! Spiridon has painted thousands of paintings and made millions of dollars. That sounds like a great career path to me."

My mom smiled smugly and raised her eyebrows like she was the Queen. The Queen of Evil Bitchery, maybe. She said, "Bill, would you care to explain it to your daughter in logical terms she can understand?"

What, did she think I was stupid? I huffed and rolled my eyes.

My dad nodded. "Sam, what your mother is trying to say, I think, is that Spiridon is, well, how can I put this?" Dad spread his hands apart and a pained look tightened his features. "Uh, Sam, well, Spiridon is amazingly talented, and I think, if I had to characterize your skill, well I guess, you see, the thing is…"

Mom placed a stilling had on Dad's knee. "Your father is trying to tell you that you're not talented enough. You're not a Spiridon, or even a Christos."

CRACK!

That was the sound of my heart breaking in half. I was frozen in place where I stood. I couldn't speak, or even breathe, like all of my internal organs had suddenly exploded into fragments along with my heart. I had the distinct impression that if someone were to cut me open right at that moment, they'd find a hollow person with small piles of red glass shards pooled in the empty feet. Those red shards would be the broken remnants of my broken heart.

Mom continued, "Not that I'd want any daughter of mine painting pornography for a living like Christos, but I have to admit, Spiridon's landscapes are very good."

I was so hurt by what my mom had just said, I couldn't respond. I stood silently and gaped at the two monster impostors pretending to be my loving parents. They were evil. I wanted to run out of the room, but I couldn't move when my heart was broken and my insides were hollowed out.

"I don't know that I would say 'not talented enough', Sam," Dad said quietly, "but it's clear to me that Spiridon and Christos have both been painting for a long, long time. And I suspect that Spiridon had a large hand in educating Christos in art from birth. Sam, you're starting late in life. You're nineteen years behind Christos. More if you factor in Spiridon's instruction. In my estimation, for you to pursue art would be an unsound business decision. Conversely, you've been surrounded by numbers and accounting principles since birth," my dad smiled.

He was so fucking proud of his accounting.

He continued, "In the same way that Spiridon has given Christos a head start, I'd like to think that your mother and I have given you a head start in business. You are well suited for a career in Accounting. You will excel and make good money while you're at it."

Something about my dad's logic infuriated me beyond belief. I'd been hearing it all my life. He was always missing the point. I was so angry, I think the heat of my irritation melted those red glass shards in my feet and they melded back together. Now my heart was pumping red hot resolve through my entire body.

"You don't get it, Dad," I said. "I never wanted to be an accountant. Don't you see that? You don't, do you? You and Mom have never been able to see what I wanted out of life. You just dumped all your ideas on me like I'd automatically love them. Like I was a junior version of you two. But I'm not. I'm a different person. I don't want what you want out of life. I have my own dreams, my own ideas. I'm going to live life my way. Not yours."

"Then don't expect any more money from us," my mom laughed.

"I told you before," I said stridently, "I don't want your money. I don't need your money. I'm doing fine on my own."

"Even if you manage to sell some paintings," my dad said, "how much do you really think you'll earn over a lifetime? You told me yourself that Christos has made over six figures already. How much have you made selling your art, Sam?"

"I DON'T CARE!" I shouted. "I don't care if I never make ANY money! It's not about the money! I HATE accounting! I want to do something I enjoy. Maybe you guys like what you do, but the idea of going to the office every day makes me sick. I can't live like you, and I don't care how much money I do or don't make!"

My mom chuckled sarcastically, "I'm sorry you feel that way, Sam."

"Sam," my dad pleaded, "Art isn't a wise career path. I'm doing my very best as your father to show you that. Can't you see where I'm coming from?"

"Shut up, Bill," Mom snapped at him. "You're giving into her and I won't have it." She stood up and glared at me. "I don't care what you think. We should never have let you choose San Diego in the first place. But I let your father talk me out of making you go to American University. If you'd gone there, you could've lived at home and we wouldn't be in this mess. You wouldn't be shacking up with some two-bit tough like this Christos Manos and his hippie grandfather."

"They're not hippies," I insisted.

She took a menacing step toward me. Her eyes narrowed viciously. "I don't care what they are. They're a bad influence on you. They're turning you into a rebellious little bitch, and I'm tired of it. I won't have you throw your life away because Christos and his muscles get your panties hot."

I felt hate pouring off of her in waves.

I almost crumbled at that moment. I almost made a comment about how my mom was trying to debase my love for Christos, like that was a bad thing. But that would've been going on the defensive.

I was tired of my mom's rants. I was going on the offensive.

I was going to attack.

For once in my life, I was going to show my parents how much fight I had in me.

===

"You're just jealous, Mom!" I growled. "You see that I'm living a life that isn't boring and bland! You see that I have a romantic boyfriend who loves me with all his heart. And for the first time in my life, I'm happy." I narrowed my eyes accusatorially, "And you can't stand it," I hissed knowingly. "You want me to be as miserable as you are." I suddenly realized the implications of what I was saying, that I was comparing my dad with Christos. And it was pretty obvious who won that contest.

My dad, who wasn't a complete idiot, frowned thoughtfully. He opened his mouth to speak, then closed it with a long sigh.

"Don't start pointing fingers, Sam," Mom growled. "This isn't about your father and I. It's about you and how you've become an ungrateful, spoiled little child."

I laughed in her face. "Don't you get it? I'm not a child! And I'm not spoiled! I have a job! I'm paying my own way! You! Aren't! Paying! For! ANYTHING!!! Why are you even here? Why did you have to come to San Diego in the first place?"

My mom's brows knit together and her lips pulled back in a terrible smile.

Dad's head hung between his shoulders where he sat on the couch. He looked up at me, his face weighed down. "Sam, your mother and I think it's time for you to come home."

I was stunned and confused. "What?"

"You've made it clear that this entire San Diego University outing was a grave mistake," Mom said confidently. "You've had your fun with your boyfriend. I have no doubt he's screwed your brains right out of your ears. It's the only possible explanation for your terrible decision making over the last several months."

Wow, my mom was offensive beyond belief today. The thing that made it worse was that she acted like it was no big deal for her to talk to me this way, like Christos was a worthless nobody who didn't matter. She had no idea how important he was to me. How he had changed my life for the better. She was so out of touch.

She continued, "Now it's time for you to leave that boy behind and get serious about college."

"I'm not leaving Christos! You're crazy!"

"I am not crazy," she said. "Christos is a distraction. You'll be better off without him."

My heart ping-ponged in my chest for the fortieth time in the last ten minutes. I wasn't surprised that my parents were trying to ruin my life. It was how they did things.

"Your father and I have already looked into it," she continued, "you can transfer your credits from SDU to American University and start there in the fall."

I wanted to launch into a tirade and tell her how awful her idea was. But if I did, I knew I'd lose this argument. I had to stay strong. I took a long, deep breath. Then everything fell into place. I wasn't a child anymore. I didn't need to let my parents control me. I had a choice. And I was going to make it. Smirking, I said, "I'm not going to American."

"You are," Mom said with certainty, "and that's final."

I think she'd missed the calm resolve in my voice. "You can't tell me what to do," I said firmly. "I'm nineteen."

"Oh, we can't, can we?" Mom said archly. "And how do you plan on paying your tuition in the future?"

"With the loan money I'm already getting and the job I have," I said defiantly.

"Oh, is that so? Are you forgetting that your father and I have to sign your loan application each academic year for you to renew the loan?"

Oh, shit. My mom had headed me off at the pass.

I was screwed.

===

CHRISTOS

Blood red salsa blurted out of the squeezable red plastic container and drenched my carne asada burrito.

"You sure you got enough hot sauce?" my grandad asked

sarcastically.

I chuckled. "You know I like it hot. This is just for the first bite."

He smiled and took a bite of one of his chicken tacos, which had only a light drizzling of hot sauce.

We sat at a table outside the Roberto's on the Pacific Coast Highway overlooking the San Elijo lagoon, having dinner. It had been my suggestion we go out and give Samantha and her parents some space to talk. I think Samantha had made sure she was never alone with them the whole week on purpose.

"Are you worried about *Samoula*?" my grandad asked.

"Yeah," I muttered.

"It's good we left them alone. Her parents probably want to talk to her. I can't blame them. She is their daughter, after all."

I sipped on my Jamaica tea. "Do you think they're arguing right now?" I asked.

My grandad chewed then swallowed. He chased it with a gulp from his big cup of horchata. "Probably."

Man, I wish I'd brought a flask so I could spike my Jamaica with some vodka or whatever went with hibiscus tea. The odd thing was, I'd cut back on my drinking more and more since Samantha's parents had arrived. I'd wanted to spend Spring Break with Samantha so she didn't have to endure an entire week alone with them. It had been so easy to forget about Brandon and my gallery show. As those pressures had faded from my awareness, the urge to drink had faded with them.

But now that Spring Break was coming to a close, I could feel all those old obligations ready to nip at my heels. I was itching for a drink. But the real reason I wanted to get bombed was because I was scared shitless about what I'd find when I got back to the house tonight.

I took a bite of my burrito and chewed thoughtfully. When I was finished, I said, "I've been waiting for her parents to go off on her all week. If you'd heard them on the phone when Samantha told them she wanted to move in with me, you'd be pissing your pants right now like I am. They were totally irate and made all kinds of threats about what they would do if she moved in with us. I wouldn't be surprised if we get back to the house and she's gone. Probably cuffed and gagged and thrown into a big duffel bag so her parents can haul her ass back to the east coast."

"Relax, *paidí mou*," my grandad smiled. "*Samoula* is a strong girl. I have a feeling she's standing up to her parents right now. If they think they can corner her and bully her into giving up and going home, they've bitten off more than they can chew."

He took a big bite of his taco and chomped on it.

"I hope you're right," I said before taking a huge bite of my burrito.

I couldn't bear the thought of losing her.

===

SAMANTHA

A big boulder dropped down into my stomach, reminding me that my insides were more intact than I'd realized. I wasn't a hollowed out husk.

Yet.

But my mom was working on it.

She was right. Without my parents' signature, I wouldn't get any loan money at all. I'd have to earn every cent of my tuition and books. I'd never be able to find jobs that paid for everything. But there was no way I was going back to D.C. As far as I was concerned, San Diego was now my home.

Maybe I could plug my parents' PIN number into the form online and sign it myself? I knew what their number was.

"And don't think about using our PIN to forge the electronic signature," Mom chuckled. "We've already changed it."

Wow, Mom had read my mind. I wasn't surprised. I'd learned most of my dirty tricks from her.

My dad was leaning his elbows on his knees. He looked very tired. "Sam, this was our last resort. We've tried reasoning with you, but nothing has worked. We can't in good conscience let you continue as an Art major. Come back home to American University and get your degree in Accounting. Your mother and I will make sure you don't have to work and you can focus entirely on your studies. Maybe you'll even find a boyfriend who is a business major like you. After you graduate, perhaps you can pursue art in your spare time. Everyone needs a hobby."

A hobby? He was completely insane and it was making me insane. My mom was crazy too. I don't think they'd listened to a word I'd said all evening. They were ignoring me and trying to grind me down until I agreed to go home.

My head was spinning from all their arguments. I couldn't deal with either of them. I felt totally betrayed. My parents were treating me like an infant, like I was holding my fingers too close to the flame because I didn't know any better. They were wrong.

I'd had enough.

"No!" I shouted and literally stomped my foot. "I'm not doing it! I'm not moving back home and I'm not changing my major! If you don't like it, tough shit! Get out of here! Go home!" I pointed to the front doors. "I'm sure the Motel 6 has a room waiting for you. In fact, let me go pack your bags and I'll drive you there myself." I turned and marched toward the stairs, heading toward the guest rooms.

"YOU COME BACK HERE, YOUNG LADY!" Mom roared.

I ignored her.

Until her hand bit into my arm and she whipped me around.

Her other hand clamped on my other arm and she shook me violently with both hands as she screamed in my face, "YOU'RE MOVING BACK TO WASHINGTON D.C. WHETHER YOU WANT TO OR NOT!!"

After she stopped throttling me, I sneered at her. "Are you through?"

Her eyes burned hot with fiery insanity and her brows twisted into a rotten knot. She shouted, "I'VE HAD ENOUGH OF YOUR BACK TALKING!!"

I glared at her, my lips compressed into a thin line. "No, Mom," I said calmly.

WHACK!!

She had slapped me across the mouth. My cheek stung.

"YOU WILL DO WHAT YOUR FATHER AND I TELL YOU, AND THAT'S FINAL!!"

I planted my palms against my mom's chest and shoved her as hard as I could. She reeled backward, her arms pinwheeling, and stumbled into my dad. The two of them fell down on the couch in a tumbled heap.

My hands fisted at my sides. I was ready for whatever she did next. I was going to punch my mom in the face if I had to.

Her eyelids peeled back in stark horror. Her mouth was agape like I was the devil himself. Unfortunately, I wasn't the devil in this room. She was.

I felt confidence and resolve fill me from head to toe. My heart beat strong in my chest. I was a rock, and neither of my parents were going to budge me. "I'm not doing anything you say. Mom—" I sneered when I said the word 'Mom' "—Linda. Whoever you are. You're the worst parent ever. You're a bully and you're a jerk. Go back to D.C. where you belong. And take your loan money with you."

I turned and calmly walked out of the living room.

Chapter 16

SAMANTHA

Luggage banged around inside the guest room while my parents packed. After our argument, I think they'd decided to stay at the Motel 6. I imagined my mom would've been throwing dishes against the wall, or at me, if it had been her house and her dishes. Since she couldn't, the only thing she could do was assault her shoes, her clothes, and her travel kit as she shoved everything into her suitcase.

I stayed in my room with my door closed because I was convinced that if I looked at my mom one more time, I was going to vomit. My face still stung and throbbed where she'd slapped me. Every thump I felt in my cheek steeled my resolve to stay in San Diego and stay with Christos.

Eventually, I heard Mom stomping down the hallway toward the stairs. She was leaving in a huff.

Fine by me.

A few seconds later, I heard my dad mumbling as he trudged down the hallway after her. My parents were flying out the next day anyway, so it really didn't matter if they spent the night here or not. They could spend it in a gutter somewhere, for all I cared.

The front door slammed shut. Their rental Honda revved and drove off.

Good riddance.

I was just glad Christos and Spiridon hadn't been around to watch my parents' bad behavior.

I laid down on the bed and covered my eyes with my arm. I must've dozed off because the next thing I knew, Christos was waking me.

"*Agápi mou?*" he said softly. "What happened to your parents? Their car is gone and their room is empty."

I slid my arm down to my chest. It weighed about a thousand pounds. I was going to need a crane to lift me off this bed, I was so depressed. Not even ten gallons of ice cream could move me now.

Christos sat down next to me gently. "Do you want to talk about it?"

"No," I said flatly.

He smiled and nodded. My heart accelerated as I took in that beautiful grin of his. It melted my world every time. All the pain my parents had stabbed into me faded to a fuzzy pressure that was someone else's problem. At least for now. For now, I was going to bask in the blue glow of Christos' loving gaze.

He smiled more widely. "You sure? Talking it out will make it better."

I had resolved to keep my emotions in check, but with all the love pouring off of Christos, I didn't see the reason to hold them in. I sat up and wrapped my arms around him and cried softly. "Christos, *agápi mou*, my parents are evil. They want me to quit SDU and move back to D.C."

I felt Christos suddenly tighten.

"What did you tell them?" he asked cautiously.

"I told them they're crazy." I felt him relax and melt against me.

"Thank goodness. I don't think I could deal with losing you." There was a tenderness in his voice that pierced straight to the center of my being. "I love you, *agápi mou*," he said, "I don't want to live without you in my life. I can't imagine waking up to an empty bed because, once you leave it, my bed will remain as empty as my heart until the day I die. Life without you would be a dull, gray, tasteless thing without meaning. I would rather die a quick death than live a vacant life without you by my side."

Whoa. Swoon.

Yeah, my mom was totally out to lunch about Christos.

"Oh, *agápi mou*," I murmured, "I'm not going anywhere."

===

Two days later, I was back at work at the Eleanor M. Westbrook art museum.

"Samantha," Mr. Selfridge said, "I need to go out for a little while. I have a meeting with the Provost of Adams College. I'll be gone for about an hour. Can you handle things while I'm gone?"

"Sure," I smiled at him from where I sat behind the counter in the lobby.

"See you shortly," he waved as he walked out the front doors.

I really loved my job at the museum and really liked having Mr. Selfridge for a boss. I only wished the museum could give me more hours. I'd asked Mr. Selfridge about it at the beginning of my shift today, but he had apologized that the museum had no more hours to give.

Now that Spring Quarter classes had started, and my remaining loan money had been eaten up paying the first of my monthly installment payments, I needed more cash in a hurry. I'd have to find a second job once again. With any luck my job hunt wouldn't eat up all my study time. The last thing I needed was for my GPA to drop low enough that my loans got suspended.

With my parents back in D.C., I actually felt a sense of relief, despite my heinous financial predicament. My parents were just one more hassle that I wouldn't have to deal with. I was going to figure things out without their help.

Somehow.

No customers had come into the museum today, so I had some down time. I pulled out my laptop and started searching for jobs online. As much as I hated the idea, it was time to suck it up and look for a math tutoring job. There had been tons the last time I'd looked for a job.

Unfortunately, it didn't take long to realize that Sheri at the Financial Aid offices had been right. Jobs in general were scarce these days. The numerous math tutoring listings I'd seen a few months ago were all gone.

Great.

I sighed and closed my laptop. I'd do more job searching later. At least I had my museum job, which meant a little money coming in to offset my hemorrhaging budget crisis.

One of the glass front doors of the museum opened and Tiffany Nofun-Poophouse walked inside wearing a tight dress and platform heels. There went my good mood. Not that I had much of one to begin with, but she definitely knocked it to the bottom of a deep and dreary well, the kind of well with slippery slime on the sides you couldn't climb back out of, the kind where they had to call the rescue crews to pull your muddied mood out.

"Hey, Tiffany," I groaned as she clacked toward the counter in her hooker heels.

She smirked but said nothing.

"What brings you to the museum?" I asked blandly. At least I didn't have to say "Welcome to Grab-n-Dash. How can I brighten your day?" And she didn't have a big drink in her hand to throw in my face. I smiled as I realized there was little Tiffany could do to me here at the museum to actually ruin my day.

"I need a ticket," she said brusquely.

"Are you an art major? Because if you are, you don't have to pay."

She slammed her huge purse on the counter and yanked her wallet out. There must have been more than a dozen credit cards inside. She peeled one out of the wallet and punched it at me.

"I didn't know you liked coming to the art museum," I said meekly, trying to make conversation. "It's really nice. I find it very relaxing here, especially if you've had a bad day."

She glared at me.

"Okay..." I muttered and rang her up. When she signed her receipt, I handed her a ticket.

She ripped it from my hand and walked toward the main gallery.

"Oh, um, Tiffany?" I called after her. "You need to leave your bag behind the counter."

Tiffany stopped in her tracks and slowly pivoted to face me. I was expecting one of those horror movie reveals where her face suddenly looked monstrous, with dramatic up-lighting and dripping fangs, but it was just regular old Tiffany, not that there was a huge difference.

After sneering at me for about an hour, Tiffany stalked toward me and jammed her purse in my hands.

I squeezed it into one of the cubbies behind the counter.

About twenty minutes later, I realized I needed to go to the bathroom to change my tampon. Normally, Mr. Selfridge was always around and I could get him to cover the front desk. But he was still out on his errand.

How long was he supposed to be gone again?

I took a step and could tell I was on the verge of dripping. I hated how a tampon could up and quit on you without any warning like that.

Where was Mr. Selfridge?

I really needed to go to the restroom.

It wasn't like I was going to change my tampon behind the counter. What if someone walked into the museum? If I had been wearing a skirt, I might have considered it. Might. But in jeans? Not bloody likely! I imagined how it would play out. I'd be squatting behind the counter, my pants around my ankles as I tried to plug a fresh tampon inside the hole in the dam, and BOOM! someone would walk inside and accuse me of public indecency.

No, thank you.

I bit my lower lip and used my ESP to will Mr. Selfridge to walk through the front doors. Where was he? I took a tentative step toward the waist high swinging door at the end of the counter, ready to make a run for the restrooms the second he walked in.

Squish.

Any second now, Mr. Selfridge was going to walk through those front doors…

I really couldn't wait any longer.

I took another step toward the swinging door at the end of the counter.

I glanced back at the front doors, and switched over to my telekinetic powers. I used them to draw Mr. Selfridge, wherever he was, toward the museum.

Crap. It wasn't working. My telekinesis was as bad as my ESP.

Another step.

Squish.

This was not good.

Where the fuck was Mr. Selfridge?

I looked at the clock. He wouldn't be here for at least ten minutes. In ten minutes, I would need to throw my panties *and* jeans in the laundry. But there was no washing machine at the museum and I didn't have any sweats to wear while I waited anyway. I'd have to go home, but I had classes later today. I wouldn't have time to make it to home and back before they started. So much for my day running smoothly.

I picked up a pen off the counter top and waved it in the air like a magic wand. I pretended I was Hermione from a Harry Potter movie. It was the intention that made all the difference. "Mr. Selfridge, please appear, so my panties remain clear." It was the best

I could come up with on short notice.

Sadly, Mr. Selfridge did not magically appear in a puff of smoke.

Screw it. I couldn't wait any longer.

The only person in the museum was Tiffany. What damage could she do while I was in the ladies room? She wasn't one of those lunatics who would slash a painting with a knife, was she? I hoped not. Besides, I had her bag behind the counter, and I don't think she had any room in her tight dress for a knife. And I didn't think she was likely to pull a painting off the wall and carry it out. She hired workmen to do things like that, and I hadn't seen her come in with a work crew.

Okay. I was going to risk it. I walked carefully out from behind the counter and bee lined for the restroom. I swear I only moved my legs from the knees down so as to minimize possible leakage. There was a lot of heel-toeing involved, but I was amazed by how fast I could move without the use of my knees.

I made it into a stall in the restroom and heaved a sigh of relief when I saw that my panties had but a single red blotch. Apparently, my magic wand waving spell a minute ago hadn't kept my panties clean. I would've made a terrible wizard.

At least the leakage had been minimal. And I'd made it just in time. My tampon was ready to burst when I dropped it into the bowl. I blotted the red dot on my underwear with toilet paper until there was no moisture. Wow, I'd been close to bleeding out, no pun intended.

When I finished my business, I washed my hands and jogged back behind the counter.

The museum wasn't on fire, the ceiling hadn't fallen in, and there wasn't a riot of people throwing molotov cocktails, so I figured everything was okay. Nobody could have gotten into the cash register, because I had the key for it around my wrist on a springy elastic band.

I was good.

I heaved a sigh of relief.

Mr. Selfridge walked in ten seconds later. Good timing, Mr. Selfridge. Not that it mattered.

"How was your meeting?" I asked him.

"Excellent," he smiled. "Thanks for asking."

Tiffany walked out of the museum gallery and up to the counter.

"I need my bag," she grumbled.

"Oh, let me get it for you," I said enthusiastically. I dug it out of the cubby and handed it over.

Tiffany snatched it from me and walked out the front doors without saying thank you. Such a bitch.

Mr. Selfridge frowned. "I guess that young woman didn't like the museum?"

"I don't think she likes anything," I said.

Mr. Selfridge furrowed his brows, confused. "It wasn't anything you said to her, was it?"

"No, she just has a bad attitude."

Mr. Selfridge nodded uncertainly. "Okay, then. Well, I'm going back to my office. Ring my phone if you need me." He started walking across the large lobby toward the side hallway that led to the offices in back.

One of the museum doors burst open.

"You!" Tiffany blurted as she stalked across the lobby to the counter where I stood.

I wasn't surprised she'd come back. She hadn't managed to ruin my day, so she was going to call me names or demand a refund because she hated the art in the museum.

Mr. Selfridge had stopped at the other side of the lobby to see what was going on. Tiffany noticed him.

"Hey, you!" she shouted.

Mr. Selfridge was startled. "May I help you, young lady?"

She cocked her hips and jammed her fists against her sides, "Your employee stole my credit card!"

I'd spoken too soon. Never put it past Tiffany to do her very best to ruin my life.

Mr. Selfridge walked over to the counter. "I'm sorry," he said to Tiffany, "what did you just say?"

"I said," Tiffany huffed, "your employee stole my credit card."

Mr. Selfridge leveled a look at me over his glasses.

I sighed. At least Tiffany was crazy, and it would only take a second to prove to Mr. Selfridge that I was innocent. I mean, why would I take Tiffany's credit card? This was proof she had finally cracked.

"She must've taken it from my bag when she made me put it behind the counter," Tiffany growled.

Mr. Selfridge raised his eyebrows at me.

"She's crazy," I laughed defensively. "I didn't take her credit card."

Tiffany slammed her bag on the counter, opened it, and wrestled with the contents inside like her bag was full of rabid chipmunks. Eventually, she pulled her wallet out. She opened it and presented the missing space. "See? I keep it right here. It's gone."

Tiffany had so many other cards of every sort in her wallet, it was like she was pointing at a lawn and accusing me of stealing a blade of grass.

More importantly, I didn't steal it.

"How do you know you didn't lose it someplace else?" I scoffed. "Maybe it fell out of your wallet. It's probably in the bottom of your purse."

Tiffany narrowed her eyes. "I looked," she hissed.

"Look again," I sneered.

Mr. Selfridge watched all of this with neutral interest.

"I didn't take her credit card, Mr. Selfridge."

"You're such a liar," Tiffany sneered.

Mr. Selfridge cleared his throat and said to Tiffany, "Perhaps you'd be willing to place the contents of your hand bag on the counter top, young lady?"

Tiffany glared rusty daggers at me. "Fine." She up ended her bag and everything spilled out like a garbage truck emptying its load at the dump. I was surprised a cloud of dust didn't billow up. How did she find anything in there? I thought my purse was bad.

Tiffany spread the contents out on the counter until it looked like landfill. "It's not here," she grunted.

"You're sure you didn't lose it someplace else?" Mr. Selfridge asked.

"Yes. I used it to pay for my museum ticket. I have the receipt right here." Tiffany held the slip of paper up to show Mr. Selfridge. "See?"

Mr. Selfridge nodded. "And the card is not in your wallet?"

"No! Do you want me to pull out every credit card to prove it?"

"Yes, as I matter of fact, I do," Mr. Selfridge said calmly. At least he was on my side in all this. "May I see your receipt from purchasing your museum ticket?"

Tiffany jammed it in his hand.

He examined it. "We'll check the number on the receipt against the cards in your wallet."

This was such a waste of time. Tiffany had run out of good ideas about how to ruin my day so she was grasping desperately at anything she could think of to piss me off. Whatever. I was over it and over her. She was a nuisance at best.

Mr. Selfridge meticulously matched the numbers on each card with the number on the receipt. When he was finished, he sighed and looked at me gravely. "I don't see the card here anywhere. Could it be in your pockets?"

Tiffany laughed in his face. "Do I look like I have any pockets?" She motioned toward her tight dress. While it was true she had no pockets, I wouldn't be surprised if she'd shoved her credit card up her butt just to get me in trouble.

"Maybe you dropped it outside," I suggested. Or threw it in the bushes or a garbage can on purpose.

Tiffany snarled, "I told you, she took it from my bag when I left it behind the counter while I toured the museum."

Mr. Selfridge raised an eyebrow and folded his arms across his chest. He stroked his chin with one hand. "Samantha?" he asked expectantly.

"I promise, Mr. Selfridge," I sighed, "I didn't take it."

"Check her bags," Tiffany insisted. "She must have stolen it. Where else could it be?"

"This is crazy," I said absently. "I didn't take her credit card, Mr. Selfridge."

"Do I have to call campus security?" Tiffany demanded.

Mr. Selfridge looked between me and Tiffany. He said, "The simplest thing to do, Samantha, is for you to turn out your own bag. If you didn't take this young woman's credit card, we won't find anything, correct?"

"Yeah," I said. I just hoped Tiffany didn't demand a strip search after going through my book bag failed to turn anything up. "I've got nothing to hide." I reached under the counter for my book bag and set it on the other side of the counter from Tiffany's pile of crap. I didn't want her claiming that her stuff had been in my bag. I pulled out my laptop and my books.

"What about the side pockets?" Tiffany demanded.

"I don't have your credit card, Tiffany," I said as I grabbed everything out of the side pockets and added it to the pile of my stuff on the glass counter. Amongst pens, my keys, a tube of lipstick, crumpled receipts, a nail file, an eyeliner pencil, two tampons, and twenty other things, was only my wallet. "See? No credit card."

"Check her wallet," Tiffany insisted to Mr. Selfridge, like I wasn't even there.

"Do you mind, Samantha?" Mr. Selfridge asked.

"It's not in my wallet." I opened my wallet and showed it to both of them. "Do I have to go through every pocket?"

Tiffany gave me a dirty authoritarian look. "Yes, you do."

"Fine." I began peeling cards out of my wallet and slapping them down in a row on the counter. "MY Driver's License," SLAP! "MY SDU Student ID," SLAP! "MY MasterCard," SLAP! "MY Frequent Buyer's Card for Bath & Body Works," SLAP! "MY Debit Card," SLAP, "and…"

SLAP.

Why was there a fancy black VISA card in my wallet?

Tiffany's lips curled into a victorious smile. "That's my card. Just like I thought. She took it."

What? I glanced at the black VISA card. How had it gotten into my wallet?

Mr. Selfridge reached over and picked up the card and examined it closely. "You are Tiffany Kingston-Whitehouse, correct?"

Tiffany pulled her SDU student ID and her driver's license out of her wallet, which Mr. Selfridge had never checked, and showed it to him.

Mr. Selfridge examined both, then looked at me over his glasses. "This doesn't look good, Ms. Smith," he muttered.

Why had Mr. Selfridge gone from calling me Samantha all the time to Ms. Smith all of a sudden? The answer was obvious. I had been framed by Tiffany Kingdumb-Sleazehouse and Mr. Selfridge thought I was a criminal.

"I told you she stole it," Tiffany growled.

"Yes," Mr. Selfridge sighed, "I'm afraid this doesn't look good at all, Ms. Smith."

And that was how I got fired from my job at the campus art museum.

If somebody had offered me a job working nude in a rat infested dungeon as a math tutor for convicted rapists, I would've gladly taken it.

===

Mr. Selfridge didn't have a choice. It was academic policy at SDU that any student employed at an on-campus job would be terminated if caught stealing. Mr. Selfridge was very apologetic, but said that because of the evidence, he had to let me go.

The good news was that Tiffany had her credit card back, and I know I hadn't used it to pay for anything. And I'm sure no one else had used it between the time it was sitting safely in her purse and mine.

The bad news was that Tiffany had filed an official grievance with the Dean.

What a surprise.

Mr. Selfridge said he would tell the Dean that I was a model employee the entire time I'd worked for him. Hopefully, it would inspire the Dean to believe my version of events. With any luck, I might get my job back. Eventually.

I just wished Mr. Selfridge could tell the Dean that Tiffany was a rich bitch who hated me because I stole Christos from her, and she'd snuck her credit card into my wallet when I'd been changing my tampon, but I didn't think that would mean squat to the Dean. Shit, I should've squatted behind the museum counter like I'd imagined and changed my tampon in plain sight. Then I wouldn't be up Menses Creek without a paddle. Yeah, it was a gruesome image, but somehow it captured Tiffany Blingston-Douchehouse's scheming to a tee.

Tiff the Bitch was the all time epic bitch of the universe. Apologies to female dogs everywhere.

I made an appointment to see Dean Livingston.

A few days later, I sat in the waiting room to his office.

While I waited, I sketched yet another cartoon of Tiffany being murdered in yet another heinous way in my sketchbook. This time I had her buried up to her neck in sand while shiny black DeathStalker scorpions (which were the second most poisonous in the world, I'd learned) stung her in the eyeballs and dungeness crabs performed sloppy plastic surgery all over her grimacing face.

"The Dean will see you now," his secretary said from her desk.

I gasped and slapped my sketchbook closed, realizing it was

starting to resemble a serial killer's hatebook. Maybe I needed to tear my Tiffany drawings out, lest someone notice them and cite them as evidence of my guilt.

I shoved my sketchbook in my bag and walked into the Dean's office. It looked like your classic wood and books Oxford College office. It seemed out of place in San Diego, yet there it was.

Dean Livingston was standing behind his desk. He was a tall, older man with clean cut silver hair and a conservative navy suit. "Have a seat," he motioned toward the leather chairs facing his desk.

As I walked across a huge Oriental rug, I noticed the Dean had a big antique globe mounted in one of those huge round wooden floor stands. Sitting on one of the bookshelves was one of those brass sextant things ship captains used. Probably in case the Dean suddenly needed to explore the new world. He certainly looked old enough to have been on Columbus' boat. I just hoped he considered himself the nice kind of explorer who brought exotic silks and spices to trade, not the mean kind who brought conquistadors or small pox infested blankets to invade.

I sat down while the Dean opened a folder on his desk and flipped through the papers inside it. I think it was my file. My legendary permanent file. The one they always told you about in high school that haunted you your entire life. Great. Now they were going to add petty criminal to my list of transgressions.

The Dean continued to examine the papers while he spoke, "I see here that you've had a bit of a problem with your job at the art museum?"

I had the distinct feeling I was nothing more than a number to him, one of thousands who went to SDU. The university had over thirty thousand students, so I wouldn't be surprised.

"Yeah," I said.

"You are aware that any student caught stealing at a work study job will be terminated?"

"Yes."

"And that there are no exceptions to this rule?"

"Yes."

"And that San Diego University has a zero tolerance policy toward theft?"

"Yes," I rolled my eyes. Did they pay him to just read from the manual? Heck, I could do this guy's job. I bet it paid pretty well, and I'd make more than enough to cover my tuition.

"This is a very serious offense, young lady. What do you have to say for yourself?" he asked.

I suddenly felt like every criminal ever who professed their innocence while nobody believed them. The only difference was, a jury hadn't convicted me. Tiffany had. How to explain? I was going with the obvious, "Tiffany framed me."

"Who is Tiffany?"

"The girl who says I stole her credit card," I sighed.

Was he even listening? Or just doubting? I did my best to explain what Tiffany had likely done. Of course, I could only guess. But it was all I had to work with.

While I talked, I noticed the Dean slowly slouching farther and farther down in his slippery leather chair. His cheek was leaning against the hand he'd propped on an armrest.

To my horror, he slipped so far down in his chair while I spoke that his knuckles were driving the skin of his cheek up the side of his skull in wrinkly accordion folds. His lips were stretched so far up now that it made a gap in one corner of his mouth that couldn't be closed. I could clearly see his bridgework.

"Mmmm," he mumbled absently.

I waited for him to say something more in response to my theory about Tiffany.

Another wrinkle folded into place on Dean Livingston's cheek as he continued to slide in slow motion down his chair. There were now sixteen folds. I know, because I had time to count while I waited politely for him to respond.

I glanced around and watched dust motes floating in the sunbeams pouring through the windows to my right. They danced. I always liked dust motes.

Hello! Dean Livingston? Anybody alive in there? Was he asleep with his eyes open? He certainly looked old enough to have come across the Atlantic on the Santa Maria with Columbus.

"The girl…" he said.

Uh, yeah? What the heck was I supposed to say to that? I raised my eyebrows expectantly.

He raised his a tad in response.

I raised mine a bit higher.

Back and forth we went, our eyebrows going up a millimeter higher at a time. He had the advantage because the eyebrow on the side of his face with the wrinkled cheek had an inch head start.

Okay, was this a game of who can raise whose eyebrows the highest? Did I win if mine touched my scalp? Because that's how high they were now.

Any day, Mr. Livingdeadston!

I'd had it. I blurted, "Tiffany! Remember her?"

"Who?"

Had he forgotten already, or been asleep the whole time? Either was possible.

Exasperated, I blurted, "I told you, Tiffany was the girl who came into the art museum on my shift, and when I went to the ladies room, she must have put her credit card in my wallet so she could accuse me of stealing it."

"The museum..." he sighed like a deflating gas bag.

Wow, was that as far as we'd gotten?

"Which...museum?" he burped.

I mean burped, an actual burp.

"Excuse me..." he slurred.

Wow, I think I saw his breath smoking out the gaping corner of his mouth, it was so thick and rank. And tinted brown. Ew. I think a housefly flew right through it and spiraled down to its death. So gross. Any second, spiders were going to crawl out of his mouth like it was a tomb. At least his corpse was showing signs of life. Except I think he was dozing again.

"Mr. Livingston?"

He was literally staring right at me, but didn't say a word.

Wake up, Mr. Livingston! This was useless.

"Is this a bad time?" I asked carefully.

He blinked.

Was that it? Geez, I could totally do this guy's job. I wondered what his job interview had consisted of? Blinking more than twice an hour?

Lameballs!

"Mr. Livingston, I really need my job back," I pleaded, "and I didn't take Tiffany's credit card. Isn't there anything we can do? I really need the work or I won't be able to pay my tuition," I gulped, suddenly worried that admitting I was having trouble covering my tuition bill might be digging a grave for myself. The university didn't want broke students who couldn't pay. Then again, I suspected Mr. Livingston was intimately familiar with graves, seeing as how he had one under his desk and kept one foot in it at all times.

He blinked three times, a record for him, then yawned, "You will need to make a formal appeal to the University, at which time," he yawned again, "you will have an opportunity to state your case before a tribunal of administrators." He was now fully awake. People usually were when they were bending you over and going to work with the broom handle.

"Until then," he admonished, "you will not be allowed to work on campus. You will also be placed on academic probation until your name has been cleared. If the tribunal finds that you are indeed guilty of theft, or if you are caught committing any other crimes on campus, you will be subject to expulsion."

Gulp. What? Had I heard him right?

Why had I gotten out of bed this morning?

Stupid Tiffany!

Chapter 17

SAMANTHA

The warm spring weather was perfect in contrast to my mood. I sat outside at one of the tables at the Student Center with Madison, Romeo and Kamiko. We were all eating fish tacos for lunch.

"I'm screwed, you guys," I sighed.

"You say that like it's a problem," Romeo quipped. "In my world, getting screwed is the most desirable outcome of any encounter."

"Even if Tiffany Kingston-Whitehouse is the one doing the screwing?" I asked skeptically.

"Now that you mention it, I always suspected that girl had a dick," Romeo cackled.

"She's way too much of a bitch to be a man or have a penis," Kamiko said as she dipped a tortilla chip in her salsa.

"Female dogs everywhere are cringing because we're comparing them to Tiffany," Madison giggled.

"Maybe we could compare Tiffany to toxic waste or puppy murderers," Romeo suggested.

"Don't kill any puppies!" Kamiko pleaded.

Romeo frowned at her. "How is it that me saying 'puppy murderers' means it has actually happened? What, did a puppy somewhere in the world just die because I said it?"

"I don't know," Kamiko said sheepishly, "just don't say it."

Romeo rolled his eyes, "You've been watching way too many cartoons, darling." He took a bite of his fish taco.

I sipped my iced tea, "What am I going to do, you guys? I can't even find a math tutoring job. There's no jobs anywhere right now. And, until my case with Tiffany goes up for review in front of SDU's academic tribunal, Career Services won't give me another on-campus job. I'm tainted goods."

"Have you tried looking for work as a sex slave?" Romeo asked.

"Who wants a tainted sex slave?" Madison joked.

I glared at her, "Thanks a lot, Mads."

She smiled, "Do you really want to work as a sex slave?"

"If the pay is good, I'll do anything," I sighed. "But I already checked the sex slave want ads. All the sex slave masters are looking for someone with experience."

"Slave experience, or sex experience?" Romeo asked innocently.

"I'm assuming both," I joked. "Most of the ads mentioned ball gag *and* whip experience. I've never used either."

"If you need any pointers," Romeo said, "let me know."

"Yeah, Sam," Kamiko smiled, "if you need practice whipping someone's ass, I can demonstrate for you on Romeo."

"Is it just me," Romeo smirked, "or would Kamiko make a good dominatrix?"

I looked at Kamiko, who had her hands in her lap while leaning over her drink cup, which was sitting on the table, while she sucked on her drink straw. She looked like a little kid. The only thing missing was a twirly crazy straw. I said, "Maybe a cartoon dominatrix."

"Butter lettuce?" Romeo said to Kamiko suggestively, like he was trying to seduce her. "Locally grown?"

I wasn't sure what he was talking about.

Neither was Madison.

"You mean the butter lettuce party?" Kamiko asked. "Those weren't dominatrices. Those were male stripper unicorns."

"DominatriCEES?" Romeo enunciated forcefully. "When did you become Ms. Dictionary, Kamiko?" Romeo asked skeptically, as if Kamiko's word pronunciation was weirder than male stripper unicorns.

I was so lost.

"Yes," Kamiko said, "dominatrices is the primary spelling for the plural version of the word."

Madison frowned at me, "What are they talking about?"

I shook my head, "Cartoons? The dictionary? I have no idea. My friends are insane."

"Butter lettuce party from Bravest Warriors?!" Kamiko suggested with maximum frustration. "Episode three?! Season one?!" She slapped the table top for emphasis. "Don't you guys watch the internet?!"

"Yeah," Romeo glared at me and Madison sarcastically, "Duh!"

"Mads," I said, "I can't decide who is more cray cray. Them or us."

"I'm just eating my fish tacos," she giggled. "I don't know any of you."

===

I plugged my debit card into one of the ATMs on campus near the Student Center. I needed to check how much cash I had left in my account because my monthly tuition payment was barreling toward me at the speed of light. I was going to owe more than $5,000 to SDU in a few short weeks.

After I entered my PIN, I pressed Check Your Balance. Instead of a number, the ATM machine laughed at me and told me to get a job. I'm surprised it didn't shred my card and flash the words YOU'RE BROKE repeatedly.

There were people waiting behind me in line to use the ATM, so I canceled out and took my card.

Where the hell was I going to find five grand? I had combed through the job search websites with a microscope and hadn't found anything yet. Maybe I needed to go back to Grab-n-Dash and beg for my job? A scent memory of hot dogs and urine colored polyester wrinkled my nose.

Maybe not.

Short of selling a kidney or other parts of my body to the highest bidder, the only other thing that occurred to me was checking online for scholarships.

I walked to the Main Library and set up my laptop near a window on the seventh floor. I sighed as I logged onto the library's wi-fi network and searched through scholarship websites. It didn't take long to realize that most of the application deadlines had already passed. Not that it mattered. Most of them didn't pay any money until the fall.

I sat back in my chair and sighed. I glanced out at the amazing view of San Diego. I'd always loved the Main Library's wrap around windows. From the seventh floor where I sat, you could see for miles.

Usually, the view lifted my spirits. Too bad nothing short of a construction crane could lift my spirits today.

I sighed and went back to my job hunt. Trying to remain optimistic, I narrowed my internet search by application deadline. There weren't many scholarships left on the list.

I found one for bagpipe majors. It paid seven thousand bucks! Bagpipes couldn't be too hard to play, could they? I would totally double major in bagpipes if it meant seven grand. The only problem was I couldn't even afford a set of bagpipes. Even if I could, I wouldn't be surprised if Christos or Spiridon kicked me out of the house for taking up the fartbags. But I would play them every damn day if it meant $7,000. Crap. Who was I kidding? I don't think I could deal with all that quacking.

Next.

There was one scholarship for people studying the Klingon language. I'd watched Star Trek. Didn't Klingons just grunt? I could grunt.

There was also one for the American Nudist Research Library. No, seriously. I read it on the internet. What did nudist researchers research, anyway? Increased incidences of skin cancer among the nude? Early onset droopage, for both men and women? Because you know drooping was the biggest problem faced by nudists. I seriously would've applied if it wasn't for the fact you had to live in a nudist colony to qualify. I didn't even know where to find a nudist colony, unless you counted art models. Hey! Maybe with all the girls coming to Christos' studio every day, the Manos house qualified! I was totally submitting an application.

I searched the scholarships for another two hours and applied to a dozen more. With any luck, I might actually get picked for one, but I wasn't holding my breath.

I had to assume that I was no closer to covering the $5,000 I owed SDU than when I started.

Droopyballs!

Ew.

===

My spring classes consisted of: Sociology 3, History 3 (which focused on 20th Century America), Plein Air Painting (which Kamiko told me to take because she was), and Drawing the Costumed Figure (which Romeo and Kamiko both were taking).

I'd managed to gets B's in Sosh and History during Winter Quarter, much to my surprise. I think all the cramming I did for mid terms and finals made up for my tendency to doodle in my sketchbook during class. With my current financial problems, I vowed to pay total attention and take notes during Sosh and History this term. No more doodling. The last thing I needed was a bad GPA making my financial aid situation worse than it already was.

I met Kamiko outside the Visual Arts building for our first Plein Air Painting class. It only met once a week, on Wednesday afternoon. How awesome was that? We both held portable easels that collapsed into the size of a suitcase. I'd borrowed mine from Christos. He had several in the studio. I couldn't afford to buy one, and it was a requirement for the class, so I was in luck.

"Why do we have these easels?" I asked.

"You'll see," Kamiko grinned as we walked into the Visual Arts building.

"You know," I wrinkled my nose, "Plein Air sounds kind of boring." I was pronouncing it like 'plain' because I had no idea how to say it. "Are we going to paint plain things? Like vanilla ice cream and white rice? Because I don't see how we could paint plain air. Unless we paint the sky? And because it has to be plain, we only paint cloudless skies? Isn't that just squeezing blue paint on a canvas?"

Kamiko smiled at me indulgently as she held the door open to the classroom. "No, silly."

Unlike my previous art classes, which had taken place in rooms that were obviously artist's paradises, the Plein Air room was small and bland. The walls were blank. There was a teacher's desk at the front of the room, one of those ancient metal ones that looked like a gray battleship that had seen several wars. And of course, a bunch of student desk chair combos with mustard yellow plastic seats crammed together. I had been right about the plain thing. This looked like any random high school classroom in America. Wasn't this supposed to be a University?

"Why do I feel like we're going to spend the next three hours in detention?" I asked Kamiko.

She arched her eyebrows, but said nothing.

A few students stood against the walls with their portable easels. There wasn't much room to set them up. Maybe that's why we had the portable easels, so we could squeeze them into the scant remaining available space?

A few minutes later, a middle aged woman walked into the room. She had curly hair and a big smile. She wore a wide brimmed hat and a khaki hunter's vest with a bunch of pockets over a long sleeve shirt and jeans. Hiking boots completed her outfit. Were we going on a safari?

"Hello, everybody," she said. "My name is Katherine Weatherspoon, and I'll be your Plein Air instructor for spring term. If you haven't figured it out by now, we're going to be painting outdoors for the next ten weeks. *En plein air*," she said it with an accent that sounded like she was saying 'on plain air', "is a French expression that means 'in the open air'. Everyone, gather up your easels. We're heading out."

The students picked up their easels and followed Katherine Weatherspoon out the door.

I leaned over to Kamiko and whispered, "I was right, we're going to be painting the blue sky all quarter."

"It's worse than that," Kamiko whispered, "we're actually going to be painting air, like oxygen. So it's just clear. Did you remember to bring a tube of transparent acrylic glaze? Because that's the only color you're going to need."

"What, like see through? We're just going to put clear paint on canvases?"

Kamiko shrugged her shoulders.

This was going to be really boring. I guess not every aspect of painting was a winner. "Where are we going?" I asked Kamiko as we filed in behind the last of the students.

"I have no idea," she said.

We walked across campus, through Adams College, and out to North Torrey Pines boulevard. We crossed at the light when it was green.

"Are we going to the cliffs?" I asked.

"I guess," Kamiko said.

Sure enough, we ended up out at the cliffs west of the SDU campus. They overlooked the beach and the Pacific Ocean. There was lots of plain air for the painting. Yay.

"Here will be good," Professor Weatherspoon said, setting her portable easel down. "Everyone, find a place to set your easels up, then I'll begin a demonstration."

Kamiko and I found a spot together. It didn't really matter where I set up because there was oxygen in every direction.

A few minutes later, the professor had us all gather around her easel. She had a very small canvas mounted on it, about four by six inches. With her portable palette already covered with little dollops of oil, she began painting. She used a little metal spatula, which she kept referring to as a palette knife, to mix colors on her palette and smear them onto the canvas. It didn't take long for her to cover the canvas with colors. I realized half way through that she was painting the curve of the Torrey Pines cliffs to the south, the beach, the ocean, and the sky. Her painting was really amazing, resembling a sloppy photograph made of cake frosting. If I squinted my eyes, it looked like the real thing.

When the professor was finished, she turned to the students and smiled, "Now go ahead and start your paintings. I'll be walking around helping everyone out."

Kamiko and I walked over to our easels. Now that I realized we weren't going to be painting invisible oxygen all term, I adjusted my easel so I was facing the south cliffs, like the professor had.

I didn't have a palette knife, so I just used brushes. I wasn't used to working on such a complicated subject likes cliffs and waves. There were ten million different things to paint in my field of vision. I was getting a little flustered. I set my brush down and rubbed my forehead with the back of my wrist.

"Having troubles?" Professor Weatherspoon asked.

I was so used to Marjorie Bitchinger's bitchiness and sarcasm last quarter, I was afraid to say anything for fear of incurring Professor Weatherspoon's wrath.

"It's okay," she said in a kind voice, "there's a lot to figure out all at once," she smiled. "What you want to do is focus on the big shapes first. Work from big to small and add detail last. May I?" she asked, reaching for my brush.

"Yeah, totally," I smiled.

She picked up my brush, dabbed it in some raw umber on my palette, and blocked in a few lines for the cliffs. "Since you're using a brush, paint thin. You don't want too much paint making a mess all over your canvas." She rinsed the brush in my little jar of Turpenoid, then went in with a thin mix of white and ultramarine blue. "Put in the horizon line, like this," she painted a faint blue horizontal line, "so you know where it is." She cleaned the brush again, dipped it in some yellow ochre, and scribbled in the line of the beach where it met the water. My painting now looked like colored outlines of the view. "Now all you have to do is fill everything in," she smiled and handed me my brush before walking away to help other students.

My good mood was back. I turned to Kamiko, "Is this even a real class? It seems like way too much fun."

"I know, right?" she grinned while she mixed a pile of phthalo green with cerulean blue on her palette.

"Maybe we can both drop out of school and be Plein Air painters for the rest of our lives."

"Sounds like a plan to me," she grinned as she applied her blue green paint to her canvas where the greenish waves met the golden sand of the beach. "We can hitchhike across America and paint whatever we see."

"Then we can publish a book of our paintings," I suggested.

"Totally," Kamiko grinned.

Plein Air Painting was awesome. When class was over three hours later, we packed everything up and walked back to SDU.

I had totally forgotten about my financial woes the entire time. And for that, I was grateful.

But they hadn't forgotten about me.

===

Five people stood in front of me in line for the teller at the bank in Del Mar when I walked in the next morning.

From what I understood, if you handed a note to the bank teller that you had a gun and wanted money, they gave it to you. They didn't ask if you had a gun. They just assumed you did, and paid you, which meant I was in luck because I had no gun. I'd considered stopping at a 99 Cents Only store to buy a toy gun, but I didn't have 99 cents to spare, so I decided to wing it.

Of course, when you handed the note to the teller, they also stepped on the floor alarm button and the cops showed up, but I was fast on my feet. I could be gone before the SWAT team arrived and guns started going off.

Besides, this was San Diego. Did they even have SWAT teams in San Diego? The security guard at this bank was an old guy. I'm pretty sure he had a banana in his holster. I would be fine.

And I was only going to ask for $10,000 to cover my tuition. Not a penny more. I liked to think of it like a scholarship, because no one expected you to pay scholarships back.

The person in front of me was a bulbous man in a sloppy windbreaker and saggy slacks. He kept clearing his throat every five seconds. I think he had a hairball. I was waiting for him to squat down on the marble floor, head hanging between his shoulder blades, and hack it up like a cat, but he never did. He just kept hacking.

Eventually, the teller called Hairball up to the counter. He pulled out a stack of cash, which he counted out in front of the teller, coughing after every fifth bill he laid down like clockwork. I think he was making a cash deposit. I didn't understand why he was counting it. That was the bank's job. But he insisted. It took forever. He was hacking so often, I was getting the urge to clear my own throat. Were there toxic spores in the air? Whatever Hairball had, it was catching.

I was getting more and more nervous by the second because I was next. For a minute, I considered leaving, but didn't. I had to go through with this. As soon as Hairball was gone, I was asking for that ten grand.

About ten hours and a million hacks later, Hairball was finished. I stepped up to the teller window and opened my mouth to speak.

What came out was a hack. Stupid Hairball. It really was catching. I cleared my throat several times. When I finished, the teller was looking at me like I had tuberculosis. I probably did. Thanks, Hairball Hackmaster.

"Ahem," I hacked a final time. I wrung my hands together. I was going to do this. I needed ten grand. My heart was pounding. It was time to ask for my money.

"Can I help you?" the teller asked like she was about to call the Center for Disease Control so she could have me quarantined.

My throat was tickling again, but I willed it to relax. "Yes," I said hoarsely, "I need to speak to someone about getting a loan?"

"Certainly," the teller fake smiled dryly. "I'll have one of our loan officers speak with you. If you could take a seat over there," she pointed to the far corner of the bank, "someone will be out to talk to you shortly." She couldn't wait to get me out of her breathing space.

"Thanks," I said and sat down in one of the chairs. My throat was still tickling, but I refused to start hacking again while I waited.

It was ten in the morning, and I'd decided to cut classes today and try to solve my money problems. I mean, what was the point in studying if I couldn't pay my tuition bill when it came due?

Sadly, I hadn't been able to find a single job online, and the scholarships weren't looking any more promising. I still hadn't told Christos about losing my museum job. It had been two weeks already, but the last thing I wanted to do was bother him with my money problems. With all of the paintings he needed to finish for his next gallery show weighing down on him, he had more than enough stress already, and it was eating away at him. His continued drinking was proof.

When the loan officer finally called me into his cubicle, I was bummed to discover I needed a cosigner for a $10,000 loan.

Great.

Where was I going to find a cosigner? My parents? Ha! That was the funniest thing I'd ever heard. Christos? I couldn't ask him. It was one thing to live in his house rent free, another to make him liable for a huge chunk of change. I couldn't do it. And I couldn't ask my friends. They didn't have any money to spare.

Maybe I needed to head to Las Vegas on the weekend and pour some money into the slot machines? Oh, wait. I didn't have any money to blow on gambling.

Wasn't there some kind of college hooker organization that represented young college women like myself, and only paired you with hot guys? Nah, I think I read that in a romance novel somewhere. It couldn't possibly be real. Besides, I had a boyfriend.

I was out of options.

Sane ones, anyway.

I sat in my car in the parking lot outside the bank and cried while I leaned my head against the steering wheel. My hair draped around my face and stuck to my wet cheeks. When I was out of tears, I drove to UTC, the shopping center just east of SDU. I walked from store to store, asking about jobs, just like I'd done with Romeo a few months ago.

No one was hiring.

Not even Hot Dog On A Stick. I considered waiting around until one of the hot dog girls took a break so I could knock her out and steal her multi-colored uniform. I was so desperate, I would gladly wear one of their clown outfits and re-subject myself to smelling like hot dogs if it meant I had some money coming in.

Since UTC was a bust, I drove to Mission Valley and hit up the Fashion Valley Mall, Hazard Center, and the Westfield. I filled out several applications and left them behind with promises from the managers they'd give me a call if anything opened up.

When I went home that night, I was exhausted. I had job searched for nine hours straight. My feet were killing me.

I checked the studio for Christos but he wasn't there. I trudged upstairs and found him passed out in our bedroom. He reeked of booze. He was getting sloshed every day now.

When in Rome.

I was so tired and hungry and frustrated and disheartened from my failed job search today that I decided to get sloshed myself.

I drove to the grocery store under the cover of darkness and bought an armload of ice cream. When I got back to the house, it didn't take long for me to stuff myself so full of ice cream that I was sloshing when I walked into one of the downstairs bathrooms. I unloaded my freshly consumed ice cream in private and prepared for round two. I walked back to the freezer and pulled out another pint.

Mmmm, ice cream.

Gag.

I ate two more pints before I'd had enough and went to bed.

===

A few days later, between Sociology 3 and American History 3, I spent several hours studying in the Main Library. When it was time to head to my history lecture, I closed my laptop and headed for the stairwell door.

There was a huge staircase that spiraled around the square cement tower that supported the fourth through seventh floors of the Main Library. From the outside, the Main Library resembled a squat cement squared-off oak tree with a narrow base that supported the four floors on top.

Going down the stairs inside the three-story base always reminded me of descending into a giant crypt, like in the pyramids, but without cool hieroglyphics on the walls. It was gray and dreary.

Too bad I wasn't going to find any gold sarcophagi at the bottom of the stairs, or whatever other treasures grave robbers always found when they broke into pyramids. Oh well.

At least it was exercise.

When I walked out of the stairwell next to the elevators, I passed through a corridor that had glass cases on both sides. The cases contained an ever-changing collection of museum style exhibits of all kinds of things: old antique books, ceramics, folk art objects, or sometimes actual art. Today, I noticed that there was a new display in several of the cases.

To my surprise, when I read one of the placards, I discovered it was original art from the Dennis the Menace comic strip.

I stopped to look at the art more closely. I had only ever seen Dennis the Menace art in the pulpy newsprint paper my dad looked at every morning. Up close, the original inked art was magnificent. The lines were so precise and crisp, yet stylized and very geometrical. I would never have made an observation like this before I'd started studying drawing so intensely six months ago. I used to just think of Dennis the Menace as a cartoon with cute drawings. Now I had something vaguely profound to say. I was so proud of myself.

Maybe I *had* found treasure at the bottom of that library staircase.

"Hank Ketcham is amazing, isn't he?" Justin Tomlinson asked.

"Oh!" I gasped. I'd been so engrossed in the art, I hadn't noticed him walk up. "Hey, Justin."

Justin wore a sporty lightweight leather jacket over a V-neck print tee, and skinny jeans. He looked like he was ready to walk up to the podium at the Grammys and accept an award for best male vocalist.

"The library just got the art in this week. I've been dying to see it in person," he said.

Art? What art? I was busy admiring Justin's impeccable fashion sense. He was stylish and hip without over doing it. I bet he had his own personal dresser and style consultant. His hair was carefully mussed in a sexy way that looked easy and relaxed but probably took an hour to arrange.

One look at Justin and my profound art observations had flown right out the window.

"What do you think of it?" Justin smiled.

His hair? It was amazing. His smile? Even better. "Uh…"

Justin frowned, "The art? What do you think of the art?"

"Oh! The art! Yes! The art is amazing!" I think it was common knowledge that guilty people ended every sentence with an exclamation point. Not that I was guilty. I wasn't guilty of anything. So what if Justin was adorable?

Justin slowly nodded with an odd look on his face. I think he didn't know what to say because he was trying to decide whether or not I was clinically insane.

I wasn't sure what to say either, so I nodded back at him. Nod, nod, nod. I could go on nodding all day like a Bobblehead doll if I had too. Nod! Nod! Nod! Big smile! Lots of teeth! So not guilty of finding Justin adorable! NOD! NOD! NOD!

"Why do I feel like I'm stuck in the middle of a Dennis the Menace comic strip?" Justin asked.

Because we were? Except in this case, it was Denise the Menace, and I was Denise.

I shook my head, trying to get a hold of myself. That just made the bobbling worse. Hold still! I grinned so wide my cheeks hurt. I had a moment to realize that although I had an amazing boyfriend, some men had cuteness powers granted by the devil. It wasn't my fault Justin was dazzling me. Any woman who took one look at him would go Bobblehead the second they saw him.

"So, uh," Justin stammered, sounding uncomfortable, "did you do any more wombat sketches?"

What was a wombat again?

Okay, I'd had enough of my brainlessness. I bit the inside of my cheek, shocking myself out of my boy crazy stupor.

Wincing, because now the inside of my cheek really hurt, I said, "I was going to ask you, did you guys vote yet?" It had been a few weeks since I'd given him all my designs for Potty the Pot Smoking Wombat.

"Not yet. Some of the other artists are still working on ideas."

"That's good," I nodded. Nod, nod, nod.

STOP NODDING!!

My cheek hurt too much to bite again, and I wasn't going to bite the other side, so I sighed, rolled my eyes, and said, "I wanted to submit a few more before the vote."

"Do you have them now?" he asked.

"Uh, no. I've been sort of, ahh…busy lately?" Guilty people also ended their sentences with question marks. Or was it broke people whose parents were pricks? I forgot. One or the other.

"Well, get any new drawings in to me as soon as you can."

Yeah, I was into him. NO I WASN'T!!

Justin continued, unaware that I was schizophrenic, "I'll probably take a vote at the end of the week."

"Okay," I smiled, doing my best not to bat my eyelashes. It was Justin's sexy devil powers that made me do it.

"By the way, have you and Romeo come up with any ideas for comic strips yet? We're already putting together the next issue for print. The deadline for submissions is right around the corner."

"We have a few, but we've both been pretty busy. Romeo always has theater major stuff taking up his time."

"Well, even if you guys don't make the deadline, Romeo still seemed like a good guy. Lots of funny ideas. You should totally bring him to the next staff meeting."

"Okay," I nodded. I meant, tilted my head to indicate agreement without nodding, nodding, nodding.

STOP!!

"Anyway," Justin said, "I've gotta run to class. Email me any new material if you come up with something?"

"Okay."

Before walking off, he flashed a grin and said, "Laters!"

Wait, he had ended his sentence with an exclamation point! And the one before that with a question mark! Did that mean he was feeling guilty? Or was it just me feeling guilty? Well, 'Laters!' was only one word and didn't count as a sentence, right? Did Justin like me? Or did it mean I was crazy?! Maybe both?!?

Oh, um, hmm. That might complicate things for me. Him liking me. And me being crazy.

GET A HOLD OF YOURSELF.

Note the absence of guilty exclamation points. That was my sane voice telling my cray cray ones to shut up.

Sigh.

I needed a lobotomy.

I walked outside into the fresh air hoping that would help clear my head and that Justin was long gone so he wouldn't think I was stalking him.

I wasn't stalking him! Was I?

I promise I wasn't!?!

Where was that lobotomy? I heard you could use an ice pick through the eye socket and it worked fine.

Groanballs.

Anyway, I really hoped Justin wasn't being nice to me just because he was interested in me. He wasn't a jerk like Hunter Snakeley, but he was the editor of The Wombat. I didn't want him fudging the vote in favor of my wombat drawings just because he thought it might make me like him. And I didn't want him fudging the vote against me if he thought I didn't like him. I wanted to win fair and square.

Wait, I just remembered Justin had been the one who approached me in the first place last quarter. He'd been drawing stalking me for who knew how long. You didn't stalk someone you weren't interested in, did you?

Groan!

Why was my life so complicated?!?

Not guilty!

I swear!

I mean, I swear.

No exclamation points or question marks that time.

===

The hot yellow sun rolled across the surface of the Pacific Ocean as I parked my VW in the driveway of the Manos house. I walked to the front door with my keys jingling in my hand. I always felt a sense of relief wash over me when I came home. As I was about to slide my keys into the lock of the double front doors, the door was ripped open from the inside.

"Thank god you're here!" Sophia blurted, standing in the doorway. Sophia was one of Christos' other models. I'd met her several times before. She had Eastern European eyes and full lips. Normally she was quite beautiful, but at the moment worry cut her face into ragged lines.

"What's wrong?" I asked, immediately frightened by her panic.

"Christos is passed out," she said nervously, pulling me into the house, "I didn't know what to do. I was about to call 911."

My heart tripped into overdrive. "Is Christos hurt? Did he fall?" He'd been drinking so much lately, I wouldn't be surprised if he had. I knew drunk people were supposed to be so relaxed they were less likely to get hurt if they fell down or whatever, but that didn't matter if you fell through a window and landed on shards of glass or off a balcony onto cement.

"Sort of," Sophia winced.

"Sort of fell?"

She shook her head, obviously worried. "I don't know how to explain..."

"What happened?" I did my best not to lose my cool.

"Maybe I should show you," she grimaced.

I was suddenly thinking Christos had had a seizure and his mouth would be covered with foamy blood. Could alcohol give you seizures? Or was it something worse?

As we stepped into the studio, Sophia said in a low voice, "I think he's drunk."

Shit, was that all?

Sure enough, Christos sat slumped over in a chair in front of the painting of Sophia he'd been working on. There was a huge red streak running across the canvas, cutting down the middle of the face and across the chest. A brush loaded with the same red paint dangled from Christos' hand.

He was snoring.

"He just fell onto the painting while he was working about an hour ago. I'd told him this morning maybe he should stop drinking, but he ignored me. Who was I to complain? I'm just the model, and I need the job."

I could relate to that.

"I didn't know who to call," she said, "and no one else was here. I almost left, but I thought I should stay until someone showed up. I didn't want him choking on vomit or whatever."

"Thanks, Sophia," I said sincerely. "I totally appreciate your hanging around and keeping an eye on him. If you want, you can take off now. I can handle it from here."

"Oh, uh, I'm supposed to stay and model until six."

"Don't worry about it," I said dismissively. "I'll tell Christos you were here the whole time," I winked. "Either way, I don't think he'll know when you left."

She nodded nervously. "You're sure?"

"Yes," I smiled, "I promise."

She heaved a huge sigh of relief, "Thank you SO much! I was starting to worry no one would show up and I'd be stuck here until whenever he woke up. I've got a photo shoot in L.A. tonight, and with traffic, I'm probably going to be late as it is. If I get a head start now, I might actually make it. Do you need any help moving Christos before I roll?"

Sophia's arms looked like pencils. Despite her compassion, I didn't think she would be much help in the lifting department.

"I think I'm going to need a crane," I joked. "Or I can just wait until he sleeps it off."

"Totally," she grinned.

After Sophia left, I took a good look at Christos. I wanted to make sure he kept breathing and didn't choke on vomit. Considering he was snoring like a saw mill, I think he was fine. But if the saw mill shut down operations, I'd slide him out of the chair and onto his side.

In the meantime, I took the brush with the red paint out of his hand and folded his arms into his lap so he looked more comfortable.

I examined the red streak on Christos' painting of Sophia. I dabbed at it with my pinky finger. It was oil, so it was still wet. Should I wipe it off? I can't imagine he'd be mad. It looked like an accident. Considering Sophia said he'd fallen asleep while painting, it probably was.

Unless he'd intended to ruin the painting? Like the way he'd trashed the painting of Isabella the day my parents had arrived? Oh well. I was going to wipe the red off, just in case it was an accident. If he had meant to ruin it, he could ruin it again in the morning with a clear head.

First, I cleaned off the brush with the red paint on it. Then, I found some clean paper towels and carefully wiped away at the red slash until it was completely gone. I stood back from the painting and examined it from a distance.

Good as new.

Then an irrational fear seized me. What if Christos had meant to put that red slash there? What if it was some genius breakthrough he'd finally discovered and I had gone and cleaned it off?

Oh no.

I remembered that Christos had become frustrated with his

paintings of all the models and he was trying to find a way to spice them up. What if that red slash was the first step in a new creative direction that I was too dense to fathom? Maybe he'd had a flash of brilliance and decided to combine abstract art with his realistic portraits in a whole new way? Considering I still didn't know much about the history of art or how new styles and art movements developed, and I didn't know the first thing about abstract art, it was entirely possible.

Oh no.

What had I done?

Had I erased the only mark of his newfound genius? I didn't even have a cell phone picture of it in case he wanted a reminder.

Oh no.

I eyed the glob of red paint still on his palette, and the now clean brush that had been loaded with said red paint. Should I load up the brush with more red, try to recreate the red slash, then stick the brush back in his hand?

He'd totally think my red slash was his red slash. I mean, it was just a slash, right?

Who would know the difference?

Who was I kidding. I knew people liked to say that a baby or a monkey could paint abstract art, but I'm pretty sure that was an exaggeration and one abstract artist could tell his or her work from another's. When Christos sobered up, he was going to recognize that my lame red slash wasn't his genius red slash.

Fuck, fuck, fuck.

My panic level was up to my eyeballs. I was swimming in panic. I needed a panic snorkel or I was going to drown in it.

Deep breath.

I took another breath, and another. I reminded myself that Christos had been so drunk, he'd fallen asleep. That wasn't how a genius worked, was it? Then I gasped as I remembered all those famous artists and writers and poets who had been alcoholics. What did I know about genius?

What had I done?

Where was my ice cream?

RED ALERT! RED ALERT!

I needed to strategize. What was I going to do when Christos woke up in the morning and asked me where his red slash had gone?

I know! I could squeeze some red paint out of the tube right onto the canvas, then push Christos in his chair into the painting, and lean his face into the glob of red. It would smear the paint, he'd have red paint on his face as proof, and he'd never know what I'd done! He'd assume he'd ruined his genius red slash himself! It was genius! I was genius!

Oh, wait. What was it I'd said earlier about guilty people ending their sentences with exclamation points? Christos would figure out something was wrong, especially if he woke up tomorrow and I answered all his questions about the red slash with exclamation point sentences.

I needed a better idea.

I looked at the pile of red stained paper towels in the trash can. His red slash was on those towels. What if I carefully unfolded them and pressed the red slash back onto the canvas, like a sticker? Who was I kidding. The slash was ruined. Christos' genius was smeared beyond recognition.

I felt like a complete idiot. Like I'd just walked into Picasso's studio the day he'd decided to leave behind the realistic painting style of his early days and began his legendary blue period, and I was the idiot who had the nerve to say, "No, no, no, Pablo. This is way too much blue. You need to use more color. Trust me, I know what I'm talking about."

Yeah, right.

I had the sinking feeling that today Christos had embarked on his own journey to worldwide acclaim, and the painting of Sophia would have been remembered forever as the very first painting of his legendary Red Slash period, had I not wiped it away.

I was the worst girlfriend of all time.

I could only hope Christos forgot all about it when he sobered up. If he said anything about red slashes, I would suggest it was the liquor talking, and maybe it had been dancing red elephants he had seen?

Except for the mountain of dirty red towels in the trash can. I needed to bury the evidence somewhere quick.

Why did I feel like a murderer?

Oh, yeah. Because I'd just murdered Christos' burgeoning art career.

I swiveled Christos around in his chair so his ruined painting wouldn't be the first thing he laid eyes on when he woke up. I didn't want to shock him into a heart attack.

Two hours later, when he finally blinked himself awake, I led him upstairs before he could ask me any incriminating questions about his missing red slash.

When I dropped him into bed, I noticed he smelled like a bourbon distillery. His sweat must've been at least sixty proof.

When he was safely asleep, I dashed downstairs and stashed the dirty red towels in a neighbor's garbage can down the street. Did the soiled towels look like bloody rags used to mop up after a stabbing? Err, I meant, slashing? Mmm, kind of. But DNA testing would not reveal a match with the corpse of Christos' dead career.

No one would ever know I was the killer.

Except me.

I had nightmares about red slashes all night long.

===

I was awake before Christos.

I tiptoed to the kitchen and quietly made us breakfast in bed. After we finished eating, we made love for two hours, despite the remnants of his hangover. Did I orgasm multiple times? Of course. Did I exaggerate my screams in an attempt to keep Christos in the bedroom longer with more sex? Maybe a tad. But I didn't want him to go down to the studio and see his slashless painting.

After Christos came for the fourth time, he said he wanted to get back to work on his painting of Sophia. Desperate for another distraction, I suggested we stay in bed and experiment with some light bondage. Not that I was into S&M, but I needed an excuse to tie Christos to the bed so he couldn't leave the room.

"Tempting," he smirked, "maybe next time? I really need to get back to work."

"Oh wait! You haven't seen the new lingerie I bought!" I jumped out of bed and grabbed it out of my chest of drawers. I ran into the bathroom before he could object. "It'll only take a second for me to put it on!"

"When did you buy lingerie?" he called from the bedroom.

"Last week," I hollered as I tried not to trip over myself while I hastily threw it on. "I went shopping with Mads."

I walked out of the bathroom decked out in a black lace babydoll tied at the throat, black thong, and black thigh high stockings. I'd planned on saving it for a special occasion. Sparing Christos the tragedy of his missing red slash seemed as good as any.

"Holy shit!" Christos blurted. "Why didn't you tell me you had sexy lingerie!"

The lingerie was good for another hour of love making. But I couldn't keep Christos in our bedroom forever, as much as I wanted to.

While we showered together after sex, I considered sneaking out and calling in a bomb threat on Christos' studio. But I was pretty sure you weren't supposed to tell the police the bomb threat was in your own house.

I was out of options.

When Christos was dressed, he beelined for the studio. I followed him, ready for disaster. I kept an eye on my exits in case I needed to beat a hasty retreat.

He stood in front of the canvas.

Moment of truth.

If he murdered me for ruining his painting, I wouldn't press charges. It was the least I deserved.

"You're frowning," I said nervously, "Why are you frowning?"

"I'm not sure," he said absently. "Something about the painting of Sophia…"

Crap. I'd been right all along.

I'd ruined it.

Christos was going to dump me and kick me out on the street for ruining his career. I'd end up one of those broken old homeless women with leathery skin who kept all her possessions in a grocery cart. I'd tell anyone who was kind enough to give me spare change or a half eaten sandwich that I'd once been in love with the greatest artist on the planet, until I'd ruined his life and his career.

Christos picked up a brush from the work table beside his easel. "It's not really working for me," he said thoughtfully. "What do you think?"

I walked around and stood beside him. "Oh, no! It's perfect! I mean, this is a work of genius! I've never seen anything more amazing!" Wow, were my exclamation points as obvious to him as they were to me? I figured I was four seconds away from being covered with red slashes after Christos stabbed me to death with the blunt end of a paintbrush for what I'd done. I wouldn't put up a struggle, no matter how much it hurt. I deserved a slow painful death.

Christos set the brush down and smirked at me. "Okay, *agápi mou*. You can be honest with me. You don't like it, do you?"

Did he mean the painting as it was now?

He hadn't said anything about the red slash.

"Err, no?" I said with what I suspect was an incriminating degree of guilt. "I mean it's really good? What's not to like? I can't imagine anyone not liking it? Can you?" I stopped myself before I used any more guilty question marks.

He chuckled. "Thanks, but, I don't know. It seems lifeless to me. Like it needs something to spruce it up."

Like a red slash?

Shit! Had I said that out loud?

Fuck!?!?!

I took a deep breath. "It's amazing, Christos. I mean, I couldn't paint anything this nice."

"Thanks, *agápi mou*. I know it doesn't suck, but it's not grabbing me. There's millions of good paintings in the world, but less than a hundred, maybe less than a dozen, that people remember. I mean, how many famous paintings can you name off the top of your head?"

"The Mona Lisa? Van Gogh's Sunflowers? Munch's The Scream? Monet's Water Lilies? Dali's Melting Clocks? Uhh...Rembrandt's Night Watch? Uhh, I'm running out! Help me here?"

I didn't sound nervous, did I?

"See what I mean?" he said casually, "It doesn't take long for the average person to fall short. Most people don't get past the Mona Lisa. Beyond that, about the only other thing people remember is Picasso's Blue Period, because it sounds funny."

Oh geez, he was dangerously close to putting the clues together. I needed a distraction quick! Guilty exclamation point! D'oh! I meant, d'oh. I'd already used my body to full effect in the bedroom, and it hadn't stopped the inevitable. All I could do now was string together the first ideas that popped into my head. I said, "I know, right! A blue period? The first thing I think of when I hear 'blue period' is pulling my tampon out one day and it's Cerulean blue! And that's like, the most expensive paint of all, right? I could turn myself into a paint factory if I bled Cerulean blue! But I could only sell paint once a month because it's such a rare color!"

What was I saying?!? I was crazy!!!

!?!?!?!?!?!

Guilt! Guilt? Guilt! I needed to have my brain removed! ASAP?

Christos chuckled, "Blue period. Have I ever told you how much I enjoy your bizarre ideas, *agápi mou*?"

Bizarre was too kind a word. I giggled nervously.

He put a loving arm around my shoulders. "All this talk about blue periods has got me thinking. I need to come up with my own thing, like Picasso. Have any ideas? I bet you could think up something no one's ever thought of."

How about a red slash period? Oh wait! You already thought of that!?!?!?!?!

I was three seconds away from collapsing into a puddle of tears. I couldn't take it anymore. I cracked like fine china on cement.

"I DID IT, CHRISTOS! I WIPED AWAY YOUR SLASH OF RED GENIUS YESTERDAY! I'M SO SORRY! BUT YOU WERE DRUNK! I THOUGHT IT WAS A MISTAKE! I WANTED TO CLEAN IT OFF BEFORE IT DRIED AND RUINED YOUR PAINTING!!!"

I sobbed.

He wrapped his other arm around me. "What are you talking about, *agápi mou*?"

After I calmed, I looked into his loving eyes. They welcomed me with warmth and affection. I wiped tears from my cheeks and sniffled, "When I came home yesterday, you'd fallen asleep drunk. There was a big red slash of paint on the canvas. I cleaned it off, thinking you'd done it by accident, but then I thought maybe you hadn't! Now I've ruined it!" I sobbed some more.

"A red slash?" he said thoughtfully. "I don't even remember that." His face darkened into a frown.

Oh no, this was it. This was the moment he realized what I'd done.

He smirked, "I feel like an idiot, *agápi mou*."

Him?

I thought I was the idiot.

He shook his head with disgust, "I've been drinking so much lately I can't even remember what I'm doing anymore."

Hope. Maybe I hadn't snipped off Christos' red slash period at the bud.

"So," I said, "you don't think you put the red slash on the painting on purpose?"

"Are you kidding? I was probably so loaded I didn't even know what color paint was on my brush," he chuckled.

"So I didn't destroy your genius?"

"My genius?"

"It was a pretty awesome red slash," I quipped.

His face went serious and he arched an eyebrow, "Then maybe you should've left it alone? Sometimes genius works in mysterious ways..."

Gulp. I wondered if I could commit suicide by holding my breath until I suffocated. It was the only escape option I had while wrapped up in Christos' arms. Tears welled in my eyes, so I buried my face in Christos' shirt out of embarrassment and guilt.

Guilt!?!?!?!?!!!!!!!

I inhaled deeply. Christos had been drinking so much, I assumed he would smell of booze, and I was hoping I could inhale enough booze fumes to get a contact buzz and finally calm down. Nope. Apparently, he'd sweat all the alcohol out of his system during our vigorous lovemaking earlier. I would have to go back to holding my breath until I suffocated. But, after our shower, he now smelled like the sexiest man on the planet. There was no way I could hold my breath if it meant not getting to inhale more of his manliness at close range.

When I looked up into his loving, affectionate eyes, my guilt eased several notches.

"I'm totally kidding, *agápi mou*," he smiled. "If all it took to make a painting genius was adding a red slash, people would be adding red slashes to everything. Loaves of bread. Smart phones. SUVs. Saucepans. The world would be filled with red slashes. But do you see red slashes everywhere? Nope. And no, this wasn't the start of a worldwide red slash phenomenon. I think you're safe." He kissed the top of my head lovingly.

"You're sure?" I mumbled inhaling his intoxicating sexiness. I could definitely get drunk or high off of Christos' manly scent. "I didn't sabotage the beginning of your red slash period?"

"No," he chuckled, "I think we're safe."

I relaxed into his arms at last.

"But I do need something," he said.

"Oh, what?"

"I need some fresh ideas, some fresh perspective. Otherwise, I'm going to grind all these paintings into the ground until I can't stand to look at them or they're all covered with red slashes. And I don't mean the kind of slashes that sell paintings. I mean the kind that says, 'This painting is crap, next!'"

"Where do we go to find good ideas? The idea store? I hear they're having a sale," I grinned.

"Funny," he smiled, "but that would mean everyone would be able to buy the same good ideas. They wouldn't be good anymore. They'd be run of the mill. I need to talk to someone who really is a genius and can suggest something truly special."

"Who?" I asked, my interest suddenly piqued.

"You need to talk to your father," Spiridon said, suddenly standing in the doorway to the studio. "He knows what you're going through better than anyone."

I glanced at Christos. He had gone white and his eyes were wide with what looked like fear.

After a long pause, Christos looked down at me and swallowed hard.

In a crackly voice he said, "He's right."

Chapter 18

CHRISTOS

My '68 Camaro dipped and bobbed over the picturesque rolling hills of Rancho Santa Fe as we neared my dad's house. Rancho Santa Fe was an exclusive upscale community hidden a few miles inland from the coast. Suburban three bedroom houses on cookie cutter lots were replaced by lavish ranch style homes surrounded by oceans of acreage.

"There's a lot of horses and mansions out here," Samantha observed as she took in the countryside.

"Yeah," I said.

"It sure is beautiful. How come you don't go out to visit your Dad more often?"

I glanced at her briefly. It was the only answer I could give at the moment. The subject of my dad was guaranteed to piss me off or break my heart. I wasn't in the mood to do either. I just wanted to get his advice and get through the visit as quickly as possible.

"Oh, uh, sorry," Samantha said sheepishly.

"It's okay, *agápi mou*," I said softly. "Do me a favor, when we get to my dad's place, don't mention my drinking, okay?"

"All right," she said uncertainly.

I wanted to tell Samantha that it would bother my dad if he found out I was drinking all the time. Sure, that was part of the truth. Who wanted to find out their kid was getting trashed on a daily basis instead of making something of themselves? But the rest of the truth was I felt like an idiot for drinking so much. After watching my dad destroy his marriage with his own drinking, I should've known better. Right?

Like father, like son.

Man, I had become a fucking cliché.

But it went deeper than that. My dad hadn't really started

drinking until he'd felt bound by his golden handcuffs.

My grandad had once told me that when my dad was young, he'd made a clear headed decision to paint abstract art because he knew it sold well. He had a family to support and he didn't want to tough it out as a realist painter and hope that he'd make money someday. That's what my grandad had done. Sure, now my grandad was successful, but in the beginning, he'd had plenty of lean years and my dad lived through most of them as a kid.

So my dad went for the sure thing. Not that Joe Anybody could make money as an abstract artist. Tons of artists tried the 'easy' route over the decades and failed miserably. But my dad knew exactly what he was doing. His career blew up from the start and it started raining money.

But it didn't take long for him to feel bound tight by those golden cuffs. He got sick of abstract real quick. Maybe because it was so damn easy for him. He never did figure out a way to Houdini out of doing the abstract art and transform his career into doing the realistic stuff he really wanted to do. I guess it wasn't in the cards for him.

Ironically, I'd already made a good chunk of change at my first solo show at Charboneau Gallery selling realistic art. I was living the dream my dad had hoped to live from the day he'd picked up a paintbrush. And here I was, drinking because things weren't going perfectly.

The last thing I wanted to do was walk into my dad's house and say to him, "Hey, Dad, I'm doing what you always dreamed of doing, but I can't hack it because that fuck Stanford Wentworth said my paintings didn't have any heart, and he was right. So instead of manning up and fighting through the pain, I'm crumbling like a sand castle in a slight breeze."

Yeah, like I wanted to tell my dad I was pussing out on an opportunity he would've killed for twenty five years ago.

Hence, all my drinking of late and my reluctance to face my dad today.

I wheeled the Camaro onto a paved private road and drove until we came to the gates and stopped. The iron gate had a circle set in the center. The circle held a fancy polished gold letter M. I could never decide if it was cheesy or awesome. Mainly, I didn't really care. My dad could spend his money on whatever he wanted. He'd paid for it the hard way when his drinking had chased off my mom. After she left, he'd painted like crazy and raked money in by the truckload, trying to fill the void. No matter how much he made, all the cash in the world couldn't replace my mom. Not for me or my dad. Eventually, the drinking took over so bad, my dad stopped painting altogether and just drank.

I grimaced while punching a code into the little box bolted to a pole coming out of the ground in front of the gates.

A second later, the gates swung slowly open.

I'd only been here a few times in the last four years.

Why did these gates make me think I was about to get swallowed? Maybe because the last time I'd been in my dad's house, it had been a dark dungeon. You could feel the sadness seeping out of the walls in every room. All the curtains were closed, bottles of alcohol were scattered around on every flat surface in the place. Any sign that my dad was a painter was nonexistent. No art hung on the walls. There was no studio space set aside. As far as I knew, all of his painting supplies were stashed in a storage locker in Encinitas. That was thanks to Franco Viviano, the owner of Spada Gallery in L.A. Viviano was the guy who sold my dad's work and had helped make my dad rich. My grandad had told me the whole story.

Apparently, when my dad had gotten the idea in his head to burn all his paintings and his art supplies in a drunken stupor a year ago, he called Franco and told him he was quitting. That was kind of funny because my dad didn't work for anybody. Franco just represented him. But my dad told Franco he was quitting and burning all his art and supplies.

According to my grandad, Franco had jumped in a car and driven down from Beverly Hills the second he'd gotten off the phone with my dad. Franco had called my grandad while he was driving south and the two of them met up at my dad's house. They didn't want Dad doing something stupid. In the end, after calming my dad down, Franco had hired some guys to remove everything and put it safely in a storage unit in case my dad ever decided to paint again.

Sadly, before my dad had started going downhill, his house had been a painter's paradise. Now it was a drunkard's tomb. I hated it.

I pulled my Camaro to a stop in front of the house. It was still nice on the outside. It was only about eight years old. Give it another decade, and it would show signs of wear if he didn't do any maintenance, which he probably wouldn't. He couldn't even keep himself showered and shaved, let alone take care of a huge mansion. Eventually the outside would catch up with the inside.

"Oh my gosh," Samantha gasped, "is this your dad's house? It's huge."

"Yeah." Should I warn Samantha what awaited us inside? Or let it hit her like a hammer? I didn't think it mattered.

"How long has it been since you were here?" she asked.

I squinted into the sunshine, "At least a year?"

"Are you nervous?"

"That's an understatement," I said sarcastically.

We walked up to the cut glass front doors. I rang the doorbell. It played a Bach piano sonata or some shit. The things people did with too much money.

I could see the silhouette of someone walking up to the front door.

Moment of truth.

The door opened smoothly and silently. None of that horror movie creaky hinges shit. Yet. Give it time for the rust to set in.

"Paidí mou!" my dad beamed, all smiles "So good to see you!" He attacked me with a bear hug and slapped my back. "It's been a long time since you've been here! I'm so glad you've come."

I hugged him back, but after a second, I said, "All right, Dad. I think you're going to break something." He seemed even stronger than when he'd hugged me in court at my trial. And he looked even healthier.

He released me, "Are you getting soft on me?"

"Yeah, as if," I quipped. "But I think you've been hitting the weights again. Am I right?"

"I have," he smiled.

Man, I don't think I'd seen my dad this happy since before my mom left. But something told me this was all an act and the second we walked inside the dungeon, the truth would come out.

"Samantha!" my dad said. "So good to see you again!" My dad went in for a hug, but I think he saw that Samantha was a little overwhelmed, so he patted her gently on the shoulder. "Come inside, you two. Can I get you something to drink?"

I almost said, "Something without alcohol?" but I bit my tongue. Since I was old enough to know better, my dad's drinking had driven me nuts. I'd always given him shit about it in the past. Who was the asshole now?

"Sure," Samantha said. "I'm pretty thirsty."

We walked into the huge entry hall with the big spiral staircase. The chandelier overhead was the size of the Eiffel Tower if it were made of crystal and hanging from my dad's ceiling. Everything in the room was so damn bright and white.

What happened to the dungeon?

We walked down a marble hallway to the big kitchen. It was clean too. No booze bottles anywhere. My dad opened the Sub Zero. No bottles of vodka. Just bottled water, fruit juice, and milk.

"What can I get you two?" Dad asked.

"I'll take a water," Samantha smiled.

"What she's having," I said.

My dad uncapped the waters and poured them into clean glasses from the cupboard.

"Dad," I asked, "what did you do, dip this place in a bottle of bleach?"

He chuckled as he poured the second water. "No, that much bleach would've burned a hole in the ozone layer," he chuckled. "I've got a maid coming in five days a week. She's got elbow grease to spare."

"Five days a week?" Samantha marveled. "How much are you paying her?"

My dad frowned but smiled. "You really want to know?"

"Err, I mean," Samantha stammered, "I need to find a job. I used to work at a convenience store but that didn't work out."

"A convenience store?" my dad gawked. "That sounds terrible."

"It was," Samantha groaned. "But maybe being a maid would be better. I wouldn't have jerky customers coming in all day long. Anyway, I just wondered what a maid gets paid."

"I pay the maid well. I hired her from an agency. I can give you their number and put in a good word for you. Maybe they can find you some work."

"Really?"

"Sure. But I imagine most maids work during the day," Dad said. "Don't you have classes at SDU?"

"Yeah," Samantha sighed.

"Well maybe the agency has some of those maids who clean office buildings at night. I'll look into it."

"Could you?" Samantha asked hopefully.

"Definitely," he said. "Hey, I've got something I want you to see, son."

"I'm all eyes," I quipped.

My dad smirked at me and nodded. "Funny. You know, Samantha, this boy of mine is quite the character."

"You're telling me," she smiled as we walked through the house.

He had so many rooms and hallways it was like walking through a museum. For the first time in years, there were paintings everywhere hanging from all the walls.

"Man," I said, "there's a shitload of paintings in here. It's starting to look like the Sistine Chapel."

"Is this all your art, Mr. Manos?" Samantha asked.

"Call me Nikolos," Dad smiled. "Some of the paintings are mine, others are from fellow artists. I always like to trade paintings with artists I respect."

Sam joked sarcastically, "Is that why I don't see any of Christos' paintings?"

"Whoa!" Dad laughed, "she has a tongue, doesn't she!"

I sort of expected that to rub me the wrong way, but Samantha said it with such affection, it was obvious she didn't mean it harshly. And my dad had no idea what I'd been going through lately. At least I hadn't told him. Maybe my grandad had? It didn't matter. I wasn't going to bring it up.

"So what did you want to show us?" I asked.

"In here," Dad said as we entered a huge room at the back of the house.

Light poured in from outside. The room was walled in by glass. It was white and clean and inviting. Things were organized, unlike the constant mess he'd worked in back in the day when he was doing abstract, even before the drinking had started. In those days, the studio had been messy but exciting and flamboyant. The perfect setting for an "Artiste's Studio."

This studio was calm and thoughtful. No raucous bullshit. All the painting supplies were racked and organized. Canvases were lined up in neat rows. Any supplies not in use were neatly arranged or put away in drawers. Yet it had this inviting feeling, like I wanted to dive in and start painting right here myself. It was the perfect balance halfway between a disaster area and an antiseptic surgical theater.

I noticed dozens of glass bottles containing dry pigment of every color in the rainbow resting along a counter top. "Are you mixing your own oils?" I marveled. Nobody mixed their own paint. It was such a pain in the ass. I ordered mine online.

"Yeah," Dad answered. "I got tired of having to reorder everything. Besides, it connects me to the work more if I mix the paint from scratch myself. The old masters like Rembrandt had to make their own paint. Why shouldn't I? Anyway, it's my own personal protest against all the modernization in the world. Everything is too detached nowadays. I know a guy who gets his ultramarine pigment straight from the lapis lazuli mines in Afghanistan. That guy has some hair raising stories about buying pigment, let me tell you."

"I can't even imagine," Samantha said. She looked like a kid at a campfire listening to mythical tales about gods and monsters.

Dad continued, "I'm thinking about flying over with him to Afghanistan the next time he goes, just to see the mines and thank the guys who are breaking their backs digging up rocks so I can paint in a cush studio."

"Warn me in advance if you do," I said. "I'll come with you."

"You'd go to Afghanistan?" Samantha asked in disbelief. "Isn't that super dangerous?"

"Imagine the stories you'd bring back," I said.

My dad said, "Samantha, you should come with us."

"Oh, I couldn't afford it," Samantha said, "Besides, I've never done anything like that. I don't know if I could, even if I had the money."

"Sure you could," my dad said.

I winked at Samantha, "Now you know where I get my sense of adventure, *agápi mou*."

"That's an understatement," she chuckled.

I glanced around the studio, feeling like a kid in a candy store. That was when I noticed the paintings on all the easels were portraits. My dad hadn't painted portraits since before I was born.

I walked over to one of the easels. "Holy shit. This is grandad."

"Yeah," my dad said. "He's been sitting for me the last several weekends."

"This is where grandad has been coming?" I asked.

"Yeah."

The painting was amazing.

Samantha walked over to look at it. "Oh my god, that's Spiridon!" She reached out to touch the painting. "I mean, that's him! It looks like he's standing behind the picture frame."

She wasn't kidding. I'd always known my dad was fucking unreal when it came to painting realism. I got all choked up. Who had stolen my alcoholic dad and replaced him with the heroic guy standing beside me?

If my mom could only see him now. She'd flip. This version of my dad was the man she'd married, not the one she'd left.

I asked, "Do you guys mind if I use the bathroom?"

"You remember where it is?" my dad said.

"Considering there's like, what eight?" I said.

"Ten," dad chuckled.

"Ten," I nodded, "I'm sure I'll find one or two before I piss myself."

Samantha and my dad laughed and continued talking as I walked out of the room. The second I turned the corner, tears were dripping down my face.

Mom.

I missed my mom like fucking crazy.

She never would've left the man standing twenty feet behind me and split our family apart.

I wept silently as I made my way to the closest guest bathroom. I locked the door behind me, put the lid down on the toilet seat, and dropped on top so I could bawl silent tears as I clenched the sides of my head in agony.

Sadness tore me apart.

Mom.

I missed her so much.

Why couldn't she have stayed?

I hitched and sobbed in silence for another twenty minutes.

===

"Did you fall in?" my dad asked me as I returned from the bathroom.

"Almost," I joked liked I was kick back happy. "If it wasn't for the rescue crew that lowered the rope ladder down from the helicopter, I would've been a goner."

My dad chuckled.

"I thought maybe you were constipated," Samantha blurted, then clapped a hand over her mouth.

"I like this girl," Nikolos grinned.

"Me too," I said to him. "She cuts straight to the point. But yeah," I said sarcastically, "after the rescue crew pulled me out, they got the guys with the oil drilling rig to bore down into my ass until the turd came out. I had my butt cheeks up in the air when the thing blew. You should've seen it. Brown rain."

"That is foul," Samantha grimaced and stuck her tongue out.

"Hey," I chuckled, "you brought up the constipation."

"And you ran with it across the finish line," she smiled.

"If these jokes get any dirtier," my dad laughed, "I'm going to have to go get my hip waders. I'm already up to my knees in shit jokes."

Samantha cackled with laughter.

We spent the next two hours in the studio trading jokes like old pals and talking art. I could tell Samantha was having a blast.

"Anybody want dinner?" my dad suggested as the sun was going down for its nightly nap.

"What's on the menu at Chateaux Manos?" Samantha joked, making the S in Manos silent, like it was French.

"We're going out," Dad said.

"What, is it the chef's night off?" Samantha said sarcastically. She was totally comfortable with my Dad after only a few hours.

"It is," he said. "I *could* stir something up in the kitchen, but I was thinking of going out."

"I hope you have someplace fancy in mind," Samantha said.

"I was thinking 'berto's," Dad said.

"As in Roberto's?" Samantha said.

"Of course as in Roberto's," he laughed. "What other 'berto's could I mean?"

"I don't know," she said, "Alberto's or maybe Rigoberto's, or Tio Alberto's or Filiburto's?"

"Wow," I chuckled, "you're really turning into a local San Diegan, *agápi mou*."

She nodded proudly.

"That's all well and good," Dad said, "but we all know Roberto's is still the best."

We climbed into my Camaro and I drove the three of us to the Roberto's in Encinitas.

My dad ordered for everyone while Samantha and I grabbed the salsa bottles and napkins and found a table outside.

"Okay," Samantha said, "your dad is like totally awesome." She was grinning from ear to ear. "Why have you been hiding him from me all this time?"

After spending several hours with my dad, seeing the studio, and touring his house, it had become clear it wasn't an act. He'd literally transformed himself since my last visit. "This is the new and improved Nikolos Manos. Remember I told you about his drinking?"

"Yeah?"

"He is a changed man. I haven't seen him like this since years ago."

"Well, he's awesome now, that's for sure."

"True that," I smiled.

"How awesome is it that he's like a billionaire, and he wants to have cheap Mexican food for dinner?"

"He's not a billionaire, but he is epic awesome," I grinned.

My dad carried two trays with carne asada burritos outside a few minutes later. "I got chips and extra guac for everyone," he smiled as he set the trays down on the colorful mosaic table top.

We chowed down on our grub.

"So," Dad glanced at me and said, "your grandad tells me you've been having a little trouble with your new paintings?"

With my mouth still full of delicious carne asada, I mumbled, "Fucking kill me now." It came out like I thought it was funny, and my dad chuckled. But inside, everything tightened up. Now that my dad had thrown away the booze and turned into a tea totaling ass kicking painter, I couldn't tell him about my downhill slide. It would kill him.

Sam flashed me a quick look. She knew the score, but I knew she wouldn't talk.

"What's been giving you grief?" my dad asked.

In the past, I would've dodged the question. My dad had had so many problems of his own, we never had time to talk about mine. But he had opened the door. By the look in his eyes, he wanted to know. Where to begin? Fuck it. I was going balls deep on the ass fucking that my painting had been giving me lately. "Did you hear that Stanford Wentworth came by the studio?"

"*The* Stanford Wentworth?" Dad marveled. "I didn't realize you'd gotten famous so quick."

"More like infamous. Wentworth hated my new shit."

"Bullshit," my dad spat. "I saw your work at the solo show. It was beautiful."

"Wait till you see my new stuff," I grinned cockily. I knew I'd made substantial progress since doing those old paintings. "Technically, my new shit's way better. Anyway, Wentworth hated them."

"Then he's an idiot," my dad chuckled around the food in his mouth.

Talking about Wentworth should've sent me searching for a fifth of bourbon. It would have yesterday. But the stress I had around the topic of Wentworth had up and vanished.

As lame as it sounded, I think it was because of the simple fact I was sitting across from my dad like not a day had gone by since things were still good with him and Mom, when we were still a happy family. The happiest ever. I'd felt those good feelings coming back throughout the day today. Well, half back, which was fucking awesome because half of the greatest family unit on the planet seemed pretty incredible to me. Plus, I had Samantha.

What more could a guy ask for?

(*mom*)

"Two things," Dad said. "One, we're hopping on a plane to wherever the fuck Wentworth is at the moment so I can break his jaw."

I grinned, "I hear he's in St. Petersburg looking at some Russian painter's new work. Cold as shit that far north of the equator. Wait until Wentworth heads down to Italy. I hear that's where he spends Spring. Then I'll join you."

"That sounds like a fun trip," Samantha smiled after wiping salsa from her lips. "Do we go to the ultramarine mines in Afghanistan afterward?"

"Totally!" I joked.

"Perfect," she said before biting delicately on more burrito.

"What was the other thing?" I asked my dad.

"The other thing is, I need to see your new work so I can figure out what made Wentworth say that. As much as I've always disliked the guy, he knows what he's talking about. I want to figure out why he said what he did. But I can't make any comments until I see your new paintings in person. Otherwise, I'll be blowing smoke up your ass, and you know how much I hate to get my lips close to your puckered butthole." He leaned over toward Samantha and whispered conspiratorially, "This kid was a fart factory when I used to change his diapers."

Samantha blurted laughter.

"Puckered butthole?" I asked doubtfully.

"I hear how the kids talk. No reason why I have to sound like an antique."

"No kids talk like that," I laughed.

"So I'm a fucking trend setter," Dad smiled.

He was that. You didn't make millions by being an also-ran copycat or an idiot.

===

"I think I see what Wentworth was talking about," my Dad said thoughtfully as we stood in front of my painting of Sophia in the studio at my grandfather's house.

Samantha stood next to me. My grandfather was right behind us.

"Technically," Dad continued, "it's incredible. But it's stale." He said it with no judgment. It was an observation, like he was thinking things through out loud. I knew my dad well enough to know he would say more when he had a clear concept in mind.

My grandfather chuckled, "You should've heard the way Wentworth was telling Christos to change things on the now-defunct painting of Isabella. If I hadn't walked out of the room, I would've thrown Wentworth out of the house."

I rubbed my grandad affectionately on the shoulder, "Thanks, *Pappoús.*"

"I really wish you hadn't trashed that painting," my grandad said. "It was excellent."

Boom. Silence.

My grandad had accidentally let the cat out of the bag.

My dad knew exactly what caused an artist to trash a painting. He'd had plenty of personal experience.

"I'm sorry," my grandad said. "I shouldn't have—" he stopped short. "I'm going to go make some lemonade. Anyone want a glass?"

"Uhh…" Samantha stammered, "I'll help? Don't we need to pick some fresh lemons first? I think I saw a lemon tree down the block."

"It's spring," I said sarcastically. "The lemons don't come in for another couple months."

"We'll wait?" Samantha said. "Let's go, Spiridon, before we miss the lemons ripening?"

The two of them walked out of the room.

My dad raised his eyebrows at me. "When did you start trashing paintings?"

"It was just one," I said with a combination of guilt and defensiveness. "The one Wentworth didn't like. I had to agree with him."

My dad pulled a couple of chairs in front of my painting of Sophia and sat us both down.

"Was it like this one?" he motioned to the painting of Sophia.

"Better."

"So why'd you trash it? And what did your grandad mean by trash? You weren't drinking, were you?"

I could've blown a smokescreen and denied it, but come on, he would know. He'd been through it all himself. "Yeah," I sighed.

"How bad is it?"

"The drinking or the painting?" I joked.

"I'm sure your painting was terrific."

I clamped my hand around my jaw and rubbed the stubble nervously, "Like you said, technically, it kicked ass."

"And the drinking? Is it kicking your ass?"

"Nothing I can't handle."

My dad shook his head. "That's what I told myself. Remember where that put me?"

My stomach suddenly felt like someone had run a sewer line right down my throat and it was pumping toxic waste into me by the gallon. I needed a tub to vomit in.

"That good, huh?" Dad said.

I hung my head and shrugged my shoulders.

"You've gotta make a choice, *paidí mou*. The longer you slide down hill, the harder it gets to stop yourself from crashing into the bottom. You've got to take the reins or the drinking will."

If it wasn't for the fact that my dad obviously knew what he was talking about, I would've written off everything he'd just said as a bunch of empty platitudes. But he'd lived at rock bottom for years. I'd seen it myself. It was sort of hard to believe he'd turned himself into the clean and sober man sitting next to me in a year's time. But he had.

I needed to take what he said seriously.

In that moment it hit me that I'd been trying so hard to convince everyone for the last couple years that I had my shit together, I'd started believing my own bullshit. Deep down, that same old self doubt still ate away at me. Time to change that. My dad's successes, both as an artist and a human being, gave me the confidence to finally speak with total honestly. "I don't know what I'm doing, *Bampás*," I said softly. Saying that out loud was the hardest thing I'd done in a long time.

I noticed my father's eyes moisten when I called him *Bampás*.

His voice caught when he said, "None of us ever does, *paidí mou*. All any of us can do is keep moving forward and hope for the best. Sometimes things work out, sometimes they don't. But you have to keep trying until you run out of try. That's all there is to it."

"That sounds fucking stupid," I chuckled as silent tears dripped down my face.

My father laughed softly. "I know, but it doesn't make it any less true." He placed a comforting hand on my shoulder.

The next thing I knew, I was opening up about everything to my father. "I'm running out of money, *Bampás*. I'm burning through cash paying Russell to work on my defense against that guy Hunter Blakeley. My paintings are shit, and Brandon is barking up my ass about having everything ready for my next solo show yesterday. At the rate I'm ruining paintings, I'm never going to finish them. Everything is spinning out of control and I can't stop it."

My father looked at me thoughtfully for a long time. Eventually, his eyes lit up and he nodded. "I think I figured out why."

This was the point where my father always dropped some big piece of wisdom that made me think about what he'd said for weeks if not months afterward. He was good at that sort of thing.

"Why?" I asked.

He tapped two fingers lightly against my chest. "Your heart."

"My heart?"

"You left your heart out of every one of these paintings." He motioned at the canvases surrounding us in my grandfather's studio. "These are Brandon's paintings, not yours. Did you pick any of these models?"

"I approved them. I mean, I picked them out of a bunch of headshots Brandon sent me."

"But you don't care about any of them. It's obvious. I can see it. I'm sure they're all nice women. But you don't care about painting beautiful young women like you used to."

"Nope," I grinned. He was right.

"You've changed. You know why, don't you?"

I did, but he was going to tell me like he was reading my mind.

"When you were younger, all you did was chase skirt. You were obsessed. You were in love with the idea of beautiful young women and the thrill of the hunt. That's why the nudes you painted in the past are still good. You put your youth into them. Being a horny young man is a fine thing any man can appreciate."

I chuckled. He knew what he was talking about. He had a thousand stories about chasing girls before he met my mom.

He continued, "But at some point, that started to change when you started growing up, didn't it?" My dad stood up and walked over to the painting of Tiffany that hung on the back wall. "When did you paint this nude of Tiffany? I haven't seen it before."

I stood and walked over next to him. "That? Probably six months ago?"

"Uh huh," he nodded thoughtfully while looking up at it. "It's not like the nudes you painted a few years back. You've grown as an artist. Tell me, why do you think this portrait of Tiffany is different?"

"The main thing is, I've been friends with Tiff forever. She's not some girl I was chasing," I chuckled.

"That is a substantial difference," Dad said. "And let me guess, you painted Tiffany before you met Samantha, didn't you?"

"Yeah. How can you tell?"

"Well, your painting of Tiffany has a clear, singular message. Despite Tiffany's obvious beauty, the message that comes through the painting loud and clear to me is respect and caring. And love."

I huffed a chuckle.

My dad smiled, "I don't mean romantic love. I mean the love of genuine friendship. I know Tiffany has turned into a spoiled princess since she was a little kid. But she wasn't that way when the two of you met in grade school. She was an innocent little girl with a big heart. You two were fast friends for years. And you put the purity of that friendship into your portrait of her. It's unmistakable."

"Yeah," I nodded. When it came to art, my dad read me like a book.

"Anyway," Dad said, glancing around, "all these new paintings of random beautiful young women you're doing for Brandon don't mean anything to you. Because now your focus has changed, hasn't it?"

That's when everything came together in my head. I said, "That's why your painting of Grandad you're working on is so amazing, isn't it? He's been going to your house every weekend for the last year, hasn't he?"

My father nodded.

"He was helping you clean up and get your life back in order, wasn't he?" I asked.

My father nodded as tears began dripping down his face.

"That's why your portrait of him is so powerful," I said.

My father rubbed the tears from his eyes with the side of his hand. "I put my heart into that painting. It's a reflection of the love your grandfather has given me continuously since I was born. He has never stopped being my father. Even now, when I'm a big shot artist and a father in my own right, your grandfather is still there for me like I just fell off my tricycle and skinned my knee for the first time. I don't think I could've cleaned myself up without his devotion. He has been there for me through all of it. When you have a child of your own someday, *paidí mou*, you'll be able to understand how deeply I love you and how deeply your grandfather loves me." My dad's face knotted with emotion. His shoulders skipped in time with his restrained sobs.

I threw my arm around his neck and he leaned into me.

After awhile, he said, "I'm okay." He faced me and a smile spread across his face. "Now you know why none of your paintings of Brandon's models are working for you or Stanford Wentworth, don't you?"

I nodded, "Samantha."

"She was right in front of you the whole time," he smiled. "I see how much you love that girl. I see it in the way you look at her. You've never had eyes like that for anyone. Well, maybe your mother, but that's different. She was your mother." He waved a hand, "You know what I mean. Anyway, your mother was a good woman. The best. I mean, is. Is a good woman." My dad choked up when he said it.

I nodded.

"Look at that," he chuckled and slapped my knee vigorously, trying to hold back more tears, "you answered your question yourself."

I could tell that my dad was running away from the topic of my mom like it would kill him if he talked about it for one more second. I knew he still loved her like crazy. He'd never stopped, even after she left us.

I couldn't blame him. If Samantha were ever to leave me, I'd be acting the same as my dad was right now. It would kill me for sure. Whoa, that was the last thing I wanted to think about.

I sniffed back some of my own tears and chuckled. "You just went all Platonic dialogue on my ass and made me figure things out myself, didn't you?"

"Can you blame me? That Plato was one smart Greek. Am I right?" My dad was laughing as he said it.

I started laughing too.

"Come here, *paidí mou.*" My dad threw his arms around me and gave me a big hug.

When he released me, he squeezed my shoulders and looked me in the eyes. "Your heart has changed. You're not a boy anymore. Your art needs to reflect that. Put the true love in your heart onto the canvas, and the whole world will appreciate it. It's that simple."

I nodded, "It is."

"Now you know how to fix your paintings," he grinned.

I did.

Art was all about heart.

Chapter 19

SAMANTHA

A cool pool of light illuminated my drawing table and my sketchbook. I was sketching cartoon wombats with various drug and bowel problems when Christos walked up behind me the next evening.

He started massaging my neck and shoulders.

"Oh, that feels good," I sighed, setting my pencil down. "I didn't realize I'd been so tense."

"When aren't you," he chuckled.

"Hey! I've been getting better. I'm not the anxious girl you met months and months ago."

"No, you're not. You're turning into an amazing woman."

I really liked the way he said that. "So, what's up?" I asked.

I felt Christos' hot breath caress my ear, "I need to paint you…in the nude."

"Do you mean you'll take all your clothes off while you paint a picture of me?" I grinned. "Sounds like fun to me, but I don't know if I'll be able to sit still."

He chuckled softly. "I meant you in the nude. But if you like, I could be nude too."

"Mmm, I like the sound of that. But do we need the painting part? Maybe we could just focus on the part where we both get naked," I purred. It had been awhile since we'd made love and I felt a burning need for Christos.

"I like where you're going with this," Christos said, "but I'm serious about this. I want to paint a nude portrait of you."

"What?!" I practically jumped out of my chair. Sitting nude for a portrait was fine when someone else was doing it, but I didn't think I could. "Why?"

"I want to paint you nude for my upcoming solo show at

Charboneau."

"Nude?" I gulped. "As in fully?" I winced.

"Is there any other kind?"

"You mean nude nude? Not just bathing suit nude?"

"Nude nude. Fine art and bikinis don't go together. Bikinis usually go on hot rod magazine covers."

"I know you talked about doing things differently after hanging out with your dad the other night. But I was thinking maybe you meant finding different models or something."

"I did," he grinned his dimpled grin.

Nervously, I said, "I didn't think you meant me."

"You," he murmured seductively.

I squeezed the neck of my T shirt together, as if it were hanging wide open like an unbuttoned shirt and I was braless. But I was covered. Why did I feel the desire to wrap myself in blankets or maybe step into a deep sea diving suit with one of those giant old fashioned diving helmets? Oh yeah, because Christos was suggesting not only that he paint me nude, but that he show off the painting in a public gallery where anyone could come in and see it. Worse, someone was likely to buy it and hang it over their mantelpiece.

How to break the bad news to Christos that his idea made me a tad uncomfortable? "Ahh…It's awesome that you want to paint me. I'm totally flattered. But can't we do it with me all dressed up? Like a regular portrait? Like your dad's portrait of your grandad? He's all dressed up."

"I could do that, but I don't think it would be the same."

"Of course it wouldn't," I joked, "it would be a painting of me. Problem solved."

He shook his head and smiled his dimpled grin. As always, it had panty dropping powers. But I wasn't going to let it work its magic on me this time.

I shook my head defiantly.

"Here's the thing," he said confidently, "there's a woman inside you that I've seen from day one. But usually, she only comes out when you're backed into a corner. Most of the time, that woman you are meant to be is hidden from the world. You've spent so many years hiding that strong, confident side of you, you barely know she's there. But I see it all the time. I want to paint that woman and share her with the world. I want everyone to know how amazing Samantha Smith is. Not can be, but is. You are amazing, *agápi mou*. And I want everyone to know it. I suspect that if you can find the courage to sit nude, your confidence will shine through in the portrait."

"Can't I be confident with my clothes on?" I asked nervously.

"You can, but it'll be that much harder for your confidence to shine through," he said.

"Why?"

"Because posing clothed doesn't require the same courage as posing nude. If you're gonna pose nude, you're gonna have to dig deep and bring out your courage."

"What if I end up being nervous while you're painting me nude? Won't that show up in the painting?"

"Yup. That's why I'm asking you, not telling you. Feel free to say no. Because if you're doing it because you feel obligated, that will show through too. You have to dig deep and find that intrinsic strength of yours and willingly bring it out so I can capture it in paint. You have to *want* me to paint you nude. Then we can show the world together how amazing Samantha Smith really is."

"Wow," I smiled, "I kind of like the sound of that! You know what would make me really look strong?"

"What?"

"If I wore a Viking helmet."

"Huh?" he frowned.

"Like one of those Valkyries from Norse mythology? They're totally badass. I would look awesome!"

He made a funny face. "Take a moment and picture a portrait of you, sitting in the nude, wearing a horned Viking helmet, and tell me that's not ridiculous."

My brows pinched together. "You were the one who suggested I look strong. Horns are cool."

"Yeah, but nude? Maybe with a sword and chain mail armor and a big shield. But that would look like you were pretending to be strong. Strength doesn't come from armor or weapons. It comes from inside, from your heart and your determination. That's what I want to paint."

"You have a point. But I still think nude with a Viking helmet could be awesome."

He raised his eyebrows skeptically.

I frowned and folded my arms across my chest, "You're the artist. Figure out a way to make me look awesome. It would be a first. I mean, you said it yourself, how many nude portraits of women wearing Viking helmets are there?"

"I'm guessing none," Christos said.

"See? It'll be a first!" I was totally into my idea now.

"I'll have to think about it," he said thoughtfully.

"Really?" I was kind of surprised.

"Really. Let me mull it over. It might actually work. But you'll have to wear pigtails like Brunhilda."

"What? I hate pigtails. They make me look five."

"That's the deal," he grinned.

"Seriously?"

He shook his head. "Maybe not. Pigtails might be a bit much. But I'll think about that helmet. So you'll do it?"

"I guess?" I smiled nervously. "But no spread legged crotch shots, right?"

He grinned, "What, no wide open beavers?"

"You keep talking like that and you can forget it," I giggled.

"I'm kidding. You only see beavers in porn, or maybe tattoo art. I don't want to scare off the fine art buyers."

"What! Are you saying my lady bits are scary?" I stood up from my chair and turned to face him.

He jumped out of range. "I'm sure some men might feel that way..."

I lunged at him, but he dodged. "Take that back!"

"I was thinking of gay men!" he said as he jogged out of the studio. "They're probably afraid of your beaver because they're worried about getting their dicks too close to those huge teeth!"

"Huge teeth? Is that supposed to be an apology?!" I shouted as I chased after him. "Anyway, mine doesn't have any teeth! And it doesn't look like a beaver! Come back here! I'm going to tear your nuts off and feed them to the squirrels outside!"

"Wouldn't you rather feed them to your beaver?" He called as he ran into the living room.

"It's not a beaver!" I shouted as I followed him around the couch. "It's a pussy! You said so yourself!" As I was about to grab his shirt tail, he jumped over the couch, out of reach. "At least you could call mine a lion or a jaguar. There's nothing sexy about beavers."

He ran to the far side of the living room and stopped. "What do you mean? I bet male beavers think female beavers are totally hot. The guy beavers are probably like, 'Dude, check out that chick's tail. It is so big and flat and rubbery, you could use it as a swimming pool cover.'"

"Swimming pool cover?" I scoffed, creeping toward him, one step at a time, hoping he wouldn't notice I was stalking him like the jungle cat that I was.

Christos frowned, backing up a step. "What? Beavers spend a lot of time in the water. They think about these things."

"Beavers build dams! What does that have to do with swimming pools?" I asked skeptically, inching toward him.

"Duh. A dam causes water to pool up, hence pool covers."

I shook my head, moving slowly forward. "I don't think so. Anyhow, why the obsession with beavers all of a sudden?"

"You're the one who's been drawing wombats all the time."

He was almost at the base of the stairs. If I moved slowly enough, maybe he'd be lulled into a false sense of security so I could catch him. I cracked a smile, "You're incorrigible." I took another step toward him.

"What are you and your jaguar gonna do about it?" he taunted.

"My jaguar is going to eat you alive," I growled. If he ran upstairs, he was mine. There was no way he could escape.

At the last second, Christos dodged right and ran toward the front doors. He was outside quicker than a cheetah.

"Come back here!" I shouted as I ran after him, right on his heels.

===

My breath pumped in a steady rhythm under the covers of darkness. The movement of my body and the liquid feeling of my limbs consumed my focus.

Christos was only a few paces ahead as we ran along the dark streets outside the Manos house toward the trailhead nearby. I meant, our house. Where we both lived.

I still managed to find time to run three days a week, despite all the craziness in my life over the last several months, and was in good shape. But Christos stayed several steps ahead no matter how fast I went. Despite all the drinking he'd been doing, he was still an amazing athlete who put me to shame. I could tell he could leave me in the dust if he wanted to, but he didn't. He teased me with the proverbial carrot on a stick. In this case, it was a hunk of man meat on the stick. Or should I say his man meat on a stick. Either way, I wasn't letting him or his stick get away.

When we reached the trailhead, he bounded up the slope like a weightless gazelle. Now he really did leave me in the dust, but I pumped my legs hard to keep up.

My heart pounded and my lungs burned when I reached the top of the trail. Christos stood at the edge of the small clearing, taking in the view. I took note of Spiridon's old wooden bench, the one where Christos and I had kissed many moons ago under the stars. I think it had been the first time I'd ever been topless outside in my entire life.

I'd shared so many wonderful firsts with Christos since we'd met. And I hoped that we would share thousands more over our lifetimes.

This clearing was also the place where Christos had first sketched a picture of me, the caricature showing me as a painter with the inscription, "World Famous Master Artist Samantha Smith. You can totally do it!" I still had that picture. Christos had bought a frame for it and it hung next to my drawing table in our studio.

Our studio.

This clearing was the place that Christos had said that only his family ever visited. I had been such a bitch that day. I'd wrongly accused him of bringing all his girlfriends up here to get their pants off and screw them. I'd been too dense and too angry to realize he was already calling me his family when he barely knew me.

Wow, how prophetic that had been.

And of course, this clearing was the place I had mocked Christos and told him his nude paintings were just trashy trophies of all the women he'd had sex with. I'd said that his paintings were an invasion of the women's privacy, nothing more than exploitation porn on fancy canvases. Funny. That's exactly what my mom had said when she saw Christos' studio during Spring Break.

"That's not art," Mom had said, *"That's pornography. I hope you would never consider debasing yourself by deigning to strip for Christos. I should hope I've taught you better than that."*

I chuckled softly to myself as my mom's words echoed in my head.

"What's so funny?" Christos asked.

"I was just remembering what my mom said about your nude portraits when she was visiting."

Christos smiled and nodded. "It seems to me she sounded a lot like you did back when we met."

"Like mother, like daughter," I sighed.

"We don't have to do the nude portrait if you don't want to, *agápi mou*. It's totally up to you."

"Thank you, Christos. But I don't want to be like my mom anymore. It's time for me to finally leave all that behind. I'm my own woman now."

"Yes you are, *agápi mou*. You are all woman." His eyes flashed darkly in the silver blue moonlight. "And that's the woman I want to paint."

"All you want to do is paint me?" I teased.

He tore his shirt over his head and tossed it on the bench. The heavy shadows on his face and muscled body from the moonlight made him look savage. The jagged lines of the tattoos on his rugged shoulders enhanced his dangerous appearance. His abs were sharp and rigid. I could imagine being chased through a forest by this awesome specimen of manhood a million years ago. I would gladly have let him ravage me.

"I'll do anything you want," he growled.

"Anything?" I whispered.

"Anything," he hissed.

"Take me," I said seductively.

He stalked toward me, crouched low. His eyes burned from under his brows. He looked ready to snarl like a beast.

I started to shiver with anticipation and a little bit of fear. The flames in his eyes were more intense than I'd ever seen them before. They were the blue fire at the core of the flame, the darkest, hottest part of him.

He stopped inches away from me and dug his fists into my long sleeve T shirt at the collar. His fingers knotted into the cotton. The muscles of his naked chest bulged and his shoulders knotted. Roped tendons and coiled veins popped on his forearms. His eyes held mine. I was mesmerized by his masculine power.

There was a sharp tearing sound as the savage man holding me in his fisted grip tore my shirt open. His lips peeled back over his teeth as cotton ripped and popped, splitting my shirt right down the middle. Hot passion glowed in his eyes as he forced the tattered shirt down my arms, binding my arms. I was at his mercy and I didn't want to be any other place in the universe at that moment. I was his to have.

He tore my shirt open the rest of the way, freeing my arms. A month ago, I might have covered my bra and breasts with my arms out of shyness. Instead, I shrugged off the remnants of my tattered T shirt and stood proud while I thrust my chest at my man.

He stared at my breasts, devouring them with his hungry gaze. They were his. I reached behind me and unhooked my bra, letting it fall. He caught it before it touched the ground like an expert hunter and tossed it onto the bench like a slingshot. It landed on his shirt like an arrow hitting the bullseye.

The cool night air tightened my nipples into rigid buds.

I felt his manly desire washing over me. That desire was for me. For *my* womanhood. Mine, and mine alone. In that moment, I understood. My perfect man was *all* man. His lust had driven him to seek out the finest specimen of womanhood he could find. And he had found me. He had chosen me out of all other women to be his woman. Because *I* drove him wild, *I* ignited his passion, *I* made him crazy. *I* turned him into a desperate caveman. And now, I would be his cavewoman.

With his hard hands he cupped my breasts delicately. He kneaded them gently, worshipping them and treasuring them because he knew they were a woman's tools for sustaining newborn life. Without my womanly breasts, his young offspring could never survive. For all his animalistic strength, his masculinity was nothing but a brief moment in history without my womanhood to carry his seed into eternity, passing our life force on and on to future generations.

Heat burned between my legs.

He squatted down and threw his arms around my hips, lifting me up like I weighed nothing. He held me high in the air with his powerful arms like a primitive idol, then lowered me so that my stomach slid down his chest. His hair tickled my skin until he squeezed my breasts against his face. As he nuzzled my chest and inhaled my scent deeply into his lungs, I coiled my arms around the back of his head, pulling him into me. He groaned as his nose skimmed across one breast and his tongue followed, licking up from the swollen curve at the bottom and tripping across the knotted nipple.

Wetness rained down inside me.

He worked my breasts over with intense attention, licking, sucking, twisting, squeezing. Primal pleasure waved out from my chest as my legs squeezed around his waist. I buried my nose in his thick hair as I dug and twisted my fingers into his thick locks. I inhaled the erotic smell seeping from his pores. The scent of his naked desire arrowed into my brain and sent spears of ecstasy down my spine. The muscles deep inside me throbbed with need.

I sighed audibly and it turned into a long, loud moan as I threw my head back to let the energy of need flow out of me into the world. I was completely unconcerned with who could possibly be listening to us up on this mountain top. I was alone in a jungle somewhere with this heathen who was burying his face in my breasts, crudely licking and suckling sustenance from me like a barbarian.

He lowered me until my face was level with his. Our noses touched delicately in soft contrast to the hot heat that had consumed him earlier. There was gentleness inside this beast. The blistering passion in his eyes remained, but the tenderness of his lips as they brushed against mine was that of a loving mate who would be kind to our offspring. This brutal beast who could hunt and protect could also nurture and love.

We kissed in a quiet, soft way, drinking up the refined, complex pleasure of lips and tongues. Heat passed between us, our breath mingling, our life force combining. We were connected on every level.

Words and thoughts melted away as we became pleasure together.

He released our kiss and squatted down and set me on the ground. He knelt before me, his face in line with my pelvis. With ceremony and reverence, he unbuttoned my jeans and slid them and my panties down to my ankles. He kissed my naked womanhood with the same careful appreciation he'd shown my mouth. He breathed heat into me as my wetness dripped onto his face and into his mouth.

He swallowed me like a thirsty animal, his tongue licking and lunging into my wet hole.

I thrust my hips into his face as pleasure overtook me. His stiff fingers squeezed my ass, holding me as my knees gave way. I would've fallen to the ground if he hadn't been supporting my weight with his strong hands. I was taken by the pleasure that blotted out my consciousness. I became the essence of femininity and ecstasy as he ate me, and nothing more.

I erupted into a violent orgasm, a volcano of heat splitting my body open like the birth of the planet. Like Mother Earth, I came alive as intense energy broke me open.

I screamed my awakening and came fully alive for the first time.

I was a woman.

I roared.

And I came.

I *came…*

===

Infinite light and infinite dark bounced off of each other, vibrating and fighting against each other.

I vibrated between their two extremes.

Slowly, sensuously, I returned to human awareness.

A hulking man had his face buried between my legs. Now he was standing up, looking me in the eyes, supporting my limp, spent body. His mouth was smeared with wetness. With the fluid of life.

We kissed deeply as I regained consciousness.

Strength and desire surged through me. I yanked my shoes off and pushed my pants and panties off until I was completely naked. I tossed my pants and socks onto the bench.

I lowered my head and glared up at him, my lips curling with anticipation.

His own lips twitched with challenge.

I lunged at him and clawed at the belt around his waist and tore his pants off, pushing them down to his ankles. His cock stood tall and proud as I kneeled before him. It was thick and veined and rugged like his powerful arms. He was masculine power from head to head.

His cock throbbed with need as he stood over me. I couldn't

allow him to suffer another moment without my heat. Our eyes locked as I worshipped him. I tongued, licked, teased, inhaled, and swallowed.

He allowed me to worship him.

Soon, his approval transformed into submission as he groaned and moaned. His huge, muscled thighs shook. He could barely stand up. All his strength was in my mouth. He was powerless to fight me off.

I consumed all of him greedily, taking him in deep.

He couldn't stop me.

And he couldn't stop himself.

A roar thundered from him, his chest flexing and his abs contracting, shaking his entire muscled frame.

His manhood poured into my mouth as his body quaked with pleasurable release.

I gripped his cock tightly in one hand as I drank him in. He quivered against my tongue and the back of my mouth.

When his spasms slowed, he bent over, hands on knees, breathing heavily.

I licked the head of him clean, then finally released him.

A final drop of cum dribbled out the tip of him. I dabbed at it with the tip of my tongue and swallowed.

I wiped the side of my hand across my mouth.

I was still hungry.

I stood and we kissed deeply for a long time, swallowing each other, drowning in desire. When I felt him pressing hot and hard against my abdomen a few minutes later, he shoved me toward the bench. I stumbled onto it. Then I was on the bench, on all fours, my tangled hair hanging in my face. I threw him a taunting look. I bit my lower lip.

He stood tall and strong. His cock was engorged once again. He kicked each boot off and peeled his bunched jeans off each foot until he too was completely naked under the moonlight.

He sauntered toward the bench and walked around behind me.

I narrowed my eyes and looked at him over my shoulder, sending him a sultry gaze. His manhood twitched expectantly. I lowered my hips and bent my knees, presenting my womanhood to him.

He stepped forward and took me from behind.

My core was slippery and ready. He slid deep inside me, until his hips pressed against my ass. I clenched him tightly as he slowly withdrew. His hands grabbed my hips from behind as he thrust forward. I pushed my hips back, meeting him in the middle.

I squeezed his manhood each time he withdrew, letting him know that I didn't want him going anywhere. He fell into a steady rhythm, pumping into me as I thrust back toward him.

Pleasure built inside me. Soon, any conscious control faded away, any desire to perform or please disappeared as the ecstasy he gave me claimed me. I gave in to the wanting, I gave in to the ravishing. My back arched as my breasts pressed into the pile of clothes beneath me, giving him full access to take me and overwhelm me with his dominant male energy.

Energy tornadoed inside my body as I let go of reality. The most perfect man in the history of men hammered into me like an animal. My pulse pounded in my ears and accelerated as his thrusts intensified. Again I roared, a lethal lioness in the throes of a timeless mating ritual.

The ground split open beneath our feet and fire raged from the center of the earth, bathing us in a geyser of magma as our orgasm shattered us to dust.

We cried out together as we renewed the eternal bond between masculine and feminine.

Union.

===

Christos was on top of me, squashing me into the pile of our clothes on the bench as I struggled to heave in a breath.

"Holy shit," he said hoarsely. "I can't stand up." His heavy torso was pressing down on mine.

"Ack!" I hissed. I couldn't get enough air to force out a complete word.

"You okay?" he asked, concerned.

"Gick!"

He rolled off me and plopped onto his ass in the dirt beside the bench. He twisted onto his knees and kneeled beside me while caressing my cheek. "Samantha? Talk to me? Did I break something? Do you need CPR?"

I rolled onto my back, completely naked, and stared up at the stars overhead. "I'm fine," I whispered. "Did we fall asleep?"

"I think we passed out." He smiled.

"Seriously?"

"Yeah, I think after we came I fell on top of you and we both passed out."

I frowned. "That's ridiculous."

"If you have a better explanation, I'd love to hear it."

"Not really," I smiled, "I'll have to take your word for it."

"I think I broke a testicle that time."

I winced. "You didn't hurt yourself pounding so hard, did you?"

"No," he chuckled. "I meant when I came. I don't think I've ever come that hard before. I mean, like, ever. You don't have any bullet holes in you, do you?"

"What?" I asked, confused.

"From when I shot my load?"

"Not getting it."

"It felt like bullets to me."

I laughed. "That's lameballs."

"I was thinking flameballs."

"I thought you said it was bullets."

He snickered, "Flameballs sounds way better than bulletballs, don't you think?"

I rolled over on the bench to my side and smiled at him. "You're such an idiot, *agápi mou*."

He grinned, "That's why you love me." He leaned forward and kissed me softly.

Before I knew it, our kiss had deepened sensually and I felt turned on all over again.

After awhile, I pulled away and smiled, "I've never had sex on a mountain top before."

"I've never had sex on this bench before," he said.

"Really?"

"I told you before, this place is sacred. I've never brought any women up here."

"But you brought me," I smiled.

"Yup. And now this place is officially consecrated ground. If any other women ever comes up here," he chuckled, "I think the ground will swallow them up."

"I think we were almost swallowed up when you were inside me earlier," I grinned.

"You keep talking like that, and I'm going to have to do it again," he purred.

"Okay, but how about we do it back at the house? It's cold out here." By cold, I meant I was completely naked outside in the middle of the night and I was chilly. If this had been D.C., we probably would've had frostbite and hypothermia by now. As it was, my teeth were wanting to chatter and I needed to warm up.

"Sounds good to me." Christos stood up.

"You have dirt all over you."

"Do I?" He looked down at himself. "I didn't even notice."

I had dirt on my knees and feet too, but he had a big patch on his ass, which was butt white, unlike the rest of his tan body. We'd both been getting sun since the start of Spring. "I can't decide if I like the speedo tan you've got going or not."

"If you want, we can go down to the nude beach by SDU where I saw you that time with Madison and Jake. Then we can lay out and erase our tan lines together."

Madison and I had never gone back to that part of the beach since we realized it was nude. "Mmm, maybe not. How about we go with tan lines?"

"We can always lay out on the deck at home when my grandad is out."

I loved how he called it our home. I smiled to myself as I put clothes on.

We both dressed.

I realized my T shirt was destroyed, but I managed to knot the ends together at my waist, over my bra. "You like?" I asked.

"You sort of look like Mary Ann from Gilligan's Island. But blonde and hotter. And after what we did on the bench, way dirtier."

I almost asked him uncertainly if that was good. But that was the old me. The new me chuckled confidently, "And you loved it."

"I did. And I love you, *agápi mou*." He leaned over and kissed me.

"And if you want any more of my dirty, you're gonna have to catch me!" I turned and ran down the hill in the darkness.

I could feel Christos' cum dripping into my panties as I ran. I didn't care. I still felt like some primal woman from pre-history. I didn't care about things like dirty underwear or doing laundry. All I cared about in that moment was the perfect specimen of manhood chasing after me, the one who had just mated with me. I felt so alive, I wanted him to take me again and prove his manliness.

The trail was rough and uneven, and I felt gravity pulling me faster than I was comfortable running, especially considering how dark it was.

But Christos' boots were pounding right behind me.

I didn't want him to catch me so easily.

I sped up my pace, focusing on where my feet fell and keeping my center of gravity low and balanced.

A thread of my old insecurity knitted my brows and a string of my ingrained civilized sanity spooled through my thoughts. I realized that my desire for Christos had me so turned on, I was being stupid. I mean, I was barreling downhill in the darkness. I could easily break an ankle or a leg. It scared me. I wondered if Christos might destroy me with his unrelenting abandon someday. I expected my old friend fear to snatch my confidence and devour me at any moment.

But I wasn't that frightened girl any longer. I wasn't going to let fear run my life.

I was a woman, and I was strong.

A powerful feminine force reared up inside me like a champion mare or a lioness on the tundra and it stomped out my fear decisively. Adrenalin and excitement poured into my veins and swam through my body.

Christos could only have me if he was strong enough to catch me.

I ran as fast as I could down the trail. I jumped over rocks and divots like an experienced huntress in her element until I was on the street below. Then I sprinted toward the house, Christos close behind.

===

We pounded up the stairs of our home together.

I knew Spiridon was out, so I wasn't worried about the noise bothering him.

I stumbled into the bedroom and crashed onto the bed. We stripped our clothes off while giggling at each other and dove onto the bed, heedless of the dirt from the trail.

We knelt on the bed together, facing each other. I was brimming over with confidence because I was thrilled that I hadn't tripped on the trail. I had navigated the rugged terrain in the darkness like a master. My success fueled my throbbing excitement.

I traced the script of the Fearless tattoo on Christos' chest with my fingertip. "Maybe I should get a tattoo across my chest that says Fearless," I grinned.

"What, and mar those perfect breasts? Nothing made by the hand of man could ever compare to your breasts, *agápi mou*. To tell you the truth, I'm a bit worried about capturing their perfection when I paint them."

"You can totally do it," I said dismissively. When I'd first met Christos, I would've cringed at his words and asked for reassurance he wasn't lying. Now I took it in stride. But the truth was, I wasn't really into tattoos for myself. I joked, "Okay, how about I get a tramp stamp that says Fearless instead?"

He chuckled, "Definitely go with the tramp stamp. That way, when I'm taking you from behind, I'll be reminded how badass you are."

"Because we both know I have a bad ass," I quipped, "in a good way."

"The best way. You have an ass that launched a thousand ships."

I frowned, "Wait, that sounds like something having to do with farts. Like my ass shoots cannon ball farts or rocket fart blasts that blow the sails that power the ships."

"All thousand of them," Christos grinned and shook his head. "Your imagination knows no bounds, *agápi mou*. Neither of limits nor of propriety."

"And you love it," I laughed.

"I do," he smiled.

We began kissing, naked on our knees, chest to chest on our bed. The passion from the mountain top erupted once again, having never completely cooled. But this time it was sweetly, silkily different. Our love making was quiet and intimate in contrast to the savage intensity and wild abandon before. This time, not just our bodies, but our hearts beat together in that timeless, ancient rhythm of man and woman in perfect union.

The bonding of our hearts brought a powerful immediacy. I was intimately aware of Christos as he thrust tenderly into me over and over again. His heat, his scent, his weight. But also his compassion, his tenderness, and his love. I felt our souls joining as our bodies came together. I could tell he felt it too. Our eyes were locked as pleasure swept through us in a shower of orgasmic release.

We lay in each other's arms on our bed as the embers of our fire cooled and the bond between our hearts strengthened, much like bedrock after the erupted volcano finally comes to rest. Our ritual of love was complete, body and soul.

Together, Christos and I had laid the foundation for our renewal and rebirth. Like Adam and Eve, we were Man and Woman.

We were Creation.

We were Love.

Love.

Chapter 20

SAMANTHA

"Do you think pirates ever used their peg legs as dildos?" Romeo asked thoughtfully.

I gawked at him.

An old guy with grizzled white stubble who was dressed in a pirate costume stood on the dais in the center of the room. He struck a classic pirate pose: hands on hips, one pirate boot up on a box, like he was at the front of a pirate ship. A cutlass hung in a scabbard from his belt and he had one of those black pirate hats and a fancy captain's coat with hundreds of buttons.

The students were all circled around the dais, drawing the pirate, sitting on these cute little benches called drawing horses, which you straddled long-ways like a horse, hence the name. A vertical plank stuck up on the front end, much like the neck of a horse, and you leaned your drawing clipboard on it. I didn't think they were big enough to be called horses, so I dubbed them drawing ponies. I would need to get a saddle for mine and properly bedazzle it with glitter and silver buckles in my spare time.

The class was Drawing The Costumed Figure. Professor Walt Childress, who had taught Life Drawing last fall, was our professor once again.

"I totally think pirates used their peg legs as dildos," Romeo whispered as he sketched on the big drawing pad in his lap with his charcoal stick.

"He doesn't have a peg leg!" Kamiko hiss-whispered while she sketched her own pirate drawing.

"But if he did," Romeo muttered thoughtfully, "he would use it as a dildo."

The old guy in the pirate costume suddenly coughed. Or was it a laugh? I wasn't sure. But I did know that he was facing us and stood close enough to overhear Romeo.

Kamiko dropped her charcoal dusted hands in her lap, confused, and gaped at Romeo. "What?"

"I mean, seriously," Romeo whispered, "pirates are gay. All of them."

This time, the old pirate made a pfft! noise like he was trying to get Romeo's attention, like maybe he wanted Romeo to stop talking. I couldn't blame him. It was hard to concentrate once Romeo got going on a tangent.

Romeo was, of course, oblivious. He was totally going to get busted at the rate he was going.

I glanced around the classroom, trying to determine if we were bothering the other students or not, or if the professor had noticed we were talking when we were supposed to be drawing. Luckily, the professor was sitting at a drawing horse on the far side of the room with two students leaning over his shoulder while he explained how to draw the wrinkles of the captain's coat just right.

Kamiko whispered, "That makes zero sense, Romeo. Pirates aren't all gay."

Romeo rolled his eyes, "Oh yeah? Why would any straight man lock himself away on a ship for months at a time with nothing but guys? Sounds gay to me."

"What does that have to do with dildos?" Kamiko whispered, frustrated. "With all those dicks around, why would a bunch of gay pirates need any dildos? Duh!"

Romeo titter whispered, "When it comes to an orgy, you can never have too many dicks, darling. Wooden or otherwise."

Kamiko grimaced and shook her head. "I've found that one is usually plenty."

"I concur," I grinned.

Our old pirate model cleared his throat. His face was turning red. He was totally listening and I think embarrassed. He probably thought our immature banter was offensive.

The young guy sitting and drawing next to me smirked and shook his head at Romeo and Kamiko's running pirate commentary.

Yes, their commentary was slightly embarrassing. For now. But I trusted Romeo to take it from slightly to extremely in no time. He was the embarrassment express train, and once he got up to speed, there was no stopping him until everybody arrived at the humiliation station. Picture a giant steam train barreling along the tracks with Romeo's face filling up the big circle on the front of the locomotive, his monocle in place while he smiled maniacally with his mouth wide open. His tongue would be dangling out the side and whipping in the wind while drool droplets flicked off. Smoke would be blurting from his smokestack in clouds shaped like letters that spelled out offensive comments.

Yes.

Romeo, The Loco Locomotive.

"TOOT! TOOT!" blows his whistle.

And we all knew how much Romeo liked to blow things.

I did my best to repress my snicker at the thought. I just hoped Romeo didn't go off the tracks and kill everybody onboard his shame train.

"Wait," Romeo said to Kamiko, "I thought your only dick experience was with cartoon penises. Have you finally taken the plunge? Walked a man's fleshy gang plank?"

The young guy beside me snickered, but did his best to repress it and keep drawing.

"Fleshy gang plank?" Kamiko scoffed. "Only a man could draw a connection between a pirate ship gang plank and a penis."

"You're kidding, right?" Romeo frowned. "Gang planks are long, stiff and they stick straight out from the hull of the ship. How is that in any way unlike a dick?"

"But gang planks are made of wood," Kamiko protested.

"Where do you think the term 'woody' came from?" Romeo whispered. "Or 'morning wood'?"

"Not from gang planks," she scoffed.

The pirate model blurted out a grunty, "Ahem!" He sounded like he could be clearing his throat or trying to get Romeo to shut up.

"Are you okay, Mr. Underwood?" Professor Childress asked the model from the other side of the room. "Do you need a glass of water? Or perhaps a break?" The professor sounded sincere. The model was an old guy, after all, and he could be overheating from embarrassment in that big pirate coat of his.

"I'm fine," Mr. Underwood, the pirate model, said.

The professor returned his focus to the students beside him.

Romeo whispered, "See? The pirate's name is Underwood! That proves my theory! Every man keeps wood under his pants!"

I repressed a titter as I glanced at Mr. Underwood to see if he was offended by Romeo's comment. I couldn't tell. He stared straight ahead, eyes locked in the distance. He was probably doing his best to block out Romeo. Poor Mr. Underwood. This was his job after all. He was paid to hold still and pose. He shouldn't have to endure Romeo's shenanigans.

"We were talking about gang planks," Kamiko hissed at Romeo. "Gang planks have nothing to do with sex. People are forced onto them at sword point and ordered to jump to a watery death in shark infested waters."

"Sounds like my last blind date," Romeo grinned casually while he continued to draw his costumed pirate on his drawing pad. "But I wasn't forced. And it wasn't sharks. It was crabs. Good thing they aren't fatal. But hey, I'm always looking for a good reason to shave my pubes."

Kamiko gagged. "OMG! TMI! I think I'm going to be sick."

The model held in one of those clicking laughs that people do when they want to explode with laughter but are forced to sneeze it out instead.

"Do you need a tissue, Mr. Underwood?" Professor Childress asked.

"I'm—" Mr. Underwood said, red faced and doing his best not to laugh, "—fine. I'm fine." He shook his head, smiling big, like he was trying to shake away his remaining laughter. He screwed his face into a serious look. But his cheeks still quivered with repressed laughter.

The professor nodded, then went back to helping the students.

Well, at least Mr. Underwood wasn't offended. I felt a little better, but I tossed Romeo a shocked look over Kamiko, who was folded over, clutching her stomach. If Romeo didn't stop, we were going to get busted.

Romeo winked at me and whispered, "I'm kidding, Kamiko. It wasn't crabs. It was barnacles. I had no idea that barnacles were a sexually transmittable disease. Lesson learned. Don't have sex with crusty old pirate ship captains. Butt barnacles are the worst. Do you have any idea how hard it is to wipe when your butt is covered with barnacles? Barnacles shred toilet paper like nobody's business."

"HA!" the model shouted. Then he started coughing elaborately. But I could tell he was just trying to maintain a professional demeanor by hiding his laughter.

Romeo was going to get poor Mr. Underwood fired at this rate.

The professor stood up from his drawing horse and said to Mr. Underwood, "Let me get you some water." He walked to the corner sink and filled a clean styrofoam cup from the tap.

Kamiko suddenly sat up, her face red, looking like she had diarrhea or was ready to barf after hearing Romeo's barnacle comments. She turned to Romeo and mimed projectile vomiting in his lap with her hands, cupping them and moving them up and down in front of her mouth repeatedly. She made a choked sound, "Gack!"

"Are you sucking off a giant dick?" Romeo whisper tittered. "Or is it a giant wooden dildo?"

The young guy next to me blurted a restrained, whispery laugh.

The professor walked past us and handed the cup of water to Mr. Underwood, who thanked him and drank the water down in several swallows before resuming his pose.

Kamiko dropped her hands in her lap and looked at me, shocked with embarrassment. She was even redder than before.

"Ahem," Professor Childress said as he turned around, standing right in front of us with a frown on his face and holding his arms behind his back in a teacherly pose. "Would it be possible for the three of you to focus your energies on your drawings rather than socializing during class? You're distracting the model. And your classmates."

"Geez, Sam!" Romeo growled, "I'm trying to draw! Stop distracting me!" He hunched over his pad and frantically shaded in his drawing of the pirate's jacket with his charcoal stick like he was innocent.

"Me?" I squeaked. "You were the one who—!"

Professor Childress stared at me and arched his eyebrows expectantly.

I winced and smiled back at him. I'm sure I looked like a guilty idiot. I wanted to explain it was the Loco Locomotive's fault, not mine.

The professor flicked his gaze from me to my drawing pad,

hinting I should get back to work. I nodded and started sketching out the lines of my pirate's hat like a good girl. My face broiled with embarrassment. I think I was now redder than Kamiko.

Out of the corner of my eye, I noticed Kamiko was biting her lip, looking terribly frightened, like she was going to get detention, or maybe even expelled. She was drawing so furiously she was tearing holes in her paper. She folded back the torn sheet with shaky hands and started a new drawing. She whimpered while she worked.

The professor stepped around behind us. For the next two minutes, he loomed over us, making sure we were working diligently.

I was pretty sure his glare was burning holes in our backs.

After another minute, the professor leaned forward so that his face was right beside Romeo's ear. In a low voice, he muttered, "Next time, young man," he said to Romeo ominously, "I suggest you choose your pirate lovers more carefully."

Romeo's eyes goggled.

"But," the professor quipped, "from what I've heard, the best way to remove butt barnacles is to chip them off with a pickaxe. Just be careful of your nuts, young man," he said seriously, "I wouldn't want you chipping them off in the process." He straightened up and smiled at us. "You didn't hear it from me," he winked.

I glanced from Romeo to Kamiko and the three of us burst out laughing.

Professor Childress was awesome.

Mr. Underwood snickered without restraint, his face turning beet red.

The professor chuckled and winked at Mr. Underwood, "Keep up the good work, Dick." Then the professor walked away to circulate amongst the other students.

Old Dick Underwood, I mean regular Dick Underwood, nodded and smiled at the Professor.

"The model's name is Dick!" Romeo hissed. "Dick Underwood! I told you! I was right! His middle name is probably Wooden Dildo!"

Kamiko gawked, "Dick Wooden Dildo Underwood?"

Romeo, the Loco Locomotive, had finally gone off the tracks.

The young guy next to me let out a long, loud laugh.

Professor Childress stood on the other side of the room. He

shook his head at us and chuckled before helping another student with their drawing.

I loved this class!

===

After class that afternoon, Romeo and I sat at one of the tables outside Toasted Roast, brainstorming ideas for comic strips for The Wombat. We still hadn't come up with much since going to The Wombat staff meeting weeks ago.

"How about Gay vs. Gay?" Romeo asked, tapping his pen against his lips. "It'll be a parody of the classic Spy vs. Spy comics from Mad Magazine."

"I don't think I've seen that one," I said as I sipped my coffee. "What's it about?"

"It's these two spies, one wears black, the other wears white, and they're always trying to kill each other with clever booby traps. And I think they're birds because they have these long pointy triangle noses."

I doodled in my sketch pad as I asked, "How would it work if it was Gay vs. Gay?"

"They'd always be trying to sleep with each other?" he suggested.

"I'm confused. Wouldn't they *want* to sleep with each other, if they were gay? What would be the challenge?"

"Maybe they hate each other?"

"Then why would they be trying to sleep with each other?"

"Hmm. Maybe you're right. How about Peabutts, a gay parody of Charles Schultz' classic Peanuts? Or we could call it Peanis."

"That sounds horribly wrong," I chuckled. "We'd probably get sued."

"How about Dickey Mouse?"

"Same problem," I said, taking another sip of coffee.

"Daffy Dick?"

I rolled my eyes.

"What? All cartoon birds are gay. Why do you think Daffy was so angry? He wasn't getting laid. And you know Tweety Bird was gay."

I shook my head.

"Gayfield the Cat?"

"No."

"Come on! Cats are totally gay man's best friend."

I arched an eyebrow doubtfully. "Do all gays loves cats?"

"I don't know about the rest of us, but I sure do. They're the only kind of pussy I really like," he snickered. He paused in thought, drumming his pen against his notebook. "How about Queer Family Circus?"

"I'm sensing a theme here," I sighed.

Romeo's monocle fell from his eye in disappointment. "I'm trying to be contemporary, Sam. There's tons of TV shows with gay couples in them. Why not gay comic strips?"

"Okay. But Queer Family Circus sounds way too pedo. With clowns," I shuddered.

"Clowns are funny."

"Clowns are scary," I insisted.

"All that garish makeup is pretty creepy," Romeo grimaced, squinching his monocle back into his eye. "Maybe you're right. How about Penis the Menace?"

"That sounds like porn."

"Family Gay?"

"Like Family Guy?" I asked skeptically.

"Why not? Gays have families too."

I sighed. "Do we have any other ideas?"

Romeo's eyes lit up and his monocle popped out again. "I know! Jugs Bunny! It wouldn't be gay. Jugs Bunny is a college coed with huge boobs. She's always getting into trouble because they're so large."

"You know, that comment proves that gay men are men, not women trapped in men's bodies."

Romeo looked confused. "What do you mean? Huge boobs are hilarious."

I shook my head dismissively. "Exactly."

"All right, Debbie Downer. Why don't you come up with something? You're shooting down everything I've got."

I smirked, "What, aren't you going to suggest a comic strip about a college coed who gives lots of head, and her name is Debbie Downer?"

Romeo's eyes lit up again. "That's genius, Sam! I love it!" He scribbled down some notes in his notebook. "Can you start drawing sketches of her? What would she look like? Does she have a huge mouth? A really long neck? Muscular lips? Maybe she has a sideways mouth that looks like a vajay-jay?"

I rolled my eyes and my head in unison. "You're kidding, right?"

"No!" he said, smiling from ear to ear. "Does she have to shave? Have a curly beard? A clit for a nose and only one nostril that she can pee out of? The comedic potential is infinite!" Romeo pounded his fist on the table, his eyes gleaming with excitement. He looked ready to take over the world with his comedy mastermind.

I grimaced. "That all sounds like a bit much. Couldn't you just make her a regular girl with an animal friend, like Calvin and Hobbes, or maybe Snoopy and Woodstock?"

"That's perfect! But the bird's name will be Woodcock! And Woodcock would, of course, be gay! Because he's a cartoon bird! You're a genius, Sam!"

I groaned. We had a ways to go with our comic strip idea.

====

I pulled the mail out of the mail box at the Manos house the next day. I had been bringing in the mail and doing lots of little things around the Manos house to show my appreciation to Spiridon and Christos. It was my house too. So I did my part to take care of it.

I sorted through the stack of mail and one letter jumped out at me.

San Diego University Cashier's Office.

Oh shit.

I tore the letter open.

I'd forgotten to make my monthly tuition payment! I'd been so crazy busy lately, the deadline had slipped right out of my mind. My first thought was that I was going to get booted from school. With Tiffany's accusation about me stealing her credit card hanging over my head already, I was skating on thin ice. The last thing I needed was a late payment weighing me down. Now I was on the verge of cracking through the ice and sinking into the freezing water.

I needed to take care of this immediately. Maybe I could put some of my tuition payment on my credit card? It was the last thing I wanted to do, but I was desperate.

Out of habit, I reached into the mailbox, making sure I hadn't missed anything. I suddenly had the idea that the mailbox would clamp shut on my fingers like a greedy maw, and chew them off.

With my other problems mounting, it seemed a likely scenario.

"Did the mail come?" Christos asked as he walked outside.

"Oh!" I jumped.

"Something wrong?"

"Uh, no?" Guilty question mark. "I mean, no! Everything's fine!" And the exclamation points too. "I mean fine. Everything is fine." I didn't want to tell him about my money problems. I'd vowed to take care of them myself, and I was going to follow through. It was all part of proving to my parents and myself that I wasn't foolish for choosing art.

"All right," Christos said. "I'm going to run to the art supply store. I need some new sable brushes. Do you need anything while I'm there?"

Not that I could afford anything. I was beyond broke. And Christos had already spent a ton of money setting up my drawing table with supplies in our studio. I couldn't ask for more. "No, thanks," I sighed.

"Do you want to come with, anyway?"

"No, I have to go to campus."

"You were just there. I thought your classes were done for the day."

"I have to take care of something with my, uh, financial aid! Some new loan papers!" I lied. I hoped Christos didn't know the first thing about how financial aid and loans worked, or he'd start asking questions and find out real quick.

"That's cool. Do you want a ride? We could go to Blick Art down in Little Italy after."

"No! That's okay!"

He frowned. "You sure?"

"Yes!"

"All right. In that case, I'm taking the Duke. The weather's so nice, I feel like a ride."

I was about to ask if he'd been drinking, because I didn't want him riding his motorcycle if he'd had even a sip. But ever since that visit with his dad, I don't think Christos had been drinking much at all. "Okay," I said.

He pushed his Ducati out of the garage and put his helmet on. "Wanna have dinner when I get home?"

"That would be awesome."

"And don't forget, we need to start your painting soon."

Oh, that. Me, nude. For everyone to see. Naked on a mountain top at night was one thing. A well lit portrait hanging in a crowded gallery was another. "Sure!" Notice the exclamation point.

"Maybe we can start tonight," he suggested.

"Maybe?" Notice the question mark.

He nodded and smiled his dimpled grin. "Later," he said as he revved the bike and rode off.

I envied that Christos was back to his usual carefree self. It had happened almost overnight, like all his troubles had vanished. He'd returned to being the Christos I'd fallen in love with. It was amazing what the love of a supportive parent could do for one's confidence and self esteem.

(Subtle jab at my own parents)

Sigh.

I wished my troubles would vanish like Christos', so I could be carefree too. Unfortunately, mine weren't even close to free. They cost thousands of dollars that I didn't have.

At least I had my credit card. I could now begin the time honored American tradition of sinking into a pit of debt I might never be able to climb out of.

===

"What do you mean I can't pay my tuition by credit card?" I asked in horror.

The cashier, a middle aged guy with a pepper gray beard and glasses, stood behind the counter at the SDU Central Cashier's Office. He said, "We can only accept payment by cash, check, money order, or student loan checks."

"But I'm out of student loan money and I don't have any cash," I groused. "The bank won't give me a loan because I don't have a cosigner." I was ready to cry and plead for mercy. I think it showed on my face and desperate tone of voice.

The cashier smiled sympathetically. "I'm sorry, there's nothing I can do. Have you spoken with someone at Financial Aid? They can help you explore all of your aid options in depth."

"I have," I sighed. "I can't get any more loan money until next year."

"That's a problem," he nodded sympathetically.

"What happens if I don't pay?"

"There is a grace period. You have another week to pay before you incur a late fee of fifty dollars."

Shit, I didn't have fifty dollars to spare, let alone thousands. "What happens if I don't pay by then?"

"You'll incur a hold on your account."

"What does that mean?"

"It means you'll have to pay a $35 fee to clear the hold and make your payment."

"You mean I'll have to pay $35 so I can pay the $50 late fee AND my tuition?"

"Yes," he said somewhat sheepishly.

I shook my head. Great. More money I didn't have. "What happens if I don't clear the hold?"

"Eventually, you'll be subject to cancellation of your classes."

"What do you mean? Like, permanently? I don't want to get kicked out of SDU," I said with feeble dread.

"No," he smiled. "It's not that dire. But you won't be able to receive any credit for this term. You'll have to retake all the classes you're enrolled in now."

"But they don't offer History 3 and Sociology 3 again until next Spring! That'll totally screw up my schedule next year!"

He spread his hands apart. "I'm sorry."

"What can I do?" I said, panicked.

"I know this sounds harsh, but if you can find a way to cover your monthly installment payment, you won't have anything to worry about. Try talking to your parents."

Them. Yeah, right. They weren't going to do shit.

"Is there anything else I can help you with?" he asked, glancing over my shoulder at the people waiting in line behind me.

"No, thanks."

My shoulders slumped as I trudged out of the Cashier's Office.

I was going to find the nearest lamppost outside and wait until dark so I could start turning tricks. I was pretty sure one trick would cover my late fee and my hold fee.

I walked down the stairs outside the Cashier's Office right as Tiffany Cum-dumb Butt-spouse walked by with a pair of her sorority hobots flanking her.

Great.

As always, she was dressed in new clothes, her platinum blonde hair was perfectly arranged, and I expected paparazzi to jump out of the bushes and start snapping photos of her any second. She exuded celebrity, even though I think the only thing she was famous for was being a bitch.

I ducked my head, hoping she wouldn't notice me.

"Well, if it isn't little miss Scumantha Banana Shit," she sneered.

I wondered for the second time how she'd found out my full name was Samantha Anna Smith. She probably had spies everywhere. I had no doubt she could afford to hire the very best.

We were walking in the same direction, so I walked quickly, hoping to put some distance between us. I heard her tittering with her two minions behind me.

"Having a bad day, Scumantha?" she sneered at my back.

I rolled my eyes to myself and kept walking, doing my best to ignore her.

"Find any good jobs lately?" she jabbed.

What a bitch. She had totally gotten me fired out of spite, and we both knew it.

I turned and glared at her, "Shut up, Tiffany."

She and her hobot friends cackled at me.

The thing that pissed me off more than anything was that Tiffany never had to worry about money, she never had to work for anything, and she was still the biggest bitch on the planet.

"Oh," she cooed in baby talk, "did I hurt widdle Scumantha's feewings?"

Her friends laughed heartily.

I pivoted on my heel and marched right up to Tiffany and her friends. The three of them stopped short, eyes bugging out.

"Hey," one of the hobots muttered.

Tiffany frowned at me, "Hey, back off—"

SLAP!!

I smacked her right across the face. Her cheek was white where I'd hit it. I'd learned that trick from my mom. At least she was good for something.

"Oh my god!" one of the hobots gasped, covering her lips with her fingers.

The other hobot was stunned into silence.

Tiffany huffed a wordless shriek. Slowly, she raised her hand and gingerly touched her cheek with her fingertips.

I narrowed my eyes at her. "Don't call me Scumantha."

I turned around and walked away, expecting her and her friends to jump me or throw knives in my back. Knowing Tiffany, her daddy probably gave her a fancy hand gun she would use to gun me down.

Instead, Tiffany shrieked, "I'm really looking forward to our hearing in front of the SDU tribunal!!! I can't wait to tell them all about how you stole my credit card AND attacked me on campus!!! I'll make sure you're expelled, you sniveling cunt!!!!!!!"

That hadn't gone quite the way I'd hoped.

Sigh.

===

A black Firebird Trans Am was parked in the driveway when I came home. It had a huge gold firebird decal on the hood and gold pin striping around the windows. The T tops were off. It was an old muscle car, but in perfect condition. I had no idea whose it was.

I hoped it wasn't Tiffany's. She drove a black Mercedes, but you never knew. Maybe she was trying to impress Christos and win him back by buying him a muscle car as a present. She could certainly afford it.

Stupid bitch.

She was making my life miserable without even trying. Yeah, I hated her.

I put my key in the lock of the double front door and discovered it was already open.

"Anybody home?" I called uncertainly.

"Samantha!" Nikolos smiled as he walked out of the kitchen. "I was waiting for someone to get here. I let myself in."

"You have a key?"

"Yeah. I've had it forever."

"How come you never use it?" I smiled.

He arched an eyebrow and shrugged his shoulders. "Oh, you know," he said casually.

Boy, I was still putting my foot in my mouth from time to time. I guess growing up took longer than six or seven months. But I was doing my best. "Is that your car outside? It's beautiful."

"Yeah. Seventy-seven Firebird Trans Am, Special Edition. Same one they used in Smokey and the Bandit."

"Smokey and the what?"

"You haven't seen Smokey and the Bandit?" Nikolos gasped.

I shook my head.

"That movie is a classic. We're going to have to have movie night at my place. Bring Christos over. We'll put it on my big TV."

"Sounds like fun!' I grinned. "Do you want something to drink?"

"I already helped myself to some of Dad's lemonade in the fridge. I can pour you a glass."

"Oh, I'll get it. You sit down." I walked over to the cupboard and grabbed a glass from the shelf and poured some from the pitcher perspiring on the counter.

"Did you ever hear back from my maid service?"

I sat down at the kitchen table across from Nikolos. "I didn't. Did they try to call me?"

"I told them to call the house since I didn't have your cell phone number. Did you not get a message?"

"No," I said.

"Do you still need a job?" he asked.

"Are you kidding?" I blurted. "I would kill for a job right now. I would clean skunk toilets if it paid."

Confused, he asked, "Skunk toilets?"

"You know, the ones the skunks use? They probably smell awful. I hear that public skunk restrooms are the worst."

Nikolos laughed. "Skunk toilets. You always have the strangest ideas."

"Is that good or bad?" I asked uncertainly.

"Definitely good. It shows you have a creative mind."

"You think so?"

"I do."

I rolled my eyes, "My parents never did." I felt like I was sinking back into my own self doubt as I talked to Nikolos. I so wanted to be over it, but all I had to do was close my eyes for a second and I could see fifty foot tall red neon numbers blinking in my mind's eye:

-$5,000

-$5,000

-$5,000

I was never going to find that kind of money.

"So, when am I going to see some of your art, Samantha? My

dad says you've really been coming along since he met you."

"Yeah," I smiled, suddenly in a better mood thinking about how nice Spiridon was to me all the time. At least I had him and Christos watching my back. But I would never dream of asking either one of them for $5,000.

I said, "I have my sketchbook, if you want to see that?"

"Sure," Nikolos grinned.

I walked into the studio and grabbed my sketchbook off my drawing table and returned to the kitchen.

Nikolos started flipping through it on the table top from the beginning so we could both look. He didn't say much at first. "I can see the progress right away. I'm guessing this page marks the point you started getting instruction?"

"Yeah, that was stuff I drew right after I started taking Life Drawing with Professor Childress."

"Walt Childress?"

"Yeah. I took his class in the fall. Now I'm taking Drawing The Costumed Figure from him. Do you know him?"

"Very well. I haven't talked to him in a few years though."

"What's up with Walt and Spiridon, anyway?"

Nikolos cracked a wide grin that had the same dimples as Christos. "Ahh, Walt and my dad go way, way back."

"Was there some kind of drama between them? Whenever Walt's name comes up, Spiridon hints around the bush, but never says anything."

Nikolos nodded. "They have, how should I say it? A history together." He emphasized the word history like it hid buried treasure.

"Really?" I leaned forward on my elbows, all ears.

Nikolos arched his eyebrows.

And...he wasn't going to say anything.

"Aren't you going to tell me?" I asked. "I'm dying to know!"

He shook his head and smiled that stupid Manos dimpled grin. "Sorry, it's not my story to tell. You'll have to ask my dad some time."

I groaned and smiled. "Fine."

Nikolos turned back to my sketchbook and continued flipping. When he got to my pot smoking wombat sketches he stopped and laughed. "What is this?"

"It's my ideas for a logo for The Wombat."

"The what?"

"The comedy newspaper at SDU."

"Oh, that Wombat. These are really funny, Samantha. How come you have so many?"

"The editor of the paper asked me to design some new ones."

"Really?"

"Yeah," I smiled.

"Which one did he pick?"

"Oh, they're going to have a vote. Everyone on staff gets to vote. And other people are submitting ideas."

"Well, yours should win. These are hilarious. And your design sense is beautiful. You draw very elegant shapes, yet they have humor and wit without being crude."

"Wow, thanks!"

"Based on all this work in your sketchbook, I can see that you truly have talent. No wonder my dad has said so many nice things about you."

I was blushing like a school girl, which was okay because I was still in school, even if it was college. It was okay to blush when someone was complimenting you this much, right? I was totally on cloud nine.

-$5,000

-$5,000

-$5,000

There went my good mood.

"Something bothering you?" Nikolos asked, concern on his face.

"Oh, uh, nothing."

"Don't kid a kidder, Samantha. You look like someone killed your kitten. What is it?"

Nikolos was so friendly and kind, I couldn't help opening up to him. "I owe the university a bunch of money I don't have."

"What do you mean?"

"My tuition payment is late because I used up the little loan money I already had. I was supposed to pay in monthly installments but I ran out of cash."

"Is that why you were asking about the maid job?"

"Yeah. Jobs are scarce right now. I can't even find a math tutoring job, which I would be good at."

He took a sip of his lemonade, "I thought you said you were working at a convenience store."

"I was. I was also working at the campus art museum."

He smiled, "You were working at the Eleanor M. Westbrook museum?"

"Yeah."

"That must be fun."

"It was," I winced.

"Was?" His brows knit. "What happened?"

"It's a long story," I groaned.

"It sounds to me like you're in dire straits."

"That's an understatement," I rolled my eyes. It was all pouring out now and I couldn't stop myself. I blamed it on Nikolos' sympathetic ear. Stupid ears. I'd vowed to deal with this myself and not put it on someone else.

"Have you ever considered looking for work in an art studio?"

"Oh," I sighed, "I've totally looked for art jobs. Besides the museum, which was just being a cashier, there are none. No one hires artists that I could find."

"I would."

I frowned. "Huh?"

"I could use an assistant in my studio. Mixing paint by hand takes forever. Same with stretching canvases and building frames. It's all time consuming work. It would be nice to have someone do it for me while I oversaw the process. Someone I can train, and someone I can trust."

I gave him a funny look. "Like who?"

"Like you," he smiled.

I shook my head, "Oh, I couldn't do that."

"I thought you said you needed to find a job. I'm hiring."

"I can't take your money, Mr. Manos."

"Call me Nikolos."

"You're my boyfriend's dad," I scoffed, "I can't call you by your first name."

"Sure you can. And if you work for me, it'll be part of the job requirement."

A spark of hope twinkled in my chest. I really did need a job. "Are you serious?"

"Yes, I'm serious."

My mouth gaped open. "I don't know what to say."

"Thank you always works," he grinned.

"Thank you, Mr. Manos!" I leaned over the table and hugged him, almost knocking over his lemonade glass.

He caught it and smiled, "Careful!"

"Thank you so much!" I sat back down. "You don't know how much this means to me."

He smiled. "Aren't you going to ask what it pays?"

"Oh! Yeah, duh."

"How much is your tuition payment?" he asked.

"What? No, I couldn't." I shook my head vigorously.

"How much?" he insisted.

I sighed. "It's over five thousand."

"How about I make your payment for you, and you can work it off."

"I could never do that!"

"Why not?"

"I can't take your money," I pleaded.

"Who said anything about taking? You're going to work it off. There's always things to do around the studio, believe me. You're going to become an expert at cleaning brushes."

"I don't know," I said hesitantly.

"Look, Samantha. Artists have apprentices. Apprentices do all the grunt work while watching the artist work. Not only will you get paid, you'll be learning something. It's one of those work study jobs. Because seriously, how much were you learning about art by ringing up people at the cash register at the museum?"

He had a point.

"Let's say I pay you twenty an hour. You can work off the five thousand that way. It won't take too long, I'm sure."

"How many hours do you want me to work a week?"

"As many as you want."

"Are you serious?"

"Yes."

I did the numbers in my head. If I worked part time, say twenty hours a week, it would only take about three months to cover my tuition bill. Oh wait. That only covered the one past due. I'd figure out the third one due a month from now later.

"Do we have a deal?" he asked, holding his hand across the

table.

I shook it. "Yes!"

What a pleasant surprise!

Now all I had to worry about was getting expelled from SDU for attacking Tiffany and stealing her credit card.

Screw Tiffany!

I had a job!

Chapter 21

SAMANTHA

"I had a new idea for our comic strip," Romeo said as we walked across campus toward the Student Center and The Wombat staff meeting at Toasted Roast. Although the weather had become quite warm for early spring, Romeo wore his elaborate burgundy steampunk coat with the black cuffs and collar, and his pointy, silver tipped black leather shoes. His monocle dangled in rhythm with his stride.

"What was your idea?" I asked.

"Tampon Tammy! She shoots giant tampons from her stinky skunk trunk while fighting the forces of evil."

"You don't mean Tammy Lemons, that bitchy girl at the last staff meeting? The one with the hipster glasses?"

"I totally mean her," Romeo said conspiratorially.

"Oh, Romeo, we can't do that. She'll hate us more than she already does."

"Maybe you're right," he sighed. "But if she's a bitch today at the meeting, I'm totally going to propose the idea to everyone."

"Please don't," I begged.

"Please don't what?" Justin Tomlinson said, falling into step with us.

"Hey, Justin," I smiled nervously. I hoped he hadn't heard Romeo's idea.

"I was just telling Sam—" Romeo blurted.

I cut him off, "How much fun we've been having working on ideas for The Wombat."

Justin frowned, "How does that follow from 'Please don't'?"

"Uhhh…" I stammered.

"Please don't tell Justin how awesome he is for letting us sit in with you guys," Romeo said, saving me.

Justin smiled and nodded as we walked down the stairs running beside the stepped fountain that led down to the Student Center quad. "Thanks. You guys are both pretty awesome yourselves. Most everybody loves what you guys are coming up with."

"Most everybody?" Romeo asked.

I shot Romeo a "shut the fuck up" glare. I knew he was thinking of Tammy.

"Well, I just meant that..." Justin sounded put on the spot.

"We know what you meant," I smiled.

The three of us walked up to the two tables already occupied by Keith, Micah, Alyssa, and Tammy.

"Hey guys," Justin said, lowering his book bag onto the table top as we all sat down.

"Well, if it isn't Romiet and Julio," Tammy Lemons sniveled.

Great. Maybe Romeo had been right. Was Tammy saying I was mannish by calling me Julio?

Romeo arched an eyebrow at me, then turned to Justin, "Justin, I have a great idea for a new comic strip. Want to hear about it?"

Gulp.

"Let's hear it," Keith smiled.

"Well," Romeo smiled a Cheshire grin, "it's about OW!!"

I had kicked Romeo's shin under the table.

"Ow?" Micah asked. "What's that?"

"Owl! I meant Owl!" Romeo said.

"An owl?" Alyssa asked doubtfully.

"Yes!" Romeo yelled. "It's, uh, about Obie, the OB/GYN Owl! He's a real hoot for the coot!"

"Hoot for the coot?" Micah snickered.

"And instead of figuring out how many licks it takes to get to the center of a Tootsie Pop, he figures out how many licks it takes to make Tootsie, as played by Dustin Hoffman in the movie of the same name, get off! Get it? Tootsie *Pop*?"

"Dude, how high are you?" underbeard Keith asked with an amazed grin on his face.

"I want to smoke whatever he's been smoking," emo Micah smiled.

"I have to admit," Justin grinned at Romeo, "it has potential."

"Potential to suck," Tammy sneered.

Wow, Tammy was sourballs.

"I have another idea," Romeo said, glaring at Tammy.

"Let's hear it," Micah said.

"It's called Tah—HEY!"

I had kicked him under the table again.

"Tah-HEY?" Keith asked. "I can't wait to hear where he goes with this one."

"Yeah, Romeo," I growled, "I can't wait either." The last thing I wanted to do was make things with Tammy worse. I already had Tiffany on my case. I didn't need Tammy too.

Romeo shook his head and glared at me, "I tah-hotally forgot."

"All right," Justin said, "maybe it will come back to you later. I wanted to tell everyone that I've finally got all the votes back for our new Wombat mascot artwork. It was a close race." He pulled two pieces of paper out of his book bag and set them on the table side by side. One was a copy of one of my drawings of the Wombat. And the other, wow, the other was really good.

It showed a wombat holding a baseball bat over one shoulder. The bat was cracked in half and the big end dangled from the handle by a sliver. In the wombat's other hand was a huge beer mug with foam frothing out the top of the glass. He had the SDU logo branded into his chest fur like on cattle. Next to him was a man lying on the ground, knocked out cold. He was obviously a professor because there was a chalkboard with chemistry equations on it behind him and a piece of chalk sticking out of one hand and an eraser in the other. A huge lump rose up from his forehead and cartoon birds circled it with musical notes coming out of their mouths like they were chirping.

It was fantastic, even if Tammy had drawn it.

"And the winner is—" Justin said.

Tammy? I was totally sure she had won. I would've picked hers over mine.

Micah drummed the table with his fingertips.

"—Samantha!" Justin finished.

What?

"Congratulations, Sam!" Romeo said.

Tammy folded her arms across her chest and scowled.

Romeo gave her a snooty look.

"Romeo," I whispered, "don't."

Justin smiled, "We all loved your art, Tammy, but most of us agreed we'd never get it past administration. Violence to SDU professors is not their favorite subject matter."

Tammy frowned, "Getting stoned while taking a dump is?" She was referring to my drawing.

Justin shrugged his shoulders, "The vote still went to Samantha."

Tammy rolled her eyes, "Whatever."

"Samantha," Justin said, "your drawing will now be on the front cover of the next issue of The Wombat. It'll also go at the top of our webpage. Everyone is going to see it."

"What?" I smiled. I couldn't believe it. I really hoped Justin hadn't rigged the vote because he was into me, because Tammy's art was truly incredible.

"We loved your art," Alyssa said to me.

"Yeah, a bunch of the other staff were bonkers for your drawing of Potty," Keith smiled.

"I think we should make T shirts that say 'Potty for President'," Micah grinned.

Tammy's mouth sagged with disgust.

It was hard to enjoy my victory when it came at the expense of someone else. I wanted to tell Tammy I was sorry, but somehow that seemed inconsiderate. "Tammy, I really like your drawing. It's really good."

She spat, "So why don't you withdraw yours and we'll use mine?"

I opened my mouth, wanting to say something supportive, but couldn't think of anything. I closed it in frustration.

"Maybe we should open the vote up to the readers?" Alyssa suggested tentatively.

Keith and Micah gave noncommittal shrugs.

Justin nodded thoughtfully, "If we can get administration to approve Tammy's art, I don't see why not?"

A smug smile curled across Tammy's lips.

Wow, way for her to steal my thunder. Maybe me and Romeo needed to write the Tampon Tammy comic strip after all. I would make the character look exactly like her so no one would wonder who it was supposed to be about. She totally had the face of a vajay-jay.

Groanballs.

===

"Do I get to have a closed set," I asked Christos, "like they do in the movies when they're shooting a sex scene?" I stood in my bathrobe in our painting studio. Which I thought of as ours all the time now, even though Spiridon owned the house.

"We're not shooting a sex scene," Christos smirked, "unless you want to. I can record video on my phone..." he said suggestively.

"No! Posing nude is about all I can manage. By the way, do we have to have the curtains open?" Not that I'd ever seen any curtains in the studio. The tall windows along both walls faced the backyard. Yeah, they needed curtains.

"I need the natural light coming in. It's more flattering than using studio lights."

"Speaking of," I said, "can you Photoshop me with your painting?"

"You mean hide all your imperfections?"

"Yeah," I said hopefully.

"No," he said with finality.

"Why not?" I frowned.

"Because you don't have any," he flashed his dimpled grin.

"Oh," I smiled. "Well, can you at least give me more of a crotch notch?"

"A what?"

"You know that gap between a woman's legs that's all the rage right now?"

"You mean a thigh gap?"

"Yeah!"

He shook his head, "You have a crotch notch."

"No I don't!"

He arched an eyebrow. "Have you looked in a mirror lately?"

I frowned, "Well, can you make it bigger? I really want to sell it."

"Are you listening to yourself?" he asked, irritated.

"What? I want a huge crotch notch."

He arched his other eyebrow. "You're sure?"

"Yes! I hate how my thighs touch together.

"Every woman's thighs touch together to some degree."

"But mine touch more than normal."

"No they don't," he argued patiently.

Why was I being so picky and neurotic? Oh yeah, because

Christos was going to paint me nude for the world to see. Can you blame a girl for wanting to look her best?

"Fine. I can make you look like you have sticks for legs, if that's your preference."

"Huh?"

"Your crotch notch is fine. I love it. No one is going to criticize my painting for having an underwhelming crotch notch. Besides, the way I'm going to pose you, no one is going to be able to tell what kind of crotch notch you have. They won't even be able to see your crotch."

"What? Why not?" I demanded.

"Because I'm going to make you hold a horned Viking helmet over it," he smirked.

"What? That sounds horrid!"

"Hey, the helmet was your idea."

"But not over my crotch notch!"

He rolled his eyes and smiled his dimpled grin. "Are you trying to make me insane?"

"No, I, uh. I don't know," I sighed.

"You told me to figure out a way to make the Viking helmet work. That's my solution," he smirked. "Be careful what you wish for."

"I don't want a helmet over my lady bits, that's for sure," I chuckled. I sighed, "Gosh, what is it with the thigh gap, anyway? It's like it didn't exist a few years ago."

"Blame it on stretch pants, booty shorts, and crotch selfies. It was bound to happen sooner or later. Once that pussy cat was out of the bag, it was never going back," he grinned.

"I wonder if women who wore Poodle skirts back in the day had to worry about having a crotch notch?" I asked thoughtfully.

"Nope. All they had to worry about was whether or not their poodle was as big as the next girl's."

"Are you saying it used to be the woman with the biggest poodle won? And now it's the notchiest crotch?"

"Sad, isn't it?" Christos said ironically. "So, are we going to paint your portrait, or do you want to obsess about your non-existent imperfections for awhile longer?"

I wrinkled my nose at him sarcastically.

"We don't have to do this," he said, "I can always paint you with clothes on. It's up to you."

"Really?"

He nodded, "But I think you'd be making a big mistake. I'd hate to think you missed the chance at being the world's most famous nude portrait. Because that's what I'm aiming for."

"Oh." I definitely liked the sound of that.

"Imagine," he grinned, "a work crew of guys wheeling your painting into The Louvre, taking down the Mona Lisa, and hanging your portrait up in its place."

I smiled, "That could work."

He chuckled, "Yes it could. Then The Louvre would finally have an impressive painting instead of that tiny little Mona Lisa."

"You sure are cocky," I said.

"Is that a problem?"

"No. Jerk," I swatted his arm.

"Okay, strip."

"Mmmm. I like it when you tell me what to do."

"Good," he smirked his sexy grin.

I dropped my robe to the ground. "Do with me what you will..." I purred.

Of course, we had sex in the studio.

Spiridon had left for the afternoon so I could feel like I had some privacy while I posed nude.

Christos and I had sex on the dais all the other models had sat on before me. I didn't ask Christos if he'd had sex on it, because it was possible he had, with Perfect Paisley or someone else from his past. All I knew was I was queen of this domain now, bitches! Oh, and I made him put down clean blankets first. Just in case.

Christos fucked me on my throne while I held sway over my domain. Christos came inside me like an art rockstar.

Then I gave him a blow job while he sat in front of his easel. I paused to make a joke about his cock being a tube of flesh colored paint.

"But it isn't flesh colored," he said.

"Yes it is," I argued. "I've inspected it carefully many times."

"I meant the paint. The paint inside my paint tube is pearlescent white."

"Is that even a color?" I asked doubtfully.

"It is. Look it up. You can find it online. It's a common craft paint."

"Yeah," I purred, "But are any of those paints edible?"

"Wow," he chuckled, "you get dirtier and dirtier the more I get to know you, *agápi mou.*"

"And you—" I pressed my finger against his muscled abs, "—love it." Then I teased the tip of his cock with my tongue before going back to work on him.

He slouched against the back of his chair and moaned. I tickled his testicles with my fingers as I brought him to another studio shaking orgasm. I slowed my head movements as his spasms diminished. I milked every last precious pearlescent drop from his cock.

When Christos finally recovered, he said, "Are we going to do any painting today, or just the fucking?"

"I vote for fucking," I grinned, before kissing his cock again.

Christos stood up from his chair, squatted in front of me, and lifted me by my ass until my wet folds were in his face. He started licking hungrily.

"Christos! Put me down!"

He didn't. He just kept licking. I don't know how he held me up so high for so long. But I glanced down several times at his rock hard shoulders. He was stronger than an ox. After awhile, I stopped worrying about whether or not he might drop me because the intense pleasure between my legs stole away every concern I'd ever had.

After I don't know how many orgasms, we eventually did start on the painting.

Christos didn't bother to put his clothes on after we'd made love.

"Are you going to stay nude while you paint me?" I asked.

"Sounds fair to me?"

"I don't know if I'll be able to keep my hands off you," I bit my lower lip.

"Do your best," he smirked.

Christos set me up in a standing pose on the dais. "I'm going to do a charcoal rough of you first, on paper. Just to see what I think of the pose and the lighting."

"Okay."

"Do your best to hold still," he said.

"I will," I smiled.

Little did I know that standing still for so long was really, really hard. "I think I'm getting a cramp," I said after what seemed like four days, but in reality was probably twenty minutes.

"Let's take a break," he smiled.

"Break? Can't we be done for the day?" I pleaded.

"Not if we want to get the portrait done. I'll make you a deal. You tell me what's cramping, and I'll massage it out."

"I have a feeling everything's going to be cramping by the time we're finished."

He smiled, "Okay, then I'll massage everything."

"Deal." I walked around to look at his charcoal sketch. "Holy shit! You did all that in just twenty minutes?" It looked like a rough black and white photo of me. Some of it was still unfinished, like the hands and feet, but the face was totally me. "How'd you get my face finished so quick? It looks just like me!"

"I have your face burned into my brain. I see it in my mind every time I close my eyes."

"You can remember it that well?"

"Beauty like yours is impossible to forget," he cocked his dimpled grin.

When my break was over, he asked, "Do you want to try the pose with a Viking helmet now? I'll do another sketch and we can compare them."

"We don't have a Viking helmet," I said.

"Yeah we do, up on that top shelf over there."

I loved how we were using the word "we" to refer to things in our studio. I followed Christos' gaze and noticed a Viking helmet sitting between a gladiator's helmet and a knight's helmet, the shining armor kind. "Where'd you get those?" I asked.

"My grandad bought them forever ago. It's always good to have props around. Now we can finally use one." He walked over to the shelf and pulled the horned helmet down. "Here, put this on."

We walked over to a six foot tall full length mirror in the corner that was built into a frame on wheels.

"Why do you have this?" I asked.

"It's for painting full length self portraits. Lots of painters use them. You can also use it to look at your painting in a mirror image, which makes it easy to see flaws."

"I didn't know that," I said thoughtfully. "Have you ever used the mirror for your own self portrait?"

"I haven't."

"You totally should! Hey, what if you painted yourself into my portrait?!"

His eyes lit up. "That's not a bad idea. But do I have to wear a Viking helmet too?"

"It depends how it looks on me," I snickered. "Can I try it on?"

He handed me the helmet and I set it on my head. It was way too big. It completely covered my eyes. I tilted my head back to look under the helmet's brim at my reflection in the mirror. I was nude from head to toe. In a Viking helmet. Maybe not.

Christos snickered. "It's perfect. A total winner."

"Shut up!" I took the helmet off.

"Put that back on! We're totally painting you with the Viking helmet. Nude."

I rolled my eyes. "Fine, it was a terrible idea. But what about you and me together? We could call the painting The Lovers."

He grinned and started nodding, "That's actually awesome."

"Don't we make a great team?"

"We do, *agápi mou*," he smiled and kissed me on the lips.

I wrapped my arms around his naked waist and leaned my head against his chest.

I gazed at the two of us in all our naked glory standing together in front of the full length mirror. "I like how this looks," I whispered.

"Maybe instead of calling it The Lovers," he smiled, "which sort of sounds temporary, we just call the painting LOVE, which is eternal?"

"I like the way you think, *agápi mou*," I sighed.

I had the best boyfriend ever.

===

Despite all my problems with money and Tiffany, I was managing to balance my entire schedule: classes, homework, my new job helping out Nikolos in his studio, and posing nude for Christos.

Working for Christos' dad turned out to be awesome. He was totally flexible about my hours. He worked all the time, so he didn't really care when I decided to come in, as long as I got everything done. And there was a lot to do.

Nikolos was always starting new paintings or running out of one color paint or another. So I was either mixing fresh paint, stretching new canvases, or cleaning hundreds of brushes. He went through brushes like water.

As promised, Nikolos had written me a check for my tuition payment. I was set until the next payment was due. But that wasn't until after mid terms, so I wasn't going to worry about it until I had to. With any luck, I'd figure something out.

At the moment, I was in the gardner's shed behind Nikolos' house. It was more like a gardner's house or three car garage, because of its size. It had several rooms, tons of windows (most of which were open to let in a steady breeze), two big outdoor sinks, running water, gardening tools, a riding lawn mower for the giant backyard lawn, sacks of fertilizer and plant food, and everything else the gardner, who I'd met several times, used to maintain the grounds three days a week. Everything in the room was neatly arranged and created a pleasant atmosphere.

I stood at a big work table against the open windows, busily mixing paint. Cadmium red medium, to be exact. Because you weren't supposed to inhale the dry pigments, I wore goggles, a face mask, and gloves. Despite the safety precautions, I enjoyed myself. From what I understood, the paint pigments were far less toxic than Tiffany Kingdumb-Cuntmouse, who had managed to find me at my previous jobs and give me grief. I was pretty sure she'd never find me way out in Rancho Santa Fe at Nikolos' place.

I was adding dribbles of linseed oil to a pile of red pigment dust on top of a thick glass slab, mixing them together into buttery goop with a putty knife. It was sort of like making toxic cake frosting because you definitely weren't supposed to eat the paint. Maybe I could make a toxic cake and deliver it to Tiffany's house for her birthday. She'd never know it was me. Wicked grin.

There was a trick to getting the consistency of the finished paint just right, but I'd been doing it for a few weeks and was getting pretty good at it. When I was finished mixing, I scooped the finished paint into empty metal tubes with those screw top caps and crimped off the ends with pliers.

Nikolos leaned his head in the doorway. Bright clear blue sky silhouetted him. "How's that cad red coming along?"

"Just finished," I smiled, pulling off my gloves, mask, and goggles.

"Ready for a break? Dad made some fresh lemonade." He was referring to Spiridon, who was over to sit for his portrait again, which Nikolos had almost finished.

"What is it with your dad and lemonade?" I grinned.

"I have no idea," he chuckled. "You should ask him."

I carried the finished tubes of cadmium red in a cardboard box as we walked back to the house together.

Spiridon walked out of the house with a pitcher of lemonade on a tray that also held three glasses filled with ice. We sat down at an outdoor table beneath an awning. Spiridon poured for everyone and served.

The view from the back of Nikolos' house was breathtaking. The house was high on a hillside and looked down at the rolling hills of a beautiful canyon. It was probably the nicest view I'd ever seen in a person's actual house. It was quiet and you couldn't hear any sounds of cars or modern human cacophony. It was just nature. Birds chirping now and then, and a soft, warm breeze. The usual word people used for a place like this was Paradise with a capital P for perfect.

I had thought Spiridon's beach mansion was awesome. This was the next level.

"How is your plein air painting class going, *Samoula*?" Spiridon asked before sipping his lemonade. "You said the professor was Katherine Weatherspoon?"

"Yeah," I said.

"She's good," Nikolos said.

"You know her?" I asked.

"I know most of the faculty in the art department at SDU," Nikolos said.

"Wow, you guys both do, don't you?" I grinned.

"Pretty much," Spiridon smiled. "How are you enjoying painting outdoors?"

"It's the best!" I beamed. "I'm always thinking how awesome it would be to paint outside for a living."

"Pretty awesome," Spiridon smiled.

"That's right! You painted all those landscapes over the years!"

"I've spent most of my life painting outdoors," he said.

"I still can't get over the fact that's your job." I sipped more lemonade and started crunching an ice cube. Normally, I wouldn't have spoken with my mouth full, but that was with my parents. Spiridon and Nikolos were so laid back, I didn't even realize I was breaking the rules.

"Hey," Nikolos said to his dad, "remember that time you took me up to Yosemite, and you were painting by that river, and you thought I was a deer?"

"What?" I asked, confused.

"That's right!" Spiridon chuckled, "You were a deer!"

Nikolos smiled broadly, that same dimpled grin that Christos had, and said, "Oh, you should've been there, Samantha. I was just a kid. My dad was busy painting, but I wanted to play."

"You were probably, what, seven or eight at the time?" Spiridon said.

"That sounds about right," Nikolos smiled. "So, there I was, tugging on my dad's arm every five minutes to show him another pine cone I'd found or maybe another fancy rock, and I'm walking back toward where he's set up by his easel to show him something else, and I see a full grown mama deer walk up behind my dad out of nowhere, followed by her two babies. The mama was two feet behind Dad, and she was one big deer. I was so scared, I couldn't even speak. The next thing I know, that mama deer is nipping at the back of my dad's jacket." Nikolos glanced at Spiridon, "Didn't you have an orange or something in your pocket?" Spiridon nodded agreement. "Anyway, Dad is so busy focusing on his painting, and without turning around, he says to the deer, 'That's wonderful, Nikos, beautiful. Now go see if you can find another one just like it.' He didn't even know it wasn't me!" Nikolos cried laughter.

Spiridon, already laughing said, "I did when that mama deer leaned over my shoulder and licked my palette of watercolors!"

"You should've seen him jump!" Nikolos laughed, reliving the memory. "He turned around and that mama deer was staring him right in the face, not two inches away! He jumped out of his camping chair at least four feet in the air!"

"No way!" I said in disbelief.

"It wasn't four feet," Spiridon laughed. "But I sure beat feet when I realized it wasn't you."

Both of them threw their heads back and chuckled heartily.

Spiridon wiped tears of joy from his eyes. "Do you remember that time we were visiting your aunt in Mykonos?"

"Which time?" Nikolos grinned.

"The one with the pelican on our rowboat."

"Oh," Nikolos chuckled, "you mean the pelican who wanted your lunch?"

Spiridon nodded.

"You tell it," Nikolos smiled.

Spiridon leaned over to me. "So, we had ridden bicycles from my sister's house in Mykonos down to Ornos for the weekend. This was back before all the hotels started taking over the island."

"Where's Mykonos?" I asked.

"It's in the Aegean sea, southeast of mainland Greece," Nikolos said.

"So," Spiridon continued, "I had gotten the brilliant idea of setting up my easel on a rowboat. I should've known better, with this one around," he cocked a thumb at Nikolos, "but I wanted to paint the town from a view on the water so I could capture the white plaster buildings against the sapphire blue of the ocean. Nikos and his cousin Helena were busy swimming all morning. When it was lunch time, my sister pulled out the picnic basket she'd brought to feed everyone. Nikos and Helena climbed out of the water, soaking wet. They were dripping over everything. That should've been my clue I was asking for trouble painting watercolors in the middle of the bay, but all I could think about was my sister's scrumptious gyros waiting for us. Once the food was out, a giant pelican landed on the prow of the boat to see what was on the menu. Nikos wanted to shoo him off, but I said it was okay. The next thing I know, I had set my gyro down only for a second, and the pelican hops off the stern and snatches up my lunch like it was a fish and swallows it down! Before I can stand up, Nikos shouts 'I'll get it' and lunges for that bird. The pelican flapped its wings furiously to escape and knocked my painting right into the water! Everyone is hollering and Nikos turns on a dime, shouting 'I'll get it, I'll get it!' He dove right in the water and rescued my painting. But you can imagine what a dip in the ocean does to a wet watercolor painting."

Spiridon and Nikolos were both laughing as they remembered.

"Oh no!" I laughed. "What happened to the painting?"

"The painting was ruined, but I couldn't tell Nikos that. He was so proud for saving it." Spiridon looked at his son and smiled lovingly.

Nikolos nodded, basking in the warmth of his father's love decades after the fact.

Spiridon and Nikolos traded painting stories back and forth like that for an hour. Some of them included the misadventures of young Christos as well. Every single tale was filled with excitement, fun, and love. My childhood had been nothing like it.

"And that's what you did for a living for all those years?" I said to Spiridon with an amazed smile. It sounded like a continuous vacation to me.

"Yes," Spiridon said. "For a long time."

"Why'd you ever stop painting?" I asked.

Spiridon sighed mysteriously. "That's a long story,"

I glanced at Nikolos, who raised his eyebrows before looking away. Okay, they weren't going to tell me.

"Maybe you should be a landscape painter, Samantha," Nikolos said, drawing attention away from Spiridon.

"You think?" I said.

Nikolos shrugged his shoulders, "Why not? It's a job like any other."

It never ceased to amaze me how the Manos men took it for granted that I was going to be a successful artist someday. Now Nikolos was doing it too. Christos had the most awesome family I'd ever met. I was so glad to be a part of it.

I shook my head and sipped more lemonade, which was delicious, as always, and basked in the warm spring air. It was hard to believe working for Nikolos was an actual job. It was like hanging out with my friends.

Lucky me!

===

I sat at my drawing table in the studio at Spiridon's house, working on drawing drapery. Drapery meant the way cloth folded, usually on clothing when people wore it, sometimes just hanging like wrinkled blankets or hanging tablecloths and curtains. It was part of our homework for Drawing The Costumed Figure.

It was almost like doing fashion illustrations.

I'd already drawn a bunch of pictures of princesses in fluffy dresses and hot guys in slick suits striking GQ poses. I had a bunch of internet browser windows open on my laptop showing photos of various gowns and runway models, male and female. I was really liking this whole Art major choice of mine. My parents were really out to lunch about art.

Whatever.

Christos was out, hanging with Jake. Spiridon was out too, I wasn't sure where. He tended to come and go without explanation. I could only assume he had an entire adult life he was living, but I never saw it. Maybe he was secretly a handsome Greek mafia kingpin?

I chuckled to myself.

My laptop was open next to me, playing iTunes. Wonderwall by Oasis wafted from the speakers on warm, loving waves while I drew in my sketchbook.

I was busy putting the finishing touches on a hot guy in a tuxedo who looked alarmingly like Christos. I hadn't even realized I was drawing him. I sat back from my sketchbook and realized the tux guy stood next to a girl in a wedding dress.

How had that happened?

I swear, I hadn't done it on purpose.

Maybe next I would draw babies in bodysuits.

I blushed to myself. What was I thinking?

I shook my head and stood up to stretch my legs and take a break. I started Wonderwall over from the beginning and danced alone, swaying to the groove, thinking about Christos, hugging my arms around myself.

I was so in love with Christos.

He had saved me from the horrid future my parents had planned for me. My life had opened up to possibilities I'd never dreamed would ever come true when I was a girl. Now I had hope like I'd never known hope before.

I was truly blessed.

My cell phone rang abruptly, cutting like a strident scream through the comforting music emanating from my laptop.

I jumped.

My phone was also on vibrate, and it danced maniacally in the tray of pencils attached to my drawing table where I'd left it, making the pencils rattle and clack together horribly.

Dread.

I grabbed for my phone, but it danced from my fingers.

Christos.

Something was wrong. On the third ring I got a hold of it. Oh no, Christos. My gut was churning.

Not again.

Falling, falling, falling.

I looked at the screen on my phone. It read:

"Mom & Dad"

What the hell? My heart was jumping in my chest. Images of Christos in a drunken car crash flashed through my head. So why were my parents calling me? They wouldn't be the first to know if he got hurt. Would they? No, that didn't make any sense.

So why were they calling?

I frowned. I could hazard a guess.

Did I even want to answer their call? They were probably going to bitch me out again. I sighed dramatically and answered my phone on the fourth ring, sounding irritated. "Hello?"

"Sam?"

"Dad?"

My dad cleared his throat.

I winced.

"Sam, I'm calling to inform you that your mother has moved out."

"What?" I was totally confused.

"She's taken an apartment in Friendship Heights. And she has taken a lover."

"What? Dad! What are you talking about? You aren't making any sense." My stomach, which had imploded, said otherwise. Every organ in my body had been sucked into the black hole forming in my abdomen.

"Your mother is seeing someone," he said flatly. "Another man."

"What do you mean seeing? Like for a meeting or class or something? I know she's always talking about taking tennis lessons at the country club."

"Sam, your mother is having an affair. With another man."

Silence punched me in the stomach. That black hole wasn't the only thing hammering away at me. Every atom in the universe was rushing at me in a super nova of impending disaster.

Some detached corner of my brain shouted inside my head, "Who cares! Mom is lame! You're lame!" But that voice was thin and tinny, drowned out by the cosmic thunderstorm that was unwinding inside me.

After more silence, I finally spoke in a mumble, "Mom is having an affair?" Tears dripped down my cheeks against my approval.

"Yes."

"With another man?"

"Yes. Someone she knew in college. He rides a motorcycle," Dad said with no hint of irony.

"That doesn't make any sense," I stammered.

"Yes, it does," he said softly.

I sat down in my desk chair. I should say, I fell down where I was standing and was lucky that my chair happened to be behind me, because I didn't stop to think what I was doing. I just collapsed when the strength left my legs.

Then dozens of disjointed memories all crashed together in my head. My mom had made it clear months ago that she thought Christos was not the kind of guy who stuck around. And she'd made it sound like she'd had experience with guys like him. Was the guy my dad was talking about some guy from Mom's past who'd jilted her and made her so bitter about bad boys? But now she had gotten back together with him?

I could only wonder.

I wasn't about to ask my dad for details. I'm sure the guy my mom was sleeping with wasn't Dad's favorite topic of conversation at the moment.

And then a memory of my mother's words from February crashed through my brain:

"Not yet you aren't. But you will be! Give it six months, maybe a year, and he'll knock you up! Then he'll be gone! Just like that! Make sure you have enough saved up for the abortion!"

She'd said it like she was speaking from experience. Was that possible?

Of course it was.

I suddenly remembered that growing up, people were always saying how much I looked like my mom. Nobody ever said I looked like my dad. And, my dad had always seemed so different and weird to me, I had a hard time believing we were related.

What if my mom had never gotten that abortion and had married dependable Bill Smith instead?

Was it possible that my dad wasn't my biological dad?

Was I some other guy's daughter?

Holy shit.

It was entirely possible.

No, that was crazy.

But it was all adding up.

What. The. Fuck.

Oh, gosh, it all sounded so desperately stupid. But why did it make so much sense?

I shook my head. Did it even matter? My mom was cheating on my dad and had already moved into an apartment. That much was fact.

Fuck.

I didn't need three guesses to figure out where that went.

Just when my life had been expanding with good vibes like a colorful birthday balloon, BAM! My parents popped a needle in me and took it all away. More precisely, my mom.

My damn mom.

Every single damn time.

===

"I'm so sorry, *agápi mou*," Christos said as he hugged me where we sat on the couch in the living room. "I know how hard it is when your parents split."

I'd waited two hours for Christos to come home, crying my eyes out the entire time on the couch in the dark. I was somewhat surprised I was so sad my mom had left, but I wasn't at all surprised by my anger at her. That was normal and familiar. But this sense of loss and I guess betrayal was new and made me uncomfortable. A part of me said the only feeling I should have for my mom right now was hatred.

But, no matter how much of a bitch she was, she was still my mom.

Fuck! I hated feeling this way.

"What are you going to do?" Christos asked softly. Although he'd been out with Jake for hours, I could tell he hadn't had much to drink. He wasn't even buzzed. I had that much to be grateful for.

"What can I do?" I asked rhetorically. "My mom left my dad.

Period."

"Do you need to fly home to see your parents? I'll totally understand if you do. I can come with you if you want."

I looked at him, tears dripping down my cheeks. I blotted them with a tissue from the box Christos had brought me. "I don't know if that'll make any difference. Besides, finals are coming up in a few weeks. I feel like if I went home, it would screw up all my classes and I'd have to withdraw and retake everything." Agony and indecision swept over me. "Oh, Christos. I don't know what to do!" I leaned into his chest and sobbed against him.

He caressed the top of my head and murmured, "Whatever you want to do, you let me know, and I'm there for you, *agápi mou*."

I twisted my fingers into the material of his T shirt. I looked up at him desperately, "I don't know what I'd do without you, *agápi mou*."

"Hush," he whispered. "You're never going to have to find out. I'll always be here for you."

I couldn't begin to fathom the kind of crazy person I'd become if Christos were to do what my mom had done to my dad. My gosh, what was my dad going through right now? I couldn't even imagine. Was he mad? Sad? Did he hate my mom? Was he desperately wishing she'd come to her senses and come back to him? Probably all of those things.

I gazed up at Christos, my eyes pleading for comfort and reassurance. I asked him meekly, in a vulnerable voice that was on the edge of shattering into fragile shards, "Are you sure?"

Christos cupped my cheek and caressed the side of my face. "Yes. I'm not going anywhere, *agápi mou*. Ever."

Looking into his loving blue eyes, I believed him with all my heart. The wave of energy that passed from my heart to his was confirmation.

He smoothed a lock of my hair behind my ear. That simple gesture of affection was so powerful, I broke into fresh sobs and collapsed into his muscled chest. In his arms, I felt safe. Protected. I never wanted to leave them.

I wept quietly for awhile, letting it out.

Eventually, I sniffed and said, "I think the guy my mom is seeing might be my father."

"What?" Christos gasped.

I cringed now that I'd said it out loud. "I don't know. Maybe I'm crazy. But my mom said all these things about you like she'd had experience with her own bad boy when she was young, and it got me thinking. Maybe this guy she's seeing got her pregnant twenty years ago. With me. My dad said this guy is from her college days and he is a bad boy. Maybe it's the same guy from when she was young and she wants to get back together with him now that I'm out of the house? Because she doesn't need my dad anymore?"

"Wow, that's insane," Christos said.

"You're right. I'm crazy." I shook my head. "I'm making it sound like a soap opera storyline. It's too crazy to be true. Right?" Desperate thoughts pulsed in my head, *Please tell me I'm crazy, please tell me my reasoning is idiotic. Please please please...*

Christos sighed, "Who knows. People do crazy shit. Anything is possible."

I clutched his T shirt and heaved a painful sob, "You don't think it's true, do you?"

"I have no idea, *agápi mou*," he said softly. "But whatever the truth turns out to be, I'll be by your side through all of it."

I burrowed further into his arms and sobbed.

At the moment, I was desperately afraid, half insane, but above all things, grateful I had Christos.

Chapter 22

SAMANTHA

Denial quickly became my best friend. It was the only way I could function and stay sane. I did my best to block out any thoughts of my parents' crumbling marriage and focused on school and my new job.

Kamiko and I were eating lunch at the Adams College Cafeteria.

"What's the Samantos status?" Kamiko asked before popping a french fry into her mouth.

"The what?"

"You and Christos? Duh."

"Samantos?" I scoffed. "That sounds like a breath mint."

"The fresh maker!" Kamiko quipped.

I chuckled, "We're good."

"How are his paintings coming along? Does he still have a parade of models coming in and out of the studio every day?"

"No. He's, uh, changed directions." I wasn't quite comfortable telling Kamiko that Christos was painting me nude.

I wondered if I could keep Christos' upcoming solo show a secret so I could avoid having my friends gawk at a nude picture of me. Who was I kidding? Kamiko followed the upcoming gallery shows like a hawk. She'd find out and she'd be there. At least I could appreciate her desire to show up and support.

Changing subjects, I said, "Have you done any new paintings to submit to Brandumb for his upcoming Contemporary Artists Show?"

"A bunch," she smiled.

"How are they coming along?"

Kamiko had been crushed when Brandon had rejected her first batch of submissions.

"Awesome," she said. "You wanna see them after lunch?"

"Sure," I smiled.

When we finished eating, we walked our trays over to the trash cans and emptied them into the bin then walked out the front doors.

There was a newspaper rack right outside.

Kamiko stopped and squealed, "Oh my God!" She grabbed a fresh copy of The Wombat off the rack. "Sam! It's your wombat!" She handed me the paper. "It looks so good!"

Wow, my art was on the cover, next to Tammy Lemons' illustration.

"You should totally save like ten copies!"

"But I haven't won," I said.

"So what?" Kamiko said, excited. "You're in print! That's YOUR art!"

"I guess you're right," I smiled. "But maybe I'll only take five copies." I grabbed a handful off the rack.

"Will you sign mine for me?" Kamiko asked, digging frantically through her book bag for a pen.

"Oh, I couldn't do that, Kamiko," I dismissed.

"What, did you forget how to spell your name?" she asked sarcastically and thrust her pen at me.

I frowned, "No."

"Then sign it, bitch! I'm so proud of you!" She wrapped her arms around me and hugged me tightly. When she was done, she pushed her pen at me again. "But seriously, sign it. I'm going to hold onto this until it's worth a thousand bucks. I'll sell it at San Diego Comic Con in twenty years when you're a world famous cartoonist."

I scoffed, "I think you're getting a bit carried away, Kamiko."

"Shut up and sign it. If I'm going to be a doctor for the rest of my life, I'm going to tell people I went to school with Samantha Smith, the awesome artist."

I arched a doubtful eyebrow.

"Quit being fake humble and sign it!" she growled.

I wasn't being fake humble. It just seemed weird she was asking me to sign the paper for her. I hadn't even won yet. For all I knew, the students who read the paper and bothered to vote would pick Tammy's art.

Some random guy with glasses and wavy long hair walked up

to the rack and picked up a copy of The Wombat. He chuckled when he looked at the cover.

"My home girl drew that wombat," Kamiko said to him. "She can autograph your paper if you're nice."

"Kamiko!" I hissed.

The guy looked at the pictures thoughtfully. "You drew this?" he asked.

"Yeah," I said sheepishly, "the one on the toilet. I didn't draw the one with the baseball bat."

"Oh," he nodded, examining the drawings. He chuckled, "I love that he's stoned while he's taking a shit. That's awesome."

Kamiko nudged me, "Sign it!"

"Yeah," the guy said, "will you sign it for me? I'm hanging this in our bathroom in the dorms."

I couldn't decide if that was a compliment or an insult.

He smiled, admiring my art, "The guys are going to love this."

So I signed it. I mean, a lot of people read when they were on the toilet. Sure, a bathroom stall in the dorms wasn't exactly Charboneau Gallery, but it was the next best thing, right?

===

Kamiko and I went to her dorm room in Paiute Hall.

"I'm trying something totally different," she said, sliding a big black portfolio out from under her bed. She unzipped it and handed me a stack of paintings on 1/8" thick illustration board. "These are all done with pen and ink, and acrylics."

They were drawings with washes of transparent color over the ink lines, and touches of opaque acrylic here and there on some, and more thickly applied acrylics on others.

"What happened to all your oils?"

"They're in the closet," she nodded toward the wheeled wardrobe next to her bed. "Since Brandumb didn't want them for the show, I put them all away. Maybe I'll try to sell them later. But for now, I'm doing this," she pointed her chin toward the stacks of paintings in my lap.

I sat down on the bed and flipped through them. There was a half dozen of them, all in totally different styles. One showed a dolphin jumping out of waves made of blue human hands and arms. Another showed a beautiful woman in a giant Victorian gown with hands that snaked out in looping coils that ended in bouquets of roses. Another showed three identical young girls with black pigtails and kimonos standing on a Japanese garden bridge over a pond filled with koi that had human faces. "Are these kimono triplets supposed to be you?" I asked.

Kamiko nodded. "And those faces on the koi are supposed to be Brandumb, but I don't think he'll notice. I had to work from memory."

"What is it supposed to mean?"

"I don't know," Kamiko grinned, "that I'm three times more awesome than Brandumb, who is so un-evolved he hasn't yet crawled out of the ocean with the other fishes that turned into humans a billion years ago?"

"You're not still angry at him, are you?"

"I was when I did that one," she smiled. "Now? Not so much."

The rest of her paintings were equally bizarre and amazing. "Did you do all of these? It looks like six different artists painted them."

She smiled and nodded, her eyes beaming with excitement. "I did my homework. I went through that catalog from the last show that you gave me until I had some direction, then I dove in."

I could still remember how Kamiko's confidence had been shattered by Brandon when he'd rejected her art, and hit on me right in front of her. For two weeks afterward, I had been afraid she'd never climb out of her funk. But her confidence was now back in full force.

"Well, they're all awesome, Kamiko." I handed the stack back to her. "I'm blown away."

She took them and slid them back into the big black portfolio. "Are you going to submit anything, Sam?"

"What, to Brandon's show?"

"Yeah."

"I hadn't really thought about it. I guess I've been too busy."

"Considering you're on the front cover of The Wombat, I think you probably should."

"Do you have that show catalog of Brandon's?"

Kamiko pulled it off the bookcase on her desk and handed it to me.

I flipped through it. The first thing I noticed was that Kamiko's new paintings would totally fit right in. "I don't know, Kamiko.

These are all really good. I can see you did a lot of research. I don't know if I'll have time to come up with something before the show."

"You'll think of something," she smiled.

As much as I'd improved while studying art with the help of Christos, Spiridon, Kamiko, and all my art teachers, the paintings in the catalog were probably better than I could do at the moment, especially on short notice.

"You have tons of great ideas, Sam," Kamiko said. "I bet you'll come up with something awesome."

Once again, I was super grateful that all of my San Diego friends were so supportive of me. Their confidence bolstered my own.

"You're right," I grinned confidently, "I will."

===

Madison and I were studying in the Main Library in our favorite private study room on the fifth floor, which had the best view of the ocean.

My laptop was open and my email program chimed when a new email came in. It was from the SDU Registrar's Office. Subject: A date has been set for your appeal.

I groaned.

"What?" Madison asked, looking up from her gigantic Marketing textbook.

Not only had the subject line of the email been a spoiler for the content of the message, it had also spoiled my mood. I clicked on it to get it over with.

The message read, "A date has been assigned for you to appear before the administrative tribunal of San Diego University to discuss the grievance(s) pending against you, at which time your standing as a student at SDU will be reviewed. In addition to the initial claim of theft leveled against you by Tiffany Kingston-Whitehouse (plaintiff), an additional charge of assault has been brought against you, Samantha Smith (defendant)…"

Tiffany and her stupid stolen credit card.

And my stupid slap.

I never should've smacked her.

According to the rest of the letter, Tiffany had gone to the SDU police to report my "attack" on her. At least the letter made it sound like my slapping her wasn't a federal offense with the death penalty attached. But for a second, I imagined the cops showing up in their police cars with the red and blue lights flashing so they could cuff me and haul me to jail for committing Assault and Slappery.

Wow, I suddenly felt like my situation and Christos' had been reversed. Or he was having a bad influence on me like my mom had warned. No, that was crazy because my cheating mom was crazy.

"Bad news?" Madison asked.

"Huh?"

"You look like you swallowed a poisoned pie."

"Poisoned pie?"

"Like one of those blackbird pies with twenty four birds inside? You look like they're flapping around in your belly right now, trying to get out," she smirked.

"I'd rather have that than this," I scowled.

"What is it?"

"My date for the Tiffany thing."

"Oh," Madison said morosely. She already knew the whole story. "I've told you before, give me the word, and I'll cut a bitch."

"Which bitch?" I snickered.

Her eyes went crazy, "Any bitch! Just give me the word!" She stood and waved her highlighter marker around like a knife. "Watch out bitches! I'm cuttin' mad!" she shouted.

"Don't you mean, Cuttin' Mads?"

She sat down and giggled.

I joined her and we shared a good laugh.

As always, we sat in one of the glass walled private study rooms. I'm sure the kids studying outside who were glaring at us thought we were goofing off. Some of them probably wanted to use our study room so they could goof off.

Well, me and Mads had gotten here first.

A moment later, a random girl stood up from one of the study carrels outside and walked up to our door. She had imitation blonde hair and wore a Delta Pi Delta T shirt, which was Tiffany's sorority.

Greatballs.

Sororiwhore opened the door to our study room and popped the gum in her mouth. She said, "Like, do you guys know when you're going to be finished in here? Other people are wait—"

Madison jumped out of her chair, which clattered loudly behind her, and thrust her highlighter toward Sororiwhore, who was six feet away. "Stay back!" Madison hissed.

Sororiwhore flinched. Then she popped her gum and scowled, trying to play it off like she was above it all.

Madison lunged forward again, now two feet from the girl. "Back!"

I turned to Sororiwhore and said in a casual, bland voice, "Be careful what you say next. She's Cuttin' Mads and she'll cut a bitch."

Sororiwhore's eyes goggled as she slowly withdrew from the doorframe.

The pneumatic door clicked shut gently.

Madison and I broke into laughter.

===

Later, Madison and I walked to our cars in the north parking lot.

"Oh my god, there's Tiffany!" Madison pointed. "Let's hide in the bushes and jump her!"

Tiffany was by herself and hadn't noticed us coming toward her.

"Gag," I groaned. "We should go the other way."

"We have a right to walk here just like she does," Madison growled.

"Yeah, but between Slappin' Sam and Cuttin' Mads," I joked, "Tiffany is likely to get murdered."

"I've got your back either way, girlfriend." Madison fished her highlighter out of her book bag and waved it around like a knife.

"Thanks, Mads. But please sheathe your highlighter. I don't want you drawing blood."

"Okay," Madison giggled and stuffed her pen in her bag as we neared Tiffany.

Tiffany's lip curled when she saw us. "You're still here? Shouldn't you have gone back home to Washington by now?"

How did she know where I lived? Or was she talking about going home to see my parents because of the problems they were having? No, there was no way Tiffany could know that, was there? Unless Christos had told her? No, that was impossible.

Tiffany rolled her eyes as she passed us, "See you at the tribunal, bitch."

"Hey!" Madison shouted.

I muttered a warning to Madison, "Keep your cap on your

highlighter, I'll handle this." I stopped and turned to face Tiffany as she walked away. "Tiffany! Can I talk to you for a second?"

Tiffany stopped, turned, and cocked her hip. As always, she looked like the cover of a fashion magazine with her immaculate blond hair, flawless makeup, and expensive clothes. "Why? Are you going to attack me? If you are, do me a favor and let me know if I need to call the campus police before you hit me this time," she said sarcastically.

I shook my head, "No, I'm not going to touch you."

She raised an expectant eyebrow. "Well? I don't have all day."

"Look, about the credit card thing."

Tiffany smiled merrily, "You mean the one you stole?"

"You know I didn't steal it. You put it in my wallet."

"I know no such thing," Tiffany shook her head while wrinkling her nose petulantly. "But I do know it was in your wallet. Gosh, Scumantha, how did it get there?" she gasped sarcastically.

"Please don't call me Scumantha," I said softly. Was she trying to get me to hit her again?

I noticed Madison was snarling beside me.

"Did the credit card fairy take it out of my wallet and drop it into yours?" Tiffany sneered.

I rolled my eyes, frustrated. The "let's talk this out" approach wasn't working. "Tiffany, are you still mad about your yacht painting?"

Tiffany rolled her eyes back at me.

Since talking sense didn't seem to be working, I was going to hit her where it hurt. I was tired of her bullshit. "Or are you still mad that I'm with Christos and you aren't?"

Tiffany started gnawing on her lower lip like a rabid chipmunk.

Yeah, that had hurt her.

"Tiffany," I said calmly, "nothing you do is going to break me and Christos apart. I'm not going back home to D.C. Even if you manage to get me kicked out of SDU, I'm here to stay. You need to accept that. So why don't you save us both a bunch of trouble and let it go?" I sounded way more confident than I felt. The last thing I wanted was to get kicked out of SDU. I loved taking classes with Madison and Kamiko and Romeo. I loved my art professors. I couldn't imagine giving all that up. It would break my heart to say goodbye to SDU. But I wasn't backing down, I wasn't letting

Tiffany get away with framing me. "Tell the tribunal the truth. Tell them you put your credit card in my wallet. Oh, and I'm sorry for slapping you. I never should've done that."

Tiffany's face burned bright red. Words spat from her mouth, "FUCK YOU, YOU STUPID BITCH!!!!" She had to take another breath before she screamed again, "I'M GOING TO RUIN YOU, YOU FUCKING CUNT!!!"

===

A gigantic fiery phoenix burst from the clouds of a flaming sunset. Its long, trailing tail feathers blazed behind it like the train of a glowing gown as it swooped across the sky. The phoenix was part eagle, part woman.

That woman was me.

"That looks awesome, Sam!" Kamiko said, standing over my shoulder, looking at my rough sketch.

"You think it'll work for Brandon's show?" I asked. It was still just a small pen and ink drawing in my sketchbook colored with markers.

Romeo was sitting and doing homework at one of the work tables against the wall in Christos' studio. He slid his chair out and walked over to take a look. "Wow," he smiled, "I love it, Sam."

I crinkled my nose. "Thanks." I still wasn't used to all the praise I'd been getting lately.

"Okay, now I have to take a look," Christos said. He was sitting in a reclining desk chair with his feet propped on a window sill, sketching in his own sketchbook. He was trying to work up ideas for the rest of the paintings he needed to do for his upcoming solo show, which would be hosted at Charboneau sometime after the Contemporary Artists Show closed.

Christos rested a hand on my shoulder and leaned over me to get a better look.

Romeo blurted, "Red alert! Red alert! Boo-EEEP! Boo-EEEP! Christos is putting the moves on Sam! Abandon ship before Christos fires his torpedo into her!"

"Must everything come down to sex for you, Romeo?" I asked.

"Yes," he grinned unapologetically.

Kamiko giggled. "Romeo, you are so wonky kong."

"Wonky kong?" Romeo said, "I'll show you wonky kong." He started jumping frantically in the air. Every time he did, he said,

"Boing!" His monocle danced chaotically at the end of the string attached to a button on his steampunk coat.

"What are you doing?" I laughed.

He continued jumping and started whooping, "Doodle lee DEE do! Doodle lee DEE do!"

Kamiko shook her head, amused. "I think he finally gave himself a stroke from trying too hard to be funny all the time."

Romeo paused from his insane jumping routine, "Don't you guys play video games? I'm Mario from Classic Donkey Kong!"

"Huh?" Kamiko said. Kamiko never played video games because she spent too much time watching cartoons, studying for all her insane pre-med classes, and drawing in every spare moment. I don't know if she ever slept.

"Come on, Kamiko!" Romeo pleaded. "You're the one who called me Donkey Kong!"

"I called you wonky kong," she said.

Romeo stopped jumping and jammed his fists on his hips. "What the fuck is a wonky kong?"

Kamiko spread her hands and raised her eyebrows, "I don't know," she said defensively, "Donkey Kong's crippled brother who has a gimp leg?"

Christos and I both chuckled.

"You're crazy, Romeo," I said.

He opened his eyes really wide and made them do circles while he waggled his tongue and made crazy noises. The Loco Locomotive was back.

Kamiko shook her head. "He's truly an idiot. Somebody get the butterfly nets."

"Hey, Romeo," Christos said thoughtfully, "do that jumping thing again."

"What, this?" Romeo asked as he started jumping up and down a few times.

"Yeah, that," Christos said.

Romeo did it a few more times then stopped.

"Can you do it again, with the jumping noises?" Christos asked, totally serious.

Romeo frowned, "Uh, okay." He did a half hearted jump and noise.

"No," Christos said, "I meant like before. Try to really get into it."

"Wait," Romeo said shrewdly, "you're making fun of me, aren't you?"

"No," Christos said blandly, "I'm totally serious."

Romeo looked confused.

I had no idea what Christos was doing, nor did Kamiko. I said, "It's okay, Romeo. You don't have to do it."

Romeo dropped his arms to his sides and looked at us.

"No, please," Christos said sincerely. "I want to see something." He sounded totally serious, but not in a mean way.

Romeo shrugged his shoulders. "Okay, but I need a second to prepare. I'm an actor, after all."

Kamiko looked doubtful.

"Hush, Kamiko," he said before she opened her mouth. "I've taken acting classes. *College* acting classes." Romeo shook his shoulders, rolled his neck and stuck his tongue out a bunch of times while humming. Then, he started jumping again, more enthusiastically and spastically than before. "DOODLE LEE DEE DO!!! DOODLE LEE DEE DO!!!" He stopped after a few. "Like that?"

Christos shook his head. "No, now you're forcing it. Like before. When it was spontaneous."

"What are you doing, Christos?" I asked.

"Trust me," he said cryptically. "Go ahead, Romeo."

"Okay," Romeo said. He calmed down and closed his eyes. "Kamiko, make fun of me. Say something judgmental, like you normally would." Even though his eyes were closed, he was grinning, not taking himself seriously.

"Uh..." she stammered and chuckled. "Your monocle is out of style?"

"That's perfect," Romeo said, "I think I've got it." He started to smile a big, natural smile. He nodded, "Yeah, that's it." His smile was huge now. He opened his eyes and started jumping, "Doodle lee DEE do! Doodle lee DEE do! Doodle lee DEE do!" He had a huge grin on his face the whole time.

Christos nodded, rapt, smiling his dimpled smile, that mysterious, fascinated look still on his face.

Pretty soon, me and Kamiko were giggling, then we were laughing.

"Okay," Romeo huffed after the nineteenth time, "I'm getting out of breath now."

"You can stop," Christos grinned.

Romeo sagged into the nearest chair. "Whoo! That was a lot of work! Did my unabashed athleticism bring your idea to completion?"

Christos said sarcastically, "I'm totally turned on right now."

After a moment, Romeo looked at the three of us expectantly, "Hey, aren't any of you going to stuff some dollar bills in my G string now? That was hard work!"

"Are you even wearing a G string?" Kamiko asked doubtfully.

He hooded his eyelids and asked, "Would you be surprised if I was?"

"I would be surprised if you weren't," I laughed.

Kamiko and Christos both erupted into cackles.

"I want my dollar bills!" Romeo whined. "That's the last free show you guys are getting. Sex workers never get any respect," he chuckled.

"That was sex work?" Kamiko frowned skeptically. "I think my eyes are bleeding from watching you dance. Or whatever that was."

Romeo grimaced at Kamiko. "Admit it, Kamiko, you're totally jealous of my milkshake." Romeo turned around, lifted the tail of his steampunk coat, and thrust his ass at us while resting his hands on his thighs and jiggling his butt up and down.

"That deserves a dollar," Christos chuckled and pulled out his wallet. He walked up to Romeo and jammed the bill in the belt of Romeo's black skinny leg jeans.

Kamiko fished a dollar out of her purse, and I grabbed one from mine. We both laughed as we put them in Romeo's belt. He was smiling the whole time.

Romeo finally stopped dancing. "A good milkshake always gets paid," he said suggestively.

The four of us laughed together. My friends and my boyfriend all rocked fifty-five gallon drums of awesome sauce.

===

CHRISTOS

"Aren't you getting bored of staring at yourself naked?" Samantha asked.

I stood naked in front of the big full length wheeled mirror in our painting studio with a palette covered in oils resting on my forearm.

I was working on the portrait of me that was half of our dual portrait entitled LOVE. The image of Samantha was already finished, and it looked fantastic.

Samantha stood beside me, fully clothed and wearing a painting apron.

I smirked at her, gazing into her eyes, "I never get bored of staring at perfection."

"Did you mean me?" She batted her eyelashes.

I flicked my eyes at the mirror, "I meant me." I turned to face the mirror square on and flexed my abs. All eight of them popped, as did the fingers of my external obliques. I was as ripped as ever.

"Your ego is so big," Samantha joked, "I'm surprised everything in the solar system isn't sucked right into it."

I chuckled while I padded up to the canvas in my bare feet, and applied some freshly mixed color to the canvas. "How's your phoenix painting coming along?"

Samantha had been working on it like crazy ever since she'd finished the sketch and showed it to us over a week ago. It sat on her easel in her corner of the studio. Based on my advice, she'd decided to do it in oils to give it the widest range of contrast from light to dark, and the most vibrant colors possible.

"Good," she smiled. "It's way more work than I expected, but I've got a handle on it."

I walked over to look at it. She was doing a really good job considering she'd only had one class on oil painting so far. I think all the time she'd been spending at my dad's studio watching over his shoulder was probably helping a lot. I know watching him and my grandad paint everyday growing up had been a huge help for me. I nodded supportively as I looked over the painting. "It's already kicking ass. When it's finished, people are gonna love it."

"Do you think Brandon will put it in the Contemporary show?" she asked tentatively.

"If he doesn't, he and I are going to have a long talk involving a lot of knuckles."

"I'll keep that in mind," she grinned. "I'll do my very best. For the sake of Brandon's teeth."

I walked back to the mirror and posed to match the painting. This self portrait shit required a lot of walking. I walked back to the canvas and put down another brush stroke. "You know, I've been thinking."

"Yeah?" Samantha asked from her easel.

"I really need to do a portrait of just you."

"You don't have to do that," she dismissed. "We already have LOVE. It shows the two of us. What could be better than that?"

"I'm loving the LOVE," I grinned, "but I've been getting inspired by your Phoenix painting. You've come so far since I met you. I sort of want to capture how you've changed as a person. How I see you, the woman you're turning into right before my eyes. Not just the way we are together. But you. Samantha Anna Smith. And the way you've grown so quickly into the most amazing woman I've ever known. You're my inspiration, you know that, *agápi mou*?"

She blushed and set down her paint brush. "Oh, Christos. That's so sweet. I love you so much." She walked over to me and leaned up to kiss my cheek. "But I don't know, isn't that going to be too much of me in your show? I mean, how many paintings of me do you really need? Isn't one enough?"

"How could there ever be too much of you, *agápi mou*?"

A bashful look knotted her face as she said, "Who wants to look at me all the time?"

"I do," I said. Grinning to myself, I marveled at how Samantha still doubted her own beauty. The irony was, her innocence elevated her level of sexiness into the stratosphere.

In my experience, hot women who knew they were hot tended to play it up. I had always been able to see through their acts like it was a practiced performance. Because of this, these women lacked a certain spontaneity. Knowing men worshipped them turned their beauty into a tiresome facade sooner or later, as if it had become a burden or a job, and they were bored with it. Ironically, they would never give it up, never walk out the front door without maximizing their beauty with hair, makeup and clothes. These women couldn't even go to the Emergency Room in the middle of the night without making sure they had at least a touch of eyeliner on.

Samantha was the total opposite. She had a smudge of paint on her cheek and another on her forehead, and her hair was in a messy ponytail. Her beauty was an after thought for her. The outcome was that she was a considerate, thoughtful person who was always trying so hard to be kind. She didn't think about her looks. She thought about being a good person.

Every minute I spent with her was refreshing, genuine, and inspirational.

I knew that combination of her determination and her open hearted authentic spirit was where all the magic was. She might doubt it, but I saw it every day. I wanted it to go into a painting of just her. Samantha Anna Smith.

"What do you think?" I asked.

"You really want me to pose again?" she said with considerable doubt.

"I do," I grinned.

A strange look flashed across her eyes.

"I do," she swallowed, "I mean, I will." She blinked a bunch of times and smiled up at me.

I leaned down and kissed her passionately.

Chapter 23

SAMANTHA

Brandon sat at the desk in his office at Charboneau and flipped through Kamiko's new paintings. Me and Kamiko sat in the chairs facing his desk, on the edges of our seats.

Brandon reminded me of one of those fashion magazine photos you see of a young guy in a stylish suit sitting in a fancy office, doing important things, all while looking ridiculously dashing. All Brandon needed to do to sell the image was stand up and lean against his desk while looking out a high rise window at a throbbing metropolis. But La Jolla was too quaint and beachy for that. And instead of stylish designer furnishings, the office walls were crowded with amazing paintings. But that didn't make Brandon any less hot.

He nodded thoughtfully to himself, engrossed in the paintings. I hoped that was a good sign. After he examined the last one, he looked up and said, "Kamiko, this is excellent work. You painted all of these?"

She nodded enthusiastically. "Uh huh."

"I had no idea you were so versatile," he said.

I shook my head and hid a smirk. There were a lot of things Brandumb didn't know about Kamiko. If he gave her half a chance, maybe he'd find out.

"You paint in a wide range of diverse styles, Kamiko," Brandon said. "Few artists have that ability. I'm impressed," he smiled.

"Does that mean you'll accept one of my pieces for the Contemporary Artists Show?" she asked hopefully.

Brandon leaned back in his chair and steepled his fingers in front of his face.

Me and Kamiko leaned forward an inch.

He lifted an eyebrow.

We leaned forward another inch.

Oh boy, he better say yes or I was going to jump over his desk and stab him in the heart with the brass letter opener sitting on his desk. Oh wait, if he said no, it was because he didn't have a heart, so I'd have to stab lower, where it would hurt a man the most.

Brandon opened his mouth to speak.

Kamiko and I leaned so far forward we were about to slip off our seats and fall on our butts like idiots.

I drilled Brandon with my gaze and put my ESP to work. SAY SOMETHING!!!

Kamiko glanced at me, a surprised look on her face. Had she heard my ESP? Kamiko raised an eyebrow at me. I think someone had finally heard my ESP! Yay! But Brandon hadn't heard a thing.

He took a deep breath and said, "Yes."

"Oh my god!" I started clapping and threw my arms around Kamiko. "You did it!"

"I did?" Kamiko said skeptically.

Brandon nodded, "Yes. But."

BOOM.

I knew Brandon was always too good to be true. I scowled at him.

"You've brought me a dozen pieces, Kamiko. But I only have room in the show for one more."

Kamiko looked from Brandon to me and said, "But what about..."

"I really like this one," Brandon said, pointing to Kamiko's painting of the three kimonoed Kamikos standing on a bridge over koi fish Brandons. "Something about it really works for me." He chuckled as he looked at it.

Kamiko gave me a surprised glance and bit her lip.

I wasn't going to say anything.

Brandon held the painting up to examine it more closely, "Yes, I really like this," he smiled. "It has a great sense of humor. Are these triplets supposed to be you, Kamiko?"

Oh shit, he was figuring it out!

Kamiko grimaced, "Ahh...yes?"

Note her guilty question mark.

"Who is the fish?" Brandon asked innocently.

"An old boyfriend of hers!" I blurted. "From high school!" There were those guilty exclamation points again.

"Uh, yeah!" Kamiko nodded frantically.

Brandon chuckled, "That's great. I'm sure he was a complete jerk."

Kamiko and I gaped wide eyed at each other. In unison, we both said, "Yes!"

"Love it," Brandon smiled, completely unaware. He set the painting down on the desk. "Kamiko, if you leave this with me, I'll have it framed and hung for the show."

"Okay," she smiled.

Brandon stood up from his desk and clapped his hands together once. He smiled, "This means I've got all the slots for my show filled!"

"But what about..." Kamiko trailed off.

"What about what?" Brandon asked.

"Sam's painting?" Kamiko sighed.

Brandon cocked his head toward me, "You brought a painting for the CA show as well?"

I nodded nervously. The last thing I wanted to do was for Brandon to have to decide between my painting and Kamiko's. I was afraid of this turning into a replay of our last visit. If Brandon chose my painting over Kamiko's, I would die. Then I would haunt Brandon from beyond the grave until he went mad. It wasn't my preferred choice of outcomes. I was still into this being alive thing. But if it happened, I would faithfully haunt Brandon, out of respect for Kamiko.

"Uh," I said, "that's okay. Mine's not very good. And you've got your show filled up anyway."

"Come on," Brandon smiled. "Let me see it." He motioned with his hand.

"Go ahead, Sam," Kamiko groaned.

Crap, she was worried too. I pulled my phoenix painting out of the black portfolio case I'd bought to carry it and handed it to Brandon.

He took it carefully with both hands. "Would you look at this?" he gawked. "This is amazing."

Great.

"I need to see this under good lighting," he said. "These oils are spectacular. Follow me." Carrying my painting in both hands, he walked out of his office. We walked along the upstairs hallway and into a little room that had a couch against one wall and an empty easel standing opposite. Brandon set the painting on the easel and slid some light switches on the wall. Little spotlights came to life, shining on the painting. Then he turned off the fluorescents, darkening the room, except for the painting.

There was a fricking spot light on my painting.

Brandon slid his hands into the pockets of his slacks, pushing back his stylish sport coat.

"This is really nice," Brandon nodded, enraptured by my painting.

I rolled my eyes. This was ridiculous.

Brandon sat down on the couch, on the edge of it, knotting his hands together.

"What is this room, anyway?" I asked.

Kamiko said flatly, sounding slightly annoyed, "It's a viewing room for customers who need some convincing to buy a painting. The lighting is set up to really make a painting look its best."

Brandon wasn't paying attention because, oh my god, he was literally worshipping my painting. Holy shit, I felt like an ass and an idiot. All I could think about was what might be wandering through poor Kamiko's mind at the moment.

Any second now, Brandon was going to turn to me and ask me if he could use my painting in the Contemporary Artists Show instead of Kamiko's. Then I would feel like a total jerk and Kamiko would hate me. I wouldn't blame her.

Brandon turned on the overhead fluorescents again and said. "This piece is phenomenal, Samantha, but it's not right for the Contemporary show."

I glanced at Kamiko. The frigid scowl that had etched its way into her face warmed thirty degrees.

Brandon turned to Kamiko, "I really like your piece, Kamiko. It's staying in the C.A. show." Then he turned back to me. "Samantha, you and I need to talk about you putting together some more paintings for me. For your own show."

What the what?!?

"My own?" I stammered.

"Solo show," Brandon grinned and nodded.

"Wow, Sam," Kamiko smiled. "That's awesome!"

I grinned sheepishly as Kamiko hugged me.

Phew! More than anything, Kamiko's excitement meant she wasn't bothered by all the attention Brandon was giving my painting.

That had been a really close call.

Maybe Brandon wasn't so bad.

===

I was completely naked, standing in front of Christos. He was clothed, at his easel, working on the nude solo portrait of just me.

He paused from mixing a pile of paint and looked up from his palette. He grinned, "I'm really missing the Viking helmet."

"Maybe next time?" I rolled my eyes at him, but held the pose, which was a standing one. I also had to hold my arms out wide, which was really tiring. So whenever Christos wasn't studying my pose, I rested my arms at my sides. It was really hard work. But I was determined to do a good job.

I was also high up on top of a chair, which stood atop a foot tall stage, putting my head over eight feet in the air. I looked down on the whole studio. Fortunately, the studio had a really high ceiling, so I didn't have to worry about bumping my head. "Why am I up so high again?"

"It makes you look more majestic," he smiled, back to mixing his paint. When his brush was loaded, he looked at me and said, "Ready?"

I nodded and assumed the pose, which was also on my tiptoes. I held my arms aloft and arched my back. Fortunately, Christos had made so many charcoal sketches of this pose, he could mostly work from them and from memory at this point. So I never had to hold the extreme pose for more than a minute or two at a time. If I'd had to hold it longer, my neck and shoulders would've cemented into place permanently, and no amount of massaging would ever be able to work out the kinks.

A minute later, Christos said, "Got it, you can relax."

I lowered my arms and massaged my own shoulders. "You're totally gonna owe me a hundred massages after this is done."

"Let's make it a thousand," he smiled.

"Sounds good to me," I gloated. "You're sure?"

Sitting in his chair, he leaned his elbow on his knee, holding a brush in one hand and the elliptical palette in the other. With his thick dark tousled hair, his chiseled features, shoulders bulging beneath the material of his V neck tee, and his dimpled, cocky grin, he was the consummate sexy artist. "Of course I'm sure. Having any excuse to rub my hands over every inch of your body for hours at a time is hardly what I'd call work. I think you'll be the one who gets the short end of the deal on the massages."

I grinned at him. I wasn't going to argue. "So, when do I get to see the painting?"

The canvas was huge, at least eight feet high and five feet wide. Christos would never let me look at it. I hadn't even seen the final sketches he'd done, beyond the very first rough, which just gave me an idea of the pose so I knew I wasn't flashing my lady junk at the world. My knees were close together in the pose, so it was fine.

"You'll see it when it's finished," he smiled.

I pouted, "I don't get a sneak preview?"

"Nope. No one does. Sometimes, the surprise is what makes it special."

I gave him a grinning dirty look, "You're such an ass hamster."

He chuckled. "A hamster? I like to think of myself as more of an ass weasel, or maybe an ass ferret. Something with fangs."

"Take your pick," I said sarcastically. "Either way, you're a small, sniveling, furry animal used to wipe people's butts."

He snickered. "Who in their right mind would wipe their butt with a rodent?"

"Primitive people who were tired of using leaves?"

"But hamsters?"

"Did you say butt hamsters?" I snickered.

He rolled his eyes, "You know what I mean."

"Hey, I'm sure thousands of years before the invention of quilted toilet paper, people looked around for softer alternatives than birch bark."

He grimaced, "Birch bark?"

"Scratchy as hell, I know," I smiled. "A wiggling hamster is way better. Plus the wiggling action does half the work for you."

He scoffed while smiling, "Maybe you need to go into advertising, because I'm willing to buy your line of bullshit." He chuckled, "Don't tell anyone, but your insanity is your most attractive feature."

"Are you saying I'm not attractive?" I demanded from where I stood on the chair. "Because I'll smite you if you say I'm not."

He grinned up at me. "I merely referenced your intense beauty to give your incredible insanity some context. They could fill an entire asylum with your craziness."

"Hand me a sword, because I'm about to go on a smiting spree," I giggled.

My phone suddenly rang. It sat on a work table nearby. The ringtone was for an unknown caller.

"Do you want me to answer that for you?" Christos asked.

"Nah, I don't know who it is. Let it go to voicemail."

A minute later, the phone rang again.

Christos glanced at me, "Want me to get it?"

"I'm sure it's a telemarketer," I dismissed.

Christos went back to mixing some paint. "Can you take the pose again?"

"Sure." I stood on my tiptoes and lifted my arms.

My phone rang a third time.

Christos sighed, "You sure you don't want me to get it? Or I can turn the ringer off."

"Why don't you answer it and say something menacing," I grinned.

He arched an eyebrow, "Menacing?"

"I don't know, you're the tough guy. Be tough. You're totally sexy when you're tough."

He set his brush down, walked over to the table, and answered the phone. "Hello?"

"That's tough?" I scoffed.

He nodded his head, "Yeah." Nodded again, "Uh huh." Nodded a third time. He turned to me and held out the phone, "It's your mom."

"What?" I climbed down from the chair and took the phone from Christos. If my mom could only see me now, standing naked in Christos X-rated painting brothel. It gave me exquisite satisfaction.

"Hello, Mom," I said sarcastically. I put it on speaker phone so Christos could hear everything. I didn't want to have to repeat whatever horrid words my mom had to offer. I was pretty sure I was going to be doing a lot of crying to Christos as soon as I hung up. But I was determined to do my best not to shed a tear while my stupid mom was on the line. Stupid bitch.

"Sam," she said, "Who answered your phone?" I noticed that her words were slurry. Had she been drinking? I don't think I'd ever seen my mom drink.

"Christos."

"I might have known," she chuckled.

"Then why did you ask?" I sneered. I was already on the defensive, which wasn't a surprise considering my mom had turned out to be the real harlot in our family.

Mom poured out another syrupy, drunken chuckle.

"Why did you call, Mom?" I grunted.

"I wanted to find out what stories your father has been telling you."

"Stories? He told me you left him and are living with some guy with a motorcycle." I glanced over at Christos, who watched me intently.

He winked and whispered quietly, "Guys with motorcycles are *always* trouble."

I could tell he was trying to be supportive by being funny. I wasn't really in the mood for a laugh anymore. Funny how my mom could ruin my good mood like a neutron bomb. But I flashed a flat smile at Christos and rubbed his arm affectionately.

"Did your father tell you anything else?" Mom asked in a friendly voice.

"No, that's pretty much all Dad said."

Oddly, my mom was being vaguely polite. A first for her. Was she being careful because she knew she was in the wrong? Maybe. I didn't really know. It was possible my Dad had given me a doctored version of events. His side of the story. But that didn't seem like him. No, my dad prided himself on telling the truth, even when it hurt people's feelings. He said a white lie was still a lie. Honesty was more important to him than social graces. Or my feelings when I was a little girl. And a teenager. And a young adult. But at least in this case, it meant I knew what was going on between them. If my mom was about to make up a bunch of stories that pointed all the blame at my dad, I would know she was lying.

My mom inhaled deeply over the phone, "Sam, I'm asking your father for a divorce."

CRACK!

My mom managed to slap me from three thousand miles away. She had demon powers, I had no doubt.

"Have you told Dad?" I growled, suddenly angry. I don't know why, but I felt very protective of him all of a sudden. Maybe his honesty, however harsh it may have been to deal with growing up, was worth more than I'd given him credit for all these years. My dad would never do all the sneaking around my mom had been up to lately.

Mom said, "Not yet. I wanted to tell you first."

Somehow, I felt like she was betraying Dad a second time, like she should've had the courtesy to tell him before anybody else. Maybe she was too chicken to do it. Maybe she was already trying to get me to take her side in the divorce. It was the only rational explanation for her politeness.

"Sam, do you have anything to say?" Mom asked.

"What, other than you're a bitch?"

I expected my mom to lash out at me. It was her standard strategy when I got defiant.

"I deserved that," she said calmly.

"You deserve a whole lot more than that!" I shouted. "Why did you do it, Mom? Wasn't Dad enough for you?" I couldn't stop myself. It just came rolling out.

"These things are complicated, Sam. I love your father, but..."

"But what, Mom?" I demanded. I was shaking, my heart was pounding, and I was as hot as an oven.

"But things weren't...working out," she sighed. "They haven't been working out for a long time."

"What do you mean? Things looked fine to me! You guys were fine at Christmas! How could they have gotten so bad in only a few months?"

Why the hell was I trying to hold my parents' marriage together? I'd always had nothing but disdain for them. What the hell was happening to me? I hated the way this situation was making me feel.

Christos slid his arm around my shoulders and I leaned against him.

"It's hard to explain, Samantha," she sighed softly.

Samantha? She never ever *ever* called me Samantha unless she was really mad at me. But she wasn't yelling. She sounded...sad.

"Well," I hissed and cried at the same time, "do your best to explain it." Silent tears dripped from my cheeks, onto my naked body. So much for not crying until I got off the phone. I suddenly felt way too naked. I walked over to the chair where my robe hung and slid it on.

"Samantha, the spark between your father and I has dimmed."

Then I remembered all the passion in my mom's voice every time she'd warned me that Christos would love me and leave me a broken woman struggling to pick up the pieces of my life. Had Mom been mourning the loss of a passion she had once known but had lost years ago?

Geez, I didn't know the first thing about adult relationships and marriage.

I steeled myself for what I had to ask next. "Mom," I sniffed, "is Dad my dad?"

"What?" she said, confused.

"Is Dad my father?"

She chuckled, "What are you talking about, Samantha? Of course he's your father."

Why was she making this so hard? Now I was shaking again and my robe felt sweltering. "Is Dad, you know, my biological father?"

There was a very long, drawn out silence. It lasted for months.

"Of course he is, Sam," she chuckled. "Where did you get such a crazy idea?"

Was she lying? She had to be lying. "Tell the truth, Mom."

"I am telling the truth, Samantha. I would know if you were some other man's daughter. That's crazy."

I had my lie detector turned on to the most sensitive setting. It all sounded true. "You mean it?"

My mom sighed. "Do you want to get a DNA test? If you don't believe me, I'm happy to do it. Where did you get this idea anyway, Sam?" she asked with a combination of urgency and concern. "Did your father tell you?"

"No," I said.

"Then who?" she demanded.

"I don't know." I wasn't going to try to explain my soap opera logic to my mom.

"Well it's crazy, Samantha. You are Bill's daughter, and I'm your mom. Okay? You have no idea how much your father and I love you, no matter what is happening between him and I."

Why did that make me want to cry ten times harder than I already had? Maybe my parents weren't as lame as I'd thought. "Then why are you leaving Dad?" I sobbed. I needed to sit down. I looked around for the nearest chair. But Christos had already wheeled one of the office chairs in the studio over to me. I sat down and he kneeled beside me, hugging me around my shoulders.

"It's complicated," my mom said. "Isn't that what you girls say nowadays?"

I sniffled a reply.

Mom took a long, deep breath. "I don't know how to explain it, Samantha. Maybe when you're older, you'll understand. I don't know."

Understand? When I was older? I hoped I never understood what it was like to be in my mom's shoes right now. I looked at Christos and he kissed me softly on the cheek. My heart was sling shotting around in my chest like one of those giant bungie rides at an amusement park. I couldn't even speak.

Mom said in a kind voice, "I know this is a lot to take in right now, Samantha."

That was an understatement. I was literally speechless.

She said, "It sounds like you need some time to process all this. Why don't you call me at this number if you want to talk further. It's my cell phone number. It's always on."

That was a shock in its own right. My mom had a cell phone? I wanted to make a joke about her finally stepping into the 21st century. I wanted to accuse her of using it to make secret plans with her new boyfriend, because duh, she obviously had. But I couldn't talk. My mom had stolen my power of speech.

After more silence, my mom said, "I'm hanging up now, Samantha. Call me if you need anything."

The line went dead.

My heart did too.

===

TIFFANY

I closed the front door behind me as quietly as I could. I didn't want anyone to know I was home, my mother or the house staff.

I was sick of the elaborate marble grand foyer of my parents' lavish mansion. When I was a girl, this foyer made me feel like a princess returning to her castle. Now it was like coming home to an elegant, expensive prison.

I couldn't stand it.

Everything about this house reminded me of my mother Gwendolyn, the evil queen of her domain. The mere thought of her made me nauseous. Literally. But lately, when it came to turning my stomach, this house came in a close second.

I leaned against the front door and slipped off my new $1,000 Louboutin ankle boots. As much as I liked the way they lengthened my legs, they made way too much noise on the marble floor of the foyer.

I padded toward the staircase on the right.

What was the point of having two staircases when they went to the exact same place? Vanity? Gasp! That couldn't be. Gwendolyn didn't have an ounce of vanity in her body.

She had gallons.

My father, Westin-Conrad Kingston-Whitehouse, tap danced down the opposite staircase. I swear, he always managed to keep at least thirty feet away from me at all times. "Your mother is looking for you," he said as he slid out the front door without saying goodbye.

I could never decide who was more scared of my mom: me or my dad.

I turned three corners and as many hallways on whispering feet before making it to my bedroom. I had my hand on the polished brass door handle, about to turn it.

Almost safe.

"Did you go out looking like that?" Gwendolyn sneered from the far end of the hallway.

Typical Gwendolyn.

Throwing barbs at your back when you weren't looking. But she loved the face off just as much.

"No, Mother," I said respectfully. "I changed into this outfit in the car before I walked in the door," I said sarcastically, "just to irritate you."

She strutted toward me, sashaying her hips. Gwendolyn wore stylish outfits at all times and changed them at least three times a day. I don't know who she was showing off for. The maids? I'm sure they didn't give a shit as long as Gwendolyn signed their checks.

Gwendolyn half hooded her eyelids. One of them flickered spasmodically. She was so damn good at that look. It drove me cray cray. I think her expression right now could induce epileptic seizures in the weak and subservient. It was made worse by her ugly beauty. Yes, I had been blessed with Gwendolyn's good looks. It was my cross to bear.

Gwendolyn smiled like a piranha. "Must you always be so snide? I've taught you better than that, Tiffany."

She taught me how to be snide, that was for sure. Not consciously. I'd picked that up from her along the way. It was unavoidable.

If you asked Gwendolyn, she was determined to fix all the mistakes she'd made in her own life, which she claimed were few, with mine.

Sadly, that made her a tad domineering.

Her snideness was just a bonus.

"Mother, now is not a good time," I sighed gripping the door handle to my room like a life preserver. If I could just get through this door unharmed…

"I need to speak with you about the summer gala. You still haven't picked out a dress."

She was referring to the annual gala at the La Jolla Country Club. Gwendolyn had to make a splash every year, each year bigger and bolder than the last. I was a part of her display. One of these years, I think she planned on hiring someone to build a parade float so she could drive up to the gates of the country club on a throne made of five hundred thousand fresh orchids. I'd be stuck sitting by her feet like a jewel on display.

Gwendolyn folded her hands in front of her waist and said, "Since you have been dissatisfied with the dress options I've given you, I've had Fred Segal courier down several new gowns from their Los Angeles boutique. They should be here this afternoon. I'd like you to try them on. Two of them are smashing off the shoulder numbers from a hot new designer in Beverly Hills named Rocco Ferrara, who I absolutely adore. Please try them all on and pick one, Tiffany. I won't have you attending the gala in your street attire."

She eyed my outfit with obvious disgust. But it didn't show on her face. She kept a perfectly pleasant smile in place around the clock. I think her face was frozen that way. It was just that awful flinty glint in her eyes that gave away her irritation.

I arched my eyebrows, hoping she was finished. I'd learned to say little in the presence of Gwendolyn. It gave her fewer opportunities to pick at me.

"Have you decided on an escort for the gala?" she asked.

Sometimes, the silence didn't help any.

"No," I sighed.

"Have you considered Brandon Charboneau?"

"No, Mother," I muttered. No matter how many hints I dropped to Brandon, he was always too busy. I was starting to wonder if he was gay. It was the only explanation, considering how obvious I'd been with him in the past.

"What about Christos Manos?" Gwendolyn cocked her head slightly. "I've always been fond of that young man."

My lips tightened down. I could feel my eyelids wanting to flutter from my impending tears. I was determined to hold them back. "Christos is...busy." I choked. My voice was on the verge of cracking. Gwendolyn always struck with practiced accuracy. Right at the jugular.

"I don't understand what your problem is, Tiffany. Are you scaring off all the eligible bachelors in San Diego?" She made it sound like getting a good man was as easy as filling a gas tank at the gas station.

"No, mother," I muttered.

"Speak up, dear. That mousy voice of yours is half the problem. No man wants a mousy girl. Show some confidence. You're a Kingston-Whitehouse."

"Can I go now?" I asked in a garbled voice.

"Yes. But be ready when those dresses arrive. I want to see how they look on you."

She was determined to treat me like a dress up doll no matter what I did. I opened my door and stepped into my bedroom.

"Tiffany?"

I stopped, my back to her, bracing for the usual criticism. I still clutched the brass doorknob. I imagined myself yanking it off the door and planting it right in the center of Gwendolyn's forehead.

"Is that skirt tight on you?" she asked thoughtfully. My mother had the heart and eyes of a Beverly Hills plastic surgeon.

Yes, my skirt was tight. It looked like it was painted on, and I looked awesome in it. I worked my ass off at the gym and ate like a mouse to make sure of it.

"Do you need to lose a pound or two? Your waistline is a bit puffy today."

Typical Gwendolyn.

I didn't answer.

"No matter," she sighed heavily. "Those dresses will be here shortly. With any luck, you won't burst any seams when you try them on." She sounded defeated already. Double crossed by the puffy waistline of her traitorous daughter. Didn't Gwendolyn know what a period was? Oh, wait. I think she had her uterus removed a long time ago. My guess was that she'd hired a surrogate to carry me to term rather than stretch her waistline. And I knew she would never have stooped so low as to have an elective C-section. It would've left a scar.

I quietly closed my bedroom door behind me and walk into my expansive walk in closet. It held more awesome outfits than a Mercedes-Benz Fashion Week. At least there were some perks to being a Kingston-Whitehouse. I placed my red lacquer soled Louboutins in the shoe rack amongst dozens of others.

Back in my bedroom, I pulled a photo album off of my desk and sat down on my plush comforter atop my four poster bed. I leafed through it. There were photos going back to when I was a little girl.

Certain ones stood out, and I lingered on them.

A school play in the fourth grade. Robin Hood. I played Maid Marian and Christos was Robin Hood. Of course. He was dashing even then.

An Easter Egg hunt when I was six. I had known then that I was in love with Christos. I'd even told him I wanted to marry him that day.

Christos at the beach, sometime in high school. He was shirtless and ripped. No tattoos yet, but muscled and handsome. The man he would become was already obvious. All the girls had eyes for him.

My eleventh birthday party. Surrounded by balloons and confetti and friends. The birthday cake was right in front of me and

I was blowing on the candles. Christos was leaning toward me, a sly look on his face, kissing my cheek. I hadn't washed my cheek for a week after that day, I remember.

I rubbed my cheek longingly.

Tears dripped onto the plastic sleeve covering the photos. I pulled the photo out to get a better look.

Christos Manos.

Christos.

I squeezed my eyes shut and my head dropped to my chest. I stifled my sobs. Gwendolyn had ears like a vampire bat and would no doubt sense me out and give me shit if she heard me crying in my room like a baby.

Christos was gone.

I shook my head, not wanting to believe it.

It was that stupid Samantha.

She'd ruined everything.

She'd taken him from me.

It was all her fault.

Christos and I had been getting closer over last summer, before classes had started. We'd been hanging out all the time. Almost every day. I had started to think maybe we'd had a chance. Christos had finally cleaned up his act, working on his paintings, becoming a respectable young man. It had been touch and go with him for several years. But he'd finally gotten his shit together. He wasn't an embarrassment anymore.

And Samantha had swooped in and stolen his heart.

I fucking hated that bitch.

I *hated* her.

I hated her with all my heart.

I was going to make her life miserable if it was the last thing I did.

Starting with her hearing in front of the SDU tribunal. She was getting kicked out of SDU. Whatever it took.

I stood up from my bed and walked into my closet, closing the door behind me. I went to the back of the closet and pushed aside coats and gowns. Like I needed yet another gown for the summer gala. I had three that still fit. But no, they'd been worn once. In public. Gwendolyn would be ashamed of me for even suggesting I wear one again.

Hidden in the corner, behind my ski jackets and snow pants was a duffel bag. I sat down on the carpeted floor of my closet and unzipped the bag. I reached inside and felt immediate relief.

I pulled an old, ratty teddy bear out of the bag. Her fur was tattered and she was missing one button eye. If Gwendolyn knew I still had Ms. Bear, she would've burned her. Gwendolyn had thrown out every doll and stuffed animal I had when I turned thirteen. She'd said they were childish. I'd managed to save Ms. Bear by hiding her under my bed when Gwendolyn wasn't looking.

I hugged Ms. Bear to my chest.

Still weeping, and in a shaky voice, I said, "You still love me, don't you, Ms. Bear?"

Ms. Bear stared back at me blankly with her one eyed smile.

I hugged her to my chest and sobbed silently. My body shook and spasmed with sadness.

Forty minutes later, when the gowns arrived, there was no sign left on my face that I'd been crying.

I never allowed myself to cry long enough for my face to get puffy.

Gwendolyn would never tolerate it.

Chapter 24

SAMANTHA

"Let's crash this bash!" I cheered as me and the gang walked into Charboneau Gallery on the night of the Contemporary Artists Show.

The place was packed with people. Unlike the crowd at Christos' solo show last year, which had been more upscale, this crowd was much younger and hipper. They had a DJ instead of a string quartet. People were talking much louder, and drinking more freely. I saw cans of Red Bull in people's hands instead of wine glasses. It was a party vibe for sure.

Kamiko was already inside. She'd arrived early because she was one of the artists. Christos and I had picked up Romeo and met Madison and Jake on the street before coming inside.

"Let's go find Kamiko," Romeo said, "I want to see what cosplay character she dressed up as this time."

"Okay," I said as Romeo pulled me along.

Christos, Madison, and Jake strolled behind.

Despite the bomb my mom had dropped about asking my dad for a divorce, I had managed to hold myself together in the days since she'd called. Sure, my legs were still wobbly and I wanted to throw up every five minutes most days, but I was determined to enjoy myself tonight.

"This place is packed," I said, "we're never going to find Kamiko."

Romeo was examining a piece of paper, "I grabbed one of the paper price sheets. It says she's number thirty-two. She should be over there somewhere," he pointed toward the right.

The four of us walked in that direction.

"Dude," Christos said to Jake as we wove our way through the crowd, "you still thinking about surfing the North Shore all summer?"

"Hells yeah," Jake smiled. "I'm dreaming about Pipeline every night."

The two of them were right behind me and Madison. I frowned at her and whispered in her ear, "Is Jake talking about *your* pipeline?"

Madison cackled, "No, silly Sam. He's talking about the reef break at Banzai Beach, in Oahu."

"Oh," I nodded. "I just assume when guys start throwing terms around that don't make sense, they're talking about sex."

"It's a safe assumption," Madison grinned.

Christos asked Jake, "Are you taking Mads with you?"

Jake nodded, "Of course, I would never go to Pipeline without bringing my favorite pipeline with me."

Christos and Jake both started chuckling. Me and Madison turned to each other and said in unison, "Men!"

Jake wrapped a muscled arm around Madison and said, "You know you love it." He smiled his endearingly white smile, always such a brilliant contrast against his bronze skin, before kissing her cheek.

Madison leaned into him, "If you weren't so damn cute, Jake, you would never get away with talking like a heathen."

"Does that mean I can keep talking like a heathen?"

Madison rolled her eyes for my benefit, but I could tell she was totally in love with Jake.

Christos wrapped an arm around me.

I shot him a warning glare, "Don't start talking about my pipeline," I joked.

"Whose pipeline?" Romeo asked. "I'm all about the pipeline. Laying it, boring it out, plugging it up, draining it—"

"Draining it?" Jake grimaced.

"Dude," Christos smiled, "what does that even mean?"

Romeo examined his fingernails and grinned, "You really want to know?"

"NO!" me and Madison blurted.

All the young people around us were dressed in various hipster garb or clubbing outfits. I was just waiting for the lights to dim and the neon glow sticks to come out. But it still was an art gallery. There were so many people we could barely see the paintings on the walls.

"It's this way," Romeo said, leading everyone. "Oh my god!"

"What?" I said, curious.

"I can't belieeeeve it!" Romeo singsonged.

"What, what?" I couldn't see past the people Romeo had just squeezed between.

I exchanged an excited look with Madison as we squeezed up to Romeo, who had his arms around Kamiko.

"You're not dressed like a cartoon!" Romeo cheered while hugging Kamiko.

"Okay," she grimaced, "don't break me." She may have been complaining, but she was totally giggling.

When Romeo broke the hug, I finally saw Kamiko's outfit.

"Damn, Kamiko!" I smiled. "You look totally sexy!"

Kamiko wore a sleeveless red on black colorblock bodycon zip front dress. She stood tall on black platform sandals and her hair was down.

"Whoa," Christos said. "Kamiko, you look hot, girl."

Kamiko blushed.

Jake nodded approval. "Nice dress, Kamiko."

"Does anybody want to pull her zipper down as badly as I do?" Romeo asked.

"Please don't," Kamiko pleaded.

"I'm kidding," Romeo smiled. "You look amazing, Kamiko," he said genuinely. "In no way do you resemble a cartoon character tonight. If I was straight, I would totally do you. You look fabulous."

"Thanks," she smiled bashfully.

Romeo gave her another big hug.

Christos grinned, "If you don't get at least ten phone numbers from good looking guys tonight, I'd be surprised."

"Thanks," Kamiko rolled her eyes like the idea of her meeting a guy was about as likely as the sun suddenly exploding. She said, "I just hope I sell my painting tonight." She stood right next to it.

Christos took a closer look. "Oh shit, is that Brandon's face on those koi?"

Kamiko's eyes widened and we exchanged a giggle.

"OMG," Kamiko tittered, clearly embarrassed, "is it that obvious?"

"Maybe to me," Christos reassured, "but I've known that bottom feeder for a long time."

"Which bottom feeder?" Brandon Charboneau asked, suddenly standing next to all of us.

Whoops. I guess that catfish was finally out of the bag. Well, it was technically a koi. Whatever. Either way, I hope Brandon wasn't offended.

"Brandon!" Christos said extravagantly, clapping him on the back, clearly trying to distract from the obvious.

"Greetings, everyone," Brandon smiled, looking dashing. "It's a crowded house tonight, isn't it?"

"Totally," Christos said loudly, trying to keep Brandon's attention away from the painting.

Maybe if Brandon didn't figure out he was the subject of Kamiko's painting, he would take note of how sexy Kamiko looked in her dress instead, and finally ask her out.

"Doesn't Kamiko look sexy in her dress?" I said to Brandon. I wasn't above hinting.

Brandon glanced at her outfit and smiled politely, "Very stylish, Kamiko." Then he looked at the rest of us, "Well, I've got to circulate." He raised his eyebrows and smiled as he squeezed past us into the crowd.

Stupid Brandumb.

At least Kamiko didn't seem to care. "Phew!" she whispered. "That was close!"

"What are you worried about?" Romeo asked.

Kamiko glared at him, "Are you insane? If he figures out that's him in my painting, he'll probably ban me from selling in his gallery ever again."

I started to say, "If he does that…"

Then, two things suddenly happened simultaneously in the next two seconds.

First, Brandon suddenly leaned back through the crowd toward us and said, "Oh, hey, Kamiko?"

And, I finished my sentence, "…then Brandon is a fucking asshole."

Kamiko's eyes bugged out.

Oh, fuck me backward and sideways. That foot of mine still had a mind of its own when it came to jumping in my mouth.

Romeo suddenly went into overdrive. "Uh, what Sam meant was, ahh...Brandon, you are the *opposite* of a fucking asshole!" Romeo's eyes shone like he'd discovered the cure for cancer. "Yes! The complete opposite! You're an unfucked asshole! You're the type of asshole who's never seen a day's work! You've never been used for fucking! You're tight as a drum! Couldn't pass a turd the size of a vitamin pill even if you tried! "

Note Romeo's guilty exclamation points. They were all over the place.

Brandon arched an eyebrow.

The rest of us stood and watched in mute horror as the Loco Locomotive crashed into the side of a mountain. Oh, the calamity. At least he was trying to save my ass.

Romeo continued shoveling, "Brandon, you are the most pristine asshole the world has ever known. Fresh off the rack. Untouched, like a diamond. An asshole in the rough. Ahhh..." Romeo finally ran out of steam, looking flummoxed. "That didn't come out quite right. Sorry."

Brandon nodded sourly, "I get the idea."

"What was it that you wanted?" Kamiko asked desperately, her teeth clenched in terror, doing her best to sweep the awful moment under the rug.

Brandon cleared his throat while shooting a ninja throwing star glare at Romeo and me, "I was just going to tell you, Kamiko, that a couple of buyers have already asked me about your painting. They really like it. I think we might sell it this evening."

A long moment of silence passed between the seven of us as we all stared at the ceiling, our toes, our fingernails. Anything to avoid the social disaster surrounding us.

Brandon looked at everyone, his eyebrows raised high. "Anything else?"

I shook my head, contrite.

"I did compare him to a diamond," Romeo whispered in my ear, as if that made up for everything.

I stomped on his foot.

Brandon turned away from the group of us.

At least Brandon had never noticed he was the koi fish in Kamiko's painting.

Brandon turned back a second later, "Oh, one other thing." He leveled a glare at Kamiko, "Don't think I didn't notice that was me on the koi in your painting."

Thud.

Kamiko went white.

Quick, somebody prop her up before she fainted.

"Oh, Brandon," Kamiko begged while hyper ventilating, "I'm so sorry! I didn't mean to! I mean, I, ah, oh…" She was going to pass out.

Brandon's mouth curled into a sly smile, "Why do you think I wanted your piece in the show?"

What?

He grinned, "I've got a sense of humor. How uptight do you guys think I am?"

"You're not tight at all!" Romeo said. "You're totally loose! Diarrhea loose! Like run off from a strip mining operation!"

"Romeo!" we all shouted, except Brandon.

Brandon chuckled, "Can someone turn this guy into a painting? Because I'm sure I could build an entire show around him," he laughed. "I'll check in with you later, Kamiko," Brandon smiled at her and faded into the crowd.

Wow, Brandon wasn't half bad.

"Does anyone want a drink?" Christos asked.

"After that, I need about ten," Jake smiled.

I turned to Kamiko, "Can I get you anything, Kamiko?"

"A MUTE button for Romeo would be nice," she said, "or at the very least, a bag to put over my head so nobody notices me the rest of the night. I'm dying of embarrassment."

Christos said, "Don't worry, Kamiko. Brandon is cool. He's not going to hold it against you."

"What about me?" I asked. "I was the one who called him an asshole."

"A fucking asshole," Romeo corrected. "The kind used for putting dicks in. Frequently."

I rolled my eyes at Romeo.

"What?" he said defensively. "You said it."

Kamiko mimed pressing the MUTE button on a remote control, "It's not working," she grinned.

===

After we got drinks at the bar and brought one to Kamiko, who badly needed it, Christos and I circulated around the gallery, looking at all the cool paintings.

The Contemporary Artists Show really had an eclectic mix of art. There was graffiti influenced art, screen printed digital creations, collages combining paint and found materials, even a large piece done entirely in crayons.

"Hey," I said, looking at the placard describing it, "it's a crayon painting!"

On the placard, beneath the dimensions, the card listed the medium as, "Crayola 96 color box on paper."

Christos nodded, gazing appreciatively at the piece, "This is awesome."

It was an amazingly detailed picture of a Renaissance era palace interior. It was reminiscent of M.C. Escher, but in full color. The tiles of a black and white floor transformed into birds and fish as the floor receded into the distance, with the black bird tiles taking flight and the white fish tiles diving into a blue pond. The pond emptied into a blue stream that flowed toward the foreground of the painting, and the stream morphed into a blue runner threaded with gold as it approached the bottom of the canvas. The law of gravity was not in effect, and people walked on the ceiling and the walls, going about their business. Then I noticed all the people were animals walking on two legs. Pigs, cows, horses, chickens, geese, sheep, goats, and any kind of farm animal you could imagine. There was even a wolf with an actual red riding hood cloak making out with three girl pigs in a dark corner at the top of the painting.

"That wolf is sure getting a lot of action with those pigs," Christos said.

"It's a regular porky orgy," I smiled. "Whose house do you think they'll go back to?"

"You mean the straw, wood, or brick house?"

"I think they'll start with the straw house and bang their way through that and the wood one, until they end up in the brick one," Christos chuckled. "Everyone knows a brick house is mighty mighty. No amount of bed shaking can bring a brick house down."

"Gross!" I grimaced. "Are you suggesting that wolf is going to have sex with the three little pig sluts? And instead of blowing their houses down, they're going to, uh, fuck the houses down?"

Christos grinned, "Hey, I didn't paint the painting."

"You're terrible," I frowned. "But, what I want to know is, why is the wolf wearing a red riding hood?"

"I don't know," he said thoughtfully. "Either it's the wolf who ate Little Red Riding Hood, or it's a she wolf looking for some sow on bitch action."

I grimaced. "That's uber disgusting."

"Again, I didn't paint it."

Christos and I walked to the next painting, arm in arm.

We circled the gallery, enjoying all the art and making more snappy comments about the imagery. One large painting had a crowd around it. Most of the people were talking rather than looking at the painting, so I tried to squeeze past them to get a better look at it.

"Excuse me," I said as I slid behind some woman dressed entirely in white.

"Watch where you're going!" she blurted.

I turned to apologize.

It was Tiffany Kingston-Whitehouse.

Great. Why was she here?

She wore a white sleeveless keyhole midi dress. And I had to admit, she looked really good in it. The dress contrasted nicely against her tan skin and golden hair. I also noticed she had glittery lip gloss that sparkled almost as much as her diamond earrings. It should've looked cheesy, but it was subtle, and on her, it only enhanced. Tiffany was uniquely beautiful.

"Excuse you," she sneered, holding her champagne glass out of the way. Champagne sloshed around it.

She was also uniquely bitchy. How did such an amazing bitch get into such an amazing body?

I noticed Tiffany was tipping her glass toward me and the champagne was a millimeter from spilling over the rim and pouring on my shoulder.

"Hey, Tiff," Christos said, catching her hand with his, stopping the champagne waterfall. "You almost spilled your drink," he said knowingly.

Tiffany frowned at him, staring into his eyes.

Christos stared back. He still held her hand. "Don't, Tiffany," he said quietly.

"Let go of me," she demanded. Christos did and she threw her drink back, swallowing it in several large gulps. "I need another drink now that the riff raff is here." She shouldered past me, bumping into me hard.

"Hey!" I blurted.

She ignored me.

I rubbed my shoulder where she'd slammed it with her own, "What's she doing here?" I asked Christos.

"She always comes to Brandon's openings."

"Fantastic," I sighed.

"Don't worry about her. I'll deal with her if she gets out of hand."

"That's what I'm worried about. She'll probably get out of hand just so you have to deal with her. That's what she did on her yacht New Year's Eve. I saw the way she was drooling over you just now." Did I sound jealous? I hoped only a little.

"Don't worry about her, *agápi mou*. I'm not going to let Tiff come between you and me."

"Promise?"

"Promise," Christos reassured. "Nothing will ever split us apart."

I winced as a wave of nausea sloshed through my stomach. The word "split" made me think of my parents' impending divorce.

Christos gave me a compassionate look. "You're thinking about your parents, aren't you?"

I nodded mutely.

Christos wrapped a loving arm around me and pulled me into his chest. He kissed my forehead softly. "I'm not going anywhere. I'll be by your side, no matter what happens."

"Really?"

"Really," he murmured in my ear.

I inhaled the warm loving scent emanating from his chest as I wrapped my arms around his waist. "I love you so much, Christos Adonis Manos."

"I love you too, Samantha Anna Smith," he said as he kissed the top of my head.

"Get a room!" Romeo said as he came walking up. "And stop being such a cooch mooch, Christos. You've been hogging Sam for the last hour. There's more than enough of her to go around." He slid his arm between me and Christos and pulled me to his side for a quick hug.

"Cooch mooch?" I chuckled. "Are you calling me a cooch?"

"You have one, don't you?" Romeo scoffed, releasing the hug.

"Yeah, but it's not like I go around calling you a needless penis."

"I'm hurt, Sam. Are you suggesting my good humor is not wanted?" He made a droopy, sad face, jutting out his lower lip. His shoulders sagged comically.

"Oh, Romeo," I giggled, "Your penis is always needed."

"That's what I'm told," Romeo grinned. "Do you want to swing by Kamiko's painting and say hello? I'm afraid someone is going to kidnap her in that dress."

"Awww, are you worried about her, Romeo?" I crooned.

"Of course I am, Sam. Who knew a cartoon character could be so sexy?" he quipped. "I'd do her if she had a dick."

I winced. "Wrong image."

"It would be a very feminine dick," Romeo said. "Smallish with a tiny little pink wrapper."

I winced wider. "Not helping!" I warned.

"What's wrong with dicks, Sam? You like them, don't you?"

I shook my head, and started laughing. "Romeo, please!"

"What?" Romeo looked at Christos for support.

"Don't look at me!" Christos chuckled. "I'm all about mooching the cooch."

I shook my head. "You guys have one track minds tonight. Did we walk into a brothel without me realizing it?"

"Everywhere I go," Romeo quipped, "I bring the brothel."

That was one hundred percent true.

===

Christos, Romeo, and I squeezed through the crowd toward Kamiko's painting. At the moment, she stood alone. The show had been going long enough that most people had seen all of the art and were now busy socializing and getting drunk.

"Hey, guys," Kamiko said nervously.

"How's it going?" I asked. "Has your painting sold?"

"No," she said, sounding disappointed.

I had noticed that most of the other paintings Christos and I had looked at had red dots on the placards, meaning they'd sold. I wasn't about to tell Kamiko that.

"It seems like most of the paintings are selling," Kamiko sighed.

Oh well. She'd figured it out herself. "Yours will sell," I encouraged.

"Excuse me, guys," Christos said, "I think I just saw a buddy of mine. I'm going to go say hey."

"All right," I said. "I'm going to stay here with Kamiko and Romeo."

Christos kissed me on the cheek.

"Don't I get a kiss?" Romeo smirked.

"Next time," Christos winked at Romeo before walking into the crowd.

I turned back to Kamiko. She looked increasingly distraught.

"I don't know what I was thinking entering my painting into the show," she said. "Maybe my parents were right about me being pre-med. This art thing is hard."

"Don't be silly, Kamiko," Romeo said dismissively. "Your art is awesome."

Kamiko looked at him despondently.

I didn't know what else to say.

Brandon squeezed through the crowd toward us, "Hey," he said. He didn't sound any more enthusiastic than the rest of us.

Disappointmentballs.

"How's it going?" Brandon asked Kamiko.

She rolled her eyes. "The truth?"

Brandon nodded.

"My feet are killing me. I've been standing here two hours."

Romeo said, "Kamiko, maybe you should unzip the front of your dress and say you come with the painting."

Brandon chuckled, "While that might work, I'd like to think Kamiko's art stands on it's own two feet."

"Yeah," she said sarcastically, "but my painting isn't wearing platform sandals," she groaned. "I'm the one doing all the standing."

"Maybe this will help," Brandon said, leaning toward Kamiko.

I was suddenly sure he was going to kiss her.

Instead, he pressed a red dot onto the placard of her painting. "It sold," he grinned.

"What?" Kamiko's face lit up.

"For two thousand," Brandon smiled.

Kamiko clapped her hands to her face. "Ohmygod! I don't

believe it!"

"Believe it," Brandon chuckled. "I had two buyers. The price started at fifteen hundred, but they argued their way up to two grand before one of them bought it."

"Wow!' I smiled. "You're a hot commodity tonight, Kamiko! Isn't she hot, Brandon?" I hinted with zero subtlety.

"She's on fire tonight," Brandon smiled before walking off.

I looked at Kamiko and sighed, "I tried."

"Oh," Kamiko said, "I don't care about Brandumb anymore." She looked disappointed, but then her face lit up and she started hopping in her heels and clapping, "I sold my painting! I sold it, I sold it!"

Romeo smiled, "I knew you would, Kamiko. Come here, you cartoon character," he said with genuine emotion. He gave Kamiko a huge hug. "I knew you could do it. Didn't I tell you in high school you were going to be a big artist someday?"

Kamiko's eyes were watering, "You did. You've always stood by me, you monocle wearing fairy."

They laughed and hugged again.

Kamiko said, "Who needs a boyfriend when I have Romeo?"

"Hey, guys," Christos said as he squeezed past people to get to us.

"Kamiko sold her painting!" I cheered.

"You did?" Christos beamed. "That's awesome, Kamiko."

Kamiko nodded, grinning at Christos.

A cute guy squeezed out from behind Christos. He wore a black suit vest over a gray button down shirt with sleeves rolled up to the elbows, black skinny jeans, and a red bow tie checked in black. His thick dark hair was mussed and a sexy curl dipped over his brow. On each forearm he had a tattoo of a cartoon character. Both were from Adventure Time, Kamiko's favorite cartoon. I totally recognized them from all the times I'd watched the show with her since school started last year.

Kamiko's jaw dropped, and she gasped, "What the F? Why do you have tattoos of Marceline and Princess Bubblegum?"

Hipster guy frowned at Kamiko like she was completely stupid. "Duh. Because they rock," he grinned.

His sexy smile had panty dropping potential for sure. Not that I noticed, but it went well with his emerald eyes. Again, not that I'd noticed.

But Romeo had. I think he was drooling at the guy.

"Hey, Samantha," Christos said, "remember I told you back in November that a buddy of mine did storyboards for Adventure Time?"

I nodded.

"This is him," Christos grinned. "Everybody, meet Dillon McKenna."

Dillon shook hands with everybody.

Kamiko looked like a deer caught in headlights. I couldn't decide if she was fan girling because Dillon worked on her favoritest cartoon ever, or because he was so handsome.

"Charmed," Romeo said as they shook, sounding totally girlie.

I grinned to myself as I imagined Romeo and Kamiko fighting over Dillon.

Christos said, "Kamiko is a huge fan of Adventure Time. And she painted that painting," he motioned toward it.

Dillon glanced at the painting, then did a double take. He stepped toward it and gave it a closer look. "Wow, you did this?"

Kamiko nodded nervously.

"This is tits," he said, looking at it closely. "Why does the face on the koi fish look familiar?" he asked.

We all broke into a laugh, except for Dillon.

"Inside joke," Kamiko smiled.

Dillon nodded as he scrutinized her painting further. "This is really good. What was your name again?"

"Kamiko Nishimura," she grinned.

"You sure can paint, Kamiko," he smiled.

"So," Kamiko said nervously, "you storyboard for Adventure Time?"

"You watch the show?" Dillon asked.

"Totally! I have every season on DVD! I dressed up as Marceline last Halloween!" She sounded totally nervous.

"You do cosplay?" Dillon asked her, sounding impressed.

Kamiko nodded.

"Nice," he said. "I made my own Ice King costume last Halloween. I have pics on my phone, if you want to see."

"Shut up!" Kamiko grinned like it was Christmas.

Dillon nodded as he pulled out his phone, "But I'm going to

make an Earl of Lemongrab costume for San Diego Comic Con this summer."

"What! Do you have tickets?"

"Yeah, we get them because we work on the show," he said as he thumbed through his phone.

"I can never get tickets to Comic Con!" Kamiko said. "It's always sold out."

"I can get you in this year, if you want," Dillon smiled. "They always have extras at the office."

Dillon handed his phone to Kamiko.

She examined the pictures. "Wow! Your Ice King costume rocks! You made it yourself?"

Dillon smiled a huge grin and nodded. "Totally."

Turning to me and Christos, Romeo said, "I think we need to leave those two alone. Kamiko's eyes have turned into candy hearts, or something equally juvenile."

"I think they're little pink smiley faces right now," Christos chuckled.

Christos, Romeo, and I all smiled at each other while we slowly retreated, leaving Kamiko and Dillon to geek out about Adventure Time, cosplay, and the San Diego Comic Con.

===

CHRISTOS

The DJ turned up the volume as the crowd grew more boisterous. People had to talk loud to be heard, enhancing the nightclub vibe.

I don't know why I hadn't thought to introduce Kamiko to Dillon sooner. They were perfect for each other.

Samantha demanded, "Why didn't you tell me your Adventure Time friend was so hot? And perfect for Kamiko?"

I frowned, "Are you reading my mind?"

"What?" she asked, confused.

"Never mind," I grinned. "Anyway, I guess I had other things distracting me back then." I gave her a knowing look and leaned down to kiss her lips.

Romeo grunted, "Somebody get me a bucket. There's so much true love around here tonight, I'm going to puke."

"Oh," Samantha said compassionately, "I'm sorry Romeo.

Christos, do you have any hot steampunk friends for Romeo?"

"I'll have to check," I smiled.

Brandon came walking up. "How are you all?" he smiled. "Enjoying the show?"

"Great show, Brandon," Samantha said.

I think her mood had improved ever since Kamiko had sold her koi painting. I knew Samantha was trying to keep a game face about her parents' split, but you could only fake so much. Her guts were probably flip flopping every sixty seconds morning, noon, and night. I know mine had when my mom had left my dad over a decade ago.

Fuck, my guts still knotted when I thought about my mom.

(*mom*)

"Thank you," Brandon smiled his stock Mr. Pleasant smile. "Christos, can I talk to you for a few moments?"

"Sure," I said. I raised my eyebrows at Samantha and Romeo.

"Let's go look around, Sam," Romeo said. He pulled Samantha off into the crowd.

"What up, Brandon?" I asked.

"I wanted to check in about your progress on your paintings. Care to take a stroll in the sculpture garden?"

I nodded.

We walked out back. The sculpture garden wasn't quite as crowded as the inside of the gallery, and it was outside so we had a vague sense of privacy in the hedges mazing around under the starlight. Brandon was all about appearances, so taking me back here meant he had something to say that was going to irritate either him or me.

When we were secluded, he asked, "How's that portrait of Isabella coming along? Did you make the changes like Stanford Wentworth suggested?"

I chuckled. As if.

"What?" Brandon smiled.

Did I tell Brandon now that I'd destroyed the painting of Isabella in a fit of rage? Or let him find out when it was noticeably absent from my solo show? Fuck it. I didn't feel like dancing tonight. "I've decided to go in a different direction for the show."

Brandon narrowed his eyes. "What do you mean?"

"I'm trashing the idea of using models. It wasn't working for me."

"I thought they were looking pretty good."

"You heard Wentworth," I chuckled. "You were there. He said the paintings were lifeless."

"I could sell them," Brandon scoffed.

"You could sell a car to a canary."

Brandon frowned, "Why would a canary want a car? They have wings."

"Exactly."

Brandon dismissed my comment. "Christos, you and I have known each other a long time."

I nodded.

"I'm trying to build your career," he said.

I said, "But I don't want a career painting models I don't give a shit about."

"Beautiful women sell, Christos. They never go out of style."

I arched an eyebrow and nodded at him.

"At any rate," he continued, "I can't build your career if I don't have any paintings to sell. Here's a suggestion. We sell the nudes you have now next month, at your solo show. Next year, we transition you into more meaningful subject matter. The important thing is we keep your momentum going. I have fifteen possible buyers lined up for your paintings. I even have one for the Isabella portrait. I don't care what Stanford Wentworth said, I can get us one-twenty-five K for it."

Whoops. I could use $125,000. Nothing like attorney's fees to drain your wallet down to zero. Fucking Hunter Blakeley.

Sadly, if I dug the tatters of the Isabella painting out of the dump now, I don't think Brandon would get fifty cents for it.

He asked, "How much longer do you think it would take for you to finish fifteen paintings?"

Brandon needed a reality check. He was under the impression I'd been busily working away in the studio these past few months, cranking out more paintings of his L.A. models. I'd kept hidden until now the fact that I'd fallen way behind because of the Horst Grossman trial and because I'd decided to go in a different direction with my art.

"Months," I said.

Brandon's eyes goggled. "Months? I don't have months. I've got shows lined up for the rest of the year. I can't shift things around. Christos," he said, sounding deeply disappointed, "I can't keep these buyers waiting around. If I don't close them now, they're going to go elsewhere."

"Why don't you sell them on some of your other artists?"

"These are big name buyers. They're not interested in my other artists, Christos. They're interested in you. They want the Manos magic. I need your paintings. Now. How many do you have?"

"Three are finished. The ones you've seen of Avery, Jacqueline, and Becca. I've got three more in progress." I was thinking of the LOVE painting of me and Samantha, the solo portrait of her, and the surprise I had brewing for everyone.

"Six? I thought you had seven. I know I sent you seven models and you were working on all of them. What happened?"

"The, ahhh…well…" I was going to have to tell him, "The painting of Isabella is R.I.P."

"What? Why?" He was frowning.

"I told you, it wasn't working for me."

"You didn't change it, did you, like Wentworth asked?"

"No," I scoffed. "He's an idiot."

"Good. Because I'm telling you, I can sell that painting for six figures for sure."

Fuck. He may as well know. "It's gone."

"What, did you sell it already?" he chuckled nervously.

If I had, I would be a total prick and Brandon would reconsider our business relationship. I wouldn't blame him. Lucky for me, I hadn't. "I, um, tore it to pieces."

Brandon's eyes goggled wider than before. "Why the hell would you do that?" He actually sounded angry. Brandon never lost his cool. "I had a buyer lined up. The guy buys nothing but high priced nudes. He wouldn't think twice about paying a hundred grand for yours. You're crazy, Christos." Brandon shook his head and frowned, looking half defeated. Then he paused and his angry expression eased into an easy grin. "You're pulling my leg, aren't you, Christos?"

I shook my head, "No. I tore the shit out of it and threw it away."

Brandon's eyes goggled a third time. "You're serious, aren't you?"

I nodded.

"Christos, you're killing me," he sighed. "I can't put up a solo show with six paintings. The gallery will look empty. I'm going to need more."

I felt bad. I had put myself in this position. "Look, maybe I can make it nine."

"Nine?" he asked skeptically.

"I never finished the three ones of the other models."

"Why not?"

"I told you, I started on new pieces."

"Christos, what are you doing to me?" he pleaded. "How far are you along on all the unfinished paintings?" He sounded totally exasperated. "Are you going to have any of them done in time?" Now he sounded like a disappointed parent.

Poor Brandon. I couldn't blame him. I was fucking everything up and I knew it. I sighed, "The three new ones will definitely be finished. If I hustle, I can get the other three finished too."

"You've only got a few weeks to do it, Christos. Is that going to be enough time?" He said it like he knew it was impossible but he was being too polite to call me on it.

"I hope so," I said quietly.

Brandon eyed me like I'd gone from being his hot property to a thorn in his side in the span of five minutes.

Because I had.

I felt bad. I was taking a huge risk with my new artistic direction. Brandon didn't deserve the stress I was piling on him. Despite the fact he annoyed me at times, he'd always been good to me and my family over the years, and he'd been counting on me to deliver a certain amount of work in a certain amount of time. Now I was blowing my deadline. But what the fuck. I didn't want to spend the rest of my life painting for other people.

I thought the whole point of this artist thing was to do what you wanted?

Fuck.

Maybe I was being a bit too narrow minded in my view of things.

===

SAMANTHA

Madison and Jake had already gone home from the gallery

because they were getting up early to surf in the morning. Romeo was chatting with Dillon and Kamiko out back in the sculpture garden. Now that Kamiko's painting had sold, she was ready to relax.

I wandered around in the main gallery, still entranced by all the art. It blew my mind that so many people had sold paintings tonight. Most of them were inexpensive by gallery standards, ranging between $500 and $3,000. That meant Kamiko's had been one of the higher priced pieces to sell. I was so proud of her.

Maybe one day, I'd sell a painting for a thousand dollars.

Out the corner of my eye, I noticed Tiffany stumble toward the entrance. She looked totally drunk. I think she was leaving, but she was in no shape to drive.

I ambled toward the doorway as she left, watching her sway onto the sidewalk outside. Maybe she would wrap her car around a telephone pole on her way home and I wouldn't have to worry about her getting me kicked out of college at my upcoming SDU tribunal hearing.

I sighed.

As much as I hated Tiffany, I couldn't let her drive home totally drunk.

Then I noticed her stumble into a guy smoking a cigarette outside. He wore a tattered leather jacket and was leaning against a parking meter. She leaned into him and clutched the lapels of his jacket. He looked surprised. But then he took a good look at Tiffany and a smile crept across his face. He dropped his cigarette and tamped it out with his boot. I guess Tiffany knew him because he put an arm around her waist and held her up.

There were two young women smoking outside, huddled together and talking to each other. Had the jacket guy been talking to them when Tiffany came outside? I wasn't sure. Odd.

Three guys from inside the gallery walked past me, laughing at something one of them had said as they stepped onto the sidewalk. Jacket guy stared at them. One of the three guys nodded at him and said, "Hey."

Jacket guy nodded back.

"There you are!" Romeo said from behind me. "I've been looking all over for you. I think Dillon and Kamiko needed some private time, so I left them alone in the sculpture garden. Besides, I couldn't take any more cartoon talk. They're *still* talking about Adventure Time. I think Kamiko is in love. Do you want to see if the bar has any booze left?"

"Sure," I said absently as Romeo grabbed my hand and pulled me inside the gallery.

We walked toward the bar. The crowd had thinned substantially. People were heading out the door. It wouldn't take long to get a drink. Not that I was going to have any alcohol. I was the designated driver tonight.

Tiffany.

Jacket guy.

Something about that hadn't looked right.

"I'll be right back, Romeo," I said to him, pulling my hand free from his. I danced past several people strolling casually toward the door.

By the time I was on the sidewalk, I knew something was wrong.

Tiffany and jacket guy were gone.

"Tiffany?"

I whipped my head left and right. I didn't see her. I turned to the two girls still smoking outside. "Did you see which way that girl with the platinum blonde hair and white dress went?"

One of the smoking girls said, "You mean the chick with that guy in the leather jacket?"

"Yes."

"I think they went that way," she pointed with her cigarette.

"Thanks." I took off at a dead run.

Oh my god, Tiffany.

Now that I was thinking about it, Jacket guy had looked a little too mangy to be her type.

"Tiffany!" I shouted.

I passed an alley and stopped. I peered down it into darkness. I didn't see her. And I didn't see anything they could be hiding behind like a dumpster or trashcans or whatever.

I sprinted down the sidewalk until I stopped at a four way intersection. My heart was hammering in my chest. Not from the running, but from the panic machine gunning in my stomach. I looked up and down the cross street. It had lots of bright streetlights in both directions. But straight ahead, the street was dark. I think I saw movement ahead.

Yup.

The small dot of Tiffany's hair and white dress glowed faintly in the moonlight.

"Tiffany!" I shouted. The light was red, but I ran anyway. A car blared its horn and swerved around me. Luckily, it hadn't been going very fast. I dodged clear and crossed to the other side of the street.

I sprinted down the sidewalk, screaming at the top of my lungs, "Tiffany!"

It was definitely jacket guy with her, his arm around her waist. They turned down a street before I caught up.

When I rounded the corner, jacket guy had Tiffany pinned against a brick wall. Her purse was on the ground. Tiffany was pushing at him with limp hands. She was too drunk to fight. She fell down on her knees. Jacket guy grabbed her by the sleeve and I jumped on his back, pounding the back of his head with everything I had. He stood up and stumbled backward, slamming me into the window of a parked car. White lighting shot up and down my back as pain exploded in my body.

I slid down the car. My butt thumped onto the sidewalk.

Jacket guy whirled around, looking surprised. His lips were peeled over crooked clenched teeth. He was hunched over like an animal. He swung his booted foot at my face, but I rolled to the side and scrambled to my feet. His boot clunked into the car door where my face had been, denting it. Then he lunged for me and I raked my nails across his cheek.

"You cut me, bitch!" he shouted.

I saw Damian Wolfram's face fall into place over jacket guy's. Anger blew up inside me like a neutron bomb and my vision went red. I swung my arms at him like helicopter blades, aiming my nails at his eyes. He stumbled back and tripped over Tiffany's legs. I kept swinging my arms. I had no idea what I was doing, but I wasn't going to stop.

My fingers peeled back skin from his other cheek. He scrabbled away like a squirrel on all fours. When he got to his feet, he stopped and glared at me. He touched his bloody cheek and examined the blood that came away on his fingertips.

"I'm going to cut you open, bitch," he said as he pulled a knife out of his pocket. He flicked the serrated blade open with his thumb.

Oh no. I was screwed.

He advanced toward me. If I ran, he would never catch me. But I couldn't leave Tiffany alone with him.

Jacket guy's face was no longer Damian Wolfram's. It was just ugly jacket guy who had fingernail gashes dripping red. I noticed spittle on his lower lip. I became obsessed with that spittle. It was so white in the darkness. I couldn't stop looking at it, I think because I didn't want to think about his knife. I didn't know what to do. Someone was going to get stabbed but I wasn't ready to accept that fact.

He took a step toward me.

Spittle. Spittle. Spittle.

He started to chuckle like a rusty hinge, waving the knife slowly through the air in lazy circles.

His eyes suddenly went wide, drawing my attention to them, breaking the spittle spell.

"You're not cutting anybody," Tiffany said. She was behind me. I turned and saw she sat on the ground, holding a small silver pistol in both hands. She was staring right at jacket guy. "Unless you want me to blow your balls off, asshole."

"Put the gun down," jacket guy said.

"Are you insane, douchebag?" Tiffany sneered. "I'm going to give you to the count of three to run away." Tiffany slurred her words, obviously drunk, but she held the pistol surprisingly steady. "One…"

Jacket guy smiled like a cobra, "You're not going to shoot."

"Two…"

He took a confident step toward Tiffany, "You're too drunk. You'll miss me by a mile."

"I've been taking shooting lessons since I was ten years old, you prick," she chuckled. "Which ball do you want to keep, the right or the left? Ah, fuck it, I'm going to see if I can get both with one bullet." She cocked the gun like they always did in the movies.

Cha-CHAK!

"Three…" Tiffany said.

Jacket guy ran away so fast, he was a blur.

I gulped, and felt my heart slide back down my throat.

"Asshole," Tiffany said as she lowered the gun.

I knelt next to her, my legs quivering like jelly. I couldn't stand up if I wanted to. My stomach was on spin cycle. "Are you okay?"

Tiffany took a good look at me. After a moment, recognition dawned on her face, which soured when she realized it was me. "I'm fine." She carefully eased the hammer thing on the back of the gun. I knew that meant it wasn't about to go off anymore. She slid the gun in her purse with a loud huff. She tried to stand up, but was having trouble.

"Do you need help?" I asked, hands resting on my thighs

"No," she blurted.

I watched her struggle to all fours, but that was as far as she was getting. "Here," I said, and looped my arms around her arms and stood her up.

Tiffany leaned against me.

Adrenalin still flickered in my veins. My hands shook, my knees wobbled, shit, even my hair was tingling. I was surprised I could stand, let alone hold her up too.

"Which way is your car?" I asked.

"I don't know," she slurred, totally frustrated, like I was annoying her.

"Oh my god! Sam!" Romeo squeaked behind me. "What the hell happened?"

I turned Tiffany and myself around to face him.

"What the hells bells?" Romeo gawked. "Are you and Tiffany scissor sisters?"

"Yes, Romeo," I said sarcastically. "We were just about to flick each other's beans for awhile before locking crotches."

"Can I watch?" he asked innocently.

I frowned. "I thought you were gay?"

"But this is a historic event," he said, "and someone is going to have to document it. You'll need proof. Otherwise, no one will ever believe it." He pulled out his cell phone. "I'm totally taking a picture of you two."

"Can I shoot him?" Tiffany asked.

"Please," I giggled. It only took about three seconds for my giggles to turn into tears of relief.

Chapter 25

SAMANTHA

Two of my fingernails still hadn't grown completely back after I'd ripped them down to the quick the night I'd saved Tiffany. They had throbbed like crazy for days.

But now, they were a minor nuisance.

I sat in a row of chairs in a hallway on the second floor of the History and Social Sciences building, which was near the Dean's office, awaiting my SDU tribunal hearing for supposedly stealing Tiffany's credit card months ago.

I wore the same outfit I'd worn to court the day Christos had been on trial. Black blazer, gray pencil skirt, white blouse, black hose, and black pumps. My makeup was light, just enough to look professional.

The outfit seemed appropriate because now I was the one about to be on trial.

A woman wearing a frumpy business suit opened one of the doors off the hallway and leaned out. "You can come in now," she said.

She held the door for me as I walked into a conference room. At the far end of the big wooden conference table, Dean Livingston sat at the head, wearing a suit, flanked by an older woman and a middle aged guy. Both wore suits and I assumed they were SDU administrators. Tiffany sat near them, a few seats down. Mr. Selfridge, my old boss from the museum, sat across from Tiffany. With any luck, he would be able to say something that helped my case. The woman who had let me in sat near the door, behind a laptop set up on the conference table.

I nodded at Mr. Selfridge and smiled at him.

He smiled back.

I wasn't entirely sure where I was supposed to sit. But nobody seemed to be telling me where to go, so I chose a seat closer to the door, not wanting to get too close to Tiffany. Also, If I needed to beat a hasty retreat, I could slip out the door with no one noticing. Not.

At least this wasn't an actual courtroom with the armed bailiff and the jury and the defense tables and all the rules. Knowing that I had a slight degree of control over things today eased my nerves slightly. It's not like I would get hauled away in handcuffs if things went badly.

I set my coffee on the table and my book bag on the floor. There was no way I could get through this morning massacre without caffeine. I debated pulling my laptop out, but it's not like I had case files to review, or whatever. All I was going to do was tell them what I knew, which wasn't much, and hope they believed me.

I wished Christos had been here to hold my hand, but he had too much work to do on his paintings. It wasn't like I would end up in jail if things went badly today. If I ended up getting kicked out of SDU, I'd see Christos every single day.

But I really, really hoped to avoid getting expelled. I'd worked too hard to throw it all away now. I didn't want to stop taking more awesome art classes and seeing my friends every day. Because I knew if I got kicked out, no matter what anybody said, I would see a lot less of Madison, Romeo, and Kamiko.

Sigh.

Dean Livingston mumbled back and forth with the two administrators sitting beside him, then he turned to me, "Thank you for your patience, Miss Smith. I think we're ready to begin?" He raised his eyebrows and glanced at everyone.

Nobody objected.

Dean Livingston folded his fingers on the files laying on the table in front of him. "As you know, Miss Smith," he nodded at me, "the reason we're here today is because Miss Kingston-Whitehouse has accused you of theft. Theft of her credit card, to be exact, while she was a visiting patron of the Eleanor M. Westbrook art museum, where you worked at the time."

I wanted to say "I object!" but I wasn't a lawyer and this wasn't a courtroom. I knew enough to keep my mouth shut until they told me it was my turn to talk. Only then would I dive over the table and throttle Tiffany by the neck while demanding she tell the truth.

The Dean turned to Mr. Selfridge and said, "Mr. Selfridge would like to say a few words on your behalf, Miss Smith."

I hadn't expected that. I hoped he didn't bad mouth me.

Mr. Selfridge stood up and smoothed his jacket. He clasped his hands in front of his waist and smiled at me. "Although I only had the pleasure of working with Miss Smith for a few short months, in that time I found her to be a diligent, hard working, forthright young woman. She always did her job, and did it well, was always pleasant with the visiting patrons, was never impatient, and she was always responsible." He smiled at me before turning to the administrators. "I trusted Samantha implicitly, and had no concerns about leaving her in charge of the museum when I needed to step out for errands."

Dean Livingston glanced up at Mr. Selfridge and said, "It is my understanding that you weren't present at the time of the theft?"

"No," Mr. Selfridge said apologetically, "I was in a meeting with the Provost of Adams College at the time. You know how Bill is about his meetings," Mr Selfridge grinned.

The Dean smiled at him, "Yes I do." Then his smile faded. "But you weren't at the museum at the time of the incident?"

"Regrettably, no," Mr. Selfridge said. "I was only present afterward, when Miss Kingston-Whitehouse returned for her credit card."

The Dean nodded, as did the two administrators flanking him. The woman administrator shot me a quick glance. I gave her my best smile, trying to look innocent and pleasant.

She looked away. Had she already decided I was a guilty liar? I hoped not.

The Dean glanced at the papers in front of him and said, "Mr. Selfridge, am I correct in saying that you saw Miss Smith remove the stolen credit card from her wallet?"

"Yes."

"But you never saw how it got there?"

"No."

"Thank you, Mr. Selfridge," the Dean finished. "You can sit down."

Mr. Selfridge sat down and tossed a nervous smile in my direction.

I smiled back genuinely. He'd tried. I mean, what else could he say? He hadn't seen how the card had gotten into my wallet. Heck, I'd been in the restroom when it had happened. For all I knew, Tiffany had hired ninjas to sneak into the museum and put it there.

It occurred to me at that moment that being in the restroom was possibly the worst alibi of all time. How was I supposed to prove it? Fish my old tampon out of the sewer somewhere and have it carbon dated to the time I'd used the ladies room? Yeah, right.

I had nothing.

"Miss Kingston-Whitehouse," the Dean said, "Can we hear your version of events?"

Tiffany stood up to speak. She wore a sexy silver pencil skirt and a fitted lilac colored blouse that was only buttoned halfway up her cleavage. Her blonde hair wafted across her bosom. She looked ridiculously hot. I guess it was fitting. When the Queen shouted from her throne, "Off with her head!" she usually wore a fancy outfit.

The Dean, Mr. Selfridge, and the other male administrator looked hypnotized by Tiffany's beauty. The woman administrator, rather than being catty, seemed similarly entranced.

Wasn't it a fact that people tended to trust attractive people more than unattractive ones?

Even when it was a stranger?

If that was true, Tiffany was so beautiful in this moment that the administrators were going to believe every word she said. When I got up to speak, the Dean would already have a noose in his hands, and he'd be fingering the knots in preparation for my hanging. The guy next to him would be loading a rifle for my firing squad, and the woman administrator would be drawing poison into a syringe so she could give me a lethal injection right here on the spot.

Tiffany made a show of smoothing her skirt.

I had no idea what she was going to say. Maybe, just maybe, she might tell the truth. Naw. Who was I kidding? This was Tiffany Kingston-Whitehouse. All she did in life was get her way. Oh well. Even if I got kicked out of SDU, she couldn't take Christos away from me, and she couldn't stop me from studying art.

Whatever.

Tiffany nodded at the Dean, "Dean Livingston, I don't know where to begin."

I did. How about the truth?

"You see…" Tiffany said nervously.

She better be nervous. When I lied through my teeth, I usually was.

"Um…" Tiffany stammered, "this has all been a big misunderstanding. I, uh, well…I sort of put my credit card in Samantha's wallet myself."

I think I actually heard wet popping noises as everyone's eyes jumped out of their eye sockets. That was of course ridiculous. Because I needed to get my ears checked. There was no way I'd heard Tiffany just say what I thought she'd said.

Tiffany looked very nervous while the administrators gaped at her.

"Come again?" the Dean said.

"I put my credit card in her wallet…" Tiffany said, "…as a, uh, prank. I don't know why. It was a stupid thing to do. And I let her get in trouble." Tiffany turned to me, a pained look on her face. "I'm really sorry, Samantha. I was a total jerk for doing that." She turned to the administrators. "I know, I'm probably in big trouble now. That's fine. I'll accept whatever you guys decide to do." She sat back down.

The Dean and the two administrators muttered back and forth. I couldn't make out what they were saying because they sat so far away, but I could see them raising their eyebrows in disbelief.

I was as surprised as they were.

Wow, when Tiffany had stood up to speak two minutes ago, I had thought her hypnotizing beauty had been nothing but a devilish ruse covering her rotten core. I was wrong. It had been a reflection of her change of heart about me.

It turned out Tiffany Kingston-Whitehouse was full of surprises, not shit, like I'd feared.

Wow.

I learned something new today.

People changed.

Even hateful bitches.

===

There was another Wombat staff meeting at Toasted Roast that afternoon. Justin had emailed everyone two days ago and said he was going to announce the winner of the campus-wide vote off between my drawing and Tammy Lemons' for the new Wombat mascot today. I couldn't wait to find out the results.

Was it possible for lightning to strike twice in one day? I crossed my fingers.

I met up with Romeo in front of the Main Library before going to the Student Center.

"Wow, Sam!" Romeo squeed, "you look hot as hell!"

I still wore my sexy outfit from the tribunal hearing.

"Do you have a job interview?" he asked enthusiastically. "Or are you going to walk into some corporate boardroom and wow a bunch of executives who make decisions that shape the world?"

"Stop, Romeo," I giggled. "I had to wear it for my tribunal hearing."

"How'd that go?" he asked, suddenly serious.

"Tiffany admitted to putting her card in my wallet. She said it was just a prank."

"What?" Romeo gaped. "You're totally lying."

"No, I'm serious."

"Seriously *hot*," Justin Tomlinson said suggestively, walking toward us from across the wide bridge that led back toward the Main Library. "You're dressed to kill today, Samantha." He looked me up and down.

"Yeah," Romeo grinned, "she has an automatic with a silencer in her book bag and she's going to use it later to assassinate some head of state after giving head to his state."

"Romeo!" I chastised.

"What?" Romeo asked defensively. "No head of state would ever let you get close enough to assassinate him without seducing him first. Don't you watch spy movies?"

I leaned toward Romeo and made a big show of staring into one of his ears.

"What are you doing, Sam?" he blurted, pulling away.

"I'm trying to see into that brain of yours so I can see all the crazy ideas floating around inside. It's probably more fun than an amusement park in there," I giggled. I leaned toward him again, peering intently.

Romeo swatted both hands at me repeatedly like a kitten at play. "Enough! They're my ideas, and I charge admission!" He started laughing, still flailing with his hands.

I backed away before I got slapped, "I was wrong. It was just earwax."

Justin crinkled his nose and laughed at us, looking super cute. "You guys are certifiably cray cray," he laughed.

"Totally," I said, smiling at Justin. I noticed his eyes twinkling at me. Yeah, he pretty much looked like he belonged on the cover of a teeny bopper magazine. But in a twenty year old sort of way that was swoony to all women under the age of forty.

Before I could look away, Justin turned to Romeo, his eyes still twinkling, and said, "Romeo, let me know what you charge for admission. I'd pay to see the crazy factory inside your head. Is there any way we can bottle it for The Wombat?"

"There is. I've been working with Willy Wonka, you know, the guy with the Chocolate Factory, to formulate a secret recipe. But we haven't yet decided on whether to distill my genius into hard candies or chocolate bars."

"I vote for hard candies," Justin smiled, "they last longer and cost less."

"Yes," Romeo said seriously, "but, like an evil villain, my only goal is to fleece children of their allowances worldwide, so as to pad my own coffers." He broke into a smile.

Justin was still smiling at him. "How do you do it?" he marveled. "You always have more ideas." Justin leaned toward Romeo, sort of like I had earlier. But sort of not.

"What are you doing?" Romeo asked nervously, leaning away.

Justin beamed a smile at him. "I don't believe Samantha when she said all she saw was earwax."

"Uh, okay?" Romeo said uncertainly.

Justin grinned awkwardly and suddenly backed off, "It's probably just earwax. Anyway, we should get to the Toasted Roast. It's time for the staff meeting."

Justin started walking toward the Student Center. Romeo and I followed.

We found Keith, Micah, Alyssa, and Tammy already sitting at two tables pushed together in the quad outside Toasted Roast.

"Hey, guys," Justin said, sitting down.

Romeo and I found chairs.

"Believe it or not," Justin said, "we got almost six thousand votes about the new Wombat mascot."

"Wow," Alyssa said.

"Shit," Keith said, "and I didn't think anybody read The Wombat anymore."

"We're fucking trend setters," Micah said. "Of course they do."

"What were the results already?" Tammy Lemons demanded.

Justin pulled a sheet of paper out of his book bag. It showed a screen grab printout of the poll results.

"It was a close race," Justin said. "3,277 votes for Sam, 2,649 for Tammy. Congratulations, Sam! You won! We have our new mascot! Potty the Pot Smoking Wombat!"

"What?" I said. I must have heard him wrong.

"You won, Sam!" Romeo cheered. "You won!" He threw his arms around me and hugged me vigorously.

Justin, Keith, Micah, and Alyssa all clapped, big smiles on their faces.

"Congratulations, Sam!" Alyssa beamed.

"Potty for President" Micah said, pumping his fist.

"Now I just have to figure out where Potty buys his cheeba," Keith grinned. "That blunt of his is humungous."

Micah high fived him and they both snickered like total potheads.

At the end of the table, Tammy Lemons frowned.

"Sorry, Tammy," Justin said.

I felt bad for Tammy. Sort of. But I didn't want to shove it in her face. I'd won! Lightning had struck twice today!

Whoopee!

A smile spread across my face.

I glanced at Justin, expecting to see his twinkling smile.

But his eyes were all over Romeo.

What the what?

How had I not noticed before?

===

Romeo walked me to my car in the North Parking lot after The Wombat staff meeting. The sun floated high over the horizon, drenching the sky in warm yellows and oranges. It already felt like summer weather in San Diego even though it was still spring.

"Romeo, I think Justin likes you," I said.

"Yeah, and he likes you too," Romeo said. "So?"

"No, I mean, *like* likes."

Romeo scoffed and shook his head, "No way, Justin isn't gay. I would've noticed."

"That's what I thought. But, I don't know, maybe it's because we were both nervous getting to know everyone at the staff meetings. And you were always focused on trying to come up with funny ideas to impress everyone. I know how you are. You totally get carried away when you're on a roll."

Romeo nodded thoughtfully. "Well, don't you think you would've noticed he was gay by now?"

"Maybe. But, Romeo, you exude so much gayness at all times that it scrambles everyone's gaydar."

Romeo raised an eyebrow, "You have a point there."

"So maybe you should ask him out?"

Romeo chuckled, "Why would I do that?"

"Because, for all your enthusiasm for the male of the species, I've never seen you on a date with man nor beast."

"I've been on some pretty hairy dates with some men who may have been beasts. Rawr!" Romeo quipped.

I stopped walking and narrowed my eyes at him. "When?"

"Whenever," he dismissed and kept walking toward the parking lot. "When am I *not* out on a date?"

I jogged to catch up to him. "Slow down! I'm in heels!"

He slowed until I caught up.

"Come on, Romeo. Don't you think you would've introduced me to one of your dates by now? I've known you for nine months!"

"I like to keep my personal life personal," he said while walking. "Besides, I never date anyone for very long."

I got the sense Romeo was trying to escape. I grabbed his arm and stopped him again. "How long?" I asked.

"What?"

"How long do you date them for?" I demanded.

Romeo rolled his eyes desperately and gave me a pleading look. I'd never seen him look so genuinely nervous before.

I leveled a gaze at him, but he was avoiding my eyes.

"You need to ask Justin out," I said.

He suddenly goggled at me like I was insane. "I can't ask Justin out!"

"Fine. I'll ask him out for you."

"This isn't high school, Sam," he said like he was parenting me. "I can ask him out myself. If I wanted to."

"So, why don't you? He's totally cute. And he couldn't stop staring at you during the staff meeting just now. And he loves your sense of humor. Seems like a good match to me."

Romeo rolled his eyes. "So what? You know I'm totally gayballs for Christos. I'm saving myself for him." His usual sarcasm was back.

"Romeo, you were also gayballs for Hunter Blakeley. And how did that turn out?"

"Perfectly! Christos saved me from him! I practically swooned on the spot when he tripped Hunter that day after sculpting class!"

I wasn't buying it. It was all the exclamation points Romeo was using. I knew a thing or two about them myself.

I rolled my eyes. "I think you're scared, Romeo. Justin is obviously into you. Unlike Hunter, who is straight. After today's meeting, and that weird moment when he tried to look into your ear in front of the Main Library, he's obviously gay."

Romeo flinched when I mentioned the library moment.

"And," I continued, "I get the sense Justin is available. I think it scares you."

Romeo cringed.

"Romeo, are you consciously trying to avoid dating a nice guy like Justin? Or is it out of habit?"

Romeo smiled and shrugged his shoulders squeamishly.

I nodded and folded my arms across my chest, "That's what I thought. You're all gay talk without the rainbow walk."

Romeo glanced around, making sure no one was listening to what he was about to say. A few random students walked here and there, but no one was closer than fifty feet away.

In a low, embarrassed voice, Romeo mumbled, "I may talk like I'm 50 Shades of Cray when it comes to living gay, Samantha, but it doesn't mean I have any practical experience when it comes to the ways of love."

I shook my head, "Wait, what? What are you talking about, Romeo? I thought you went to Hillcrest all the time to cruise for guys."

Romeo waved his hand dismissively, "I was just going down to the Old Globe."

"What's the Old Globe? A gay bar?"

"No," he smiled, "it's the classic Shakespearean theater in

Balboa Park. Theater in the round, outside under the stars. You should totally go some time if you want to see how Shakespeare was performed back in his day. Anyway, I help with the costumes and work as an usher when they have shows."

"So you don't go down to the Brass Rail to meet guys for vomit sex?"

He shook his head. "You have to be twenty-one to get into the Rail. It's a regular bar that serves alcohol."

I couldn't believe my ears. "And you're not hooking up with a new gay guy every weekend, or whatever?"

He shook his head again, "I haven't even been out on a date before. Well, I took Kamiko to our Senior prom, but that wasn't really a date."

"You took Kamiko to prom?" I gasped.

"Yeah, we had a blast. But it was all for fun. We went as friends. No boning after," he grinned.

"So you've never been on a real date?"

"Nope."

"With neither man nor beast?"

"Not even yaks. I swear. I've never been on a date with anyone."

His mention of yaks brought a smile to my face. Yak sodomites...that had been last year when he'd said it to bring me out of my emotional distress over Christos. Wow, my life had been as exciting as that amusement park inside Romeo's head ever since I'd started at SDU.

"Wow, Romeo," I sighed. "I'm totally surprised."

"Me too. It's pathetic actually. Don't tell anyone. Even Kamiko doesn't know. I tell her all those stories about cruising for men in Hillcrest so she won't bug me about meeting someone." He raised his eyebrows expectantly.

"Point taken," I said. "I'll stop bugging you about Justin."

"Thank you. When I'm ready to date, I will. For now, I think I just like hanging out with you and the gang." He wrapped one arm around my neck and tried to give me a noogie on top of my head.

"Stop, Romeo!" I cackled, pulling away. "You're going to mess up my hair!"

He was laughing, but he let go and smiled at me. "Come on, Sam. Let's get you to your car. I think you have some good news to share with Christos, right?"

I smiled at him. "Totally."

"And don't tell anyone about my dirty little secret."

I crossed my heart. "I won't. To me, you'll always be the gayest gay on the planet."

"And you'll be the faggiest hag of all time," he grinned.

We laughed together as we walked to my VW.

Chapter 26

SAMANTHA

Finals week breezed by. I felt good going into my exams. Ever since Nikolos had hired me to help out in his studio, my life had balanced out better than I ever could've imagined.

When my third tuition payment for Spring Quarter had come due last month, Nikolos had insisted on loaning me the money. He said I could work full time during the summer. I wasn't going to argue with him. I spent half the time at his studio watching him paint anyway. I'd learned a ton already.

I didn't tell Nikolos that even if I worked full time all summer, I wouldn't have any money left over to cover tuition payments in the fall, not after paying him back the money I owed him already.

I had no idea if my parents planned on signing my loan papers for next year or not. They were busy sweeping up the pieces of their broken marriage. I hadn't heard much from them lately, but what was there for them to tell me? They were splitting up. So? Half the kids in America had already been through it. Whatever. I'd deal. And I'd figure out how to pay for next year's tuition when the bills came due.

On Thursday of finals week, I walked into the lecture hall for American History 3. It was packed full of students anxious to start the test and get it over with.

I knew I had A's in Plein Air Painting and Drawing the Costumed Figure from talking to my professors during office hours. And I suspected I would get an A or a B in Sociology 3 based on how well my final had gone. American History was the last hurdle before my first year in college was officially over!

When I flipped through the questions on the exam sheet, I felt a surge of confidence. I knew exactly what to write for my essay answers. My hours of cramming had paid off.

After only two hours, with an hour to spare, I closed my blue book with a smile. I knew I'd aced it. I strolled down to the bottom of the lecture hall and dropped my blue book on the small pile that had already formed on the table in front of the chalk board.

I couldn't help myself. I had to do a happy dance. I squealed no louder than a mouse as I twirled around once before getting a hold of myself. I'm sure the students still writing wanted to concentrate.

The T.A. sitting behind the table smiled at me.

I smiled back before turning and walking up the stairs.

I grinned from ear to ear as I walked outside. The weather was absolutely perfect. The sun was high in the sky. It was probably seventy-five degrees. I wore shorts and a T shirt over my bikini top. Madison and I had been going to the beach every chance we got since the beginning of May.

I was tan from head to toe.

Welcome back to My Beach Life, set in San Diego, California, my favorite place on the planet! I was never going back to dreary Washington D.C.

I jumped in the air and screamed for joy. I was so excited! I'd made it through my first year in college!

"Hey, crazy girl," Christos said, walking out of the shade beneath a tree beside the entrance to the lecture hall.

"Christos!" I jumped into his arms.

The last time Christos had been waiting for me outside of a final exam had been last December. At the time, I'd thought we were broken up. After Damian Wolfram, I thought I'd never find true love. How wrong I had been.

Christos gave my butt a good squeeze while he kissed me briefly. "How'd you do, *agápi mou*?" he asked, setting me back on the ground.

"Great! I totally aced my final!"

"I think we need to celebrate," he said, flashing his dimpled grin.

"Hells yeah!" I cheered. "What did you have in mind?"

He opened his mouth to speak and his cell phone rang. "Hold on a second," he smiled, fishing his phone out of his pocket. He looked at the screen. "I need to take this call." He suddenly looked nervous.

"Okay," I said hesitantly. His nervousness was catching. So

much for celebrating.

Christos held the phone to his ear and said, "Hey!" as he walked toward the lawn across from the lecture hall. He obviously wanted privacy.

Not this again.

I was determined not to feel deflated, no matter what bad news he might have after he hung up.

Crap.

I looked skyward and started searching for silver linings. The blue sky was flawless and empty of all clouds. The only cloud in the area was the dark one inside Christos' stupid phone.

I wanted to break that stupid thing.

===

CHRISTOS

"Russell!" I said as I answered the phone, trying to sound casual. "What up?"

Russell Merriweather chuckled on the other end of the line before he said a word. It was always good to hear from him, no matter what the news. "Christos, my boy, how have you been?"

"Awesome," I said, grinning.

"Any more fights?"

"Not lately," I chuckled. "But I seem to remember you saying something about being able to kick my ass. When are you going to back that shit up in the ring?" I was grinning as I said it.

He laughed, "You don't want to mess with me, son. You know I throw bricks when I put the gloves on. I'll break your face."

"Bring your bricks," I snickered. "They'll be powder by the time I'm done hammering your ass."

"Considering that thick head of yours is made of solid rock, you might have a point," he chuckled. "But I suggest we keep your pretty face intact, for the sake of your lady friend Samantha. I like her a lot."

"Yeah, she's awesome," I smiled. "So, what's up? I know you didn't just call to harass my ass."

"Yeah, yeah," Russell sighed. "I wanted to get you up to speed on the civil suit that your pal Hunter Blakeley is still waving over your head."

Shit, I think I'd blocked it completely out of my mind. I'd been too busy with a thousand other things to give a shit about Hunter Fucking Blakeley and the bloody nose I gave him months ago. Besides, Russell was on top of things and I trusted him to handle it.

"And?" I prompted.

"And, my people didn't have much luck with the wait staff at Hooters. Those girls remember you and Jake better than they did Hunter Blakeley and his pals. Apparently," he chuckled, "you and Jake are excellent tippers."

"We try," I said dryly.

"And I think one of the waitresses is sweet on you. She remembered exactly who you were. She even had the audacity to ask my guy if she could get your phone number," he laughed. "At any rate, she mentioned she saw you and Jake having drinks with two young women?"

"Oh yeah. They were law students over at USD."

"Anything I should know more about?" Russell asked with a hint of amusement. "It seems like everywhere you go, the ladies throw themselves at you, son."

"What can I say?" I grinned. "But no, they were gone before Hunter showed up."

"Also," Russell continued, "I've had a chance to go over the statements from Hunter Blakeley and his three friends in detail. They are all very similar, and they all point to you being the aggressor in the fight. As things stand right now, it doesn't look good. I had my people check every nearby bank security camera, traffic camera, convenience store camera, everything we could think of. Nothing is on video. All we have is the word of Hunter and his friends against you and Jake, who, by the way, is a fine young man. After I had Jake come to my office to give his deposition. Rhonda and Brianna couldn't stop talking about him when he was gone. Those two were drooling over him so badly they needed bibs," Russell chuckled.

I blurted a laugh, "That's my boy. Yeah, Jake is awesome," I shook my head, smiling at the thought. Then I sighed. Back to business. "So, where are we at?"

"Where we're at is that your court date is in a couple weeks. I don't think there's much else I can do besides spend more of your money chasing dead ends. All we can do now is hope that by virtue of some miracle, we can hold our ground in court. I suggest you start practicing your sad eyes for the jury. I want them looking at you like you're Tiny Tim in A Christmas Carol."

"God bless us, everyone," I muttered.

"That's the spirit," Russell said. "I'll do what I can, Christos. But there are no guarantees. I'll be honest with you. This feels like it's going to be a closer race than I'd like."

"Thanks, man."

"We'll be in touch."

I ended the call.

So much for celebrating. I'd do my best to keep a game face on for Samantha. My sad face could wait until court.

===

SAMANTHA

While Christos was on the phone, I grew more nervous by the second. Despite the warm weather, I wrapped my arms around myself to stop from shaking.

When Christos finally hung up and walked toward me, he looked haggard.

"Who was it?" I asked. "Or do I not want to know?" I'd had enough bad news lately. Maybe it could wait.

"I'll tell you, if you want," he sighed.

What was love without a few troubled spots along the way? "I may as well know."

"It was Russell. About the Hunter Blakeley trial."

"Oh."

"It's looking pretty grim," he sighed.

"Oh," I sighed with him. "What does that mean?"

"It means I might owe Hunter a pile of money after the trial is over."

"What's a pile?"

"The last estimate Russell gave me, which was over a month ago, was anywhere between two hundred fifty K and eight hundred."

"What?" I gasped.

He nodded.

"That's absurd! For a broken nose?"

"Hey," Christos chuckled sourly, "they were asking for more before. Russell has been negotiating with Hunter's attorney since this started. Russell is trying to settle out of court, have me only pay for Hunter's medical bills, which are minor, and save everyone a bunch of time and money. Because, let's face it, I hit the guy. Too bad Hunter and his attorney haven't accepted any of our offers. I suspect someone working for Hunter's attorney did some digging and found out my family has more than a few dollars to our name."

That was an understatement. Between Spiridon and Nikolos, the Manos family had mountains of money.

Christos continued, "I'm sure Hunter's attorney would like to take a big bite out of the Manos financial pie. He's probably thinking he can get to my dad's cash through me. That's never gonna happen," he said confidently.

But I could tell a vein of nervousness pulsed beneath the surface of Christos' bravado. The seriousness of his situation was sinking in. It was possible that he would lose in court this time. There wasn't a secret surprise witness like me to save the day. All the facts were on the table, as far as I knew. And I didn't think Christos was holding anything back this time. He might very well lose his case and end up owing Hunter a huge sum of money that I couldn't even imagine. Christos had said on the low end, it would be $250,000. Gulp. Who had that kind of money? I said, "Can you afford $250,000, or whatever, if things don't go well in court?"

Christos shook his head, "Not even close."

"Can you ask your dad for the money?" I asked tentatively. "I mean, if you had to?"

He rolled his eyes. "No. That would be playing into Hunter and his attorney's hands. My dad isn't a part of this."

How lame was it that both of us were having money troubles at the same time?

"If I end up having to pay out," Christos said, "I'll figure it out myself," he said grimly, a far away look in his eyes.

I didn't like the sound of that. If there was one thing I knew about Christos, when he was backed into a corner, he did whatever it took to survive, no matter how crazy dangerous it was.

Whatever it took.

Gulp.

My celebratory mood was officially dead and buried.

"Anyway," Christos said resolutely, "fuck all that shit. Fuck Hunter. It's time to celebrate!" His face glowed with a huge smile.

"You finished your first year in college, *agápi mou*! I'm so proud of you!" He squatted down, grabbed me by the hips with both of his big hands, and shot me up into the air like I was weightless. Despite his crippled financial situation, Christos was physically stronger than ever. I caught air before falling back into his arms.

"Christos!" I shrieked. "Put me down!"

He chuckled and set me on my feet before leaning down to kiss me passionately. I circled his neck with my arm and we kissed for a long time under the San Diego sun.

In that moment, my life was perfect.

I hoped it wasn't a temporary thing.

Chapter 27

SAMANTHA

"What do you think?" I asked Madison, Kamiko, and Romeo as I twirled in front of them in my new dress. It was a black asymmetrical maxi with a slit halfway up my right thigh. It had a blue zippered front and blue straps that crossed in back. I wore blue platform ankle strap sandals to go with.

They all sat on my bed in the Manos house.

My house.

"Wow, Sam," Romeo said, "I'm going straight."

I winked at him.

"I love it, Sam," Kamiko smiled.

"I'm with Romeo," Madison said. "Let's have a four way with Sam because she's so damn hot."

I grinned at them. "You guys are the best. Are we ready to go?"

"Ready when you are," Kamiko said.

They were all dressed up too. Christos had given me instructions that everyone had to wear black tie tonight at his gallery opening, including black dresses on the women. I hadn't seen any of his new paintings because he said they were top secret. I still hadn't seen the portrait he'd done of me. I was excited to finally see it.

Madison and Kamiko wore sexy black dresses. Romeo wore a black double breasted suit coat with tails. He also had a high white Victorian collar, a black top hat, and his monocle. It wasn't a tux, but he certainly looked formal enough.

I giggled, "We make those girls on Sex and the City look like fashion disasters."

We all high fived and headed downstairs to my VW. Spiridon was already at the gallery, otherwise I would've asked him to drive us in his Woody station wagon so we could arrive in style.

Next time.

When we walked into Charboneau Gallery in La Jolla, it was a much different atmosphere than the Contemporary Artists Show a month ago. It was still early, and no guests had arrived yet.

Standing right inside the glass front doors was a huge brass easel with a large card that read simply, "Manos."

Everything in the room was done in black or silver. It instantly felt more upscale than Christos' previous solo show. Waiters in black with long black ankle length aprons were busy setting things up.

The string quartet from Christos' solo show was nowhere in sight. Instead, a DJ was already behind a mixing board, playing mellow ambient dubstep soundscapes. Much hipper than a bunch of guys with violins.

The room was filled with little round cocktail tables covered in black tablecloths. The center piece on each table was an elegant black and silver metal sculpture.

Dozens of delicate silver mobiles hung from the ceiling, rotating languorously in the slight breeze coming through the front doors. The mobiles consisted of swirling shapes of metal that seemed to fold in on each other in infinite spirals. They were beautiful.

Black silk streamers draped down from the center of the ceiling, curving toward the corners of the gallery. Each painting along the walls was covered by a sheet of black silk. The gallery was filled with them.

I paused. I didn't remember so many paintings around the studio at home. Were all the covered paintings painted by Christos? That seemed unlikely, but where had they all come from? Was I missing something?

"What up, C-Man!" Romeo said.

"Hey guys," Christos smiled as he came walking up, wearing a short sleeve black shirt and tight black jeans over his boots. His muscled arms and razored tattoos were the first thing I noticed. Then I noticed his incredibly handsome face and stunning blue eyes.

"Your tattoos are showing!" I blurted. "I thought you had to keep them covered so you didn't offend potential buyers who are too conservative?"

"That was the old me," Christos said. "That was Brandon's idea. This is my show now. I'm introducing my art to the world, my way."

"I like," I said, looking around. "Why are all the paintings covered?"

"There's going to be an unveiling at eight o'clock."

"That's awesome!" Kamiko said. "I love a bit of mystery."

"How come everything is in black and silver?" Madison asked.

"So the only color in the room is in the paintings on the wall," Christos said.

"Smart," Madison winked.

"Where's Jake?" Christos asked.

"He's coming later. He's still surfing up at Trestles. He'll be late," she grinned.

"*Samoula!*" Spiridon said as he walked toward us. "So glad you're here. We couldn't have a Manos family event without you." He wrapped his arms around me in a huge hug.

After the hug, Spiridon said hello to the rest of the gang.

"Holy shit!" Romeo blurted, looking behind me. "There's three of them!"

Nikolos came walking up behind me.

"Everyone," Spiridon said, "this is my son, Nikolos Manos. Christos' father."

Romeo's eyes were bugging out. He turned to me and whisper wheezed, "He's so hot, Sam!" I think Romeo was about to cry with joy. I couldn't blame him. Nikolos was a slightly older, equally hot version of his son.

Nikolos chuckled at Romeo, "You must be Romeo. I've heard all about you," he grinned while shaking Romeo's hand.

Romeo appeared ready to faint. After the handshake, he squeed, "I'm never washing this hand again!"

"Just don't use it to wipe, and you'll be okay," Nikolos chuckled. "If you ever do end up wiping with it, don't eat with it." He winked at Romeo.

No one had been expecting such a dirty joke to come out of the mouth of someone who was all our parents' ages, so everybody busted up laughing, even Spiridon.

===

Over the next few hours, people filed into Charboneau Gallery until the place was packed. Everyone wore tuxedos and black dresses. A lot of them were older, some of whom I recognized from

Christos' solo show last year, including rich Mrs. Moorhouse.

Christos' attorney Russell Merriweather showed up and he chatted with Spiridon and Nikolos like they were old pals. Probably because they were.

As we neared the official start time of the show, Christos pointed to one couple walking into the gallery. A beautiful middle aged blonde woman and a handsome salt and pepper haired man. "Guess who that is," Christos said.

"I don't know, the Prince of Monaco and Grace Kelly?"

"Nope," he chuckled, "Close. That's Westin-Conrad Kingston-Whitehouse and Gwendolyn Kingston-Whitehouse. Tiffany's parents."

I frowned, "How many names does her dad have?"

"At least thirty," Christos chuckled.

"I can see where Tiffany gets her beauty. Her mom is gorgeous. Although she looks a bit...severe."

"That's an understatement," Christos smirked.

"Really? How?"

"You don't want to know."

"Oh, come on. Now I *have* to know," I begged.

"Do you have about four hours? I can't even begin to do justice to all the shit I could tell you about the Kingston-Whitehouses in any less time."

I bugged my eyes, "Wow. Is it that bad?"

"That family is a prime time soap opera," Christos said. He almost sounded, I don't know, sad? He had known Tiffany for years. I'm sure he would fill me in some other time.

"I have to go say hi to them," Christos said. "Care to join me?"

I said sarcastically, "I'll let you handle that. Tiffany's mom scares me."

"You and me both," Christos said over his shoulder as he walked toward them. He talked to them for a bit before greeting other guests.

I hung out with Madison, Romeo and Kamiko near the door. A short while later, Jake came walking in.

"What the fuck are you wearing, Jake?" Madison demanded, her brows knit together.

Jake wore one of those black T shirts with a tuxedo silk-screened on the front in white. At least his shirt was long sleeved and hugged his tan, muscled body flatteringly. He also wore black jeans and black Vans tennis shoes. His blond hair was golden and naturally feathered and weathered. It draped across his forehead in this way that probably made anything with a double X chromosome want to run their fingers through it.

"I don't have a tux," Jake hissed apologetically. He thrust his hands into his pockets. He looked like a giant kid out of his element.

Madison rolled her eyes and smiled at him. She tip-toed up to kiss his cheek. "I still love you, you big surf bum."

The lights overhead faded down suddenly and the DJ softened the volume on the dubstep until it was a murmur.

"Good evening, ladies and gentlemen," Brandon said over a microphone from somewhere in the room.

The chatter of conversation around the room quieted. All eyes turned to Brandon, who appeared near the DJ booth. A spotlight shone on him.

"We have a very special event here tonight at Charboneau," Brandon continued, "and I want to welcome everyone to a once in a lifetime experience. This is a first, ladies and gentlemen. You may have noticed that the placard out front read simply, Manos. All of us in the art world know there are three Manos men. How could I, Brandon Charboneau, have made such an oversight?" He paused and smiled expectantly.

The crowd chuckled.

"I assure you, it was no oversight."

I saw Christos, who stood with some of the older patrons, grin and roll his eyes at Brandon.

"Because tonight, ladies and gentlemen," Brandon said mysteriously, "we have all three Manos men in attendance. Spiridon? Nikolos? Christos? Will you please join me?"

The three Manos men worked their way through the crowd into the spotlight next to Brandon while the crowd murmured.

It only took a second before people started clapping. I mean, loudly. Soon, people were cheering. I had never appreciated how famous the Manos men really were until now. But I didn't know then that this was only the tip of the iceberg.

The Manos men now stood beside Brandon. They all smiled and waved, and they all looked so damn handsome and humble. I was truly the luckiest girl in the world to be part of their family. Well, at least an honorary member, since I was only Christos' girlfriend. It's not like I was his wife. But, boy, was I proud of all three of them right now. I started tearing up with joy.

Madison bumped my elbow and whispered, "It's okay, Sam. Let it out."

"I don't want my mascara to run," I sniffled, dabbing the corner of my eye with my pinky.

"Here's a handkerchief," Romeo said, proffering one from his coat pocket, "It's silk. Go ahead," he said affectionately. "I've only blown my nose in it once today," he grinned. "I'm kidding."

I giggled and took it to blot my eyes.

When the applause died down, Brandon said, "Tonight, ladies and gentlemen, not only do we have all three Manos men here in attendance, but we also have their masterful art."

On cue, spotlights came on throughout the gallery, illuminating all of the black silk covered paintings on the walls.

"The Manos family is back!" Brandon cheered over the mic. "Welcome to the first ever showing of the unseen art of Spiridon, Nikolos and Christos Manos!" He was yelling on his final words. He handed the microphone to the DJ so he could clap vigorously.

The entire room joined him.

"Yeah!" Jake shouted.

"Woo hoo!" Madison cheered.

"All right, Christos!" Kamiko clapped.

"I'd do him!" Romeo shouted.

I grimaced and smiled at him. "You are so Romeo, Romeo!"

He grinned wide, "I know, right?"

My friends were awesome. Normally, I wasn't the kind of girl to cheer at social events. But tonight was special. And I couldn't help myself. I cheered away, "Yay, Christos! Woo!!!!"

It didn't take long for the whole room to explode with noise. It was like being at a concert when a famous band came out on stage at the beginning of the show. The room roared with approval and applause.

It was totally overwhelming.

The spotlights still shone on The Manos Men. Christos stepped between Spiridon and Nikolos and put his arms around their necks. They bowed in unison.

After awhile, the cheering faded.

Back on the mic, Brandon said, "Anybody ready to see some art?"

"Yeah!!!" the crowd shouted.

This was hardly what I expected from an art gallery opening. But what did I know? It was frickin' awesome!

The DJ cued up a bumping dubstep track at the exact same moment all of the black silks rippled to the floor beneath each canvas.

The crowd literally gasped.

The room was filled with art. Portraits I'd seen in Nikolos' studio. Landscapes I'd seen in Spiridon's house. And Christos' nudes, and a few other paintings I couldn't see. There was so much to look at.

Everyone gazed around the room, speechless. After a moment, people gravitated toward the paintings and the conversation was soon as loud as the music.

I walked around the room with the gang, looking at all the art. I made comments about the portraits I'd seen Nikolos working on at his house. They all looked amazing and had lots of character. But my favorite was still his portrait of Spiridon, maybe because I knew Spiridon so well and the portrait practically breathed when I looked at it.

As for Spiridon's landscapes, I'd seen some of them before, but not all. In any case, I'd never seen them properly lit in a gallery. They glowed from their frames like portals to another reality. You could feel the breeze on your face or the sun in your eyes. Amazing.

"These paintings are incredible," Kamiko said. "It's almost like I can smell the ocean breeze in Spiridon's art like I'm right there. It's unreal."

"I know, right?" I said, in total agreement.

"She's just smelling my farts," Romeo joked.

"Romeo," Kamiko's face pinched into a grimace, "your farts smell nothing like an ocean breeze. Believe me, I know."

I threw my head back and laughed.

We finally worked our way through the crowd to Christos' paintings. We'd all seen the female nudes before in the studio. But none of the gang had seen the LOVE portrait of me and Christos.

"I can see your boobies!" Romeo said.

I blushed instantly. This is what I was worried about.

"Don't worry, Sam," Madison said. "Half the planet has boobies, and the other half has seen them before."

I rolled my eyes. I hoped nobody recognized me. I'd forgotten to bring a disguise. Oh well. Maybe there was too much chaos in the gallery for anyone to notice I was the naked girl in the life size painting hanging on the wall under a spotlight.

Some older guy beside me in a tux was glancing between my face and the painting, back and forth.

"Yeah," Romeo said to the guy, "that's her."

I rolled my eyes, "Thanks, Romeo," I hissed sarcastically.

"Any time," he giggled.

The older guy said, "It's an amazing likeness. That's Christos with you in the portrait, isn't it?"

I nodded.

"I've never seen an artist do a self portrait with a woman beside him," the man said.

"She's his girlfriend," Romeo said, "That's why the painting is called LOVE."

"That's wonderful," the man smiled, then turned to a woman with silver hair who was obviously his wife. She smiled at me before the two of them examined the portrait in detail.

"Romeo," I asked, "how do you know so much about Christos' paintings?"

Romeo said, "Oh, uh…"

"What the fuck!" Kamiko literally shouted. She was several paces ahead of us. "I can't believe it!"

"What!" Mads said, pulling Jake along as she moved to see what Kamiko was talking about.

I followed them until we all stood before a huge portrait. Of Romeo. Jumping in the air exactly like Mario from Donkey Kong. Romeo was dressed in his traditional black steampunk attire. His monocle hung suspended in the air on the S curve of the monocle string. Romeo too was suspended in mid flight, his arms thrust down with his fingers splayed, his jacket billowing out around him, his knees flung forward and back like he was hurdling over something. He had the largest open mouthed smiled I'd ever seen. The painting was beautiful.

"What's it say on the card?" Kamiko asked. "What's the title?"

Madison leaned down and read it. "It just says, 'Romeo'."

Romeo grinned, "Because that's all it needs to say."

Christos squeezed through the crowd. "What do you think?" he asked me.

"I love it!" I smiled. "When did you do it? I had no idea you were working on this."

He cocked his eyebrow, "Whenever you were working at my dad's house."

"It's so good, Christos," Madison said.

"Thanks," he smiled. "Hey Jake, I'm loving the tux."

Jake glanced down at his T shirt tux. "Seriously?"

Christos gave Jake a thumbs up. 'Only you, bro."

Jake grinned and nodded while they bumped fists.

At that moment, I happened to notice that two paintings between Christos' other paintings still had black silk over them. One of them was really big. "What's up with the two covered paintings?"

"It's a surprise," he flashed his dimpled grin at me.

"Oh really?"

"You're going to love it."

"Like I love the LOVE painting?"

He nodded, "Yeah."

"I can't wait!"

"Well, I've got to keep circling," Christos said. "People are asking questions a mile a minute."

"Okay," I waved as he was swallowed by the crowd.

He wasn't exaggerating. Everyone wanted to talk to him. They all looked up at him with sparkling eyes, in awe of the rockstar artist. I was so proud of him.

===

At one point, the gang had wandered off to look at more art. I stood talking to Spiridon and Nikolos in front of one of Spiridon's large landscapes.

Brandon suddenly squeezed through the crowd and stuck a red dot on the landscape. "Another one sold," he smiled at Spiridon.

"How many is that?" Spiridon asked him.

"Nine, and more on the way," Brandon smiled.

"Hey, Brandon" Nikolos said, "who's selling more, me or dad?"

"Right now, Spiridon has you by two."

Spiridon clapped Nikolos on the back, "I told you I've still got it."

"Yeah," Nikolos said to him, "but Brandon says I'm catching up. Brandon, go sell more of my paintings."

Brandon grinned and shook his head, "They're all selling."

Nikolos chuckled, "Well, just make sure more of mine sell. Can't let the old man show me up."

Spiridon rolled his eyes. "Ahh, youth," he grinned.

"So," Brandon said to Spiridon, "tell me something. I've been trying to get you to sell these landscapes for years." He motioned to the paintings on the walls. "But you said you wouldn't because they meant too much to you. You even turned down Stanford Wentworth's offer for the lot a few months ago. Why'd you change your mind now?"

Spiridon shrugged his shoulders. "You yourself told Christos he needed more paintings on the wall if he wanted a successful show. I wanted my grandson to have a successful show. It's that simple. Seeing him succeed means more to me than keeping these old paintings."

Nikolos nodded agreement. "The more the merrier, right?"

Brandon nodded. "I can't thank you both enough for agreeing to do this. And thank you, Nikolos, for suggesting it. I'm so glad Christos agreed to it. And you, too, Spiridon."

"It's the least we could do," Spiridon said, "for family."

Nikolos nodded.

"Well, thank you," Brandon said. "This is truly a historic event."

"Yes it is," Spiridon said reverently.

Everyone was in such a good mood, it was contagious.

Brandon smiled, "I need to get back to it. People are waiting for me because they want to buy more art," He raised both eyebrows and smiled before withdrawing into the ocean of people in tuxes and black dresses.

I glanced at the placard on Spiridon's painting. The price tag read, $475,000. Jesus Christ, the Manos family made money like crazy when it came to selling their art.

"Where did you paint this one, Spiridon?" I asked, motioning toward the landscape. It was a gorgeous painting of sun breaking through clouds over a huge mountain valley.

"Yosemite," Spiridon said.

"You mean you went back after that deer tried to eat your watercolors?" I quipped.

"You remembered our story about the deer!" Nikolos chuckled.

"Of course I remembered!" I grinned at him. "I remember all your stories. I'm going to write them all down someday," I winked. I looked around for a moment and sighed, overwhelmed by all the excitement and the amazing art. "Wow, you guys," I smiled, "You have so many awesome paintings here tonight. I can't believe it."

Spiridon and Nikolos smiled back at me.

Spiridon shrugged, "It's just art."

"Just art," I scoffed. Maybe they were bored with lavish gallery openings after decades. What did I know?

"Hey," Spiridon said, "remember that show you had in New York? I think it was 1984?"

Nikolos chuckled, "I've tried to block out all of 1984."

"You know the one. The one with the fire?"

Nikolos' eyes widened. "Oh! *That* show."

Spiridon nodded knowingly.

"What happened," I asked, all ears.

Nikolos said, "I got the idea that if I set one of my paintings on fire in the gallery, it would create a real buzz in the art world."

Spiridon grinned, obviously knowing where the story was going.

Nikolos continued, "Too bad the only buzz was when the fire department showed up and kicked everyone out of the gallery."

Spiridon shook his head, smiling.

"Did anyone get hurt?" I asked.

"Just my sales," Nikolos winked.

"So you won't set anything on fire tonight?" I joked.

Nikolos looked at Spiridon, "Have I told you how much I like this girl?" He wrapped an arm around my neck and gave me a friendly hug.

"Nikolos was always about the marketing from the beginning," Spiridon said. "He knew what he was doing, and he wanted to sell paintings. But setting that painting on fire wasn't the only brilliant marketing idea he had, was it, son? Remember that time you covered yourself in paint and rolled around on a canvas in the middle of the gallery opening?"

My eyes widened, "You did that?"

"Yup," Nikolos nodded. "Nude."

"While people watched?" I asked in complete disbelief.

"For a packed house," he said.

"How'd it go over?"

"People loved it." Nikolos made a funny face. "I was so 'experimental'," he made finger quotes, "I was pushing the envelope."

"The only thing he hadn't factored in," Spiridon said conspiratorially, "was how hard it was to get the paint off afterward."

Nikolos squeezed his eyes shut and cackled as he said, "Who knew peeling acrylic paint of your privates would hurt so much!"

"What!" I gasped, covering my mouth.

Nikolos nodded, "But the worst part was getting it out of my hair. I ended up shaving my head *and* my jewels."

My mouth Oed.

"I warned you," Spiridon said affectionately.

Spiridon and Nikolos laughed and shook their heads at the shared memory.

These two were full of endless stories about art adventures.

"So, did you sell your pubic painting to public?" I asked satirically.

Spiridon chuckled, "Pubic painting…"

I winked at him.

"Of course I did," Nikolos scoffed.

"Did the bonus pubic hair up the price?" I asked innocently.

Spiridon and Nikolos chuckled heartily.

"Not that I remember," Nikolos said. "But it should have. That buyer got my DNA. You can't get better authentication than that. Hey, I should use that as a marketing angle."

"What," Spiridon said, "putting your pubic hair in all your paintings?"

"Why not?" Nikolos grinned.

"Know your limits, son," Spiridon smiled smugly, patting him on the shoulder.

"So," I said, "how much did the pubic hair painting sell for?"

"Oh, boy." Nikolos looked thoughtfully at the ceiling, remembering. "I think two twenty five?"

"Dollars?" I asked.

"Thousand," Nikolos chuckled.

"$225,000?" I gasped.

"Yeah," he smiled.

"Wow, when did you do that?"

"Way back in '88, I think. I told you I wanted to forget the eighties," he grinned at Spiridon.

"Come on," Spiridon said enthusiastically, "you were young. You were having fun. In those days, that was all you and Vesile did —" Spiridon suddenly stopped himself, clamping his mouth shut.

Nikolos dropped his chin to his chest and his shoulders sunk.

"I'm sorry, son" Spiridon said to him softly, draping his arm over Nikolos' shoulders.

I wasn't entirely sure why Nikolos was so emotional. But I did know one thing from working with him in his studio all the time. He never talked about his ex-wife, Christos' mom, and I never asked. I really knew hardly anything about her. And from what I could tell, Nikolos didn't date anybody at all. He just painted and spent time with friends and family.

"Are you okay, Nikolos?" I asked, suddenly worried. He seemed really distraught.

Nikolos raised his head and blinked away tears. "It's nothing. I'm okay." He turned his head away, trying to hide the emotion on his face. "Don't worry about it," he said a moment later. "I'll be fine," he sniffed.

Wow, he must have loved Vesile like crazy if he still broke down twelve years after she'd left.

I felt so bad for him.

===

"All right everybody," Brandon said over the microphone. He stood in front of the two paintings still covered in black silk, "There's one more surprise. The final unveiling. I'm sure you're all wondering about the two paintings that are still covered up."

The crowd murmured agreement.

"I'll let Christos fill you in himself." Brandon handed the mic to Christos and stepped out of the spotlight.

Christos had been so busy for the last hour, I hadn't said a single word to him.

"Some of you may know," Christos said to the crowd, "that a very special woman came into my life nine months ago. If you haven't met her, you've already seen her in my painting entitled LOVE. That's me and her, Samantha Smith, together. Samantha, will you come up here?"

Gulp.

Christos shaded his eyes from the spotlight with his hand and searched the crowd for me.

Nervousness suddenly seized me. Did I have to stand in front of everyone? Of course I did. But maybe I wouldn't have to say anything.

"Go, Sam," Madison prodded at my elbow.

"Yeah," Romeo said, pushing my back gently, "get up there."

I didn't have a choice. I made my way through the crowd and stepped into the spotlight. It was really effing bright. I squinted until my eyes adjusted. I hoped nobody was snapping photos. I probably looked terrible.

Christos took my hand and held it in his.

I'd never felt so on the spot in my entire life. Literally.

Christos smiled at me, gazing into my eyes. He said to the mic, "What none of you know is how much Samantha means to me,"

His blue eyes burned into my heart in that moment, in a good way. Oh my god, where was this going?

"Samantha has been an inspiration to me since the day we met," Christos said. "If it wasn't for her, I don't know that I'd be here tonight."

Gulp.

"Samantha saved my life, and for that, I am forever grateful. But more than that, she has been my guide. She has shown me how to embrace myself, to be me. Not someone else. Her courage blows me away every time I think about it. She moved all the way to San Diego from Washington D.C. with the dream of becoming an artist. And she never wavered from it. She stuck to her guns, no matter what challenges life put in her way. She has come so far in such a short time. She has a natural talent for art that I've never seen before. Sadly, for all her hard work, Samantha has never had a painting in a gallery show."

Christos paused while the crowd went "Awww."

He continued, "But she should. She's an amazing artist already, and she's just getting started. So, without further ado, I introduce you all to master artist Samantha Anna Smith."

One of the two remaining black silks dropped to the floor.

I was going to cry all over myself.

It was my phoenix sunset landscape painting I'd done for the Contemporary Artists Show, the one Brandon rejected. I couldn't stop myself. Tears ran down my face.

The whole room clapped. I was overwhelmed by their energy. I leaned into Christos and hugged his chest. I was laughing and crying at the same time. I couldn't believe what was happening. My tears dripped all over his black T shirt. I buried my face in it.

Christos leaned down and whispered in my ear, "You have no idea how much I love you Samantha Anna Smith."

No, I think I did. I sobbed and laughed.

After a minute, he muttered "Are you okay, *agápi mou*?"

"Yeah," I sniffed, "I think I died and went to heaven."

The crowd was starting to make a bunch of noise. Everyone was talking about my painting.

"Hold on," Christos said into the mic. "We have one more surprise. When I saw this painting of Samantha's that you're looking at now, I was blown away by it. She's only been painting in oils for six months, and I think it's fucking incredible."

Several people in the crowd chuckled.

I spontaneously pulled the microphone down to my mouth and said, "I had a lot of good advice from all of the Manos men. I couldn't have done it without a million tips from them."

The crowd chuckled.

"It was all her," Spiridon shouted from the back.

More laughs from the crowd.

"Go, Sam!" Madison shouted.

I think it was Jake next to her who did one of those really loud whistles.

"SAAAMMMM!!!" Romeo squealed. "I want to be your baby daddy!"

I heard Kamiko laughing next to him.

I was going to pass out from happiness in about thirty seconds. I was totally, joyously overwhelmed. I'd never felt so accepted, or so important, in my entire life. It was incredible.

Christos spoke into the mic, "I've been so inspired by Samantha's transformation from a mousy little girl to an amazing artist, I wanted to immortalize the person I know her to be in my final painting of the evening." He motioned to the big painting behind him still covered in black silk. "She has a warrior spirit, and she is indomitable. I wanted to pay tribute to that."

Christos nodded to Brandon and the final black silk fell away.

The crowd gasped and went silent.

It was so quiet, not even the dropping pins made a sound.

I was almost afraid to turn around and look at the painting.

But I did.

Oh, my god.

It was amazing.

It was me, a life size painting of me as a naked angel with wings of fire. It was the most beautiful thing I'd ever seen. I stood in a graceful pose, my arms spread wide to the sides, the pose I'd held in our studio until my neck and shoulders had cramped into knots. The huge angel's wings sprouting out behind me were made of fiery red and gold feathers. I floated in the air above the surface of the earth, which was a wide curve at the bottom of the painting, running from left to right. The purple blackness of space, surrounding the golden orange flames dancing around my legs, held thousands of shining stars.

Christos' portrait of me as a fiery angel had a similar palette of colors to my phoenix sunset. They looked like a matched set. His and hers paintings honoring the energy of creation, done in red jewels and molten gold.

I was overwhelmed. My knees gave out.

But Christos caught me.

He always did.

I was the luckiest girl on the planet.

===

After Christos unveiled his painting of me as the fiery angel, everyone crowded around the two of us. They couldn't get close enough to Christos. Everyone wanted a piece of him. It was kind of scary, actually. It was this weird mob mentality fame thing. I guess this was what being famous was like. It was weird being the center of attention, but with Christos beside me, I was fine.

People were asking both me and Christos tons of questions about the paintings and our relationship. We just answered them as they asked. Everyone was entranced with the idea that we were two painters in love, inspired by each other's creative ideas. I guess maybe I took it for granted. Not in a thoughtless way. I just never really stopped to think about how special what we had really was.

One of the most common comments we heard was about the similarity of color palette and subject matter of our two paintings. When people asked, Christos told everybody casually, "I know genius when I see it. I just took Samantha's idea and ran with it." That was a total exaggeration, but every time he said it, even after the hundredth, I was stunned and flattered and blushed like crazy.

I did so much smiling, my cheeks started to hurt. Was it possible to get cheek muscle cramps? I wouldn't mind if I did. It was worth it. I don't think I'd ever been this completely happy in my entire life.

At some point during the evening, Christos whispered in my ear, "Do you realize we've been standing here talking to people for almost two hours?"

"I know. I totally have to pee," I hissed.

"Keep holding it. It's your job," he winked.

Brandon came walking up to us. "You're never going to believe this." His eyes were on fire with excitement.

"I probably will," Christos said casually.

"Everything has sold."

"You mean all of my paintings?" Christos said uncertainly. "Or all of them?"

Christos had less than ten paintings in the show, so that's probably what Brandon meant. Christos sold more paintings at his solo show last year. But between all the paintings from Spiridon and Nikolos, there were at least sixty or seventy on sale tonight. That was a lot of paintings to sell during a single show.

"No," Brandon said, "Everything has sold. Your father's, your grandfather's, all of it. Well, everything except one."

I could only assume Brandon meant my painting. It was the obvious one not to sell. Spiridon, Nikolos, and Christos were world famous artists with reputations. The Manos family had a painting legacy, and people wanted to buy a piece of their fame to hang on their walls while it appreciated in value. I was just the girlfriend. I doubted anyone actually wanted my painting. Sure, it made for a good story to go with Christos' life sized portrait of me, but that was all.

"Which one hasn't sold?" Christos asked.

I grit my teeth in preparation of the news. I'd get over it. One day, I'd sell a painting at an art gallery show. Just not tonight.

"Yours," Brandon said.

That's what I thought. Oh, wait. Was he talking to me, or Christos?

Christos said, "You mean Samantha's painting sold?"

Brandon scoffed, "Of course Samantha's painting sold. I sold it five minutes after it was unveiled."

"What? No way!" Christos blurted.

Okay, my brain must have broken, because I think Brandon just said my silly little fantasy landscape had sold tonight.

Brandon nodded and grinned at me and Christos.

"How much did it sell for?" Christos asked.

Brandon's smile peeled back charmingly and he said, "Twenty-seven thousand."

I slapped my hand over my wide open mouth, stopping my broken brains from rolling right out.

Christos grinned at me and rubbed my back affectionately, causing a shiver to run up my spine. "I knew you would," he said.

"I didn't!" I said, flabbergasted. "You know what this means?"

"What?" Christos asked.

"I'm going to be able to pay my tuition next year!" I hopped up in the air with my arms over my head. "Yes!"

Christos hugged me and kissed me. "Congratulations, *agápi mou*. It was only a matter of time until you started selling. Didn't I tell you that when we first met?"

"You did!" I said gleefully. Wow. I couldn't believe it. My dreams were coming true like I'd never imagined!

I was definitely the luckiest girl in the world tonight!

===

CHRISTOS

"So, Brandon," I said, turning to face him, "which painting hasn't sold tonight?"

"Your portrait of Samantha as the fiery angel," he answered.

"Oh," Samantha crooned. "I'm sorry, Christos. Your painting of me is so beautiful. I would totally buy it, if I could afford it. Would you take twenty-seven grand for it?" She winked at me.

"Thanks, *agápi mou*," I said reassuringly. "Save your money for your tuition. Besides, if no one buys my portrait of you, I'll fucking keep it," I smiled. "I put my heart into it." I glanced behind us at the eight foot tall fiery angel winged Samantha portrait hanging on the wall. "Yeah, I would never get tired of looking at it. It's the real you, *agápi mou*, the one I see every time I look at you, the one other people don't always realize is there."

"Oh, Christos," Samantha sighed, "I love you so much." She leaned into me and hugged me around the waist.

"I love you too, *agápi mou*," I said and kissed the top of her head. "Hold on a second," I blurted, suddenly realizing something. "Brandon, did my LOVE portrait of me and Samantha sell too?"

"Yeah," Brandon nodded. "For half a million."

"What?!" Samantha blurted

"Yes," Brandon's smile widened. "You heard me right. A half a million dollars."

Samantha clapped both her hands to her face, "Oh my god! I can't believe someone bought a picture of you and me nude!"

I grinned at her, "Believe it." I turned to Brandon, "So, who bought it?"

Brandon's eyes flashed and he looked away momentarily. "It was, uh, an anonymous buyer."

I could tell Brandon was hiding something. "Anonymous?" I said sarcastically. "It's not like we're selling porn or drugs. You can tell me, Brandon."

Brandon shook his head seriously, "I was given explicit instructions not to reveal the buyer's identity under any circumstances."

Samantha said, "Now I'm totally curious."

"I can't tell you," Brandon shrugged. "It was in the terms of the contract."

"Terms?" I asked. "It wasn't Stanford Wentworth, was it?"

"No," he chuckled.

"Who's Stanford Wentworth," Samantha asked.

She'd been spared the torture of enduring Wentworth's visit to my studio that day he'd said I needed to change up my paintings because they were shit, and had said Samantha's Calla Lily oil study was awful. Thinking about him now, all I wanted to do was punch his face in then rub it in the pile of money I was making tonight. Then I heard Russell Merriweather's voice echoing through my head, *"No. More. Fights."* I smiled to myself.

Brandon said, "Stanford Wentworth is one of the richest art buyers in the world, Samantha. He can make someone's career if he buys their art."

"Oh," she said, "That sounds like a good thing."

"He's also a prick," I said. "I don't want his sorry ass owning my art. I'm doing fine without him."

Brandon said, "What if I told you he put in a bid on your portrait of Samantha?"

"No shit," I chuckled.

"He did," Brandon said.

A smug smile spread across my face, "I guess he changed his tune about my art." Knowing it gave me a delicious sense of satisfaction.

"Wentworth was one of the early bidders. Once the other buyers started driving up the price," Brandon smiled conspiratorially, "he was mysteriously unable to get any more bids through to me."

I grinned back at Brandon. Wentworth had been a prick to him that day at my studio, too. Brandon was blocking him out of the bidding process. Wentworth had a bit of a reputation as a star maker. He would sweep up an artist's early work, before they were famous, and hold onto it. This would drive up demand on the artist's work, at which point Wentworth would often sell it for a hefty profit. Fuck him. He wasn't going to make a dime off my sweat. He'd had his shot that day at the studio and he'd blown it.

"So, Brandon," I asked, "what's the status on the bidding?"

"Actually," Brandon smiled smugly, "It's turning into something of a heated battle. Two people here tonight have insisted the painting must be theirs, and four other buyers on the phone are calling me every five minutes to find out if they need to raise their bid or not."

"I hope none of the people on the phone are agents of Wentworth's," I said.

"No," Brandon said, "I know all of them well. We're in the clear. Wentworth will walk away empty handed after tonight."

I nodded approvingly.

"Wow," Samantha said, "If you're turning buyers away, that means you're totally popular, Christos!"

"What's the bid up to?" I asked Brandon.

He grinned, "One point five million."

"Holy shit!" Samantha blurted.

I felt the same way.

Brandon's phone rang. He pulled it out of his pocket and glanced at it before turning to me, "Another bidder calls. The price keeps climbing. I've got to answer this," he smiled as he walked off, holding his phone to his ear.

"Christos, that's insane!" Samantha squealed. "You're making so much money tonight!"

"You are too," I said.

"I know," she smiled. "Twenty-seven grand! I can't believe it!"

"You're making a hell of a lot more than that."

Her brows narrowed, "What do you mean?"

"I mean, I'm splitting whatever I get on my portrait of you, and the LOVE portrait of both of us, with you."

"What?! That's crazy. Those are your paintings! I can't take your money!"

"What do you mean? I wouldn't have either painting if it wasn't for you. All I'd have is a self portrait of myself and some paintings of Brandon's L.A. models. I don't think there'd be a million dollar bidding war over any of them. You made both paintings special, *agápi mou*. You, Samantha Anna Smith. Because you're my girlfriend, you're in the paintings, and you're an amazing artist in your own right. This is the stuff art history books write about a hundred years from now. The whole story, the whole package. Us. You and me. Without you, I'd be the third Manos. With you and your art, I'm something special."

"I don't know, Christos," Samantha frowned, "it's so much money."

"So what? It doesn't mean you don't deserve it."

"I can't take your money, Christos," she sighed.

"Why not? Let me put it another way. What if I'd painted a portrait of you, spent maybe two or three hours on it, and sold it for, say, two hundred bucks. Would you split the money with me then? I get a hundred for painting it, you get a hundred for modeling?"

She frowned, "I guess."

"So what's the difference between that and this?"

"Hundreds of thousands of dollars!" she blurted.

"No," I shook my head adamantly, "That shouldn't make any difference. Do you think just because more money is involved you deserve less?"

"Well, no, I guess not."

I nodded, "In any fifty-fifty partnership, each person gets half, right?"

"But you're talking about more money than I've ever imagined," she said nervously.

"So what? Don't undervalue yourself, *agápi mou.*"

"It's just so much money," she sighed.

"Half of it is still yours," I said. "But if you really don't want it…" I didn't know what else to say. Maybe she'd change her mind later.

Romeo appeared out of nowhere and said, "I'll go halvsies with you on your painting of me, C-Man."

"See?" I said, "Romeo knows his worth." I gave him a fist bump.

Kamiko stood beside Romeo. She said, "I still can't believe someone bought that Wonky Kong portrait of Romeo."

"What?" Romeo scowled, "It's awesome. And I think whoever bought it got it for a steal at $150,000. I told you someone would pay to have a painting of me."

Kamiko rolled her eyes. "Wait til they get the portrait into their house and have to stare at you 24/7."

"You're just jealous Christos didn't paint you," Romeo sneered.

She rolled her eyes and stuck her tongue out at him.

I said to Kamiko, "I'll paint you for my next show. We'll dress you up as one of the Adventure Time characters."

Her eyes lit up, "Wow, Christos, you'd paint me?"

"Sure," I smiled. "I'd rather paint a friend over some random model."

Kamiko clapped her hands together, "I totally want to be painted as Fionna from Adventure Time! I'll make the costume myself! When can we start!"

"We'll do it over the summer."

Kamiko gasped. "That would be so totally awesome, Christos!" Her and Romeo wandered back into the crowd while me and Samantha shared a chuckle.

A few minutes later, Russell walked up to us from out of the crowd. "Congratulations, young man," he said. "It appears you're doing rather well tonight."

"Yeah," I smiled. "Samantha, you remember Russell Merriweather?"

"Totally," she grinned, shaking his hand. "Nice to see you again."

"Nice to see you too, young lady. Have you been keeping this character out of trouble?" He nodded at me.

"Definitely," she smiled.

"You know," Russell said, "I bought one of your grandfather's landscapes."

"You did?" I asked. "Which one?"

"The one of the valley behind your father's house at sunrise. I'm always telling Nikolos how much I love the view when I go out there. Since your grandfather decided to paint a picture of it, I thought that would be the next best thing to visiting. I'm hanging it in my downtown office so I can always see it."

I knew that Brandon had priced that painting at $75,000. "Wow, Russell, that was really generous of you," I said appreciatively.

"Fiddlesticks." Russell smiled.

"Fiddlesticks?" I laughed. "Who the fuck says fiddlesticks?"

Samantha giggled at what I'd said.

"I do," Russell said in his most serious courtroom voice ever, "And if you want to keep your teeth, you won't make any further issue of it. Are we clear?" He arched an eyebrow, but it only took a second for his face to relax into a big smile.

I shook my head and smiled at him.

"Besides," Russell said, "Your family has spent plenty of money on me over the years, it was the least I could do."

"Thanks, man," I smiled.

"Well, I've got to go. Good night, Samantha. Both of you please give my regards to Spiridon and Nikolos," Russell said before fading into the crowd.

"Russell is so cool," Samantha said.

"Yup."

Brandon burst through the crowd a minute later. "It sold! Your portrait of Samantha sold!"

Samantha's eyes goggled.

So did mine.

"How much?" we both asked.

"One point nine million!" Brandon was beside himself. I'd never seen him lose his cool like this. I wasn't surprised. A sizable chunk of the money we'd pulled in tonight was his.

Samantha threw her arms around me and planted a huge kiss on my cheek before saying, "Congratulations, Christos!"

A second later, my dad and grandad were pushing through the crowd.

"Congratulations, *paidí mou!*" my grandad said, leaning over to hug me. "We heard the news."

"Thanks, *Pappoús,*" I said.

My dad threw his arms around both of us, "You did it, *paidí mou!*"

"I couldn't have done it without you, *Bampás,*" I said, looking into my father's eyes. They were brimming with tears. Just like mine.

Brandon grinned while slapping my shoulder vigorously, "A number of the major art magazines have already called. They're asking to interview you, Christos. You're going to be the talk of the international art world by tomorrow morning. I told you before, if you ever painted a portrait of Samantha, it would be your Mona Lisa. Now you have it."

"Mona Lisa?" I chuckled. "You know the Mona Lisa looks like a dude in drag. At least you could've said Evening Mood by Bouguereau. The girl in that painting is actually a woman, and she's beautiful."

"But that painting isn't nearly as famous," Brandon smiled. "Regardless, this portrait of Samantha is going to make your name, Christos. I know it." Brandon marveled as he gazed at the painting on the wall.

He was entranced by it. I think knowing it sold for so much cash made it that much better in his eyes. I couldn't blame him. Brandon tore himself away from the painting and said, "Will you be sad to say goodbye to it when the buyer takes possession of it, Christos?"

"Nope." I smiled down at Samantha, "I get to keep the real thing."

"I will," Samantha said. "I love looking at it." She glanced back at the painting.

"No need to worry, Samantha," Brandon said.

I frowned, "Why's that?"

Brandon grinned, "You guys will never guess who the buyer was."

"Who?" I asked. It couldn't be Wentworth.

"L.A. M.O.M.A.," Brandon grinned.

My jaw dropped, "No fucking way."

"What's that?" Samantha asked.

"The Los Angeles Museum of Modern Art," Brandon grinned. "To hang in their permanent collection." No wonder he was so stoked about selling my painting. This was a huge feather in Charboneau Gallery's cap.

I said to Samantha, "You know what this means, *agápi mou?*"

She shook her head.

I grinned, "The whole world is going to see my painting of you."

Her eyes goggled and she started laughing. "I knew it!"

"What?" I was confused.

"Everyone's going to see me naked!"

I laughed and so did Brandon.

"No," I grinned, "everyone's going to be inspired by your bravery."

Samantha rolled her eyes, but I leaned down and kissed her passionately anyway. The crowd around us, which was still a bustling mass of men and women in fancy black tie evening wear, started to applaud and hoot.

Me and Samantha continued kissing under the spotlight for a long time in front of everybody.

It was a perfect evening, all the way around.

The only thing still bugging me was whether or not I'd made enough money after giving Brandon his cut to pay back Hunter Blakeley. If I lost his civil suit against me in court I was going to owe him enough cash to fill a bank vault. I noticed Russell hadn't mentioned the trial when he'd said goodbye tonight. He probably didn't want to spoil my evening.

Man, why did I have to hit fucking Hunter in the first place? It's not like I didn't already know I could kick his ass ten times over.

Oh well.

I'd worry about it tomorrow.

Now it was time to gather everyone up and go celebrate someplace else. There was no way I was letting Hunter Blakeley ruin my perfect evening.

No fucking way.

Besides, what where the chances of running into him tonight?

Chapter 28

SAMANTHA

The band on stage at the Belly Up Tavern rocked the house. The place was packed. After the crowd at Charboneau Gallery had finally thinned, we all drove here to unwind and celebrate.

Christos and Jake knew the bouncers outside, so they let me, Madison, Romeo, and Kamiko all sneak inside to see the band. But they made us promise not to order any drinks. Christos and Jake told the bouncers they'd keep an eye on us.

The Belly Up was a combination bar and music venue. It had a really big stage at one end, and two bars at the other. A huge great white shark statue hung over one of the bars on cables and surfboards lined the walls.

"I've never been in a bar before," I hissed to Madison.

"What?" she shouted.

The band was so loud, I don't know why I was whispering. I leaned over to her ear and said loudly, "I've never been in a bar before!"

"Me neither!" she hollered. "Isn't it awesome?!"

I nodded.

We danced casually, swaying to the music.

Romeo randomly started twerking, his butt thrusting behind him as his arms extended in front of him, stirring the butter churn. It didn't make any sense because the band played rock, not hip hop. I started giggling instantly.

"What are you doing, Romeo?" Kamiko laughed.

"Trying to lasso me a man!" He grinned and looked around, but the only people watching him looked horrified. Romeo didn't care. He twerked away like crazy.

I glanced back at the stage and noticed the drummer and the bass player looked familiar. I turned to Madison and shouted, "Hey, aren't those two guys Jake's friends?!"

"Yeah!" Madison shouted, "That's Lucas Summer on bass and his brother Logan on the drums!"

"They helped Christos and Jake move my stuff into the house!" I shouted.

Madison nodded.

The band was really good. The song they were playing started to speed up. The whole house was rocking in time to the music.

Logan was going crazy on the drums. He looked like a wild animal. A total contrast to how shy he'd been the day I'd met him. What was that old saying? Still waters ran deep? Or was it hot shy guys made great rock drummers?

Me and Madison really got into the music, banging our heads like idiots until our hair twirled around. We were both laughing and dizzy and had to stop.

I almost tripped over my platform sandals, but Christos caught me in his arms and stood me up.

He hollered, "Me and Jake are going to get some drinks! Do you guys want anything?"

"We told those bouncers we wouldn't drink!" I hollered uncertainly. I mean, I'd be happy to have a drink or two. I didn't plan on getting drunk. But I didn't want to get anyone in trouble.

"You're such a good girl!" Christos quipped.

"I can be bad!" I grinned.

"Now?! Or do I have to wait until later?!"

"Uh…" I didn't know how to respond to that. I hadn't been thinking of getting down and dirty on the dance floor. "Maybe you can have Romeo twerk for you?!"

Christos took one look at Romeo, who was in a jerky twerking trance, and blurted laughter. "No!" Christos shouted. He kissed my cheek and said, "You can show me how bad you are later!" He squeezed my butt and I jumped. "Me and Jake will get you guys some waters! And you can share my drink, if you want!"

"Okay!" I smiled as the two of them squeezed through the crowd toward the bar.

The next song the band played was a slow, heart wrenching ballad. The lights on stage faded to a mellow blue to match the mood of the music. Lucas sang on the mic at the front of the stage while playing his bass guitar. He had a smooth, sexy voice. I'd already thought he was cute with his surfer good looks and blue eyes, but hearing him sing, I had no doubt drooling packs of women chased him everywhere he went.

Based on what I could make out of the lyrics, I think the song was about a guy whose girlfriend had died or had left him. I wasn't sure which.

Lucas and Logan sang the heartfelt chorus together, in perfect harmony:

"When I awoke
You did fall asleep
Now your eyes are closed, and
I can only weep."

"Why did you go, girl
I just found myself
Now I'm all alone, and
I really need your love."

The brother's voices blended fluidly, expressing a sorrowful sense of loss perfectly. They were both total heart throbs.

After Lucas and Logan sang the chorus a second time, the spotlight shifted away from them toward the other side of the stage. It stopped on the guitar player, who I finally noticed was a young woman with long flowing hair. If I had to guess, she was about my age, maybe a little older.

She had been hiding toward the side of the stage for most of the show, not really calling much attention to herself. She was acting so shy, she almost seemed fragile. But when it was time for her guitar solo, she stood at the front of the stage, inches from the crowd.

The spotlight glimmered blue diamonds off her guitar. I saw arms from the crowd reaching up to touch her like she was a pagan shaman performing a magical ritual. Maybe she was. I thought she might be distracted by the reaching hands, but she was in her own world, totally focused. She played her heart out.

The sound of her electric guitar poured out of the speakers like a human wail, the gut wrenching sound of tears and heartbreak and it swept me away. This mystery girl seemed like she was so full of sadness that she couldn't contain it any longer, and the only way she could release it was through playing her guitar.

I was in total awe of her ability to grab my emotions and connect mine to hers with such immediacy.

As her guitar solo built to a crescendo, she threw her head back, her long hair dangling behind her, her eyes closed, her face overwhelmed with pure emotion. She wasn't fragile at all. She had to be strong and courageous to channel all the emotion inside her and project it through her guitar with such honesty and vulnerability.

I felt chills coursing through my body and my eyes were suddenly hot and brimming with tears.

This young woman was amazing.

After she finished her guitar solo, Lucas and Logan sang the chorus again, but with new words.

"Now it's time to heal
Time for me to live,
But it's hard for me to say..."

Then Lucas sang a line by himself,

"It's time to let you go..."

followed by Logan singing,

"I'll never let you go..."

Together, they sang,

"Again. No, not again."

Based on the lyrics, I wondered if Lucas had lost a girlfriend and Logan was trying to hold onto the one he had? It was all so mysterious.

The only thing I knew for sure was that I was crying and laughing when the song ended. I couldn't get over how much the band had moved me with their music.

Everyone in the bar cheered and clapped.

A second later, the band ripped into a new song, totally upbeat, and everyone was dancing to the steady, rocking groove. The girl on guitar did another guitar solo toward the end of the song, playing a million miles an hour. People cheered the whole time she played.

This time, instead of looking like she was going to explode with sadness, she had a look of primal rage on her face. At the end of her solo, she hit this one long note that sounded like a scream. She held her free hand up in the air while the note vibrated endlessly.

I couldn't help myself. I cheered as loud as I could, "Yeah!!"

It was incredibly exciting.

When the song came to a close, the band made a ton of noise, strumming their guitars and hammering the drums at the same time. The stage lights flashed through every color of the rainbow. Then, on cue, the girl and Lucas both jumped in the air. They strummed their instruments a final time when they landed back on the stage. The drums stopped at the exact same moment, the band went silent, and the stage lights went dark.

Everyone in the bar roared their approval.

When white stage lights came back on, illuminating the band, Lucas Summer shouted over the mic and pointed at the guitar player, "Victory Payne on lead guitar, everybody!" He clapped his hands over his head, applauding her while his bass guitar dangled from his shoulder strap. People whistled and screamed. "We're Lucas and Logan Summer! We'll be back in a half hour for some more music! All right!!!"

The crowd cheered again as the band walked off the stage.

I turned to Madison and said, "That girl was incredible! I've never seen anyone play guitar like that before!"

"Me neither," Madison said.

"And she's a girl!" I cheered.

"I think I've got a girl crush," Romeo said genuinely.

Kamiko said, "I thought I was your girl crush."

"What did they say her name was again?" Romeo asked.

"Victory Payne," Madison said.

"That's her name?" I scoffed. "It sounds fake."

"I think her real name is Victoria," Madison said thoughtfully. "Victoria Payne."

"Do you know her?"

"I've met her through Lucas and Logan once before. She's really nice. You'd like her."

===

CHRISTOS

The bar was so busy, I was still waiting for our drinks when the band took a break.

"I'll be right back," Jake said. "I'm gonna take a piss."

I nodded.

A minute later, someone tapped me on the back. I turned around and Tiffany Kingston-Whitehouse stood right behind me.

"Hey, stranger," she smiled. She wore standard Tiffany garb, which meant a tight top and tighter skirt. She loved to show off her body whenever she had the chance. I couldn't blame her.

As usual, she seemed happy to see me. "Hey, Tiff." Had it been a month ago, I would've given her a quick brush off, but after the way she'd told Samantha's tribunal the truth about her 'stolen credit card' I was inclined to be nice. "How they hangin?" I grinned.

"Perky as ever," Tiffany winked, subtly thrusting her chest at me. She wasn't exaggerating. She did have an amazing rack, which I knew was the real deal. But she didn't need anyone reminding her how good she looked. Her ego was plenty big enough already.

Changing the subject, I said, "I saw your mom and dad at my solo show tonight. How come you didn't come? You usually do."

"Oh," she glanced awkwardly away, "I, uh, sort of thought maybe I should leave you alone. So you could, you know, enjoy the show. With, uh, Samantha," she rolled her eyes like it took everything she had to talk nicely about Samantha.

That was progress. Sounded like Tiff was turning over a new leaf.

"What happened to you calling her Scumantha?" I grinned. "She told me about that, you know."

Tiffany shrugged. For once, she didn't have her hands all over me. She just stood a foot away, holding a girl drink in her hand, which was half gone.

I decided to be polite and let her off the hook for past transgressions. "Can I buy you another drink, Tiff?"

"I'm good for now," she smiled. "How were sales tonight? Did you clean up?"

I nodded cockily, "Hells yeah. We sold everything."

"I heard your dad and your grandfather had paintings on sale tonight?"

"Yeah, their stuff sold too."

"Congratulations," she said sincerely, "you should be proud of yourself, Christos. I bet you made a ton of money."

"I hope." The next thing I knew, I was opening up to her like I used to. "I just hope it'll cover the civil suit hanging over my head."

"Civil suit?" She sipped her drink. "What civil suit?"

"Oh, some douche bag named Hunter Blakeley. Do you know him?"

She shrugged.

"Total prick," I shook my head. "This guy Hunter Blakeley was harassing Samantha a few months back every time he ran into her. One day he does it in front of me. Tried to start a fight with me, but I tripped him into the dirt. So everything's fine, right?"

She nodded, cuing me to continue, and sipped her drink.

I gave her the run down about running into Hunter in front of Hooters, and him and his three buddies following me and Jake to our car. I glossed over the part about me and Jake stealing Hunter's bar babes and buying them drinks because I didn't want Tiff thinking she had a shot with me, because she didn't. And I'd been shitfaced that night anyway. I didn't plan on doing much if any drinking beyond one or two at a time for the foreseeable future. I had too much to lose.

I never wanted to lose Samantha.

"What happened at your car?" Tiff asked, her eyes wide with interest as she sucked down more of her drink.

I had a moment to wonder if she was trying to get buzzed so she would have an excuse to put the moves on me without inhibition. It was her usual strategy. I'd have to keep an eye on her.

"I popped the guy in the nose," I said. "Once. But I think I broke it. Anyway, this guy Hunter is a model, and it turns out he lost a bunch of work. Now his attorney is asking for close to a million bucks."

"A million!" Tiff swallowed wrong and coughed several times. "Sorry." She blotted her chin with her cocktail napkin.

I couldn't help but chuckle.

"What?" she smiled

"Nothing," I grinned.

When she finished blotting, she said, "What are you going to do about this Hunter guy?"

"Fuck, I don't know. Me and Russell think Hunter's attorney found out how much my family is worth and they're trying to bend us over.

"I'm sorry to hear that," Tiffany winced. Over the years, I knew Tiffany's family had seen their fair share of people trying to sue the shit out of them over the littlest thing, just because they had money.

She could relate.

"Thanks, Tiff. Yeah, it's pretty fucked up. We don't have any videotape evidence or anything to prove that Hunter started it. It's just me and Jake's word against Hunter and his three pals. This Hunter guy can come across totally clean cut when he wants too. A jury would probably believe him. Best case scenario, I'm hoping we can get the damages reduced. But even then, it could be a few hundred grand."

"That's awful, Christos," Tiff said, resting her hand on my arm.

I glanced at her hand.

She let it fall away.

"I wish there was something I could do to help..." she gazed into my eyes, but then suddenly got a far away look, lost in thought.

She was gone so long, I finally said, "Tiff? You still there?"

"Yeah," she smiled. "Sorry. Just thinking about something."

"Anyway, I was going to say thanks, Tiff. I appreciate you listening. But don't worry about it. I'll deal with it."

She shook her head and smirked, "You always do."

She set her empty drink on the bar and said, "I need to go freshen up in the ladies room."

I nodded and she walked off into the crowd.

A minute later, Jake wandered back to the bar. "You get our drinks yet?"

"Still waiting," I said.

While we waited, I couldn't help but wonder what was on Tiff's mind all of a sudden. I could always tell when her wheels started turning over some new scheme in her head. She hadn't changed a bit.

I'd have to keep my eyes on her.

===

SAMANTHA

"Let's go talk to the band," Madison said as Lucas, Logan and Victory walked from the stage toward the bar with the big shark hanging over it, "I'll introduce you to Victory."

"Okay," I said as she pulled me along.

Romeo and Kamiko followed.

As we made our way toward them, Madison hollered, "Hey,

Lucas!"

"What up, Madison!" Lucas grinned. "How'd you guys like the tunes?"

"Totally rockin'," Madison said.

The bunch of us were now all standing facing each other.

"You guys were totally awesome!" I said.

"Hey," Lucas smiled at me, "I remember you. You're Samantha, right?"

"Yeah," I grinned.

Lucas said, "Logan, you remember Samantha. We moved her shit out of her apartment into Christos' pad."

"Yeah," Logan smiled. He didn't say anything else. Still as shy as the first time I'd met him. But he was so cute it didn't work against.

Madison said, "These are Sam's friends Romeo and Kamiko." They both said hello to the boys.

"And this," Lucas said, "is our friend Victory."

"Hi," she said.

I shook her hand, "Your guitar playing is amazing," I smiled.

"Thanks," she smiled back, exuding a cool cat rockstar vibe.

I wasn't sure what to say to her. I couldn't tell if she was too cool for school or what. So I turned to Lucas and said, "Hey, Lucas, you guys played some really awesome songs tonight. But one of them really stuck out, and I was wondering what it was about."

"Which one?" he asked.

"The slow sad one," I said.

"You mean Now Your Eyes Are Closed?" he said, "The ballad?"

"I guess?" I said uncertainly. "It was the really sad one."

Logan nodded at his brother.

"Yeah," Lucas said to me, almost wincing, "that was Now Your Eyes Are Closed."

"Well, it was really amazing," I smiled sincerely. "But I couldn't figure out what it was about."

Logan, the shy one, glanced at Lucas, who suddenly looked miserable.

Had I asked the wrong question? I glanced down to make sure my foot hadn't stuck itself in my mouth without my approval. Yup, it had, toes and all. At least now it was jammed so far inside my mouth I wouldn't be able to say anything else to make people uncomfortable.

"Uh," Logan said, "that song is kind of personal to me and my brother. We don't really talk about it."

"I'm totally sorry," I said nervously. "I shouldn't have asked." Maybe one day, like in a few decades, my social awkwardness would disappear completely. But for now, it still lingered. Oh well.

"No worries," Logan smiled, trying to sound casual, but I could tell he was uneasy with the topic.

Lucas, the talkative one, was now all choked up. His eyes had darkened and a brooding look weighed down on his face.

Had I been right about my guess that their song was about Lucas' girlfriend dying?

Logan's features softened with sympathy as he watched his brother Lucas sinking into a deep emotional pit right in front of us. "You okay, bro?" he asked. He rested a gentle hand on Lucas' shoulder.

Lucas inhaled forcefully through his nostrils and shook it off. "I'm good." A second later, the twinkle I'd seen in his blue eyes the day we'd met returned. He turned to Victory and said, "You were on fire tonight, girl. We need to have you sit in for us more often."

"Thanks," Victory smiled quietly.

"Wait," Madison said, "I thought Victory was your regular guitar player?"

"Nah," Lucas said, "our regular guitar guy is busy doing paying session work up in L.A., so we asked Victory to sit in for our last couple gigs."

I blurted, "You should totally keep her in your band! She rocks!"

"Victory has a regular gig with another band," Lucas said.

There went my foot again.

"She's just doing us a favor," Logan said.

Victory nodded. She was so quiet. Unlike me, the blurt bomb.

Someone tapped my shoulder. I could only assume it was Christos with our drinks. I totally needed a social save before I said something else awkward.

"Hey, Sam," the voice said behind me. I turned around to face Hunter Blakeley.

Lameballs.

I meant, slimeballs.

Why was he here? Had he still not gotten the message I wanted nothing to do with him? Oh well, this was a public bar. Was there a quick way to explain to everyone that Hunter was suing my boyfriend for hundreds of thousands of dollars because he was a total ass, and we should all shun him until he went away? Maybe not. So I turned my back to Hunter, hoping he would take the hint and go away.

I should've known better.

Hunter squeezed into the circle next to me. He smiled at the Summer brothers and said, "I'm Hunter Blakeley."

They both shook Hunter's hand. They didn't know who he was.

I glanced at Romeo, whose eyes had bugged out of his face.

"Who's this?" Hunter drawled smarmily, eying Victory like a piece of meat. She was gorgeous, and Hunter was as predictable as he was obvious.

Victory arched an eyebrow at Hunter. I couldn't tell if she was interested in him or not.

He extended his hand, "I'm Hunter Blakeley."

Victory didn't shake his hand. She just stared at it for awhile, then gave Hunter an amused grin. She was kind of hard to read.

Hunter smiled at her. "Are you a friend of Sam's?"

Victory glanced at me. "Do you know this guy?" she asked me.

"Sort of," I said uneasily. I wanted to shout, "He's horrible! Run away!" But I was trying to be polite, so I didn't.

Victory narrowed her eyes at me, drilling me with her gaze.

That was weird. She seemed mad all of a sudden. Was she mad at me? I don't know why she would be, but I could feel it coming off of her in waves. I must have pissed her off somehow. Maybe she thought my question to Lucas about his song had been ultra rude, and she was offended for him? Maybe she was irritated I'd suggested she join Lucas and Logan's band? Was it a sore point between them? I had no idea. Geez, I was the First Lady of Awkwardness & Insecurity tonight.

Victory turned to Hunter and smiled at him.

Maybe she was attracted to Hunter? I hoped not. For her sake.

Victory took a step toward Hunter, until she was right in front of him. Any second, Victory was going to take Hunter's elbow, then turn to me and say sneeringly, "Let's ditch these nerds," before she and Hunter walked away. Then Lucas and Logan would laugh at me and throw things and call me names.

Instead, Victory glared up at Hunter and said, "Dude, you're making everyone uncomfortable. Samantha doesn't like you, and I can tell you're a prick." Her eyes gleamed when she said it. She looked, I don't know, dangerous. Standing in front of him, she seemed way too small, but you know what they said about Honey Badgers. She wasn't afraid of Hunter at all.

Romeo clapped a hand over his mouth, stifling a laugh.

A smile widened across my face. I couldn't help myself.

Victory said to Hunter, "Why don't you go elsewhere?"

The grin remained on Hunter's face. He was never one to listen to basic instructions. He stood his ground. He was enjoying himself way too much to leave when the fun was just starting.

"Hunter Blakeley," Christos singsonged from behind me. "So good to see you, pal" he said sarcastically.

My very own Motorknight always knew right when to show up.

Grin.

===

CHRISTOS

Hunter turned around and scowled up at me, "Christos Manos, in the flesh."

I stared him down.

Hunter was a big guy. But I was bigger. And he knew he didn't stand a chance against me in a fight. We had already proved that on two embarrassing occasions.

"How's life treating you?" Hunter chuckled like he was my best bud.

"Awesome," I smiled.

Hunter draped his arm over Samantha's shoulders, like they were together.

Samantha winced and ducked away, saying, "Get off me, Hunter!"

He laughed it off like it was no big deal.

"You want me to teach Hunter some manners?" Jake asked, cracking his knuckles enthusiastically.

"No, I got this," I said. The last thing I wanted was for Jake to knock Hunter's teeth out and have his own civil suit to deal with. Jake and his family didn't have money to spare like mine did. A big lawsuit would bury them.

Hunter said to Jake, "Easy, tough guy. Looks like your boyfriend is going to protect you. Maybe you can blow him later as a reward for standing up for you."

"You're an ass," Madison said to Hunter. "Don't you have some dick modeling to go do?"

"You remembered," Hunter smiled, like he was good friends with Madison because of it.

"I remembered you're a dickhead," she scowled. "I'm sure there's tons of dick modeling out there for a dickface like you."

"Go, Mads!" Samantha blurted before slapping her hand over her mouth.

Hunter chuckled. "Wow, I've never seen so many ballsy women in one place." He glared at me and Jake as he said it, implying both of us were women.

"Relax, Hunter," I said.

He stepped up to me until his chest was an inch from mine and said, "I don't think so."

I really wanted to crush him like an ant.

"Come on, tough guy," Hunter hissed. "Show me what you got."

This was ridiculous. Hunter was doing everything he could to piss me off. He was acting like he had invulnerability armor on because of the civil suit. Sadly, he sort of did. We both knew he would sue me a second time if I hit him again. He had the upper hand and he was playing it to the hilt.

Whatever.

"When did you become such a pussy, Christos?" Hunter asked.

I shook my head dismissively.

"You're not so tough now, are you?" he sneered.

"Hit me, Hunter," I said calmly.

His eyes narrowed.

"Go for it," I said, "I won't hit back. I know you want to."

Hunter nodded shrewdly, "I know what you're trying to do. You want me to hit you so you can file a counter suit."

"Am I?"

"I'm not stupid, Christos."

"That's debatable," I chuckled.

Samantha and the gang all snickered.

Hunter's face soured.

"Are you going to leave now?" I asked. "Or maybe you want to call some of your buddies so you can even the odds. Make it eight on two against me and Jake. Bring some guns and knives and shit, so it'll be a fair fight."

Hunter huffed derisively.

"You're a pussy, Hunter," I said. "I'll prove it. Hit me as hard as you want. I promise I won't sue."

He looked like he was considering it, he was so angry.

"I'll let you throw three shots before I retaliate. Then it'll be self defense. But I'll only swing once. You know that's all it'll take. And this time, there's plenty of witnesses."

"I'm filming all of this," Romeo said, pointing his smart phone at me and Hunter.

I kept hearing Russell's words echoing in my head, *"No. More. Fights."* It wasn't technically a fight if I just used words to win, was it?

"Fuck you, asshole," Hunter hissed in my face. "I can't wait to see how tough you are in court."

"Me neither," I said to Hunter as he shouldered past me.

===

TIFFANY

I watched the entire showdown between Christos and Hunter from a distance after I came out of the ladies room. That Hunter was a complete jerk. He really needed someone to put him in his place.

When Hunter barged past Christos, I considered joining Christos and his friends. I always liked spending time with Christos, but he was with his girlfriend Samantha. Oh well. I decided to leave them in peace.

I'd see Christos some other time.

I went back to the bar to order another drink. I was in the mood to drink alone tonight. After my double martini arrived, I sipped on it in solitude while the band played another set. Sometime later, I watched Christos walk out of the bar with his girlfriend and the rest of his friends.

Sigh.

I really needed to accept that Christos was no longer on the market. Another martini would certainly help. I signaled the bartender for another and he nodded in reply.

"Heeeyyyy, Tiffany," Hunter Blakeley drawled. The band was

taking a break, so he didn't have to shout. He squeezed up to the bar next to me, pushing some random chick out of his way.

"Hey!" Random Chick blurted at Hunter, "Watch where you're going!"

Hunter tossed a casual smirk in Random Chick's direction while giving me a look that said, "Can you believe her?" He didn't care. Hunter was totally full of himself.

Why hadn't I noticed before that Hunter could be such a lout? Maybe because his good looks were very deceiving. Maybe because when I'd met Hunter, Christos had been dating his girlfriend for a couple of months and I was lonely. I was susceptible to Hunter's quick smile and his golden amber eyes. And his ample muscles. And his washboard abs.

Hunter smiled, "How come you stopped returning my calls, Tiffany?"

I shrugged while absently playing with the red plastic sword that skewered the olive in my empty martini glass.

"I had a lot of fun that night," he said hopefully. I could tell he was fishing for another shot with me.

I was torn between distaste for his bad behavior with Christos and my own desperation. I didn't know which would win out tonight. I think the number of martinis I drank would affect my decision. I really didn't care.

When the martini I'd ordered arrived, Hunter pulled out his wallet and said to the bartender, "I'll get that. And could you bring me a Corona?"

The bartender nodded and pulled a bottle out of the bar fridge, popped the cap, and handed it to Hunter.

Hunter laid bills on the bar, including a tip.

I sipped my martini. Hopefully the gin would blot out my emotions. I was tired of feeling sad all the time. It had definitely gotten worse in the last month. The last thing I wanted to do tonight was think about things.

(*Christos*)

Hunter sipped his beer and grinned at me.

He really was a good looking guy with a friendly smile.

He lifted his beer and said, "Cheers."

I clinked my martini glass against his beer, then gulped down a swallow.

I couldn't decide if I was making a mistake drinking with Hunter or not. I mean, we'd had sex once before. He wasn't a total loss.

For the next thirty minutes, Hunter talked about himself. And talked, and talked, and talked. And talked. I almost asked the bartender for some earplugs, which they had on hand because of the live music. But the band was still on break. I didn't want to be entirely rude. So I nodded a lot, focused on his smoldering amber eyes, shaggy blond hair, and pretended to care about Hunter's boring life.

I wondered if he would talk this much during sex. He was so much better looking with his mouth shut.

"Anyway," he said, finishing some story I'd already forgotten, "that's why I spent last summer in Cannes." He pronounced Cannes as "cans."

I suspected Hunter had never been to Cannes, let alone France, or anywhere else in the Mediterranean, from the way he talked about it. He sounded like a guide book, not someone who travelled.

"You want another drink?" Hunter asked.

I held my hand over my glass, "I'm good." Then, without warning, the wheels in my head started turning. They always did, no matter how much I drank. "Hey, Hunter, how is work going?" The first time he'd taken me out, he'd told me about his modeling for two hours straight.

"Oh, I haven't done too many gigs lately."

"Oh? Why?"

"I got in a fight with this guy."

"Really," I said, all ears. "What guy?"

"Some guy named Christos Manos. Do you know him?"

"No," I lied. "What happened?"

"This guy Christos started some shit with me awhile back. So I fought him. I ended up with a broken nose. But you should've seen his face when I was finished with him."

I had. Christos' face was flawless as always, and I believed his version of events over Hunter's. "Really?" I gasped. "Did you put him in the hospital or something?"

Hunter chuckled confidently, "Close."

Such a scam artist. But then, Christos had already told me as much. I said, "Aren't you worried about getting sued for beating up this Christos guy?"

Hunter frowned, "Why do you ask?"

"Oh, people sue all the time, don't they?" I hoped I sounded every bit the dumb blonde. I giggled for effect.

"Funny thing is," Hunter grinned, "I'm suing *him*."

"Why? If you put him in the hospital?"

Hunter shook his head, "No, I *almost* put him in the hospital. It wasn't that bad." I could tell he was backpedaling and trying to shore up his lie before it fell apart.

"So, why are you suing him?" I asked innocently.

"Because he started it," Hunter sneered snidely. I could tell the truth was seeping out around the edges. Hunter was in over his head. He continued, "The guy has a ton of money. He should've known better than to start shit with me he can't finish. He's lucky I didn't really put him in the hospital." Hunter nodded a superior nod.

"What a jerk," I said ironically. Hunter didn't suspect I meant he was the jerk. I was still sober enough to realize that I should've listened to my instincts about Hunter. He was a total tool. After what Christos had told me tonight, I should've told Hunter to walk away the moment he'd walked up to me at the bar. I excused myself on the grounds that I'd been lonely and it had been a moment of weakness. "I feel like going for a walk," I said randomly.

"Okay," he said. "You want company?"

"Sure." I grabbed my purse from the hook under the bar and stood up.

Hunter followed me outside into the night air.

We walked down Cedros Avenue, past all the closed shops and parked cars, until I found an alley. I turned down it. It was dark, dingy, and cloying. Good enough.

I pulled Hunter into the darkness with both hands, grabbing him by the shirt. Once we were far enough from the streetlights on the sidewalk to be completely in shadows, I pulled Hunter into me.

He pushed up against me, grinding me against a rough stuccoed wall.

Perfect.

We kissed. I wasn't really into it, but I had a reason to be here. We made out for awhile. It didn't take long for me to get bored. Time to get down to business.

I unbuckled Hunter's belt.

"Whoa, Tiff," Hunter purred, "you don't waste any time."

I glared at him and fisted his T shirt in my hand. "Don't call me Tiff. You don't call me Tiff. Got it?"

"Whatever you say, darling," he grinned.

I could deal with darling. Whatever. I unbuckled his belt. "You're still clean?" I asked.

"Yeah," Hunter said, "I told you that the last time we had sex. I get tested all the time."

"But that was five months ago."

Hunter stopped. "Tiffany, look. I get tested regularly and I don't sleep with any old skank that comes along. I've only had sex with two girls since you, and I know them both. They're clean. Trust me."

"Fine. Let's get this over with."

"Over with? Do you even want to be here, Tiffany?"

"Yes, I most definitely do."

Hunter's amber eyes flashed. "You sure?"

"Yeah."

He grinned and leaned forward. More wet fish kisses followed. Not that it mattered. We were doing this.

So what if we ended up having sex in a dank, dark alley? So what if I was dry when he stuck it in? So what if I told him to fuck me as hard as he could before I was even into it? So what if my back was raw from him grinding me against the stucco wall behind me? So what if he came inside me?

After everything Christos had told me, Hunter was a total scam artist. A hot and sexy scam artist. But there was no way I was letting him get away with swindling Christos out of hundreds of thousands of dollars.

Hunter wasn't the only one who knew how to play games.

When we were finished, I said, "I have to go."

"What? Where are you going? Let me buy you another drink inside. Or we could go back to my place." He glanced around the dark alley, "Someplace nicer than this."

I pushed my dress down over my thong, which Hunter had torn apart and was nothing but a waist belt now. Good. I looked over my shoulder at my butt and saw my dress was nice and dirty from rubbing up against the stuccoed wall. "I have to go to the emergency room," I said, still looking over my shoulder at my dress.

"The emergency room?" he asked, confused. "For your dress?"

"Bye, Hunter." I started working up some tears. I wanted my mascara running before I got to the hospital. I started toward the lighted sidewalk at the end of the alley.

"Hey," he grabbed me by the arm and turned me around.

"Ow! Hunter!" I shouted, "That hurts! Let go of me!"

He released my arm, his eyes wide with uncertainty. "What's wrong with you, Tiffany?"

"I've been raped. That's what's wrong with me."

"What?" he gasped. "I didn't rape you!"

"You didn't? Because I could swear that's your semen inside me right now. And when I go get swabbed out at the ER, they're going to find it." I turned around so he could see my dirty dress. "And would you look at that? My dress is soiled and scuffed from where you threw me against the wall. And my thong is torn to pieces. Sounds like rape to me. And, boy," I winced, "was I dry when you put it in. I'm sure they'll find plenty of abrasions."

"What?" Fear pulled his face in twenty directions at once. "You're insane, Tiffany."

"Am I?"

"You totally wanted it," he scoffed.

"That's what the rapists always say."

"Fuck you, Tiffany."

"It wasn't fucking. It was rape."

He grabbed my arm again.

"Oh!" I jeered, "Are you going to beat me up now? Give me a black eye? Go ahead, Hunter."

He let go of my arm and scowled at me. "Why are you doing this?"

"Because, Hunter, you're an asshole. And because you're trying to sue Christos Manos when all he hurt was your pride."

His brows curled. "You know Christos?"

"Of course I know Christos, dumbass. And I know he doesn't start fights. He told me what happened."

Hunter scowled, "You bitch." Now he was figuring it out. Not that it made any difference.

"You just want his money because you're a leech, Hunter."

"That's bullshit!"

"Is it?" I asked thoughtfully. "Then why are you still suing him?"

Hunter smirked and looked away. He looked guilty as hell.

I smiled, "I'll make you a deal, Hunter. In exchange for me not pressing charges and sending you to prison for three years, you drop your suit against Christos. Deal?"

"Fuck you," he spat.

"You already did, Hunter. I have the evidence to prove it. All I need to do now is run my face into the side of a door and give myself a black eye."

"You wouldn't do that," he scoffed.

"I wouldn't? Like I wouldn't let you fuck me while I was still dry so I could frame you?"

He opened his mouth to say something, then the light went out of his eyes and his shoulders sagged. "You're serious, aren't you?"

"One hundred percent. Take your pick, you can try to rip off Christos and his family, and end up in prison, or you can forget about it and I will too."

"How do I know you won't press charges?"

"You don't. You're going to have to trust me."

"Trust you?" He laughed. "After tonight, I'll never trust you."

"Hey, I took you at your word that you haven't slept with any skanks since the last time we had sex."

"I haven't," he frowned. "Honest."

"See?" I smiled. "Look how good trust works."

"Fuck, Tiffany, you're terrible."

"That's how I felt about you when I found out you're basically blackmailing Christos."

"Now you're blackmailing me?"

"Yup."

"Fine. What are you going to do?" He sounded scared. Good.

"Well," I said, "I'm going to the ER, like I said. They'll use a rape kit to collect evidence. Then I tell them I don't know who it was. It was dark, I didn't get a good look at your face, it all happened so fast and you ran off afterward. If you don't drop your suit against Christos, I suddenly remember who you are. It's that simple."

"You've thought this all through, haven't you?"

"And you didn't? Did Christos tell you his family was rich, or did your lawyer figure it out for you? I know how lawyers think, Hunter. Lawyers like yours have been trying to rip off my family for decades. Like I said, Hunter. You're a leech, and you want what isn't yours. This is your last chance. Deal or no deal?"

Hunter clenched his jaw and glared at me like he wanted to kill me.

So what.

Chapter 29

CHRISTOS

I lounged on the double chaise under the San Diego sun the next morning. Samantha lounged beside me. We were catching rays on the deck by our pool.

We'd been out so late, we crashed when we got home. Neither of us had any energy for sex before bed. I think we'd both used up all our adrenalin during the excitement of my solo show and afterward at the Belly Up. We'd just fallen asleep in each other's arms. As long as Samantha was by my side, I never cared what we did.

After breakfast this morning, all we wanted to do was rest. It had been a long year.

"Do you want anything to drink?" Samantha asked. "Your lemonade is empty." She was laying on her back, her bikini top unknotted. She had no idea how incredibly hot she looked, all tan and brown.

"I'm good," I muttered. Luckily, we were both tan enough to lay out for a long time without getting fried.

"Good, because I'm too tired to stand up," she giggled, resting her cheek on my shoulder and her arm on my back.

"I'm going to have a Samantha tan line," I joked. "It'll be a silhouette in white of where you curl up on top of me."

"It'll look stylish. We'll invent couples tanning. It'll be all the rage by the end of the summer. Make your own fancy pattern on your lover. Unlike a tattoo, it's easily removed."

"That's genius. Why hadn't we thought of that before," I chuckled.

My cell phone rang on the glass table next to me.

"You don't have to answer that now, do you?" Samantha asked.

I picked up the phone. "It's Russell."

"More bad news?" Samantha sighed.

"I hope not. I should answer." I put it on speaker phone. Samantha may as well know. "What's up, man?"

"Christos! You're never going to believe this," Russell said enthusiastically.

"If it's bad news, I probably will." I smirked at Samantha.

She rolled her eyes.

"I got a call from Hunter Blakeley's attorney this morning."

"Fabulous," I sighed.

"He wants to settle."

"Yeah? For how much? A half million?" I said sarcastically.

"Twenty-four thousand."

I sat up in my chaise. "What?"

"You heard me. Twenty-four thousand. Eleven thousand for Hunter's medical bills and lost wages, and thirteen thousand for his attorney's fees."

After last night, I could easily cover that. Not that I wanted to throw away that much cash on an asshole like Hunter, but considering I'd hit him instead of walking away, twenty-four grand seemed a small price to pay to get him off my back for good. "What the fuck happened, anyway? I thought Hunter and his lawyer were holding firm."

"I have no idea," Russell said dramatically. "I'm as surprised as you are, Christos. There must be an angel out there watching over your ass."

An angel. I shook my head. Why not? Stranger things.

"Now," Russell admonished, "Before you go getting the idea that it always works out like this, that you always win your cases or get off easy, may I remind you that it would be far simpler in the future to avoid fighting altogether?"

I chuckled, "Hey, would you believe I actually walked away from a fight last night?"

"You did?" Russell said, all excited. "Good for you."

"And you'll never guess with who," I chuckled.

"Hunter Blakeley?"

"How'd you know?" I chuckled.

"Lucky guess. But that sure is strange."

"I can't explain it either. But I'm telling you, he got up in my face and I didn't lift a finger."

"Good for you, son. I'm proud of you. With any luck, this will be the last time you ever require my legal services for behaving like a tough guy. Promise me we can keep our relationship entirely social from here on out?" He sounded amused and hopeful at the same time.

"It's a promise. But I need to ask you one more thing first."

I could practically hear him rolling his eyes over the phone. "Christos, do I even want to know?"

I glanced at Samantha. To Russell, I said, "You know what? I'll tell you about it later."

"All right, son. I've got work to do. Let's talk again soon, all right?"

"Will do," I smiled and ended the call. I turned to Samantha and grinned.

"Wow," she said, "that's good news, right?"

"Totally," I smiled.

"I mean, it's a lot of money, but I guess you have enough?"

"Yup." I laid my head back on the chaise and gazed up at the pure blue sky. "For the first time in years, I finally feel like I can put all the shit in my life behind me."

"That's awesome," Samantha said.

After awhile, I stood up. "Want some lemonade? I'm going to go make a fresh pitcher. We finished off the one my grandad left in the fridge."

"Now you're making it too?" she grinned.

"Hey," I smiled, "it's a Manos tradition."

===

SAMANTHA

Christos and I spent the afternoon under a sun umbrella. All I wanted to do was be outside and relax with him in the perfect San Diego weather.

He made me dinner, which was fresh gyros, because neither of us wanted to bother with anything extravagant.

"Hey, where's Spiridon?" I asked. "He should join us."

"I don't know," Christos said. "He's been gone all day."

I sort of wanted to talk to Spiridon about the show last night, but it would have to wait. Christos and I ate outside at one of the deck tables, watching the ocean waves roll in. The food was super yummy.

A cooling breeze picked up around seven o'clock.

"Hey, you want to go for a hike?" Christos asked.

"Do we have to? I'm so tired."

"Come on," he smiled, "we can watch the sunset from up at the bench on the hill."

"That's a long hike," I groused. "Can't we watch the sun go down from here on the deck?" A dusty hike was the last thing I wanted to do right now.

"The exercise'll do you good."

"I ran yesterday morning. I don't need any exercise."

"I can carry you," he said.

"Don't do that, Christos. I would feel like an invalid. Can't it wait until tomorrow? I promise we'll go tomorrow. First thing, if you want."

"No, it really has to be tonight."

"Why are you acting weird?" I asked.

"It's nice out. I just want to go on a hike. Is that so weird?"

I sighed. "Why don't you go without me. I'll be right here when you get back."

"We're going," he said as he stood up from his chair at the table, bent over, and picked me up out of my chair.

"Christos! I'm too tired," I pleaded, but I was sort of laughing.

He carried me upstairs. It had been awhile since he'd carried me places. I never got tired of it. He set me down on the bed.

"Why don't we have sex instead?" I suggested as I flopped back on the bed.

"Naw, a hike is better."

I sat up suddenly. "What alien kidnapped my Christos and replaced him with the celibate version?"

He chuckled as he pulled on socks and running shoes. "Let's go for a hike."

"You're not going to let this go, are you?"

"No," he said as he pulled out my shoes and socks.

"Fine," I groaned. "But you're going to have to carry me. I don't care if I *do* look like an invalid."

"I can handle that," he grinned his dimpled grin.

"I believe you can."

Ten minutes later, we were walking toward the trailhead near the house, holding hands.

"The hill?" I groaned. "You're going to make me hike all the way up to the bench, aren't you?"

"It's good for your shapely legs," he smiled.

"Don't try to compliment your way out of carrying me," I joked as we trudged up the hillside.

Half way up, Spiridon came hiking down, followed by Nikolos.

"What are you guys doing here?" I blurted.

"Oh, nothing," Spiridon said as he jogged past. He was in a great shape for an old guy.

Nikolos was right behind him, "See you two later."

I stopped and watched them disappear down the hill. "What were they doing up here?"

"Who knows," Christos said. "Come on, before the sun goes down."

I shrugged and we hiked up the rest of the way to the family bench. To the place where Christos and I had shared so many important firsts, including crazy caveman and cavewoman sex under the moon not too long ago. I'd been a wild woman that night. I blushed just thinking about it.

As always, I was huffing after making it up the steep hill. I took the final steps around the bushes that circled the Manos family bench, and turned the corner.

The view that awaited me was, as always, stunning.

But the content of it was drastically different.

And not because of the summer sun.

But because of the rose petals that made a carpet of red leading up to a small white wooden altar that overlooked the view of the Pacific Ocean.

On top of the altar were bouquets of roses sitting on both sides of a small golden center piece. The center piece was like a little filigreed riser. On top of the golden riser was a big seashell, opened to reveal a red velvet box holding a glittering ring.

My body filled with chills. My throat tightened, my eyes burned, my knees shook. I couldn't take another step. I held my fingers to my lips, which quivered like crazy.

"Do you need me to carry you?" Christos asked, holding his hand out to me.

I nodded.

He picked me up and carried me the few steps to the family

bench and set me down on it. Then he stepped up to the altar and lifted the ring box out of the sea shell.

He turned to me and kneeled at my feet.

The ring glimmered in the dazzling sunlight, a thousand sparkling stars dancing off of it. It was the most beautiful ring I'd ever seen.

"Samantha," he said, "*agápi mou*, you are truly the most amazing woman I've ever known. The ways in which you make me happy are beyond measure. You make my life better, you make me better, and without you, I would only be half the man I've become. The first time I took you up here, I told you this place was sacred. Only family comes up here. Now it's time to make it official."

His eyes were brimming with tears. Mine were running silently down my face in rivers.

He cleared his throat, choked up with emotion, "Samantha Anna Smith, will you marry me, *agápi mou*?" he whispered.

"Yes," I whispered, my voice gurgly with emotion.

I had secretly wished that Christos and I would be together forever, but I'd been too frightened to ever say it out loud.

Now my dream had come true. I could say it as loud as I wanted, except I could barely speak.

Christos slid the ring onto my finger. I couldn't tell whose hands were shaking more, his or mine.

It didn't matter.

Christos and I were now and always forever.

Forever.

LOVE.

Epilogue

SAMANTHA

"Are you nervous?" Kamiko asked.

"I'm okay," I said, fanning my face. It was a bit warm inside the hotel room at The Lodge at Torrey Pines, despite the perfect seventy-five degree weather outside. I think it was partially my nerves. Or maybe the fact the room cost $600 a night. I guess you paid extra for the doormen wearing kilts. Yes, kilts, because they had a golf course. But it wasn't cheesy at all. The grounds were so incredibly lush, and the hotel had such a rustic, romantic charm, I had instantly loved the place when Christos and I had visited here in June.

"How can you be nervous?" Romeo asked. "It's your wedding day. After today, you'll be able to fuck Christos without having to wear a scarlet A on your chest."

"Romeo!" Kamiko groused.

"What? It's technically adultery if you're not married."

I rolled my eyes at him. "What century are you living in?"

"The seventeenth?" he smiled.

"That's what I thought," I giggled.

"I'll turn up the A/C," Madison said. I was so glad she and Jake were able to fly back from surfing in Hawaii to join us for the wedding. I'd never seen Madison so tan. She was practically dark brown.

"Can you just open the sliding glass door?" I asked. "I think it'll be quicker to get a breeze in here."

She did, and cool air drifted inside. I felt immediate relief. I loved the smell of the fresh ocean air. At least my wedding gown was off the shoulder, so I had ventilation. I just hoped I didn't sweat my makeup off. "Who thought of this whole thing where the groom can't see the bride before the ceremony? I swear, I'm going to melt by the time I see Christos."

Madison and Kamiko wore matching pale lavender bridesmaid dresses. It was a high-low pleated maxi design with a thin belt around the waist, perfect for the warm weather. I wanted my girlfriends to look as sexy as me. I didn't go in for all that business about being the star of my wedding. They were important too.

"Are we ready?" I asked.

Madison and Kamiko nodded.

"Now I'm nervous," Romeo said. He wore a matching pale lavender tuxedo.

"I can't believe you insisted Sam make you a bridesmaid, Romeo," Kamiko grinned.

"He's totally one of the girls," I joked.

We made our way out of the hotel room, and down to the Arroyo Terrace behind the hotel. It overlooked the croquet lawn behind the eighteenth hole of the golf course. Blue skies and lush green lawns surrounded us. The ocean kissed the sky in a peaceful white line on the western horizon.

"How's my makeup?" I asked desperately.

Madison, Romeo, and Kamiko looked at me and smiled.

"You look perfect," Madison said.

"Can I do you before you say I do to Christos?" Romeo asked. "Then you won't be cheating on him."

"Enough!" I said. "Let's go."

Rows of white chairs were set up on the lawn and filled with people. Most of them were friends of the Manos family. My friends were right beside me.

A carpet of white rose petals were arranged leading up to the lavender wedding arch. The petals were in a curling design that incorporated the green of the grass. The grass showed through in curving cutouts.

The music playing quietly outside transitioned into Here Comes The Bride. Some people thought it was cheesy, but to me it was a mandatory classic.

My dad stepped up to me, wearing a navy suit. He looked more handsome than I usually gave him credit for.

"Samantha," he smiled, offering his elbow.

"Hey, Dad."

Never in my wildest dreams had I imagined he would want to

be here. I'd expected him to protest and argue and tell me I was an idiot for getting married so young and before I finished my degree. But he hadn't. He just wanted to be with his daughter on her wedding day. It was a pleasant surprise, to say the least.

I blinked back tears. There was no way my makeup was going to make it through the ceremony unscathed.

We marched toward the altar, where Christos awaited. I kept my eyes on the prize because I was so nervous. Out the corner of my eyes, I noticed all the smiling faces staring at me from the crowd.

As my dad and I neared the final row, I glanced to the right. Sitting on the aisle in the front row was my mom.

It had been a huge shock when my dad had told me that Mom had moved back in with him. They were working things out. She was very apologetic to him, according to my dad, and very apologetic to me as well.

Oddly, over the summer I had discovered that I was forging individual relationships with each of my parents. They had both started treating me like an adult, but in their own way. I kinda liked it. It was like we had become equals. I realized my parents were now trusting me to take care of myself.

That really blew me away.

I couldn't believe it.

But it was true.

My mom smiled at me from where she sat. She was crying. Maybe she wasn't so bad, after all. I smiled at her briefly before locking my eyes on Christos.

Jake stood beside him in a real tuxedo for once. Beside Jake were Nikolos and Spiridon, also in black tuxes. They all grinned at me.

But I couldn't tear my eyes off Christos. He was so unbelievably handsome. Even with his muscles and tattoos covered up by his tux, he was gorgeous. The hottest guy on the planet. His sapphire eyes shone into mine like love beacons. His dimpled grin came out and blazed brighter than the sun.

My god, he was the perfect specimen of manliness.

My dad kissed my cheek before I stepped up to the altar. Christos took my hand and we faced the Justice of the Peace.

After we exchanged vows, which I barely remembered doing, we did the candle lighting ceremony. Christos and I used our two candles to light the one in the center, before blowing our individual candles out.

Two became one.

Forever.

I flashed on a memory of the one remaining candle that had been burning the morning after my and Christos' pre-Valentine's celebration in his bedroom. The rose petals, the candles, and the See's chocolates. Too bad it had been the day before his criminal trial. I had believed that morning I might lose him to prison for years. Maybe forever. I had believed that one remaining candle had been an ill omen meaning I would soon be on my own. How wrong I had been. Now I realized that one candle had symbolized our oneness even then. Silly girl. Why had I been so worried?

When the Justice of the Peace pronounced us husband and wife, Christos leaned over to kiss me.

Yes, despite all the kissing and sex we'd had, it was the most magical kiss of my entire life.

The whole crowd applauded and cheered. But Madison cheered louder than anybody. Well, Romeo was pretty damn loud, but Madison gave him a run for his money.

While everyone cheered, Christos muttered in my ear, "Now will you take your half of the money for the LOVE portrait? And my portrait of you as the fiery angel? It's only about a million bucks after Brandon's cut."

My eyes popped wide open. How could I argue with that? Well, I could. A little. "Do I have to?" I smiled.

"You're my wife. It's fifty-fifty from here on out. What's mine is yours. And you're rich."

"In that case..." I grinned as we kissed gently again, "how can I say no?"

The reception was held inside the beautiful dining room inside The Lodge. Kamiko had brought a date. Dillon McKenna, the Adventure Time storyboard artist. They were entirely cartoon cute together.

Romeo, to all of our surprises, had brought Justin Tomlinson, Mr. Boy Band editor of The Wombat. I couldn't tell how serious they were. I was sure I'd find out.

We had hired an awesome wedding DJ named Graham Gold who got everyone up and dancing after dinner. He was totally worth the extra cash we spent on him. He wasn't just a DJ, he was an entertainer. The perfect choice.

During the bouquet throwing ceremony, I think Justin Tomlinson was as shocked as everybody else that Romeo caught my bouquet.

Throughout the reception, everything continued to blur by. I did my best to talk to everyone. I hoped I didn't forget to say hello to anyone important. I said hello to Brandon, who was there, and Russell Merriweather. But I'd never met many of the people in attendance. I hoped they didn't mind I forgot their names seconds after being introduced.

At one point, Christos and I were standing by the wedding cake, talking to Nikolos.

"I wanted to explain my wedding present, before you two go on your honeymoon," Nikolos said.

"You don't have to do that, *Bampás*," Christos said. "Whatever it is, it'll be fine."

"I agree," I said. "You being here is more than enough."

Nikolos nodded. "You are so young and innocent, *Samoula*," he smiled. "But sometimes, marriage can be difficult. That's why I wanted to explain my gift."

"Did you buy us marriage counseling sessions or something?" Christos joked.

"No, I bought your LOVE portrait. The one of you and *Samoula*."

"What?" Christos and I both gasped.

"I made a special arrangement with Brandon. It wasn't a commission sale for him. We just did that so you wouldn't ask any questions. All of the money is going to the two of you. All $500,000."

Gulp. That was one big wedding present.

Nikolos continued, "And I want you both to have the painting. I want it to serve as a reminder of the special love you both feel today. I want you never to forget it." Nikolos was clearly overcome with emotion. This was an important gesture for him.

"You can't do that, *Bampás*." Christos protested.

I agreed with Christos. This seemed like too much of a wedding gift to give anybody.

"Yes, I can," Nikolos said. "You're my son. And now, you, *Samoula*, are my daughter." He looked at me. "I see the hesitation in your eyes, *Samoula*. Let me explain. I don't want you or my son to ever have to worry about money in your marriage. Money worries drove a wedge into my family that I've regretted for a long, long time." He gave Christos a heavy, sad look.

Christos nodded solemnly.

Nikolos turned back to me, "I made the decision to chase money when I was a young man so my wife and son would always have enough to be safe. But money worries became my obsession. And my beloved wife Vesile left me because of it. Now that I have money, I don't want the same thing to happen to my son. I don't want you to ever have a reason to leave him, *Samoula*."

The heartbreak Nikolos held behind his eyes was immeasurable. I was ready to cry for him. He blinked his wet eyes and turned to smile at his son.

"But we have plenty of money, *Bampás*," Christos pleaded. "I made a ton at the show."

"Now you have more," Nikolos smiled at him. "If you're smart with it, you will always have enough."

"I know all about pinching pennies," I said. "I grew up around saving money. I know just what to do," I grinned.

Nikolos smiled, "Excellent. I know you'll take care of my son, *paidí mou*."

Nikolos raised the water glass he held in his hand, "To the happy couple. The heart that loves is always young."

Christos and I didn't have any glasses at the moment, so we smiled at Nikolos.

"Thanks, *Bampás*," Christos said.

Nikolos sipped his water before wrapping an arm around his son and slapping him on the back affectionately. "I'm sorry your mother couldn't be here tonight," he said, holding back sudden tears.

Christos winced and sighed heavily, as he hugged his father and said in a thick voice, "Yeah."

Christos hadn't spoken to his mother for a year or more, as far as I knew. I don't think he'd seen her in far longer. Sadly, I don't think he'd ever forgiven his mother for leaving when he was ten years old. She had broken the hearts of both father and son that day.

When Nikolos released his son from their hug, I could see that Christos had tears in his eyes. I rubbed him on the back of his tuxedo as he hung his head.

"Sorry," he muttered.

"It's okay," I reassured, wrapping both my arms around him.

After a moment, I looked up and saw Nikolos' eyes suddenly widen in surprise.

I turned to look behind me at whatever had caught his attention.

My chest tightened into a knot.

The most beautiful woman I'd ever seen in my entire life walked up behind me across the dining room. She had flowing dark hair and brilliant blue eyes. Everyone was staring at her. She commanded attention without even trying. She could easily be a supermodel, even though she was older. Her long blue scoop neck dress draped elegantly to her toes. I had no idea who she was, but I could make a pretty good guess. My heart jumped into my throat.

"I'm sorry I'm late," she said in an elegant voice. "My flight was delayed, but I wouldn't miss this day for the world."

Christos turned to her. Shock blotted out all the expression on his face as he went white. His face sagged. He looked like he was seeing a ghost. He was absolutely stunned when he said, "*Mamá?*"

The woman opened her arms to her son, "*Paidí mou...*"

My jaw dropped.

"Vesile?" Nikolos gasped. "*Kardia mou?*"

Vesile looked between Christos and Nikolos with silent tears dripping from her eyes. She said, "I've missed you both."

THE END.

For now...

===

A NOTE FROM DEVON:

Every ending is always a beginning. I was genuinely sad to say goodbye to Samantha, Christos, Romeo, and the gang as I penned (err, typed...it's not like I used a fountain pen) the final scenes of this book. I literally slowed down in my writing because I didn't want things to end.

I have so many stories left to tell about the gang, as you may have noticed. What does Spiridon do when he's out? What happened between him and Professor Walt Childress so many years ago to make Spiridon stop painting? What about Madison and her surf shop with Jake? Will Kamiko end up a doctor or an artist? What about Romeo? You know he's destined for something flamboyantly spectacular.

And of course, there's Nikolos and Vesile. Theirs is a love that makes me literally weep when I think about it. How else can you explain how Christos turned out so awesome? He had the best role models imaginable until the stresses of life tore Nikolos and Vesile apart. Who wants to hear their story? I know I do.

And last but not least, Tiffany.

She wasn't such a bitch after all.

No wonder Christos always treated her so well.

What's going to happen to Tiffany? Her life is a total mess. I'd love to know!

Wow, there's so many stories left to tell about my San Diego homies.

But for now, they all need a rest. They've been on set, performing their hearts out for you, dear reader, for the last nine months! ;-)

Now it's Victory Payne's turn. She wants to be a rockstar. Like, really, really badly.

And who doesn't love a good rockstar story?

Want to get an email when Devon's next book is released?

Sign up here: **http://eepurl.com/B7crf**

a Rocker Romance series

starring Victory Payne and those hotties Lucas & Logan Summer

coming Spring 2014

Personal thanks from Devon Hartford:

Thank you, dear reader, for taking the time to live with Samantha, Christos, and the gang for awhile! If you enjoyed Reckless, please leave some positive feedback on Amazon, Goodreads, or any book blogs you frequent. Be sure to tell your friends about it!

If you want to drop me a line, you can find me at any of the links below. I love to hear what you have to say, and I love to talk books!

-Devon

Like me on Facebook: at Devon Hartford, NA & YA novelist

Friend me on Facebook at Devon Hartford

Follow me on Twitter @DevonHartford

Follow me on WordPress at devonhartford.com

===

ABOUT THE AUTHOR

Devon Hartford spent most of his life in Southern California, frequenting many of the locations in Reckless. Devon also paints. His background in the arts was the inspiration for this book.

OTHER BOOKS BY DEVON HARTFORD:

Fearless (The Story of Samantha Smith #1)

Reckless (The Story of Samantha Smith #2)

ACKNOWLEDGMENTS

First and foremost I need to thank fellow New Adult author Elle Casey. She has gone above and beyond in her efforts to help me get this series off the ground and get it into the hands of you, the reader. You should definitely check out her work!

Secondly, thanks to all my passionate and fantastic beta readers: Neicy Cassidy, The REAL Julie England, Kerrisha Budhu, Megan C Christmas, Sarah Welsh (a.k.a. Princess Frilly-Bottoms of the Land of Willow), Bethanie Melander, Maria Combee, Eileen Fitzharris, Mandy Karsa, Anne Berkeley, Jenene Townsley, Brandy Everard, Natasha Slater, Stephanie Svajgl, Dora Kitinas, Kimber, Muriel Garcia, Sandye, Crystal Hoffman, Darlene Weber, Whitney "sugar peas" Hutchinson, Steffini Walker Texas Ranger, Wendy Boyer, Jenny Bayes, Michele McKenzie, Sarah, Kerri-Anne Carruthers, Rosanne Triegaardt, Jo Cox, Lynn Walters, Jenn Hedge (Beta Speed Queen), Nicki Hewitt-Hart, Teresa Hamman, Ashley Lorene Hall, Nancy Byers, Tania Clark, Sandye, Kelly Hirsh, Emma Mack, and Lynnette Kucharski for invaluable feedback and encouragement!

Becs Glass and Sinfully Sexy Books for dedicated book pimping love!

Chrissy Zent Sharp for awesome book pimpery via The Book Whore-der's Delights. Be sure to check them out if you're a Romance reader.

And thanks to everybody else who has helped make this book a reality!

WHILE YOU'RE WAITING FOR THE RELEASE OF MY NEXT NOVEL:

Don't forget to read these books by my friends and fellow romance authors Jane Harvey-Berrick (*Lifers*) and Delia Steele (*Broken*).

Lifers by Jane Harvey-Berrick: After eight years in prison, twenty-four year old Jordan Kane is the man everyone loves to hate. He is the local pariah in his home town, shunned by everyone, including his own parents. But their hatred of him doesn't come close to the loathing he feels every time he looks in the mirror. Torrey Delaney is new in town, and certainly doesn't behave in a way the locals believe a preacher's daughter should. As friendship forms between Jordan and Torrey, can two damaged people find their place in the world? Is love a life sentence?

Broken by Delia Steele: Lexi has developed a very nasty shell around her BROKEN heart and picked up a BDSM lifestyle for all the wrong reasons. She hides her true self to the point of losing it completely. She is wild, angry, conceited, foul, and refuses to let anyone into her world. Until Cameron…a sweet country boy with a heart of gold. Can he help Lexi find the light in her darkest days, or will her darkness be the death of him? But how can he help her if she doesn't even realize just how BROKEN she truly is?

17+ (Language and Sexual Content may not be suitable for some readers)

www.ingramcontent.com/pod-product-compliance
Lightning Source LLC
Chambersburg PA
CBHW031304280626
47169CB00017B/20